The Winter Rose

KATIE FLYNN

The Winter Rose

C

CENTURY

1 3 5 7 9 10 8 6 4 2

Century
20 Vauxhall Bridge Road
London SW1V 2SA

Century is part of the Penguin Random House group of companies whose
addresses can be found at global.penguinrandomhouse.com.

Penguin
Random House
UK

First published by Century in 2022

www.penguin.co.uk

A CIP catalogue record for this book is available from the British Library.

ISBN: 978–1–529–13542–8

Typeset in 13/16.5 pt Palatino LT Pro
by Integra Software Services Pvt. Ltd, Pondicherry

Printed and bound in Great Britain by Clays Ltd, Elcograf S.p.A.

The authorised representative in the EEA is Penguin Random House Ireland,
Morrison Chambers, 32 Nassau Street, Dublin D02 YH68.

Penguin Random House is committed to a sustainable
future for our business, our readers and our planet.
This book is made from Forest Stewardship Council®
certified paper.

Acknowledgements

I'd like to thank the Llangollen Motor Museum for their information regarding car locks!

To the incredible women of the WAAF

The Winter Rose

Prologue

September 1941

Cadi Williams stared blindly into the darkness that engulfed her. She was certain she had heard a familiar voice crying out for help and, what's more, she was almost positive they'd called her name, but with the voice barely on the cusp of her hearing, it was hard to tell exactly what – if anything – had actually been said. She had a feeling that she recognised the voice, but she couldn't put a name to it. Not only that, but each time she tried, it filled her with a sense of unease, as though something was horribly wrong, but what? With no recollection of where she was or how she'd got there, she would have to rely on someone else to fill in the gaps. She opened her mouth to respond, but nothing came out. Before she could work out what had happened to strike her dumb, the voice called out once more and this time there was no mistaking the words, or the urgency behind them.

'Oh, Cadi darlin', please help. I can't seem to move…' The voice paused for moment before sobbing quietly, 'And I'm *really* scared.'

1

Desperate to respond, Cadi tried to shout, but it seemed she was still powerless to make herself heard. With tears of frustration seeping through her lids, she attempted to stand up, but try as she might, she just didn't have the strength. As the tears trickled down her cheeks, she impulsively went to wipe them away, but it seemed she wasn't even strong enough to do that. How on earth would she get out of here, if she couldn't move? Another thought occurred to her. For all she knew, there could be an unexploded bomb ticking its way down to detonation. She hesitated. Was that the sound of creaking timbers above her head? Would she be buried alive … was she *already* buried alive?

Feeling the fear rising in her gut, Cadi did her best to steady her nerves. Losing her head would only add to her problems, but it was hard to remain calm when you feared for your life. Screwing her eyes shut, she tried to scream, but the darkness swallowed her voice. If she was to be rescued, she would have to figure out a way of letting someone know where she was. She knew the other person was trapped, and that they too appeared unable to move, but if she could at least speak to them, then maybe the two of them could work out a way of escaping their prison.

Thinking hard, Cadi tried to remember what had happened prior to her coming to.

A picture of the Greyhound public house formed in her mind and, as with the newsreels in the cinema, the image played out in front of her. With no overnight guests staying in the B&B, Cadi had been wiping down the bar, whilst Maria – Cadi's friend, who also happened to be the landlady – bolted the doors behind the last of their customers. Maria's husband, Bill, having been invalided to a desk job a few months earlier, was enthusiastically reliving his escape from France whilst Cadi's fiancé Jez, and Jez's grandmother Carrie, listened.

Cadi's heartbeat quickened as the dreadful truth dawned. It was Carrie's voice that she could hear calling out to her. Momentarily forgetting that she could neither move nor speak, Cadi tried to do both, but found she was still powerless to do either. Desperate, but unable to reassure dear Carrie that she wasn't on her own, Cadi felt fresh tears seep through her lids as Carrie called out with greater urgency than before, 'Cadi, *please hurry!*'

The sound of the older woman's pleas gave Cadi a sense of foreboding, just as it had earlier. She frowned. Carrie was the most kind-hearted, wonderful, loving person you could ever hope to meet. The old dear wouldn't harm a fly, so why did the sound of her voice fill her with such unease?

Another image formed in her mind. They were no longer in the bar, but sheltering from an air raid in the pub's cellar. Jez had gone to retrieve the till when there had been an almighty explosion, blowing him back into the cellar. After that, everything had gone black, and it had been some time later when Cadi came to. Fearing that Jez had been killed in the blast, she had been desperate to find him, but the first person she found had been Carrie. The older woman had been in the same position she was in before the explosion. Cadi felt a shiver run down her spine as she recalled Carrie's lifeless eyes, which stared dully into space.

The grief had been all-consuming, but she had no time to sit and cry. If she was to find Jez, she needed to move – and quickly.

A new image played in her mind now. This time she was holding Jez as he wept for his grandmother.

With the feelings of grief flooding back, a sudden thought entered her mind. If Carrie had died in the bombing, then how could she possibly be hearing her cries for help now? She had been racking her brains for an answer when realisation dawned. She must have dreamed the whole thing. Which meant that Carrie was still alive and, what's more, she needed Cadi's help.

Taking a deep breath, Cadi shouted until she could hear her own voice as clearly as she had heard Carrie's. 'I'm coming, Carrie!' Struggling to move her arms and legs, she thrashed about until other voices came to her attention. It was Bill, and Maria too, and they were calling back to her. Suddenly freed of her restrictions, Cadi shot up. 'We have to help Carrie …'

Maria, who had been kneeling beside Cadi's bed, smiled sympathetically. 'Cadi, sweetheart, I'm afraid you've had another of your nightmares.'

Bill, who was hovering behind his wife, spoke quietly. 'It sounded as though you were back in the Greyhound, am I right?'

With fresh tears trickling down her cheeks, Cadi nodded, as Maria enveloped her in a warm embrace.

'Carrie's dead, isn't she?' said Cadi quietly.

Maria tightened her arms around her. 'I'm afraid so, love. Did you dream something different?'

'I dreamed that Carrie was alive,' sniffed Cadi, 'and that the rest of it had been a nightmare.'

Taking a fresh handkerchief from her nightgown pocket, Maria handed it to Cadi. 'I'm so sorry, darling.' Cupping Cadi's face in her hands, she gazed at her affectionately. 'You shouldn't have to suffer these nightmares.' She glanced at Bill from over her shoulder. 'Someone needs to stop that beast of a man.'

Knowing that his wife was referring to Hitler, Bill squeezed her shoulder gently. 'We will, love, don't you worry about that.'

Hearing a floorboard creak in the room above hers, Cadi hastily pushed the covers back. 'The guests! I need to prepare breakfast ...' But the colour drained from her face as another, more pressing thought entered her mind. 'I wasn't shouting in my sleep, was I?' One look at Maria was enough to give her the answer. Burying her face in her hands, she spoke thickly through her fingers. 'You don't think they heard me, do you?'

Maria patted Cadi's hand in a comforting fashion. 'They're in the RAF, Cadi. I should imagine they've heard worse.'

Bill, having suffered from nightmares himself, was keen to change the subject. 'And you needn't worry about preparing the breakfast for at least another hour or so.'

Cadi glanced at the alarm clock that sat beside her bed. It read four-thirty, which meant they needn't be up for another hour yet. She hung her head in shame. 'I'm so sorry. I didn't mean to wake anyone.'

Bill smiled kindly. 'Don't be daft, you can't control your dreams.' He winked at her in a playful manner, before continuing, 'Besides, I was already awake, what with our Maria snoring her head off.'

Having shared a room with Maria prior to Bill's return, Cadi's lips hinted at a smile. 'Maria doesn't snore.'

Bill pretended to be thoughtful, before curving his lips into a mischievous grin. 'I suppose it could've been be.'

Cadi's smile broadened slightly before disappearing. She knew Bill was only trying to make her feel better, but she couldn't take her mind off her troubled sleep. 'I wish there was something I could do to get rid of these rotten nightmares.'

'Time,' said Maria simply, 'and lots of it.'

Nodding thoughtfully, Cadi spoke through thin lips. 'Or revenge ...'

'Maybe,' conceded Maria. She stood up from beside the bed. 'As we're up, I might as well pop the kettle on. Would anyone else like a cuppa?'

Making sure that her nightie was in place, Cadi swung her legs out from under the covers. 'How about you two go back to bed and I bring you both a cup of tea?'

Bill rubbed his hands together in an enthusiastic manner. 'Tea in bed – I don't suppose there's any chance of toast?'

Maria arched a reproving brow. 'And have a bed full of crumbs? Not on your nelly.' She wagged a chiding finger at Cadi. 'You start giving this one tea in bed and he'll be expecting all sorts.'

Bill slipped his arm around her waist. 'All sorts, eh? Sounds good to me.'

Maria rolled her eyes. 'That'll do, William Shankley.'

6

Chortling to himself, Bill winked at Cadi. 'You know you're in trouble when a woman calls you by your full name.'

A smile tweaked the corner of Cadi's lips. 'That's what Jez always used to say.'

Bill tapped the side of his nose as he left the room. 'Very wise man, that Jez,' adding, 'I'm off to put the kettle on before I get myself into any more trouble.'

With her husband making his way down the stairs, Maria closed the door, before turning back to Cadi. 'Are you still finding life without Jez hard going?'

Cadi fiddled with the corner of her feather eider-down. 'Awfully. I know it's only been a couple of weeks, but it feels like so much longer. I honestly don't know how you coped when Bill went off to war.'

Maria shrugged. 'Much like you, I didn't have a choice – although, having said that, you and Poppy helped keep me entertained.'

As she remembered the shenanigans the pair had got up to, a reminiscent smile graced Cadi's cheeks. 'We certainly did, albeit unintentionally.'

'Looking back, I wouldn't have had it any other way,' said Maria, 'and I shall miss you dearly when you leave for the WAAF.' She glanced at the engagement ring on Cadi's left hand. 'If you're lucky, they'll post you close to Jez.'

Cadi crossed her fingers. 'That would be wonderful, but I'm trying not to get my hopes up, just in case.'

'It's been a while since you applied,' mused Maria. 'I reckon your papers should be through any day now.' She turned towards the bedroom door. 'I'll go and fetch you some warm water so that you can have a wash.'

Thanking Maria, Cadi waited until her friend had left the room before getting up from the bed. Slipping her arms into her dressing gown, she crossed over to the sash window and carefully lifted the end of the curtain so that she could peek out onto the road below without being spotted. It wasn't the scene she was used to, nor the one she wanted to see.

The Greyhound in Burlington Street was where Cadi and her best friend Poppy had made their home, after leaving the small Welsh mining village of Rhos, many moons ago. As she reminisced, she smiled at their naivety. Before leaving Rhos, the plan had been to go to Liverpool where they would stay with Cadi's Auntie Flo. Despite being underage, they were determined to join one of the services. The suggestion had been met with encouragement from some, but disapproval from others – particularly Cadi's arch-enemy Aled, who had poked fun at the very notion, saying that the services were after women, not children. Cadi's father had also made it plain that he didn't approve, but Cadi's strong will and independent nature had meant that she left anyway, regardless of his opinion. Within days of arriving in Liverpool the girls had entered the town hall intent on signing up, but to their embarrassment they had been practically laughed off the premises. Anyone else would have given up, but not Cadi. She had left Rhos saying that she was going to make something of herself, and she would be damned if she was going to return home without having done exactly that.

She continued to gaze onto the street below as she cast her mind back to the night when their youthful hopes had turned into a living nightmare. Having failed to find work, and with little money, the girls had been making their way back to the train station when Poppy had been attacked by Eric, a drunken brute of a man, who had mistaken her for his daughter, Izzy. With Eric trying to drag Poppy into his house, Cadi had jumped onto his back in a bid to rescue her friend, but Eric had thrown her over his shoulder as though she were a rag doll. She grimaced as recalled the pain of the cobbles hitting her head. Touching the back of her skull as though expecting to feel the lump, a faint smile etched her lips. It was at that point that Jez had raced to their rescue. With one thump he had knocked Eric clean off his feet. With Cadi winded, Jez had offered to carry her to his friend's pub – the Greyhound. The girls had agreed and that's when everything had changed. Maria offered them not only sanctuary, but jobs and a home to boot.

Every cloud, thought Cadi to herself now. Their new life had brought fresh opportunities, and Cadi in particular had embraced the chance to turn the pub into a B&B. They soon made friends, one of whom was Eric's daughter Izzy, and as time went by, Cadi and Poppy hatched a plan to rescue Izzy from her brute of a father.

The smile faded on Cadi's lips as she recalled the day she had said goodbye to Poppy and Izzy as they set off for the Women's Auxiliary Air Force. Their lives had changed an awful lot in a relatively short period of time. Indeed, it seemed the war was altering everything – especially when Aled turned up at the B&B, kitted out in Air Force blue. No longer the arrogant, spoilt boy that Cadi remembered, but a kind, generous and, indeed, handsome young man. And Cadi wasn't the only one who thought Aled handsome. Daphne, the Waaf responsible for driving Aled and the rest of the crew to Liverpool, was clearly smitten by him, and she had made it plain that she didn't approve of Cadi and Aled's new-found friendship, by making snide comments about Cadi and her beloved Greyhound pub.

In retaliation, Cadi had given Aled a quick peck on the cheek before he left the next morning. She had only done it to annoy Daphne, but the consequences had come back to haunt her when Daphne wrote to Jez, accusing Cadi of seeking Aled for herself. It was untrue, but the accusations had caused a lot of upset, with Cadi having to admit her childish actions. Jez had been angry, of course he had, but he had soon forgiven her, and their relationship had grown stronger as a result.

Believing that the worst was behind them, Cadi and Jez had continued with their lives, until the Luftwaffe's bombs reached the Greyhound. After that, everything changed. Not only for Jez, Cadi, Maria and Bill, but for the locals, all of whom relied on the pub as an escape from reality.

After laying Carrie to rest, Jez had returned to his RAF base, whilst Cadi, Maria and Bill looked for a new home. When an offer came for Maria to run the Belmont Hotel on West Derby Road, she had grasped the opportunity with both hands. Eager to set the wheels in motion, she had asked Cadi if she would consider staying on with her at the Belmont, but Cadi had already made up her mind to join the WAAF.

Now, Cadi cast a worried eye over her bed. What if she had the nightmares whilst sharing a Nissen hut with several other women? The very thought of waking up with strangers staring down at her filled her with dread. Should she mention it on her first night or simply hope that a different setting would free her of her troubled sleep?

Hearing the door open behind her, Cadi dropped the curtain and turned to greet Maria. 'I can't say I'm going to miss it here, but I will miss you and Bill.'

Taking care not to pour the warm water anywhere but into the basin, Maria smiled. 'You know you'd have been more than welcome to stay, if you had wanted to – still could, come to that.' She glanced fleetingly from the task in hand to Cadi. 'You do know they couldn't do anything about it, if you changed your mind? It's not like it is with the fellers, poor sods; any of them change their mind and they'd be court-martialled, but not you: you could walk away scot-free.'

Cadi gave her friend a chiding smile. 'You, of all people, should know that I'm not one to shy away from a challenge.'

Maria hugged the empty jug to her chest. 'I certainly do, but this war's already taken too many people.' She jerked her head towards the bedroom she shared with Bill. 'I'm lucky my Bill came home broken but whole, as there's many don't make it back at all.'

'Granted, but the Germans aren't going to stop until they've wiped out every last man, woman and child,' said Cadi, adding fervently, 'and I *won't* see another of my loved ones taken away before their time.'

'I'm still surprised your father didn't try and per-suade you to go back to Rhos after the bombing – I know he promised that he wouldn't interfere, after nearly losing his own life, but you are his only daughter.'

Cadi dipped her flannel into the water. 'Dad's a man of his word. He might not like me being in the thick of it, but neither would he try and interfere, not after everything we've been through.'

'War changes everything,' said Maria, 'very rarely does it change it for the better.'

Feeling the warmth of the water against her skin, Cadi glanced at her reflection in the oval vanity mirror that stood on top of the dresser. She might not have scars like Bill, but visible lines now crossed her forehead. War left its mark in more ways than one. She said as much to Maria.

'True, but with all bad things comes good. If it weren't for the war, you and Poppy might never have come to Liverpool; and if you hadn't, you'd never have met and fallen in love with Jez.' She barely fell silent before adding, 'And Izzy would still be a prisoner in her own home, with that beast of a man using her as a punchbag. And whilst I know we lost Carrie, we've gotten away with it lightly, compared to some – or at least we have so far.' She glanced towards the window. 'I loved the Greyhound, but I'll not deny that I'm glad we're further away from the docks, living here at the Belmont.' She looked over her shoulder as Bill called out to them from the foot of the stairs.

'Are you two going to spend the whole morning gassin'?'

Hissing for Bill to keep quiet, lest he wake the guests, Maria hastily descended the stairs. 'I like to think I offer our boys a good night's sleep, but you'll soon put paid to that, if you go waking them up with your big gob, William Shankley.'

Cadi heard Bill chuckle that he was in trouble for the second time that morning, and it wasn't even six o'clock yet.

Closing the door behind Maria, Cadi fetched her stockings from the back of the chair. Sitting on her bed, she began to carefully roll them up with her fingers. She'd seen Poppy as well as many other Waafs in their uniforms, and she had been very impressed with their smart appearance. An image of herself in the blue uniform entered her mind: her fair curls were pinned beneath the neat cap, and the belted jacket emphasised her trim waist. The vision caused her to smile. Being in the WAAF was going to suit her down to the ground.

With her stockings fastened, Cadi slipped the lilac shirtwaister frock over her head and began fastening the buttons. Running a hotel, on top of helping Maria behind the bar, hadn't left her with much of a social life, but she hoped that would change when she joined the WAAF. Certainly her friends were always boasting of the places they had seen, as well as the many dances they attended. Checking her reflection in the mirror, she ran a comb through her hair, then clipped it back from her face. Satisfied that she was presentable, she slid her feet into her T-bar heels, fastened the straps and made her way downstairs.

'Aha! Just in time for some toast,' said Bill, pushing a plate towards her.

Taking a seat opposite his, Cadi selected a slice, popped it onto a side plate and began spreading a thin

13

layer of butter over the toasted surface. She looked at Maria, who was stirring a large pan of porridge. 'Do you need a hand?'

Maria shook her head. 'No thanks, love, I'm doing grand.' She indicated Bill with the wooden spoon she was using to stir the porridge. 'Bill says that if you don't get your papers today, he'll see if he can gee them up, down the town hall.'

Cadi smiled gratefully at him. 'Thanks, Bill, much appreciated.'

Standing up, he took his plate over to the sink, then selected a bowl from the cupboard, which he handed to his wife, who dutifully half filled it with porridge. 'Not to worry, queen, it's the least I can do.'

Maria arched a single eyebrow at Cadi, who had finished her toast. 'Porridge?'

Cadi shook her head. 'Thanks all the same, but I couldn't manage another bite.' Seeing Maria attend to the porridge whilst slicing rounds of bread, in readiness for their guests, brought a question to the forefront of her mind. 'How will you manage once I've gone?'

'Even if you get your papers today, it's likely you'll not leave for another week or so, and I'm sure I can find *someone* looking for a spot of work.' She glanced at Bill with a shrewd smile on her lips. 'And Bill can always help me with the breakfast, until I do so.'

Bill's eyes widened. 'You want *me* to cook the breakfast?'

Maria looked at him aghast. 'Do I heck as like! I meant you could do the pots or lay the tables.'

Scraping up the last of his porridge, Bill placed the empty bowl in the sink before kissing his wife on the cheek. 'Summat I can't make a pig's ear out of, eh?' Not expecting a reply, he took his coat and hat from the back of the kitchen door. Sliding his arms into the sleeves, he pecked his wife on the cheek before picking up the packet of greaseproof-wrapped sandwiches that Maria had prepared for him. As he headed out, he called 'Ta-ra, girls' as the door closed behind him

With breakfast finished and most of the guests checked out, Maria and Cadi had begun the task of changing the bedding when they heard the snap of the letterbox. Seeing the look of anticipatory hope on Cadi's face, Maria jerked her head in the direction of the front door. 'Go on, today might be your lucky day.'

Cadi hastened down the stairs, her heart almost skipping a beat as she saw a brown envelope lying on the doormat beneath the letterbox. Picking it up, she returned to Maria, who was smiling encouragingly at her.

'Looks pretty official to me,' she said.

Slitting the envelope open, Cadi gave a squeal of delight before reading the contents out loud. 'They want me to report to RAF Innsworth for training next Wednesday.'

Maria dropped the sheet she was holding and hurried over to give Cadi a congratulatory hug. 'Cadi love, that's marvellous news.'

Tucking the letter into her dress pocket, Cadi bundled the dirty laundry into a heap. 'I'm so excited, I can't wait to break the news to Jez and the girls.'

Maria ushered her out of the room. 'There's no time like the present. You go. I can finish up here.'

Hugging the letter close to her chest, Cadi hurried to the door. 'Thanks, Maria, you're a real gem.' Trying not to thunder down the stairs, she found herself wishing fervently that her friends would be free to take her call. Picking up the receiver, she crossed her fingers as she asked the operator to put her through to Jez's base. Much to her delight, Jez's voice came down the line within moments.

'Cadi?'

'I'm in!' she trilled. 'I leave for RAF Innsworth next Wednesday.' She hesitated. 'I've only just realised that I have no idea where Innsworth is – is it close to you?'

The operator interrupted without apology. 'May I remind you that loose talk …'

Jez groaned audibly across her. 'Yes, yes, we know, but I really can't see the harm—'

Hearing the operator take a breath, ready to argue back, Cadi cut across her. 'I promise we won't do it again. Jez darling, I really don't want to spend our time arguing with the operator.'

Jez relented. 'Fair dos. As for you being close, I'm afraid not, but I wouldn't worry about it too much, because you won't be there for long anyway.'

'How do you know?' asked Cadi curiously.

Jez enlightened her. 'Initial training only takes a few weeks, after that they'll move you somewhere to do your proper training – exactly where will depend on what you're training for. Take me, for example—'

At this point the operator interrupted again, only in more exasperated tones. 'For goodness' sake! Loose lips—'

16

Jez cut her short. 'All right, all right. There's no need to get your knickers in a twist.' Hearing the operator huffing to herself, he quickly turned the conversation back to Cadi. 'How'd Maria take the news?'

Cadi leaned against the bar. 'She was delighted for me. We've already discussed my replacement. Maria's confident she'll find someone, but in the meantime she's going to get Bill to help with the breakfasts ...'

Jez roared with laughter. 'If she gets Bill cooking the breakfast, the hotel won't *have* any customers.'

Cadi giggled. 'She says he's only allowed to do the pots or lay the tables.'

'Very wise too,' said Jez. 'Have you told Poppy or Izzy the good news?'

'Not yet, I wanted to tell you first.'

She could hear from his voice that Jez was pleased with her decision. 'And much appreciated it is too.'

Hearing Maria move from one bedroom to the next, Cadi spoke hastily. 'Speaking of the girls, I'd best get a move on, cos I've still got all the laundry to do.'

'Righty-ho,' said Jez. 'Give me a call when you can.'

'Will do.'

'Ta-ra, queen, love you.'

'Love you too.'

Hearing the line go dead, Cadi asked the operator to put her through to Poppy and Izzy's base at RAF Fisk-erton. On hearing Poppy's voice come down the line, Cadi gave a small squeak of delight.

'Wotcher!' said Poppy. 'You're lucky – I was just about to go out on manoeuvres.'

'Manoeuvres,' said Cadi, her voice dripping with awe. 'It makes you sound so important.'

17

Poppy laughed. 'I'm only driving some old fuddy-duddy five miles down the road, so it's not that important. Any news on your papers?'

'That's why I'm ringing,' confessed Cadi excitedly. 'They arrived this morning. I'm setting off for training next Wednesday. I'd best not say where, seeing as Jez and I have already had an ear-bashing for being too outspoken.'

'Not to worry,' said Poppy. 'Drop me a line when you get there or, better still, give me a call – it's not so bad chatting base-to-base.'

Cadi breathed out happily. 'I'm so excited, Poppy, I can't wait to get started. I'm beginning to wonder why I didn't do this years ago.'

'Because you were happy as you were,' Poppy reminded her friend, 'and there's nowt wrong with that.' She grinned. 'Besides, you may change your mind once you've been woken by reveille for the umpteenth time.'

'I'm used to early starts at the hotel,' said Cadi nonchalantly, 'and even if I weren't, I'm that excited, I reckon I'll be awake before reveille sounds.' And she meant every word. Cadi knew that she was going to take to service life like a duck to water and, quite frankly, she couldn't wait.

Chapter One

Bill indicated the approaching train as it crawled into the platform. 'Looks like this one's yours, queen.' He winked at Cadi, who wore a hesitant smile. 'Are you having second thoughts?'

She paused briefly before shaking her head. 'Not exactly, but I'll admit I'm finding the whole affair a tad daunting, now that the time has come for me to leave, but I suppose that's only natural when I'm starting a new job in a place I've never been to before.'

Maria smiled. 'You seem to forget you've already done it once, only you were a lot younger, so if anything, this should be easier.'

Cadi still appeared doubtful. 'I had Poppy with me then, though, and it's much easier doing things with a friend by your side. I'm on my own this time.'

'True,' conceded Maria, 'but I've a feeling you're going to come up trumps, you usually do.'

Cadi pulled the rail pass that she had been issued from her pocket and examined it proudly, as they waited for the passengers to descend. It might have sounded silly to anyone else, but to Cadi the pass itself made her feel important, as if she was a part of something big, which she supposed she was. The WAAF was becoming a vast organisation, taking on thousands of women each week. She drew in a deep breath. She was going to be like a small fish in a very big pond, but Maria was right: she had left home a long time ago. If anything, she should count herself lucky; for many of the women joining up, this would be their first experience living away from their nearest and dearest. She pocketed the pass and picked up her small suitcase.

'I'm going to get myself a window seat before they're all taken.' She looked at Maria, who was blinking furiously in an attempt to stop tears forming. 'I know you don't like goodbyes, so I'll not make this any harder than it already is.' Leaning forward, she kissed Bill briefly on the cheek, before setting her suitcase back down. Taking her old friend in a warm embrace, Cadi spoke from the heart. 'Thanks, Maria, not only for coming to see me off, but for everything. If you hadn't decided to take a chance on me all those years ago, I don't think I'd be half the woman I am today.'

With her eyes beginning to glisten, Maria looked over Cadi's shoulder to Bill, who smiled lovingly at his wife as he searched his pockets for a clean handkerchief. 'None of that, Cadi Williams,' she mumbled, 'or you'll have me blubbing like a good 'un.' Taking the handkerchief that Bill held out to her, she leaned back from their embrace. A wobbly smile tweaked her lips as she dabbed her eyes. 'I hope you know how incredibly proud I am of you – Poppy and Izzy too, come to that.'

Standing behind his wife, Bill placed his hands on her shoulders. 'She's always bragging about "her girls". Anyone'd swear she was your mam.'

'She is,' said Cadi. 'Or at least she's my Liverpool mam.' She glanced at the train, which was beginning to fill up with passengers. 'I hate to go, but I really must dash or I won't get any seat, let alone one by a window.'

Bill winked at Cadi. 'Ta-ra, queen, keep in touch.'

Nodding, Cadi picked up her suitcase and hurried off before she could change her mind.

As she boarded the train she made a beeline for the first empty carriage. Stowing her bag on the rack above her, she scanned the platform for a sign of her friends. She smiled as she saw Maria pointing her out to Bill whilst frantically waving. Waving back, Cadi heard the rail guard shout something before placing his whistle to his lips and blowing hard whilst flourishing his flag. She felt her stomach lurch as the train's whistle blew its response, before pulling slowly out of the station. With Maria and Bill no longer visible, Cadi settled back into her seat. She smiled at a young brunette who had entered the carriage, without her noticing.

The girl smiled back. 'Was that your mam and dad?'

'No, that was my old employer, Maria, and her husband, Bill,' replied Cadi.

The girl, whom Cadi assumed to be in her late teens, looked impressed. 'Blimey! I wish I'd had a boss like that – mine couldn't wait to see the back of me.'

Cadi eyed the outspoken girl curiously. She seemed pleasant enough, with a cheery smile and kind blue eyes, and what Cadi would describe as a very homely look about her. Intrigued to hear why the girl had proved to be unpopular with her old boss, Cadi asked the question that was uppermost in her thoughts. 'Where did you work?'

The girl rolled her eyes. 'Blacklers.'

Having seen Blacklers Department Store – or what was left of it after the May blitz – Cadi grimaced. 'Before the bombing or after?'

'Both.'

Cadi wrinkled her brow. 'You'd think your boss would be a bit more charitable. It's not easy upping sticks and moving somewhere new, especially to the premises you're in now, which aren't nearly as grand as the one on Great Charlotte Street.'

'I think that was part of the problem,' confessed the girl. 'You see, in the old place I worked in the restaurant, but when we moved, a position to serve the customers on the jewellery counter came up and me mam said I was to go for it, because it pays a little bit more and it's a lot fancier than serving sarnies for a living.' She shrugged. 'It just wasn't for me – I am what I am, and I can't talk the same as the toffs, nor would I want to.' Pinching her nose, she put on a haughty voice. 'And Hyacinth thought I was far too common!'

'Oh,' said Cadi knowingly, 'I know the sort. Thinks she's as good as the customers that come in to buy the fancy jewellery, even though she couldn't afford to do so herself.'

The girl stared at Cadi, open-mouthed. 'Nail on the bloomin' head!' She thrust a hand towards Cadi. 'I'm Kitty Brown.'

Cadi shook the girl's hand. 'Pleased to meet you, Kitty. I'm Cadi Williams.'

Beaming, Kitty fished out a small paper bag, which she offered to Cadi. 'Everton mint?'

Thanking her, Cadi took one of the sweets, peeled the paper off it, then stowed it into her cheek. She glanced at the small satchel that Kitty had placed on her knee. 'Where are you off to?'

Kitty patted her bag. 'Seein' as I can't get me old job back, I decided to cut my losses and leave Blacklers in favour of the WAAF.' She sucked her mint thoughtfully before continuing, 'They're sending me to somewhere called RAF Innsworth to do my initial training. How about you?'

'Snap!' cried Cadi, much to Kitty's surprise and delight. 'Only I'm not leaving Blacklers, of course.'

Kitty pulled a face. 'With an employer like you had, I'm surprised you wanted to leave at all.'

Realising that an explanation was in order, Cadi told Kitty all about her work in the Greyhound and the subsequent bombing. 'The Belmont's lovely, but it's not home – or not to me at any rate,' she finished.

Kitty gave her a knowing smile. 'Bit like me, with Blacklers – only I didn't live there, of course.' She rested her elbow against the arm of the chair. 'It sounds like you'd invested a lot of yourself into the Greyhound, so it can't have been easy losing your job *and* your home like that.'

Cadi nodded. 'The Greyhound meant everything to me. It may sound silly, but I think I took the bombing personally.'

'I can see why,' agreed Kitty. 'The house my auntie rented got bombed during the Christmas blitz. She wasn't bothered about the house itself, because it wasn't hers. It was losing all her personal bits and bobs that upset her the most.'

'That's the difference,' said Cadi. 'I put my heart and soul into the Greyhound, and I know I could do the same with the Belmont, but quite frankly I don't see why I should have to start again, when I shouldn't have lost the Greyhound in the first place. Not only that, but I've got friends in the WAAF, and of course my fiancé, Jez, is in the RAF. So I guess it feels like this is the right time for me to move on,' she continued, adding as an afterthought, 'as well as to get my revenge on Jerry, of course.'

Kitty's eyes were full of admiration for Cadi. 'I don't think I would've been brave enough to leave home at sixteen, like what you did. Blimey, I'm a little nervous to do it now and I'm going to be celebrating my nineteenth birthday in a few months' time.'

Cadi sucked on her sweet thoughtfully. 'Have you any siblings?'

Kitty shook her head. 'Only child – why?'

'Just wondered if you'd ever shared a room before. When I lived with my family in Rhos I used to share a room with my three brothers. Imagine having to do that, with no privacy save for a curtain to divide up the room.' She smiled as she recalled the small bedroom. 'You share a room with three miners and,

24

believe you me, you can't wait to get away from there.'

Kitty laughed. 'I see what you mean.'

'I love them dearly,' added Cadi quickly, 'but a girl needs her privacy – *especially* when she gets to a certain age.'

Kitty gazed out of the window at the fields, which stood looking bleak after the autumn harvest. 'I've been trying to imagine what it's going to be like sharing a room with so many other women, but it's hard to envisage.' Her cheeks turned pink. 'I don't want to come across as naive, sheltered or prudish, but what do you suppose happens when it's time to get changed for bed?'

Cadi cast her a sympathetic glance 'I'm guessing you're a little shy?'

'When it comes to stripping off in a room full of complete strangers, then yes, I suppose I am ...' She hesitated. 'Aren't you?'

Cadi, having never given the matter any thought, considered this before answering. 'I don't think so. I shared a room with Maria, Poppy and even Izzy at one time, but maybe that's different because we all know each other?'

'Maybe,' mused Kitty. 'I wasn't overly shy when we used to get changed for PT in school, but having said that, I used to keep my vest on.'

Cadi coughed on a chuckle. 'True ...' Smiling fondly at her new friend, she continued, 'I think you'll have to cross that bridge when you come to it. There's usually a way around these things, and I dare say you won't be the only one who's cautious about undressing in a room full of strangers.'

With the matter settled, Kitty steered the conversation to a subject she was eager to discuss. 'Any ideas about what you want to do in the WAAF?'

Cadi shrugged. 'Poppy and Izzy are both in the MT – that's short for Motor Transport – and I think it sounds rather fun. They get to go all over the country, meeting new people, seeing new places, so I suppose I'd like to do something like that. You?'

Kitty replied without hesitation. 'I'm hoping to work in the cookhouse – it's what I enjoy doing, and I'm good at it. In Blacklers we only had the finest produce, but we had to be pretty thrifty with it.' She turned her attention from the fields back to Cadi. 'They used to tell us that every currant counts, and you couldn't afford to waste a single one. I used to enjoy serving lots of people a hearty meal from few ingredients – it was challenging, but that's what I liked about it.'

'I don't think you'll have any difficulties getting into the cookhouse,' said Cadi. 'They'd be mad to turn down someone with your experience.'

Kitty didn't look so sure. 'Square peg, round hole – that's what my father always says.'

Cadi frowned. 'Sorry?'

'Dad reckons the Army enjoys placing people where they don't belong, to test them out.'

Cadi's frown deepened. 'But that's silly. Surely you give people the jobs to which they are suited?'

'Let's hope so, because I wasn't any good at flogging jewellery – although I can't see there'll be much call for that in the WAAF.'

Cadi's brow rose swiftly. 'I jolly well hope not.' As she looked out of the window she felt a pang of envy towards Kitty, who knew exactly what she wanted from the WAAF. The more Cadi thought about it, the more the only thing she was 'qualified' to do was make meals and change beds; and while she might not mind doing that in the hotel, she didn't much fancy the thought of doing it for hundreds of people.

She wondered what she'd be like at driving. According to Poppy, it was easy enough and they gave you good instruction. Cadi smiled wistfully as she imagined herself sitting behind the wheel of a black Daimler, with Churchill himself seated in the back. She was pulling up to a set of traffic lights and the dreadful Daphne was coming towards her, behind the wheel of a dirty great lorry. When Daphne's eyes met Cadi's, she could see that the other woman was positively spitting feathers as she compared their vehicles.

When Cadi drifted back out of her daydream she was surprised to find a smile creeping up her cheeks. Was she really still affected by the other woman's actions? A vision formed in her mind of Daphne smiling in blissful ignorance at the trouble she had created. *I'm angry*, Cadi thought to herself, *and rightly so, because Daphne was never held accountable for her actions*. Daphne had been the cause of the chaos, by blowing things out of proportion, saying that Cadi had kissed Aled goodbye, but without specifying the type of kiss.

Now Cadi cursed herself inwardly. Was she angry at Daphne for telling tales, or at herself for being so silly in the first place? She had often questioned whether Daphne would have sent the letter, had Cadi not pecked Aled on the cheek.

And therein the trouble lies, thought Cadi bitterly. *You don't know, because you never got the chance to confront Daphne.* She knew it was better to let the matter lie, but if she were to bump into Daphne, she would definitely tell the other woman exactly what she thought of her behaviour, whilst hopefully getting an answer or two along the way.

By the time Cadi and Kitty arrived at their destination station, both girls were relieved to learn that they wouldn't be boarding another train.

Kitty glanced along the length of the platform as they drew into the station. 'I wonder where we go from here?' she pondered curiously. Spotting a man in RAF uniform, she pointed him out to Cadi. 'Do you think he's here for us?'

Cadi pulled her suitcase down from the rack. 'I reckon so, but I guess there's only one way to find out. Are you ready?'

Kitty swung her satchel over her shoulder. 'As I'll ever be.'

The girls waited for the guard to open the door before descending onto the platform. Walking towards the man in uniform, Cadi was pleased to see him hold up a clipboard as they approached.

He smiled briefly. 'Are you girls here for RAF Innsworth?'

They both nodded.

'Names?'

They watched as he ticked their names off the list, then used his pencil to point to one of the two army trucks parked on the street outside. 'You're in the back of that one.'

Nodding, the girls made their way to the waiting truck and, as they approached, it suddenly occurred to Cadi that Daphne could well be the driver. Crossing her fingers that this was not the case, she was relieved to see a short Waaf who greeted them with a friendly smile. 'Would either of you like a bunk-up?'

Cadi looked at the large gap between the tailgate and the floor. 'Why on earth don't they provide us with some sort of step?'

The Waaf giggled. 'Because these trucks were built for men in trousers, not women in skirts.'

Kitty, who was about a foot shorter than Cadi, grimaced. 'I could do with a ladder, never mind a step.'

Cadi took Kitty's satchel. 'C'mon, you first.' Cupping her hands together, she indicated that Kitty should place her foot inside them. 'I'll lift while you pull,' she instructed.

This proved easier said than done, and they only managed to get Kitty in by means of Cadi supporting her foot while the driver pushed her bottom and Kitty hauled herself along the floor of the lorry. Once inside, she turned to face them. She was still on her knees, and her face was beetroot from all the effort. 'I'm out of breath and I've only got into the back of the lorry,' she panted. 'God help me when it comes to parade.'

The Waaf grinned up at her. 'Don't worry, they'll soon whip you into shape. And when they do, you'll

29

be hopping in and out of the back of these things like it's nothing.'

'I hope so,' said Kitty, 'because I don't fancy having to do that in front of a load of people – especially if they're men.'

Much to her own surprise, Cadi hopped into the back with ease. She turned to face the Waaf who was handing up her suitcase. 'What's Innsworth like?'

The girl grimaced. 'Put it this way, it can only get better once you leave.'

Cadi's face fell. 'It's not *really* that bad, is it?'

The Waaf's face remained impassive. 'It's as basic as it gets, but don't worry – they're not all like Innsworth.'

Kitty arched a hopeful brow. 'Perhaps you've got really high standards ...'

The Waaf laughed knowingly. 'You only have to suffer it for three weeks, just bear that in mind.' Seeing some other recruits plodding towards the back of the lorry, she stood to one side while, one by one, they heaved, pushed, shoved and hefted each other on board. When the sergeant was satisfied that he'd ticked off everyone on his list, they raised the tailgate and set off for their new home.

If the Waaf's warnings hadn't been off-putting enough, the journey only added to their trepidation, leading some of the girls to wonder whether they'd made the right decision. Especially after hearing one of the new recruits, a red-headed girl with a face full of freckles, tell her tale of woe.

'My sister's in the WAAF and when I told her where I was going, she started laughing.'

'The driver doesn't speak too highly of it, either,' admitted Cadi. 'Did your sister say anything after she'd stopped laughing?'

The girl nodded miserably. 'She told me to enjoy my lump of coal.'

Kitty tutted. 'I may not know much, but even I know they don't give you coal to eat. I think she's pulling your leg.'

The girl, who'd introduced herself as Ronnie – short for Veronica – rolled her eyes. 'Not to eat – to use for fuel.'

'One lump!' cried a girl who was sitting closest to the tailgate. 'That's not enough to keep a mouse warm, let alone a room full of women.'

'According to my sister, it wouldn't matter if they gave you a bucketful, because they insist on keeping the windows wide open – even if it's blowin' a gale outside.'

Cadi and Kitty exchanged glances. 'Not in winter, surely?' ventured Cadi.

Ronnie nodded. 'Mandy – that's my sister – reckons they do it to stop everything going mouldy, and they don't care if there's a foot of snow outside.'

Kitty nudged Cadi. 'Remember what the driver said: it's only for three weeks – everything'll be better after that.'

One of the girls who had remained quiet until now piped up. 'Depending on where you go, of course. I used to work in a laundry, and I've heard plenty of tales from mothers whose daughters are in the WAAF. The worst one being of a woman who'd been put into an attic room with four other girls. She said they had

31

suffered from bedbugs, as well as rats the size of cats ...'
Seeing the looks of horror on the other women's faces,
she continued, 'They moved them in the end, but only
because they kicked up a fuss.'

The lorry had lurched over another pothole, causing
cries of pain from several of the passengers.

'God only knows, my bottom's got plenty of pad-
ding,' said Kitty, 'but *not* when it's being bounced
around on a wooden seat in the back of a lorry.'

When they eventually pulled up outside the base
some time later, the women descended gratefully, glad
of the chance to stretch their legs. Cadi looked around
her as she absent-mindedly massaged the life back into
her backside. 'I wonder what happens now?'

Kitty indicated a smart-looking Waaf who was strut-
ting towards them in an authoritative manner. She had
a clipboard resembling that of the sergeant's under her
arm.

Introducing herself as Corporal Moses, she ticked
the girls off the list. This somewhat amused Cadi, who
wondered whether the corporal thought some girls
might have absconded between the railway station
and the base. Satisfied that they were all present and
correct, she instructed them to follow her to the hut
where they would be sleeping for the next three
weeks, should they be lucky enough to complete the
course. As they followed behind her, the girls tried to
pay attention as the corporal indicated various buildings, such as the NAAFI, the cookhouse and the
ablutions, which, Cadi noticed, were several yards
away from the Nissen hut where they would be
staying.

The corporal opened the door to their hut and the girls filed in behind her. Once inside, she told them to claim themselves a bed and stand by it. When they were ready, she continued to talk.

'Your first task is to make your beds, after which you can nip over to the cookhouse and get yourselves something to eat ...'

Cadi listened as the woman relayed a list of instructions, many of which she felt sure she would forget. With the lecture at an end, the corporal left the girls to settle in.

The girl who'd heard the horror stories from the women at the laundry picked up the first of her three cushions and lifted it towards her nose, before hastily pushing it away with a look of revulsion. 'This thing stinks! How are we meant to make a mattress out of these?'

Ronnie deftly placed the three straw-filled cushions in a row, before spreading her bed sheet over them. 'According to Mandy, the trick is to keep the bis-cuits – that's what they call the cushions – together. She reckons that if you wrap them tightly, they aren't too bad.'

Kitty groaned as she laid her biscuits out on the bunk below Cadi's. 'I just know all mine'll be on the floor, come morning. And as for that corporal, she must be using her ears to breathe, cos she sure doesn't stop talking. Can anyone remember what we're meant to do after we've had summat to eat? I kind of tuned out after that bit.'

Ronnie, whose knowledge of the WAAF was proving to be a godsend, nodded. 'Get kitted out, then go to the large building next to the cookhouse and line up for your FFI – that's short for "free from infection" – and after that it's the medical, where you'll get prodded, poked and jabbed with all kinds of inoculations.'

Kitty stared at her in horror. 'Why do we need to be immunised? Surely Innsworth can't be that bad?'

Ronnie glanced around before lowering her voice. 'It's more like they're protecting us from each other. You get folks from all walks of life joinin' up, so there's bound to be some pretty nasty infections knocking around, and they'll get passed around like wildfire, with us all living cheek by jowl.'

Cadi tucked her blanket in, then smoothed it down with the palm of her hand. 'So more like it's better to be safe than sorry.' She smiled expectantly at Kitty. 'Are you ready to get some food?'

'More than,' said Kitty.

Cadi turned to Ronnie. 'Fancy joinin' us?'

Ronnie, who was happy to be included, beamed. 'Rather.'

As they headed for the cookhouse, Ronnie voiced her concerns prior to joining. 'I did worry that I might not make any friends, so thanks for inviting me.'

'I think everyone feels that way when they're starting summat new,' said Kitty. 'Cadi and I were lucky because we came on the same train.'

They entered the cookhouse and joined the back of the queue. 'I can't wait to see what I look like in my uniform,' mused Cadi as she eyed the back of the svelte Waaf in front of her.

Kitty cast a critical eye over the food on offer. 'I wonder what the food tastes like? I'm not expecting anything fancy, but ...'

Drawing on the experience of her sister, Ronnie grimaced. 'You'll not be disappointed then.'

Cadi gained the cook's attention by pointing out one of the sandwiches. 'I'll take that one with' – she hazarded a guess – 'some sort of meat?'

Sighing heavily, the cook handed over the sandwich. 'Corned beef and onion.'

'That'll do. Of course we'll not get a chance to experience anything hot until they give us our irons.'

Kitty continued to stare at what she believed to be a huge saucepan of stew. 'What do you mean by "irons"? You can't eat food with an iron ...'

'We each get our own set of cutlery, they call them "irons" – my pal Poppy told me about them,' said Cadi. She indicated a large tub of hot water as she continued to speak. 'You have to wash them in that, after you've eaten.'

Kitty pulled a face. 'Doesn't look very hygienic.'

'Poppy reckons they often come out with more on them than they went in with,' agreed Cadi.

Ronnie glanced into the tub of water and grimaced. 'No wonder we need inoculations.'

Armed with a sandwich and a cup of tea each, the girls selected a table close to the counter, so that they could keep an eye on the time.

'Flippin' Nora,' mumbled Kitty through a mouthful of bread. Hastily taking a swig of her tea, she managed to swallow, albeit with difficulty. 'This sarnie's as stale as stale can be.' She glanced at Cadi's. 'How's yours?'

Cadi pulled a face. 'The same, but then Poppy did warn me the food wasn't up to much.'

Ronnie examined her own cheese sandwich. 'Mandy said the stuff in the NAAFI's better, but you have to pay for that out of your own pocket.'

'Well, if I get into the cookhouse I shan't be serving sarnies like this,' announced Kitty firmly. 'If the bread's stale, you use it to make bread-and-butter pudding, not sandwiches.'

Having finished their supper, the girls collected their kit, before making their way to the hut where the FFIs were being carried out. They joined the back of a long line of women, all looking anxiously ahead of them.

Watching the girls at the head of the queue, Cadi spoke the thought uppermost in her mind. 'Have you noticed that some of the girls go into that room over there,' she indicated a room on the far left, before adding, 'whilst others just walk out?'

'I have,' said Kitty. 'I wonder what's wrong with them?'

'Head lice,' said Ronnie matter-of-factly. 'They get rid of them straight off the bat – that way they don't have a chance to spread.'

'I think this FFI thing is a jolly good idea,' said Cadi firmly. As children, both Cadi and Poppy had suffered with head lice. Despite their mothers' reassurance that the lice only went for clean hair, both girls had found the whole affair thoroughly embarrassing, as well as infuriatingly itchy. She winced as she remembered the vicious steel comb that her mother had used to get rid of the pests. Her train of thought was interrupted by Kitty, who was eyeing another queue of girls.

'I wonder what else they check you for?'

'Everything, from disease to pregnancy—' Ronnie began, only to be cut short by Kitty, who shrieked in surprise.

Blushing madly at the attention her outcry had drawn, Kitty hastily lowered her voice. 'You *have* to be joking?'

'Men and women all sharing the same base, miles from home?' Ronnie arched an eyebrow pragmatically. 'The inevitable is bound to happen to at least some of them.'

'If they're married maybe,' conceded Kitty, 'but surely not . . .'

Ronnie shot Kitty a wry smile. 'I think you're going to learn a lot as a Waaf, not all of it in the guidebook, either.'

Cadi simply knew Kitty was about to ask if there was a guidebook, so she broke in quickly. 'And no, there aren't any guidebooks,' she answered to the unasked question.

'Crikey,' hissed Kitty, 'me dad would have his shotgun out, if I turned up with a bun in the oven.'

Ronnie stepped forward as the girl in front of her moved up the queue. 'I don't think there's any fear of that, do you?'

'No, I do not!' sniffed Kitty primly.

Cadi's engagement ring caught Ronnie's eye. 'I didn't realise you were married.'

Cadi followed her gaze. 'I'm not – this is my engagement ring. My fiancé's a mechanic in the RAF.'

'Where do you come from, Ronnie?' asked Kitty, who was eager to get away from the subject of shotguns and weddings.

'Blackpool,' replied Ronnie. She glanced at Kitty. 'I know you're from Liverpool, I'd recognise that accent a mile off.' She turned to Cadi, with an air of uncertainty. 'I'm not entirely sure, but are you from Liverpool too?'

Cadi nodded. 'Kind of. I grew up in Wales, but moved to Liverpool when I was sixteen.'

Ronnie blinked. 'When you say moved, do you really mean you ran away?'

Cadi hastily shook her head. 'No, nothing like that. I just wanted to move to the city – you know, for more opportunities.'

'Flippin' 'eck,' gasped Ronnie, 'your parents must be very broad-minded.'

Cadi laughed. 'Not my father; he was dead against it at first, but I managed to win him round in the end.'

'Cadi ran her own B&B,' said Kitty, 'made a real success of it too.'

'Impressive,' said Ronnie. Hearing a voice call out from behind her, she grimaced. 'Looks like it's my turn – fingers crossed they don't find summat they shouldn't.'

It was much later that same day, and the girls were preparing for bed. Cadi, like most of the women, had never been to the dentist and was currently admiring her teeth in the hand-held vanity mirror that Maria had given her as a going-away present. She turned to Kitty, who was undressing beneath her bed sheets. 'What did you think of the dentist?'

'Not a lot,' said Kitty, her voice muffled as she pulled her vest over her head. 'He kept hittin' my teeth with a bit of metal to see if they were loose. Quite frankly, I'm surprised I've got any left, the way he was goin' at it.' She hesitated. 'I don't see how that's meant to be good for your teeth.'

Cadi put the mirror away. 'I think the fear of what he was going to do was worse than the actual procedure, or it was for me at any rate.'

Ronnie, who was already in bed, yawned audibly. 'I heard tell one of the girls actually bit one of the dentists.'

Kitty gave a harrumph from under her sheets. 'I hope she bit the bugger that done mine.' There was a muffled pause. 'Did she get into trouble?'

'I don't think so,' said Ronnie. 'Apparently it's one of the hazards of being a dentist.'

Cadi stifled a yawn behind the back of her hand. 'I'm absolutely shattered. I dread to think what I'm going to be like tomorrow.' She glanced at Kitty, who'd emerged from beneath the sheets fully clothed in her issue pyjamas. 'Very nice!'

Red with the effort from getting changed, Kitty pushed her dark curls back from her face. 'Hardly what I'd have chosen, but they're surprisingly comfort-able – warm too, which is just as well, if we're going to be forced to sleep with the windows wide open.'

Cadi cleared her throat, indicating that Corporal Moses had just entered the hut.

As the corporal passed their beds, she glanced sidelong at Kitty. 'Maybe not wide open, what with it being your first night.'

Blushing silently, Kitty waited until the corporal was out of earshot before continuing. 'She's got the hearing of an elephant, that one. I can see we're going to have to watch what we say when she's around.'

With the corporal retiring to her own bed, Ronnie spoke in lowered tones. 'She seems a good sort, don't you think?'

Kitty shrugged. 'I s'pose so, but I don't really know any others, so it's hard to judge.'

Cadi brushed the last strands of her hair free of knots, before smothering another yawn behind her hand. 'I don't think I've been this tired since the May blitz.'

Kitty climbed back beneath her sheets. 'Thank God they stopped when they did. I can't imagine what it's been like for them poor souls down south.'

Ronnie blew her cheeks out. 'A never-ending nightmare.'

Cadi gave a sharp intake of breath as she removed her engagement ring in readiness for bed.

Kitty froze. 'Have you seen a spider?' She swallowed, her eyes growing round. 'Or a rat?'

'Neither,' Cadi assured her. 'I was meant to telephone Jez to let him know I'd arrived safely, but what with all the rushing round, it completely slipped my mind until I went to take off my ring.'

Kitty relaxed. 'He'll realise you've been busy. You can always give him a quick phone call in the morning.'

'It looks like I'll have to—' Cadi began, only to be interrupted by Corporal Moses.

'If you run, you can make it to the NAAFI before they shut up shop.'

Unperturbed by the fact that the corporal had been able to hear every word they'd said, Cadi thanked the corporal as she donned her coat and rushed out of the hut.

Once outside, she stopped short as she desperately tried to remember which of the buildings was the NAAFI, but it was no use – everything looked the same in the dark. She was about to head back when she saw a man walking out of one of the buildings. Hoping that he'd be able to point her in the right direction, she hurried over. 'Excuse me ...'

Stopping short, the man turned to face her. 'Can I help you?'

'I hope so. I'm looking for the NAAFI?'

The man shoved his hands into his jacket pocket. 'You're new here, aren't you.' It was a statement, not a question.

Cadi sighed irritably. 'Obviously, otherwise I'd know where the NAAFI is.'

He tapped his lapel. 'And you'd also know how to address a flying officer in the appropriate manner.'

Cadi nearly dropped on the spot. She'd just been rude to an officer. She began to gabble an apology, but he waved her into silence.

'Seeing as you're new, I'll let it lie.' Pulling his hand out of his pocket, he pointed to a building further on. 'That's the NAAFI over there ...' He hesitated. 'Haven't I seen you somewhere before?'

Cadi shrugged. 'I only arrived today, but I'm sure I've been in just about every building, so it's quite possible.'

He pulled a face. 'Probably.'

Thanking him for his assistance, Cadi left the officer to his thoughts as she trotted towards the NAAFI. Keeping her fingers crossed that the telephone would be free, she made a beeline for the counter. Picking up the receiver, she spoke swiftly to the operator, who put her through. It seemed like an age, however, before Jez's voice came down the line, sounding slightly out of breath.

'Cadi? Is that you? Is everything all right?'

She relaxed. Simply hearing the sound of Jez's voice had brought her comfort. 'Everything's fine. I would've rung you sooner, only I've been rushed off my feet.'

'You daft mare. You should've waited till tomorrer morning,' he chuckled softly. 'Believe me, you're going to need all the sleep you can get.'

'I know, but I said I'd call, and I wanted you to know that I'd arrived safely.'

Jez smiled. It was typical of Cadi to put the feelings of others before her own. 'And much appreciated it is too. And now that I know you're all right, you can tell me how your first day went.'

'Good! Even though we've not done any actual train-ing per se, we have been busy getting kitted out, as well as being checked out for any medical issues.' She hesitated. 'I don't remember any of you mentioning the dreaded inoculations?'

'Didn't we?' Jez laughed. 'Probably tried to forget – after all, it's not the most pleasant of experiences.'

'No, it's not!' said Cadi with verve. 'My arm feels like a pincushion, and I've not even heard of half the things they're injecting me against.'

'You don't want to, either,' Jez assured her.

'The food's diabolical, just as Poppy said it was, and even though I've not gone to sleep yet, those biscuits are as hard as nails.'

'You get used to them after a while,' said Jez, adding, 'at least you won't mind getting up early.'

Cadi gave a small yawn. 'I'm whacked. I should think it's going to take more than a hard bed and reveille to wake me up.'

He grinned. 'Don't worry, you'll be awake. Have you made any new friends?'

'Yes, lots. One of the girls – her name's Kitty – boarded the same train as me in Liverpool.'

'That's good,' said Jez. 'You'll find life in the services a lot easier with good pals. What's your corp like?'

'She seems really nice. In fact it was her suggestion that I try and phone you now.'

'Well, that's half the battle won then,' said Jez. 'You'll go through a ruck of corporals, sergeants and officers. Some good, some not. A good corp can make the world of difference.'

'If I make it to corporal, I'd like to think I'd be just like Corporal Moses,' mused Cadi.

'Better that than some of those buggers who like to throw their weight around,' conceded Jez. 'They never get the most out of their men acting like that …' He hesitated as Cadi's words caught up with him. 'You make it sound like you're already thinking about a promotion?'

'I know I've not been here more than a few hours,' said Cadi, 'but I think I rather fancy the role of corporal one day.'

'You're a natural leader,' praised Jez, 'and the services are crying out for women like you.'

With her cheeks beginning to colour, Cadi tried to swallow her smile. 'You're biased.'

'Maybe I am, but that doesn't mean to say I'm wrong.'

The operator cut across them, letting the two know that their three minutes were up.

'Some things never change,' said Cadi. 'I had rather hoped that base-to-base might buy us more time.'

Jez laughed. 'Some hope! Although it's probably for the best, seeing as you must be dead on your feet.'

'I am that,' agreed Cadi. She smiled. 'Goodnight, Jez.'

'G'night, queen – sending all my love, as always.'

Cadi managed to get out the words 'I love you too' before hearing the familiar click of the operator ending the call.

Her smile broadened as she replaced the receiver. Just hearing Jez's voice had meant the world to her, and she was glad she'd taken the corporal's advice to nip across to the NAAFI. Going to sleep in a room full of strangers was going to be a lot easier with Jez's goodnight-wishes fresh in her ears.

It was the morning after their first night, and Cadi had been awake since five-thirty. Despite her fears she had slept well, without nightmares, something she hadn't done since the bombing.

Now, as she lay in her bed, she mulled over what she would be doing if she were still at the Belmont. Her first task would be to light the fires, after which she'd put the kettle on, so that she could get washed and dressed, before getting breakfast ready for their guests.

Sitting up, Cadi looked around at the other girls, who were still sleeping soundly. Not wishing to disturb anyone, she slung her greatcoat over her shoulders before wandering off to the ablutions, where she had an unpleasant wash in cold water before brushing her teeth and fixing her hair.

Back in the hut, she dressed swiftly and, with nothing left to do, decided to put pencil to paper. After writing letters to Bill and Maria, then to Izzy, Cadi turned her hand to a letter to Poppy:

Day One was an absolute whirl! You didn't warn me of the dreaded inoculations, or the dentist, both of which came as a horrible surprise. I will say the services take good care of their men and women, but not when it comes to the food …

Cadi started as reveille sounded. Tutting irritably, she did her best to erase the line that now crossed the page.

'Flippin' heck,' mumbled Kitty sleepily as she knuckled her eyes. 'Did you go to bed last night?'

Cadi gently rubbed the line. 'I've always been an early riser.'

Kitty yawned audibly. 'I wish I was. I don't feel as though I've had a wink, with that dreadful mattress they gave us.' She prodded one of the biscuits with her forefinger. 'Look at that! My finger doesn't even go in. I might as well be sleeping on the floor.'

'Each to their own,' chuckled Ronnie. 'Morning, girls.'

Kitty frowned at the cheery-faced Ronnie. 'How can you be so chipper? Surely you weren't comfortable?'

Ronnie shrugged. 'I've been homeless a couple of times in my life and, believe me, this,' she nudged the mattress, 'is a thousand times better than cobbles.'

Blushing, Kitty mumbled an apology. 'I didn't realise ...'

Ronnie sat down on her bed. 'Not to worry, and maybe "homeless" was a bit of an exaggeration, seeing as I was only sleeping rough for a night or two,' she ran her fingers through her thick red locks, 'depending on how long it took my old man to calm down.'

'Your dad sounds a bit like my friend Izzy's father,' said Cadi. She hesitated. 'Only maybe not as bad, because he would've killed her, had she stayed out all night.'

Ronnie's eyes grew wide. 'Not really?'

Cadi gave her new friend a dark look. 'He took his belt to her, giving her a black eye and a split lip, just for finding a photograph of her mam.'

'Didn't you say Izzy was in the WAAF?' asked Kitty curiously.

Cadi nodded proudly. 'Poppy and I helped her escape.' She leaned forward. 'We even hid her overnight in the B&B.'

'I can see you're made of stern stuff,' said Ronnie approvingly.

46

Eager to fill her new friends in on the rest of her daring deeds, Cadi continued, 'Eric – that's Izzy's father – came to Lime Street Station to try and get her back, only he bumped into me first.' She arched an eyebrow coolly. 'I gave him a piece of my mind, so he tried to thump me, but when I ducked, he ended up clocking a soldier at the back of me. It looked like all hell was going to break loose, until I talked the soldier out of walloping him back.'

'Why?' chorused Kitty and Ronnie together.

'From what I heard, it sounds as though he deserved a good thumping,' added Kitty.

'He certainly did, but not in the middle of a train station, with Izzy looking on,' Cadi replied.

Kitty relented. 'I s'pose not, but it doesn't seem fair that men like him always seem to get away with everything.'

'My old feller's got a temper on him,' admitted Ronnie, 'and I'll not deny I've felt the back of his hand on more than one occasion. But he's never taken his belt to me.'

Suddenly aware of the deathly silence, Kitty gazed around her. 'Where's everybody gone?'

Ronnie jumped to her feet. 'The ablutions!' Grabbing her washbag and towel, she gestured impatiently for Kitty to do the same. 'Come on, or we'll still be getting dressed whilst this lot are getting brekker and we'll be last in line again.'

Cadi smiled as the girls hastened out of the hut. She was about to continue erasing the line on her letter when a voice spoke up from behind, startling her.

'The early bird catches the worm.'

Cadi turned to see Corporal Moses smiling down at her.

'I'm used to getting up early,' explained Cadi as she hastened to her feet.

'That's as maybe,' said the corporal, 'but it won't go unnoticed by those who matter.' She looked at Cadi's bed, which was already stripped and stacked. 'Do you hail from a military background?'

Cadi shook her head. 'Before coming here, I ran a B&B and I found it helped if I got a good routine going ...' She paused. 'Quite a few of our guests were servicemen on manoeuvres, and they often complimented me on the efficiency of the business.'

Corporal Moses nodded. 'They're used to having things done in a certain way. That way, they can be ready to go at a moment's notice.'

'Exactly,' said Cadi. 'I always made sure their breakfast was ready, so that they had plenty of time to eat before heading off into the wide blue yonder.'

Corporal Moses eyed her thoughtfully. 'Do you know what you want to do when your basic training's over?'

'I'd quite like to become a corporal one day,' confessed Cadi, 'but I'm not sure how to go about it.'

Corporal Moses arched her eyebrow. 'I think you'd easily pass muster ...' She paused. 'Your job meant you had to get on with people from all walks of life, without instruction – would that be a fair assumption?'

Cadi nodded. 'I'd say so.'

Corporal Moses rocked on her heels as she spoke. 'Things are moving at one heck of a pace, and the War

Office is having to build new air bases to keep up with demand. They're in need of people who can work without instruction and think on their feet, making improvisations where necessary.' She nodded at Cadi. 'Am I right in thinking that sounds like you?'

Cadi's heart hammered in her chest. It hadn't been twenty-four hours, but already it seemed as though she was being considered for promotion. 'I'd like to think so.'

Seeing the other women begin to file back into the room, Corporal Moses tapped the side of her nose. 'I know so.' With that, she walked up the rows of beds, instructing the women to stack their bedding and straighten their clothing.

Cadi would have turned her attention back to her letter, but she decided instead to help Kitty and Ronnie out by making their beds for them. After all, if she hadn't kept them talking, they'd never have been late going into the ablutions.

Puffing as she jogged towards Cadi, Kitty removed her greatcoat and began dressing with, Cadi noticed, no qualms as to who might see her in her vest and knickers. 'Thanks, Cadi, you're a pal.'

Cadi placed the pillows on top of the biscuits, before turning her attention to Ronnie's bed. 'Where's Ronnie?'

'Here!' Ronnie called as she trotted towards them. 'Never again! When you wake up tomorrow, do me a favour and wake me too.'

'And me,' cried Kitty. 'I'd rather be twiddling me thumbs than rushing round like a headless chicken.'

*

49

It was the end of their second day in Innsworth and once again the girls were grateful to see their beds.

'I don't care if I never see another gas mask again as long as I live,' sighed Kitty as she tried to pummel some life into her mattress. 'I know they say it's necessary in case of attack, but who in their right minds would take their mask off, *knowing* the air was filled with toxic gases?'

Cadi shrugged. 'I haven't the foggiest, and while I know it was horrid, I must admit I'm rather enjoying myself.'

Ronnie stared at Cadi in shocked admiration. 'You're a breed in itself, Cadi Williams.'

'You can't tell me this is better than making beds at a hotel, or serving behind the bar of the pub?' asked Kitty in disbelieving tones.

'It's certainly more interesting,' considered Cadi. 'Anyone can make a bed or serve up a cooked breakfast. Knowing how to react in extreme conditions isn't just interesting – it *matters*. Not only that, but it could save your life as well as someone else's, and I can't think of anything more important than that.'

Ronnie brushed her hair ready for bed. 'If I see a fire I tend to run away, but you, Cadi, are the sort of person who runs towards it.'

Kitty was about to say that Cadi wouldn't do anything so silly when she recalled Cadi's words regarding her encounter with Izzy's father. Kitty knew that if she'd seen Eric on the platform, she'd have ducked down, hidden – done whatever it took to get away; what she wouldn't have done was confront him. 'Ronnie's right,' Kitty said decidedly, 'you're a different breed from the rest of us.'

Cadi felt her chest swell with pride. 'I dunno about that, although ...' She paused as the corporal's words came back to her. 'Corporal Moses did mention something earlier this morning.'

Kitty's brow rose. 'Oh?'

'She asked me if I'd given any thought as to what I'd like to do after basic training, and I told her I rather fancied becoming a corporal. She thought I'd be a good candidate, even suggesting that I try out for one of the new bases springing up around the country, because they need people who can work on their own initiative.'

'She's right,' agreed Ronnie. 'That sort of thing would suit you down to the ground.'

Cadi turned her thoughts to the day her papers had come through. She had thought at the time that she would take to service life like a duck to water, and it appeared she was right.

The girls had been at Innsworth for the best part of a fortnight and, despite finding the work hard, Kitty and Ronnie were also beginning to enjoy themselves.

'Dances in the NAAFI,' cooed Kitty as she pinned her hair back from her face. 'They're worth the square-bashing alone.'

Ronnie raised an eyebrow quizzically. 'The dances or the men?'

Kitty giggled. 'Both!'

Cadi looked at Kitty via the reflection in her mirror. 'You've certainly changed your tune. You were shocked at the thought of a man kissing a woman out of wedlock when we first arrived.'

'I was sheltered,' admitted Kitty. 'The way my mam went on, I wasn't sure whether kissing got you pregnant, but after them talks we had ...'

'Telling you how *not* to get pregnant,' reminded Cadi. 'The information wasn't meant as a guide on how to date every man you meet before you're twenty.'

Kitty objected. 'Be fair – I've not dated one man yet.'

'Not for want of trying, though,' said Ronnie. 'Blimey, Kitty, you're like a kid in a sweet shop every time you step through that door.'

'Because the room's filled to the rafters with handsome fellers, and I'm an eighteen-year-old woman who's never been kissed!' wailed Kitty. 'I'm goin' to end up a spinster if I'm not careful.'

'You've plenty of time as yet,' said Cadi. 'I was the opposite of you. I never wanted to go near a feller, for fear of ending up like my mam.' She elaborated. 'Living in a little village with four kids and not a penny to spare.'

'And yet here you are, betrothed to the man of your dreams, and you're the same age as me,' Kitty reminded her.

'I hadn't thought of it like that,' admitted Cadi. 'I suppose living away from home at such a young age meant I had to grow up quickly. Not only that, but I achieved everything I wanted earlier than most.' She thought for a moment before adding, 'Not that I'm done yet. I still want to do things, and I know Jez won't try and stop me. Far from it – he encourages me to live my life the way I want. He'd never stand in my way or try and hold me back.'

'Sounds like the ideal man,' mused Kitty.

'He is, and I'm lucky to have him,' said Cadi. 'I know he's the one for me because I wouldn't want to be with anyone else.'

Ronnie spoke thoughtfully. 'And it's not like you've not got options. Men are always asking you to dance, even though you turn them down.' She glanced at Kitty. 'Maybe that's it – maybe men like the thrill of the chase?'

'So you're saying let them come to me?' hazarded Kitty.

'Yes,' said Ronnie simply. 'It certainly seems to work for Cadi – not that she's trying.'

The girls headed for the NAAFI and, once inside, they selected a table close to the dance floor.

As Kitty took her seat, she noticed a man eyeing Cadi from across the room. Not wanting to draw his attention, she gently nudged Cadi with her elbow. 'Don't look now, but that feller by the door's got his eye on you,' she muttered. 'Do you know him?'

Cadi immediately peered over to where the man sat. He looked vaguely familiar, and she supposed the feeling must be mutual because, as their eyes met, he got to his feet and began walking towards her. 'Oh, great,' she mumbled. 'Why did you tell me to look?'

Kitty furrowed her brow. 'I didn't! In fact I told you *not* to look.'

Cadi was about to argue that, by asking her if she knew the man, Kitty was really telling her to look, when he arrived at her side. She was on the verge of telling him politely that she wasn't interested in dancing, when their eyes met.

'You were the girl looking for the NAAFI a couple of weeks ago, am I right?'

Cadi nodded. 'That's right.' Still embarrassed by the way she had spoken to him on that occasion, she blushed. 'I really am sorry, I was in a dreadful hurry ...'

He drew up a chair and sat down beside her. 'Don't worry about it. With hindsight, I suppose it was a bit of a silly question.' He smiled, revealing a set of dazzling white teeth. 'I said then that I thought I recognised you from somewhere, and I stand by that.' He gazed curiously at her. 'What did you say you did before joining the WAAF?'

Cadi smiled politely. 'I didn't, but as you've brought it up, I used to run a B&B.'

He snapped his fingers. 'Got it! You ran the Grey-hound. I *knew* I recognised you.' He patted his chest. 'Don't you remember me?'

Cadi shook her head shyly. 'I'm sorry, but we used to get a lot of people through our doors.'

The man continued, determined to jolt her memory, 'I asked you whether you'd thought of joining up, and you said you'd been turned down because you were too young.'

Cadi brightened as her memory of their conversation came back. 'I remember. You told me that the WAAF was the best of the services, and that I should join them.'

He slapped his knee. 'That's right. Only what made you join? I was under the impression you were happy where you were?'

'The pub got bombed,' said Cadi bluntly.

His face fell. 'I'm sorry to hear that. I hope nobody was hurt?'

She gave him a grim smile. 'I'm afraid my fiancé's grandmother was killed in the blast.'

He hung his head momentarily before looking back up. 'Is that why you joined up?'

'Partly,' admitted Cadi. 'My friends are also in the WAAF, and my fiancé's in the RAF.'

'Really?' Taking a cigarette from a silver case, he placed it between his lips before holding the case towards Cadi, who shook her head politely. 'What does he do?'

'He's a mechanic,' said Cadi, 'so he has both feet firmly on the ground, and that's where I prefer them to be.'

'Still a dangerous job . . .' He lit the cigarette. 'I don't believe we were ever formally introduced. I'm Flying Officer Grainger – Mike to my friends. And you are . . . ?'

'Aircraftwoman Williams,' she said with more than a hint of pride, 'but everyone calls me Cadi.'

'I'm glad I remembered who you were. I never forget a face.' Standing up from his chair, he smiled down at her. 'I wonder what you'll be when I see you next?'

'I'd like to make corporal,' said Cadi.

He eyed her shrewdly. 'As I remember, you ran a tight ship at the Greyhound. So I have no doubt you'll do the same in the WAAF.' He smiled round at the three women. 'I shall leave you to enjoy your evening.'

Cadi waited until he was out of earshot before turning back to Kitty and Ronnie, both of whom were eyeing her enviously.

'What a corker!' breathed Kitty.

'He's the most handsome feller I've ever seen,' agreed Ronnie. 'You never told us you'd met him?'

'Didn't think it relevant,' said Cadi guardedly.

'And why did you apologise?' asked Kitty.

Grimacing, Cadi told the girls what she'd said to the officer.

Kitty stifled a shriek of laughter by pinching her nose.

'Oh, Cadi!' giggled Ronnie. 'No wonder you didn't mention it.'

'I'd never normally be so rude,' said Cadi, 'but it seemed like such a stupid question when I was in a hurry.'

'You're lucky it was him you bumped into,' said Kitty. 'Had it been someone else, they might not have taken it so well.'

'Some girls have all the luck,' Ronnie observed as she watched the handsome flying officer laughing with his friends. 'And Cadi's one of them.'

'I dunno about that,' replied Cadi.

'You're right, Ronnie,' said Kitty. 'She's a catch – men can sense stuff like that.'

Cadi frowned. 'Would you mind not discussing me as though I wasn't here?'

'Sorry, but it's true,' said Kitty. 'Men take one look at me and warning signs start flashing in their eyes, but it's not like that with you, is it? I bet you've been fighting them off with sticks all your life.'

Cadi wanted to refute this statement, but if she was honest, Kitty was right. Cadi hadn't been in the least bit interested in Jez when she first met him, yet he had been carrying a torch for her since the moment they met. And, as it turned out, so had Aled. She felt her cheeks warm. 'Not exactly fighting them off with sticks,' she mused, 'but I've had a couple of suitors.'

'See?' cried Kitty. 'Well, from now on, I'm going to be like Cadi. If a man comes near me, I shall look the other way.'

Cadi and Ronnie shared amused glances. Both women knew full well that any prospective suitor would be leapt upon before he'd had a chance to introduce himself.

It was their final day at Innsworth and the Waafs in Cadi's hut had gathered round to hear where their futures lay.

'That's the worst part of being a Williams,' whispered Cadi to Kitty and Ronnie, 'you're always at the bottom of every list.'

Ronnie was about to reply when she was called forward. After a brief conversation with the corporal she returned to her friends, papers in hand. 'I've been selected for training as a wireless operator, in the London Radio School. How posh is that?' she gabbled excitedly.

'It certainly sounds it,' breathed Cadi. 'Well done, Ronnie.'

Kitty's heart was racing in her chest. 'I won't get nothin' like that, because I'm not as brainy as Ronnie,' she whispered. 'I hope they send me to the cookhouse, cos that's where I want to be. I don't care where it is, as long as I'm there.'

The girls fell silent as Kitty was called forward.

She turned to face her friends. 'Wish me luck.'

Cadi crossed the fingers of both hands, holding them up for Kitty to see. 'Good luck.'

They watched as Kitty spoke to the corporal, her dark curls bouncing as she nodded her head fervently.

Cadi tucked her arm into Ronnie's. 'I hope it's good news – it would be awful for her to jump out of the frying pan into the fire.'

Ronnie wrinkled her brow. 'How do you mean?'

Cadi elaborated. 'Kitty only joined up because she was doing a job she hated.'

'Of course – the jewellery counter,' said Ronnie. She smiled as Kitty turned away from the corporal. 'If that grin's anything to go by, I'd definitely say it was good news.'

Kitty returned at a trot, a broad beam splitting her face in two. 'I've been selected to work in the officers' mess as a cook.'

'That's brilliant news, Kitty,' said Cadi with a relieved sigh. 'I bet you'll have better ingredients than the stuff they serve to us mere mortals.'

Kitty was looking at her papers, her eyes shining with delight. 'I hope so.'

Waiting patiently for her turn, Cadi's heart leapt as Corporal Moses called her forward. She turned to the girls. 'Shan't be a mo.'

As she approached the corporal, Cadi felt her heartbeat quicken in her chest. She had thought she wouldn't be bothered where she ended up, as long as she was near her friends, but now that it came to the crunch, she found herself hoping she didn't end up in the cookhouse. *I want to do something important*, Cadi told herself, *something that matters – something that will change people's lives.*

The corporal handed over her papers. 'You've been posted to RAF Cardington to train as a driver in the MT.'

Cadi glanced down at the instructions in her hand. She knew, from what her friends had told her, that being a driver was an important job, but she'd become quite taken with the idea of being a corporal in charge of her own hut. 'Oh,' she said before continuing dejectedly. 'So I'm not going to be working on the new bases then.'

'In order to work on the new projects, it's imperative that you are able to drive, which is why I put you forward for the MT. You need to be able to get from A to B in all manner of vehicles, as well as helping to get a base started from scratch.' Corporal Moses smiled encouragingly. 'Driving's just the start of your journey.'

Cadi brightened. 'So you still think I could make it as a corporal?'

'I do indeed, and I'm not the only one who thinks you're worthy of promotion.' The corporal raised her eyebrow. 'It seems you have friends in high places.'

Cadi looked perplexed. Could the corporal be referring to Jez, Poppy or Izzy?

Seeing the lack of comprehension on Cadi's face, Corporal Moses enlightened her. 'I'm referring to Flying Officer Grainger.'

Cadi's jaw dropped. 'Oh.'

The corporal eyed her quizzically. 'You seem surprised?'

'I am,' confessed Cadi. 'Are you *sure* he had something to do with it?'

'Positive.'

'I've only met him a few times.'

The corporal gave her a shrewd smile. 'You obviously made quite an impression.'

Tapping the instructions against the palm of her hand, Cadi recalled the officer's words. He had certainly been impressed with her work at the Greyhound, and maybe that was enough for him to see her potential? She smiled brightly at the corporal. 'I suppose I must have. Thanks for everything – I won't let you down.'

'Good luck.'

Cadi turned to join her friends, who were waiting impatiently, both of them eager to hear her news.

Kitty was the first to speak. 'You took your time. What did she say?'

'I'm off to RAF Cardington to train for the MT.' Cadi paused. 'Do you remember Flying Officer Grainger?'

Ronnie pretended to swoon. 'How could we forget?'

'Gorgeous Grainger,' giggled Kitty. 'Why d'you ask?'

'According to Moses, Grainger recommended me for promotion. Is it me or is that odd? It's not as if we're good pals.'

Wriggling her eyebrows in a suggestive manner, Ronnie nudged Cadi playfully. 'Maybe he wants you as his chauffeur?'

Kitty grinned. 'Lucky so-'n'-so.'

Cadi rolled her eyes. 'Don't be daft. Besides, he knows I'm betrothed.'

Ronnie tucked her arm through Cadi's. 'I'm only teasing. If Grainger put you forward, it's because he knows a good Waaf when he sees one.'

Cadi looked around the hut that she had called home for the past three weeks.

'I'll miss this place ...'

Kitty and Ronnie stared at her, open-mouthed. 'Surely you jest?' asked Kitty incredulously.

'Maybe I should rephrase that,' considered Cadi. 'I'll miss the camaraderie with the girls – you and Ronnie in particular.'

'We can still meet up,' Ronnie assured her, 'and there's always letters and phone calls.'

'We might even end up on the same station,' said Kitty reasonably.

Cadi was about to say she thought this highly unlikely, then reconsidered. 'I suppose it's possible, as every station needs wireless operators, cooks and drivers.'

Kitty hooked her arm through Cadi's. 'It may have been only a few weeks, but it feels as though I've known you my whole life.'

'It's spending twenty-four hours a day in each other's pockets,' said Ronnie.

'Tonight's our last night,' said Cadi, 'and I say we go out with a bang.'

'Dance until we drop,' sighed Kitty, adding, 'You watch, because it's my last night I bet I'll be surrounded by fellers.'

Cadi knitted her brow. 'And that's a bad thing?'

'Yes, cos I won't see them again after tonight.'

Ronnie wagged her finger in an authoritative manner. 'Patience is a virtue.'

'Well, I don't want to be virtuous,' pouted Kitty.

Cadi emitted a shriek of laughter. 'Kitty!'

'I don't mean like that,' she replied. 'I meant … oh, never mind what I meant.'

Cadi led their way out of the Nissen hut. 'Let's make the most of our last day before the real training starts.'

Chapter Two

November 1941

When she had first entered the MT, Cadi had taken Poppy's words to heart.

'Driving's a doddle, you can't go wrong – all you have to do is turn the wheel in the direction you're going,' Poppy had assured her friend. 'The hardest part is map-reading, especially when they've taken all the flamin' signs away.'

This conversation had taken place the day Cadi got her new posting. Believing every word that had left her friend's lips, Cadi had approached her first lesson with gusto. However, she soon discovered that driving wasn't quite as easy as Poppy had made out, the hardest part being the gears or, rather, the ratio between the clutch and accelerator as she changed gear.

'I never mentioned the gears because it didn't cross my mind,' Poppy explained truthfully.

'Well, all I do is lurch up the road,' replied Cadi bitterly, 'and that's if I'm lucky. Half the time I just stall the stupid thing.'

'Maybe you're overthinking it,' suggested Poppy helpfully.

'It's hard not to,' wailed Cadi. 'If I don't get this right, what then? Corporal Moses said it was imperative for me to drive, if I'm to achieve my goal.'

Keen to assure her friend that everything would be all right, Poppy spoke encouragingly. 'Chin up. It's only your first day. I'm sure you'll get the hang of it tomorrow.'

Determined to be successful, Cadi persisted and it wasn't long before she had conquered the Hillman. Believing she had got the knack of changing gear, she was disappointed to find that she was back to square one when she was introduced to the larger vehicles.

Now Cadi ran her tongue over her bottom lip as she attempted to pull forward without stalling. The lorry she was driving was similar to the one Daphne had turned up in when she collected Aled from the Greyhound. Cadi knew that the thought of Daphne having succeeded where she seemed to be failing was adding to the pressure. She could not, and would not, let Daphne get the upper hand. Gripping the steering wheel tightly, she concentrated with all her might as the lorry slowly inched forward. With the vehicle gaining speed, she carefully took her foot off the clutch pedal, only to hear the engine cut out. She slapped the steering wheel with the palm of her hand. 'I'm going to scream if I don't get this soon.'

The corporal teaching her raised his eyebrows fleetingly. 'That makes two of us.'

She groaned. 'I swear I don't do it on purpose.' She glanced at him shyly from the corner of her eye. 'Have they sent you over because all the others have given up on me?'

Chuckling softly, he turned to face her. 'You're not that bad. You mark my words, three weeks from now you'll be changing gear without giving it a second thought – just as you do when you're driving the Hillman.'

Cadi gave a resigned sigh. 'I'm fine once I'm moving – it's the pulling-away bit I have difficulty with.'

'It's all about feeling the bite. Once you find that, you'll be able to drive anything, regardless of whether or not you've driven it before,' he said confidently.

Cadi huffed irritably. 'That's what they all say. And even though I can do it in the Hillman, I still don't really know what the bite is. Quite frankly, it all feels the same to me.' Taking a deep breath, she put the vehicle into neutral, started the engine and attempted to pull forward, only to be stopped by the corporal.

'Are you even breathing?' he asked, a half-smile twitching his lips. 'As for that steering wheel, you're holding on to it as if your life depends on it.'

'Does it matter, if it helps me concentrate?' said Cadi, who felt the corporal was adding to her woes unnecessarily.

'Yes, because it means you're not relaxed, and that won't help your driving. You need to loosen up – not only your hands, but your legs too.' He demonstrated Cadi's driving position by holding his arms stiffly out in front of him. 'How can I drive properly if my arms are locked into position?'

'It's difficult to relax when you're trying not to make any mistakes,' whined Cadi. 'I'm halfway through my training and I'm still getting it wrong. I'm beginning to think I'm not cut out for this driving malarkey.'

He held up his forefinger. 'I've got an idea.' Without further explanation, he pulled his tie from around his neck. 'I want you to use my tie as a blindfold.'

Cadi's brow shot towards her hairline. 'You *what*?'

The corporal leaned forward, indicating that Cadi should do the same. 'Trust me.' With the tie secured in place, he continued, 'I want you to put her into gear and tell me when you feel the bite.'

Cadi shook her head vigorously. 'I daren't. What if someone steps out in front of me? I could end up killing them.'

The corporal continued, unperturbed by her concerns, 'You're making excuses. Now do as I say and pull forward, until your foot is free of the clutch.'

Wiping her forehead with the back of her hand, Cadi put the lorry into gear. Believing that everything was about to go hideously wrong, she went through the motions, only this time she felt the clutch bite.

'I've got it!' she cried as she gently lifted her foot off the clutch before applying the brake.

'Excellent!' praised the corporal. 'Now I want you to do the same, but in reverse.'

Slipping the lorry into reverse, Cadi went through the same process. With the vehicle gently creeping back, she applied the brakes. Beaming happily, she lowered the blindfold while voicing her thoughts. 'I don't understand. I *never* look at the pedals, so why did the blindfold make such a big difference?'

'You *felt* the clutch,' explained the corporal. 'By being blindfolded, you had to rely on your other senses.'

'You're right, I did. And now that I know what it feels like, I really will be able to drive anything.'

He winked at her. 'Ah well, that's the difference a good instructor can make.'

She knew he was only joking, but at the same time he was right. 'What made you come up with the idea of the blindfold?'

He shrugged. 'We're expected to get all kinds of people driving anything from lorries to motorcycles. You have to be quick to adapt and find solutions where you can.' He looked at the road ahead of them. 'Fancy giving it another go?'

Cadi handed his tie back. 'Only with both eyes on the road this time.' She put the lorry into gear and began to push the accelerator down while easing off the clutch. In truth, she had half expected that she would have to close her eyes in order to feel the bite, so she was pleasantly surprised when she recognised it instantly. Pulling forward with ease, she beamed proudly. 'I can't believe I've finally got it! I thought I was doomed to fail, but not any more.'

With the lesson over, Cadi headed straight for the NAAFI so that she could telephone Jez. As she waited for him to come to the phone, an image of her beau formed in her mind: tall, dark curly hair, deep-brown eyes and cheeks that dimpled when-ever he smiled. The image vanished as his voice came down the line.

'Cadi?'

She gave a small squeal. 'I can do it, Jez! I can move a lorry without stalling or kangarooing my way into second gear.'

'Well done, queen. I knew you'd get there in the end – you always do.'

Cadi leaned against the counter. 'I can finally look forward to my leave, without worrying about the course. I can't wait to see everyone; it's been way too long.'

Jez agreed wholeheartedly. 'I couldn't agree more, and I know Maria feels the same because I spoke to her this morning. All she talked about was spending Christmas with us all under the same roof.'

'I'm glad Izzy agreed to come,' said Cadi. 'She shouldn't have to stay away because of Eric.'

'Too right she shouldn't,' said Jez bitterly. 'I wonder what changed her mind?'

Cadi grinned. 'Her exact words were "If my father comes anywhere near me, I shall give him a piece of my mind, and he won't like what I have to say." It seems our Izzy's not the scared, browbeaten girl she once was, but a confident independent woman with a mind of her own and a tongue to match.'

'Good for her!' cried Jez. 'It'd almost be worth seeing Eric again, just to see his face when she pulls him down a peg or two.'

'I'd certainly pay good money to see Eric learn a few home truths – not that I think he'd listen,' said Cadi. 'The last time I spoke to him, it was clear he thought himself to be the injured party.'

'Until you mentioned his stash of cash,' Jez reminded her.

'Eric's money box,' said Cadi slowly. 'I'd forgotten about that.'

'I wish I'd seen his face when you asked him where he got the money from.'

'He certainly wasn't keen on hanging around after that.' She hesitated. 'I still reckon he must have nicked it.'

'Agreed, but where – or rather who – from?'

'Black market?' suggested Cadi. 'Eric was always down the docks, and everyone knows that's a prime location for smuggling.'

Jez, who used to be a supervisor down the docks, found this doubtful. 'To be a successful smuggler you need a lot of mates and, as far as I know, Eric hasn't got any.'

'True, but he got the money somehow, and I'd wager it wasn't legally.' Cadi tutted beneath her breath. 'It infuriates me that he got away with it,' adding sourly, 'just like he got away with treating Izzy like a punchbag.'

'I know, but we simply have to be grateful that we got her out when we did, and that she'll never have to see or hear from Eric again for as long as she lives.'

Cadi knew that Jez was right, but she hated to see an injustice, and Eric had never been held accountable for any of the wrongs he'd committed.

The operator broke the news that their time was up.

'I'll give you a call in a couple of days,' said Jez. 'I can't say too much, but I'm going to be off base for a day or two.'

'Sounds interesting,' mused Cadi. 'Make sure you take care of yourself. I don't want any hiccups between now and Christmas.'

He grinned to himself. 'I always do. Ta-ra, Cadi – love you.'

'Bye, Jez, love—'

The operator ended the call.

'You could've waited until I'd completed my sentence,' snapped Cadi irritably.

The operator ignored her words, responding with the usual reply: 'Caller, please replace the handset and allow the next person in line—'

Sighing, Cadi didn't bother to repeat herself. Instead she gave the operator a taste of her own medicine by replacing the handset before she had a chance to finish her sentence.

When she got back to her hut, Claire Williams – one of the girls on Cadi's course – walked towards her. 'Sorry, Cadi, I have told them, but it seems they're hell-bent on putting your post in with mine.' She handed Cadi a bunch of envelopes.

'Thanks, Claire.'

With everyone in her hut knowing that Cadi was struggling with the gears, Claire spoke tentatively. 'How'd you get on this afternoon?'

Cadi looked up from her envelopes, a large grin giving the other girl the answer she had been hoping for.

'Well done, you! What changed?'

'Different instructor,' said Cadi simply. 'It's right what they say: it's not always *what* you know, but *who*.'

'I'm so glad you got the gist,' said Claire, before acknowledging a woman who had hailed her from the far side of the room. She turned back to Cadi. 'Catch you later.'

Cadi fanned out the envelopes. Glancing at the writing on each one, she marked them off in her mind: *Poppy, Izzy, Jez, Maria, Kitty, Ronnie, Mam and Dad and ...* She stared at the last one. *Aled?* She sank slowly onto her bed. Continuing to stare at the envelope, she tried to work out why on earth Aled would write to her, when he'd not done so for ages. The last time they had spoken they had more or less agreed to go their separate ways, albeit on friendly terms.

She recalled the day in her mind's eye. She had returned to Rhos after hearing that her father and brother had been trapped in the collapsed mine, only to find that Aled had also returned home. Annoyed that he had seemingly followed Cadi to Rhos, Jez had been quick to voice his thoughts to her. Furious that Jez would accuse Aled unfairly, Cadi had retorted vociferously and the conversation had ended in a huge argument, with Cadi slamming the phone down on Jez before storming out of the post office, leaving the villagers – all of whom had feigned temporary deafness whilst she was on the phone – to gossip amongst themselves.

It was only when she told Aled of Jez's accusations that she finally learned the truth. Instead of denying Jez's suspicions, Aled confirmed that her fiancé had been right to be jealous. As the conversation progressed, it turned out that Aled had been holding a torch for Cadi for some time. Knocked sideways by his revelations, Cadi had explained that she loved Jez – and Jez alone. Aled had accepted her words, agreeing to bow out. Or so it had seemed. But if that was the case, why had he chosen to write to her now?

She sighed. There was only one way to find out. Slitting open the envelope, she pulled out the letter within:

Dear Cadi

I do hope this letter finds you well. I realise you probably never expected to hear from me again, and in truth I had decided to leave well alone. So why the change of heart, I hear you cry? The short answer is: 'the war'. I can't go into too much detail, else this letter will look more like a sieve than a piece of paper, but we got pretty badly messed up the other day, and I'm sad to say we lost our mid-gunner. It was a terrible blow to the crew, as we've been together since the start. For some reason it made me think about the mine collapse, and the trouble my presence had caused between you and Jez. I've often wondered what happened after I left you that day. Did you manage to smooth things over?

I know it's none of my business but, when all's said and done, we've known each other for the longest time, and I wouldn't want to think of you being unhappy – quite frankly, life's too short! I must say, I was rather surprised to find that you'd joined up. I did write to you at the Greyhound, but got no response. As your brother Alun's still working for my dad, I asked him, and that's when I learned you'd joined the WAAF.

Any road I hope you find the time to drop me a line or two because I'd really like to know how you're getting on, and what you're up to, but at the same time I wouldn't want to cause any trouble between you and Jez, so I'll

understand if you'd rather not. All I'll say is: friends are
precious and I'd like to keep the ones I have. I hope you
feel the same way.

Fondest wishes,

Aled

Cadi blew her cheeks out. What should she do? His letter seemed innocent enough, but she didn't know whether Jez would see it that way. She stood up. There was only one thing for it, at a time like this. Letter in hand, she strode to the NAAFI so that she could telephone Poppy.

'Hello?'

'Poppy!'

'Hello, Cadi. I must say, this *is* a nice surprise. How's things going at Cardington?'

'Wonderful! I've finally got the knack of pulling away without causing whiplash or sending someone hurtling into the windscreen.'

Poppy laughed. 'I should imagine that'll come as a relief to everyone on base – although I always knew you'd get there in the end.'

'They're ever so good, and they've got the patience of a saint. But that's not why I'm calling.'

'Oh?' Poppy's voice was full of intrigue.

Cadi gave Poppy a brief outline of Aled's letter. 'So, what d'you think? Do I reply?'

'Never mind what *I* think – what do *you* think?'

Cadi wound her finger around the telephone wire. 'If you'd have asked me that *before* Aled wrote to me, I'd have said I wanted to let sleeping dogs lie, but I'm not so sure any more. His letter made sense. You can't

73

afford to lose contact with someone over one silly mistake – life's too short for that – and Jez shouldn't have a problem with it, because Aled's already admitted defeat as far as he and I are concerned ...'

Hearing the hesitation in her friend's voice, Poppy spoke for her. 'I'm sensing a "but".'

'You are indeed, probably because you know me so well,' said Cadi. 'And that's why I rang you, because you know me better than anyone else.'

'Bezzies since we were knee-high to a grasshopper,' said Poppy fondly. 'So go on then, what's the "but", or should I guess?'

Cadi smiled. 'Guess.'

'He put in that bit about wondering whether you and Jez had made it up, and you're curious as to whether he's hoping the answer is "no", so that he can see whether the coast is clear for him to move in.'

Cadi laughed. 'I couldn't have put it better myself! Honestly, Poppy, I sometimes think you can read my mind.'

'Close, but not quite. So go on: what're your thoughts?'

'In my heart of hearts, I don't think Aled would pursue me, after everything we've been through. Which is why I think I should write back, because I'd feel awful if I didn't and something happened to him. It's only letters, so Jez has no reason to object, but at the same time ...'

'You'd rather Jez didn't know,' confirmed Poppy.

Cadi nibbled her thumbnail. 'Only because I believe he'll blow it out of proportion. What do you think?'

'You're right. Jez won't like it at all, which is silly, because there's no harm in writing someone a letter.

But the real question is whether it's right for you not to tell Jez, and I reckon you already know the answer to that one.'

Cadi heaved a sigh. 'You're right, I do. But if I tell Jez, do you really think he'll see things from my point of view?'

'Probably not,' said Poppy flatly.

'Poppy!'

She chuckled softly. 'What? Don't you like my answer, despite the fact that you know it's right?'

'I was hoping you'd say I was being silly, and that Jez would understand,' said Cadi.

Poppy smiled. 'Only he won't. Jez will make a mountain out of a molehill – and for what? A letter between friends. Hardly the crime of the century!'

'So you think I should keep it under my hat?'

'Definitely! When all's said and done, you'd be upsetting Jez for no reason.'

'You're right,' replied Cadi slowly. 'I hate the idea of keeping things from him, but Aled's reaching out to a friend, and I wouldn't consider myself to be such if I didn't write back.'

The familiar voice of the operator came down the line, and Cadi blushed as she realised that the operator might have heard some of the conversation and, if so, was it the same operator who had been on duty when she had telephoned Jez earlier? That was the trouble with making a telephone call – you were never guaranteed privacy.

'I'll let you know what, if anything, happens,' promised Cadi. 'Do give my love to Izzy.'

'Will do. Ta-ra, Cadi.'

Cadi said 'TTFN' before replacing the handset. As she made her way back to the hut, she had already made up her mind that she would write to Aled, letting him know everything that had happened since she'd seen him last. *I'm positive his reasons for writing are genuine*, she assured herself, *but if I let him know that Jez and I are still an item and his letters do start to ease off, then I'll know he was only fishing to see if I'm available. If not, then I'll know his reasons for writing were genuine and that I've done the right thing by responding.* Aled hadn't mentioned Daphne in his letter, so she assumed the two of them were no longer in touch. *Just goes to show*, Cadi thought now, *all that trouble and she still didn't get what she wanted.*

It was the day of Cadi's passing-out parade and, despite the best efforts of all those concerned, the continuing snowfall had ensured that the yard was covered.

As she stood to attention, feeling frozen to the bone, she stared fixedly at the sergeant, praying for him to give the order to dismiss. Having already had her instructions to report to RAF Coningsby – which was a lot closer to Poppy and Izzy – in the New Year, Cadi thought life couldn't get any better. Christmas was in two days' time and she couldn't wait to celebrate it with her friends. Her smiled wavered. It was a shame she wouldn't be seeing her own family, but with Rhos and Liverpool being so far apart, she simply wouldn't have the time to visit both.

After what seemed like an age, the sergeant bellowed the order for them to dismiss and, without hesitation, the entire parade ground headed for the warmth and comfort of the NAAFI.

Stamping the life back into her feet, Claire joined Cadi at her table. 'Roll on the spring, that's all I can say.'

Cadi pulled a grouchy face. 'Bah, humbug.'

Claire laughed. 'Not at all. I *love* Christmas. I just don't like cold, wet, miserable weather. Who does?'

Cadi, having taken a mouthful of the stew, swallowed before answering. 'All right, I'm with you on that one. Snow's pretty, until somebody asks you to stand in it for hours whilst freezing your bits off.'

Claire nodded. 'It's not fun to drive in, either.'

'Better than ice,' noted Cadi, 'especially black ice.' She shook her head. 'I hit a patch yesterday and it scared the flamin' life out of me.'

'What did you do?' asked Claire eagerly, a forkful of mashed potato poised before her lips.

'Turned into it, like they tell you to.' She shrugged. 'I dunno whether it made it better or not, but the instructor reckons I'd have been spinning like a top had I not done so.'

Claire grimaced. 'I hope I don't hit any.'

They continued to eat in thoughtful silence.

'What are your plans for Christmas?' enquired Cadi as she used her bread to mop up the remaining stew.

'Home to see the folks – me mam was made up when she heard we'd got Christmas off.'

'We certainly have been very lucky. I'm going to meet up with the others in the Belmont. Mam and Dad were disappointed, but I can't be in two places at once and, in truth, I'd rather be in Liverpool than in Rhos.'

Claire pretended to be deep in thought. 'Hmm, let me see, stay in a lovely warm hotel or share a bedroom with my brothers ...'

Cadi folded her arms on the table. 'Exactly! I love seeing my folks, but I'm a grown woman now and there's no way I'm sharing a room with my brothers, not any more. I did ask Mam if they could come to us, but she said Dad couldn't get the time off from the mine.'

'That's a shame,' said Claire, before adding, 'Still, there's always next year.'

Cadi knew full well, from her own experience, that another Christmas wasn't always guaranteed, not for everyone. She turned her thoughts to the letter she had sent Aled and his subsequent reply. He hadn't said much about his own life, and he'd certainly not mentioned Daphne. She understood that he couldn't discuss his operations or where he'd been – none of them could. Even so, he could have talked about dances he'd been to or films he'd seen, yet he'd done none of that, instead opting to fill her in on everything that was going on in their home village of Rhos. Cadi found this strange, especially for someone who'd been as desperate to leave as she had. Could it be that Aled was feeling homesick? She wouldn't blame him if he was, especially after losing their mid-gunner.

Claire cut across her thoughts. 'What time are you off in the morning?'

'Our leave starts at midnight, or at least mine does, doesn't yours?'

Claire wrinkled one side of her nose. 'I can't get a train home until tomorrow, so I'm stuck here till the morning.'

'Tough luck,' said Cadi. 'My train leaves not long after supper, so all in all, it's worked out rather well.'

Claire finished the last of her stew. 'It's a shame you're going to miss out on the passing-out dance.'

'I know, but seeing my friends will more than make up for that,' said Cadi, 'and, quite frankly, I can't wait!'

Jez stood on the platform of Lime Street Station. He was clutching a bouquet of hellebores whilst anxiously eyeing the line, eager for a glimpse of Cadi's train. He hadn't seen his belle for nigh on three months, but it felt a lot longer than that.

He turned his thoughts back to the last time the two of them had been together in Liverpool. They had just got over the situation with Aled and the subsequent letter from Daphne when the Greyhound had been bombed. In the blink of an eye he'd lost his entire family, for Carrie – even though she wasn't his real grandmother – was the only family Jez had ever known.

When Carrie had found the baby on her doorstep, with no note or explanation as to how he'd got there, she hadn't hesitated to take him in. Loving Jez as though he were her own, she had refused to cast judgement over his parents' decision to desert their child. As far as Carrie was concerned, they must have been desperate to abandon their baby, and she wouldn't hear otherwise.

Now Jez turned his eyes to the skies outside as a Spitfire, probably on a test run, flew overhead. He might not be able to bring his nan back, but he sure as hell could avenge her death, and he'd do that by making sure that the planes in his care were the best they could be, which is why he'd volunteered to go to Africa. He winced as the thought entered his mind. It had seemed like a good idea at the time, and he still believed it was, but he knew that Cadi wouldn't see it that way. She was fond of telling folk that she liked him with both feet firmly on the ground in good old Blighty, because she believed it to be a lot safer than the alternative.

Hearing the distant squeal of brakes, he looked towards the train, which was just visible. Straightening his tie, he stepped forward so that he might have a better view of the carriages that were drawing near.

As he eagerly awaited the arrival of his fiancée, a niggling doubt came to the forefront of his thoughts. With trains becoming increasingly unpredictable, and arrival and departure times being disrupted by bombed lines and air-raid sirens, there was no guarantee Cadi had not missed the train. Seeing the first carriages roll past, with no sign of Cadi, he had begun to fear he might be right, when he saw her waving to him from the last carriage. Beaming with a mixture of joy and relief, he followed the train along the platform until it had come to a complete standstill. Without waiting for the guard, Jez opened the door to Cadi's carriage and helped her down.

Picking her up in his arms, he kissed her deeply. His passion fired by the thought of going to Africa, his lips lingered on hers. As they broke apart, he gazed lovingly into her eyes. 'God, how I've missed you!'

'And I you,' cooed Cadi. 'I wish we weren't stationed so far apart.' She rested her cheek against his chest. 'Having said that, now I'm a fully trained driver, who knows where I might end up? I've been posted to RAF Coningsby for now, but by all accounts I shall be travelling the length and breadth of the country, so logically speaking, I'm bound to move closer to you at one time or another.'

Jez grimaced. He'd always known he'd have to tell Cadi of his impulsive behaviour at some point. He'd only hoped it would be later rather than sooner – preferably after Christmas – but if he didn't tell her after such an opening, she'd never forgive him. He tried to smile, but there was nothing to smile about, so instead his grin became more of a rictus. 'Not unless they're posting you to Africa?' he said, in what he hoped was a jovial manner.

Cadi gazed up at him – Jez had obviously misheard her. 'Sorry? You've lost me.'

His jaw flinched as he prepared himself to speak the truth. 'I did mean to tell you before, but the time never seemed right.' He paused briefly, before blurting out the words. 'I'm going to Africa.' Seeing the pained expression on Cadi's face, he continued to speak hastily. 'It won't be for long, or at least I don't think so – you see, they're having dreadful trouble with their engines and they've asked for our best mechanics to go over.' Noticing the look of disappointment clearly etched on her face, he added, 'It's a compliment really.'

The words had come out as if they were being expelled from a machine gun, and Cadi felt as though every one of them had wounded her. Her bottom lip trembled as she spoke. 'Why you? When there're plenty of good mechanics out there already.'

'Because they want the best,' said Jez, 'and I'm honoured to think I fit the bill.'

'We'll never get to see each other,' muttered Cadi miserably.

He turned to face her. 'If we're quick to resolve the problem, then we'll be back in Blighty before you can say "knife".'

Cadi forced her lips into a reluctant smile. 'You're the best mechanic I know, which is why they've chosen you. I shouldn't be angry with you – it's not as if you could've turned them down.'

It was at this point that Jez realised Cadi had got hold of the wrong end of the stick. Should he correct her or should he keep quiet? If she knew he'd volunteered she might not be as accepting, but if she continued to think he was only doing as he'd been instructed, where was the harm? Jez hated himself for not putting her right, but as it was such a small detail, did it really matter?

Cadi interrupted his thoughts. 'When do you leave?'

He gave a grim smile. 'The fifteenth of January.'

Relieved to hear that he would at least be around for Christmas and the New Year, she asked her next question. 'And are you on leave until then?'

His brow shot towards his hairline. 'I wish! I have to go back to RAF Finningley on the fourth of January, so that we can prepare for the off.'

Cadi smiled bravely up at him. 'Looks like I'll have to make the most of you whilst you're around, then.'

Picking up her suitcase, Jez remembered the hellebores. 'I almost forgot!' He presented her with the bouquet he had chosen. 'I hope you like them.'

Cadi admired the delicate flowers. 'They're beautiful.'

Pleased to see his fiancée smiling once more, Jez slipped his arm through Cadi's and together they walked out onto the concourse. Now was not the time to upset the apple cart. If he admitted to volunteering, she'd want to know why, and if he used his nan as an excuse, Cadi would quite rightly point out that Carrie would have wanted him safe and sound, back in Blighty. Which was all well and good, but Jez wanted to make the Germans pay. Given the opportunity, he'd shoot them down, just like Aled. He frowned. Why had he brought Aled into this? *Because Aled's a real hero*, said his inner thoughts, *who's probably shot down more Jerries than you've had hot dinners*. Jez's frown deepened. Why was he being so hard on himself? He was doing the best he could. After all, a reliable aircraft was as crucial to the operation as the men who were flying it. Once again his inner thoughts made themselves heard: *You're jealous; you wanted to protect the woman you love, and you failed. Cadi deserves a real man, someone who can protect her – someone like Aled.*

Cadi cut across his thoughts. 'Do you know what problem they're having with the engines?'

'Something to do with the conditions over there, that's all they've said.' He shrugged. 'My guess would be the sand, but I won't know until I get there and see it for myself.' He gestured to the line of taxis. 'Do you want to ride in style or would you prefer to take the bus?'

'Walk,' said Cadi simply. 'I've missed being in the city.'

'Me too,' conceded Jez, 'even if half of it is lying in ruins.'

'It reminds me of what we're fighting for,' said Cadi. 'When I was learning to drive I was trying so hard to get it right that I sometimes forgot what I was training for.'

'I know what you mean,' agreed Jez. 'You don't get to see much, when you spend most of your time up to your elbows in grease.' An image of a Wellington bomber appeared in his mind. The fuselage had flak marks from one end to the other, and the engine itself had a gaping hole where the cylinder head should have been. How the pilot had managed to land the heavy bomber was quite beyond Jez, and why he had made it sound as though he wasn't affected by the war also eluded him. He saw the results of war every day. In fact it was a rare occasion when all of the planes made it back from an operation without some kind of damage, if they returned at all. His mind's eye turned to an empty space where a Blenheim had once stood. The absence of an aircraft was more significant than a damaged one. So why had he made out to Cadi that he didn't see much of the war? *Because you don't want to upset her*, he thought. *There's plenty of time for Cadi to realise the horrors of working on an airfield, and until then she's best left in blissful ignorance.*

'Have you seen Maria and Bill yet?' asked Cadi, once again cutting across his thoughts.

Grateful to be leaving the subject of war behind, Jez nodded enthusiastically. 'I certainly have and, I must say, I think the Belmont's rather something, don't you?'

'There's no denying it's a lot grander than the Greyhound and it's in a much better part of Liverpool, but the Greyhound was my home, so to me the Belmont can never compare.'

Jez squeezed her arm in his. 'Loyal to the core, that's my girl.'

Remembering the letter she had written to Aled, Cadi nodded, but kept her gaze lowered. It wasn't that she was being disloyal, but Jez might not see it that way.

Whilst both she and Poppy had agreed to keep quiet regarding Aled's letter, Cadi had had second thoughts since then. It didn't matter how innocent the letters were; lying would only make things worse, and she'd be a fool even to consider it. Having decided on the train that she would come clean as soon as she saw him, Jez's news that he was off to Africa had caused her to have a rethink. If Jez knew she'd been writing to Aled, albeit innocently, he'd want to know why, and did she really want him worrying about what was happening at home whilst he was in the middle of Africa, with goodness only knows what going on around him? No. To tell him would only ease her conscience; it would do nothing for Jez but cause him concern, and that was the last thing she wanted. *I shall stop writing to Aled*, Cadi told herself. *I'll tell him that I think it's unfair for me to be writing to another man whilst my fiancé is out of the country, no matter how innocent it may be.*

With the matter temporarily laid to rest, she relaxed in the knowledge that she and Jez were about to have the best Christmas ever.

It was Christmas Eve and Cadi had gone to the station to meet Poppy and Izzy, whilst Jez helped Maria and Bill back at the hotel. Having not seen Poppy since the May blitz, Cadi was eager to see if her oldest friend had changed. As the train drew into the station, she saw both girls waving frantically at her from their carriage window. Standing outside the carriage, she waited eagerly for the guard to open the door. As soon as he had done so, Poppy and Izzy alighted onto the platform and all three girls greeted each other with gusto.

If Cadi had wondered whether Poppy would look different, that was nothing compared to Izzy. Cadi stared at her friend, open-mouthed. 'Izzy, you don't even look like the same woman.'

Izzy blushed shyly. 'Amazing what three square meals a day can do for your figure.'

Cadi couldn't have agreed more. Her friend's once wafer-thin frame had filled out nicely, and her previously gaunt cheeks had vanished, leaving her with a fresh and healthy complexion. The biggest difference, however, was in the scar that Eric had given his daughter. It was still visible below her left eye, but only just.

Seeing that Cadi was staring at the scar, Izzy spoke up. 'A touch of powder,' she said informatively. 'I was amazed at the difference it made, but Poppy thinks eating properly helped almost as much.'

Cadi turned to Poppy. With her dark hair and dark eyes, Poppy had remained relatively unchanged, save for the deepening of the premature lines that marked her forehead. 'Still my Poppy, beautiful as ever!'

Poppy grinned. '*And* I've got a boyfriend.'

Cadi's jaw dropped. 'Since when? And why wasn't I the first to know?'

Izzy giggled, faint dimples forming in her cheeks. 'Because she hooked him whilst we were on the train.'

Cadi shook her head. 'Talk about a fleeting romance ...'

Poppy was looking smug. 'That's where you're wrong. We might've met on the train, but he's going to be staying in RAF Fiskerton, same as us – he's a mechanic, and his name's Geoffrey.'

Cadi eyed her friend incredulously. 'And he actually asked you to be his belle whilst you were en route?'

Poppy shrugged. 'He's asked me on a date, so maybe it's a tad premature to be calling him my boyfriend, but it's the closest I've come to having one and so, as far as I'm concerned, that's what he is.'

Cadi laughed. 'That's my Poppy!' She jerked her head to the row of taxis. 'Unless you'd prefer to walk?'

Both Poppy and Izzy shook their heads. 'We're shattered,' explained Poppy. 'Our train was full to the rafters.' As the girls headed onto the concourse she continued, 'How's Jez? And why isn't he with you?'

Cadi relayed the tale of Jez's new posting, adding, 'He's stayed behind to help Bill prepare the rabbit for Christmas dinner—'

Poppy interrupted without apology. 'We're having rabbit?'

Cadi nodded.

'As in *Peter Rabbit*?'

Cadi looked at her friend in horror. 'He's not someone's pet, if that's what you're thinking.'

Poppy smiled. 'Glad to hear it.'

Trying to shake the image of Peter Rabbit being chased around the kitchen by Bill and Jez, Cadi continued with what she'd been saying, prior to Poppy interrupting. 'Like I started to say, Jez is staying behind, and I'm glad he did.' Cadi went on to tell the girls of Jez's subsequent posting to Africa, finishing with, 'So I've decided to tell Aled I'm not going to write to him any more.'

Izzy got into the back of the first taxi. 'Because of Africa?'

Cadi slid into the seat beside her, followed closely by Poppy, who instructed the driver to take them to the Belmont.

'Yes,' said Cadi plainly. She went on to explain that she had decided to come clean to Jez, only changing her mind when she heard his news about Africa. 'I don't want Jez to start putting two and two together, only to come up with five. So I've decided to make a clean break – that way no one gets hurt.' She shrugged. 'It's not as if Aled hasn't got other people to write to ...' She glanced thoughtfully at Poppy. 'Has he written to you?'

Poppy raised an eyebrow perceptively. 'Nope.'

'Has he known you longer than Poppy?' asked Izzy.

'Not really—' Cadi began, but Poppy cut her short.

'Not at all! Come on, Cadi, when you look at it, it's obvious why Aled started writing to you and not me.'

'Then why didn't you say summat when I asked for your advice?' cried Cadi.

'Because it wasn't obvious *then*,' said Poppy coolly.

'There's no point in crying over spilt milk,' said Izzy evenly. 'The way I see it, there's been no harm done, so why not forget about it and move on?'

'You're right,' said Cadi. 'I'm getting my knickers in a twist for no reason.'

'You've got a conscience, and there's nowt wrong with that,' said Poppy.

'Probably explains why Aled didn't have much to say in his reply,' conceded Cadi. 'He didn't talk about his life at all – only what everyone at home was doing.'

'Odd,' said Poppy, 'especially when you consider how keen he was to get away.'

'That's what I thought,' agreed Cadi, 'but with the benefit of hindsight, his letter was small talk, as if he had to think of things to say. And that makes perfect sense, if he was only fishing for information regarding my relationship with Jez.'

'Can't blame a feller for trying,' said Izzy.

Cadi stared at her. 'That's exactly what Aled said when we were riding the overhead railway.'

Izzy's brow rose. 'When was this?'

'Before the blitz.'

Izzy's brow continued to rise. 'So he's been after you for a while then?'

'Yes, but I didn't take him seriously – not at first. We used to be such fierce enemies; it didn't occur to me for one minute that he might actually be keen on me. If anything, I thought he was teasing.'

'Sounds like he's smitten,' said Izzy. She stared absent-mindedly out of the window. 'I know you told me what the city was like after the blitz, but I hadn't realised how truthful you were being.' She turned to face the girls. 'Do you think my old house is still standing?'

'Possibly. Men like Eric seem to have all the luck,' muttered Poppy.

'Never a truer word said,' agreed Izzy. 'When I think back to the stuff I let him get away with, it makes my blood boil.'

'Men like that lie, cheat and steal their way through life with no consequences,' said Cadi bitterly, 'whilst the rest of us seem to get punished for sticking by the rules and toeing the line.'

'His luck will run out one of these days,' said Poppy confidently. 'What comes around goes around.'

Rounding the corner of West Derby Road, the taxi driver pulled up outside the Belmont. The girls chipped in their shares of the fare before alighting from the cab.

Poppy looked up at the grand façade. 'Flippin' Nora!'

'It certainly makes the Greyhound look small,' observed Izzy.

Maria came rushing out of the pub, a tea towel over her shoulder, and ushered the girls into a group hug. 'I can't tell you how good it is to have you all safely back under one roof.'

Bill stepped out onto the pavement. 'Hello, girls. Come on inside and warm your cockles in front of the fire.'

The trio followed their hosts inside.

'Where's Jez? I'd have thought he'd be champing at the bit to see the girls,' said Cadi.

As if on cue, Jez appeared from the hallway. 'I thought I'd say hello in the warm.' He grinned at them, his smile broadening as his eyes fell on Izzy. 'By all that's holy!'

Izzy blushed.

Maria nodded her head approvingly. 'My sentiments exactly.'

'That so-called father of yours should be hanged for what he did to you,' said Bill gruffly.

Lowering her voice, Maria laid her hand on Bill's forearm. 'He's still her dad.'

Izzy was shaking her head. 'I've always made excuses for him, but that's because I didn't know any differently. Since joining the WAAF I've met lots of girls, and there's not one of them who isn't shocked to hear how I got my scar. I blamed myself for *years*, thinking that Dad was the one who'd been hard done by, and that I should have had more sympathy for him. He even had me believing I was lucky he'd looked after me.' She gave a mirthless laugh. 'That man brainwashed me into thinking I deserved everything I got, which was a wicked thing to do to a child.'

Bill gave a single nod. 'Well said, that girl!'

Cadi's eyes shone with admiration. 'I knew your joining the WAAF was a good idea, but I didn't realise how much it would change your life – until now, that is.'

'Please don't think I don't appreciate what you, Poppy and Jez did for me,' said Izzy firmly. 'Without

91

friends like you, I'd never have got away from Dad, and for that I'm eternally grateful.'

'I'm glad you came back, but what made you change your mind?' asked Bill curiously.

Izzy's eyes glittered as she smiled at each of them in turn before replying simply, 'I wanted to spend Christmas with my family.'

Maria blew her nose noisily. 'Oh, Izzy, bless your heart.'

Izzy smiled happily as Maria took her in a tight embrace. 'You've been more of a family to me than my father ever was. I know we're not blood-related—'

Jez was quick to cut across her. 'My nan wasn't related to me in any way, shape or form, but she did more for me than my parents ever did. She was my nan and, as far as I was concerned, she was my family – blood or not.'

'So blood be dashed,' said Bill succinctly, 'family's family.'

Izzy gazed at the brightly lit Christmas tree that stood by the parlour window. 'I've never had a Christmas tree before.'

Cadi's face fell. 'What did you use to do for Christmas? I can't imagine Eric showering you with gifts or cooking a roast dinner.'

Izzy sank down into one of the chairs beside the tree. Admiring the many glass baubles that hung from the branches, she gently touched one with her fingers, causing it to spin gently, reflecting the light as it rotated. 'In a word?' said Izzy. 'Nothing. In fact I'd say that for me it was the worst day of the year.' She glanced at the paper-chains that hung around the picture rail of the parlour. 'I used to hate Christmas,' she continued, 'especially when I'd see people hanging up their decorations or rushing home with their Christmas shopping, all excited for the big day.' She tutted beneath her breath. 'All I ever got for Christmas was a fat lip.'

Maria's jaw flinched. 'Then we must show you what a real Christmas is.' She turned to Cadi. 'Can you show the girls to the room the three of you will be sharing?'

In answer, Cadi jerked her head in the direction of the stairs. 'Follow me.'

Picking up their bags, Poppy and Izzy followed Cadi up a flight of wooden stairs. 'Maria's closed the hotel for the holidays so that we can have the place to our-selves,' she told them.

They entered one of the bedrooms and Izzy placed her kitbag on one of the spare beds. 'Maria would make a great mam. It's a such a shame she never had any children of her own, don't you think?'

Standing at the window, Cadi looked down onto the street below. 'My Auntie Flo couldn't have kids – not sure why – but she's another one who'd make a good mother.'

Poppy indicated the chest of drawers. 'Are any of these free?'

Cadi nodded. 'I've taken the top one; you and Izzy can have either of the other two.'

Poppy started placing her things in the second drawer down. 'Have you heard from your auntie lately?'

'A couple of weeks ago,' said Cadi. 'Flo's still flitting around the country, but won't say where.' She glanced at Izzy. 'Poppy used to think my aunt worked for the secret service.'

'Still do,' said Poppy plainly.

Cadi rolled her eyes. 'As usual, we shall have to agree to disagree,' she replied, before turning her attention back to Izzy. 'Have you thought about what you're going to do, should you run into your dad whilst you're home?'

'Not really. I suppose I'll cross that bridge when I come to it.' She eyed her friends levelly. 'I've been thinking about my dad a lot lately, and the things he used to say.'

'Like what?' asked Poppy.

'Like saying my mother had abandoned me, so that she could run off with her lover,' said Izzy.

'I wouldn't waste a single second thinking about him, if I were you,' intervened Cadi.

'I can't help it,' said Izzy flatly. 'You see, the more I think about it, the more I question why I ever believed a word that came out of his mouth.'

Poppy shrugged. 'In all fairness, any woman who runs off leaving her baby behind must be pretty selfish.'

'Or beaten,' said Izzy. 'Let's face it, my dad took joy in knocking seven bells out of me, so who's to say he didn't do the same to my mam?'

'Still no excuse,' said Cadi. 'If anything, it should've made her more determined to take you with her.'

But Izzy was persistent. 'I'm telling you straight, there's more to this than meets the eye – it just doesn't sit right.'

'Supposing you're correct,' reasoned Poppy, 'how on earth do you intend to prove it, when you don't even know who your mam is?'

'I'm not suggesting I can do anything about it,' said Izzy quietly. 'What I am saying is that I think Dad was lying.'

'I see ...' said Cadi and paused. 'Joining the WAAF's done you the world of good.'

'It's certainly been an eye-opener, and in more ways than one,' agreed Izzy. 'All those tedious tasks give a girl plenty of time to think.'

Poppy grinned. 'You can do mine, if you like.'

Laughing, Izzy shook her head. 'Thanks, but no thanks – I've done all the thinking I need to.'

Turning her attention back to the street below, Cadi watched the snow begin to fall. 'It's snowing,' she told the others. 'I do hope we have a white Christmas.'

'I love snow at Christmas,' remarked Poppy. 'It seems to make everything that bit more magical, don't you think?'

'Especially when you've got a roaring fire to go home to,' agreed Cadi. 'They're holding a carol service at St Michael's later, do you fancy going?'

Both Izzy and Poppy agreed they would very much like to go.

'I love a good old sing-song,' said Poppy. 'And carols are so much jollier than hymns, don't you think?'

Izzy shrugged. 'I've never been to church, so I wouldn't know.'

The girls both gaped at her. 'What, *never*?' said Poppy, the disbelief clear to hear in her voice.

Izzy gave both her friends a sceptical look. 'Don't tell me you thought Eric a churchgoer? Crikey, I should think he'd burst into flames as soon as he set foot over the threshold!'

Cadi and Poppy both burst out laughing.

'When you put it that way ...' giggled Poppy.

'It's a shame you've never been, though,' added Cadi.

Poppy pulled a nonchalant face. 'She's not missed out on much. If I'm honest, I was never keen on going to church on Sundays: sitting on them hard benches, listening to Father what's-his-name drone on and on about the same old stuff.'

Standing up from her bed, Izzy began to unpack her things into the bottom drawer. 'Then why did you go?'

Cadi looked at Poppy, who shrugged. 'Because everyone else did?'

'You have to go to church to thank God for keeping us safe and ...' Cadi's voice faded as they all listened to her words.

'God forgives you for your sins if you go to church,' intervened Poppy. 'It doesn't matter what you've done – if you go to the confessional, the priest will give you three Hail Marys, or summat like that, and all's forgiven.'

'And if you don't go?' asked Izzy curiously.

'I suppose it depends on how bad you are, but *our* priest was always saying that we'd go to hell if we didn't do as it says in the Bible,' admitted Cadi.

'So,' Izzy began slowly, 'if my dad went to confession, he'd be forgiven for everything he'd ever done to me and still go to heaven?'

Poppy nodded mutely. She had a horrible feeling she knew what was coming.

'Do you think breaking into your father's money box and pushing him down the stairs could be seen as a sin?' enquired Izzy.

96

Cadi's cheeks bloomed; she also had a feeling she knew where Izzy's conversation was going and she didn't like the look of the destination ahead. 'The Bible says you mustn't steal,' she said slowly, 'but I'm pretty sure you can't steal what's yours in the first place, and those papers were yours.'

'And you only pushed your dad off because you knew what would happen if you didn't,' said Poppy. 'You never meant for him to fall down the stairs.'

Izzy grew pale. 'But I did drug him with sleeping tablets. I don't think that can be considered the right thing to do.'

'You had to …' began Poppy, but Izzy wasn't listening.

'How can it be right that God would forgive Eric for beating me within an inch of my life, just because he went to confession, and yet if I don't go, I could be sent to hell for trying to escape?' Cadi opened her mouth to speak, but Izzy was on a roll. 'And what about Hitler? *Look* at the evil he's committing, yet according to you two, three Hail Marys – whatever they are – and he'll be forgiven for everything.' She frowned. 'How can that *possibly* be right?'

'It can't,' said Cadi simply. 'But as my mother likes to say, ours is not to reason why.'

'Well, it should be,' said Izzy firmly, 'because that's sending out the wrong message.'

'Only Eric doesn't go to church,' offered Poppy.

'Neither do I!' cried Izzy. 'So what does that mean? That we'll both go to hell, unless I start?'

Cadi looked into the far distance and at the buildings that lay in rubble. 'I don't know what to tell you,

Izzy, I really don't, because you're right. All I can say is that having faith helps a lot of people; whether it's misguided or not doesn't really matter, if it brings them comfort through their darkest hours.'

Izzy joined Cadi at the window. 'I'm rather looking forward to going to church. Will the priest be there?'

'Of course. Why d'you ask?'

'I'd like to ask him what he reckons God thinks about Hitler, and why he's allowing him to do everything he's doing.'

Poppy blew her cheeks out. 'I think we'd all like to know the answer to that one.'

As Cadi settled down to sleep she mulled over the evening's events, starting with Poppy and Izzy, who had quizzed the priest over his beliefs and thoughts when it came to God and Hitler. She got the impression the priest wasn't used to people questioning him in such an in-depth manner and that he was rather enjoying the attention. When they had finally come away, Cadi had asked Izzy whether she was satisfied with his explanation, but it seemed she was still thinking things through, although much later that same evening, as they settled beneath their bed sheets, Cadi heard Izzy, her voice just above a whisper, offer up three Hail Marys, probably to be on the safe side.

On the way back from the church Jez and Cadi had decided to go for a stroll through nearby Newsham Park, so that they might have some time alone.

'It's good to be back,' said Jez, 'but even better to be with you.'

She glanced up at him. 'You missed me then?'

He chuckled softly. 'Like you wouldn't believe.'

'It's not like we haven't been apart before,' mused Cadi. 'What makes it so different this time?'

'I worry about you more,' replied Jez truthfully.

'Why? Because I'm in the WAAF?'

He nodded. 'Lots of people struggle to come to terms with service life, and they're unhappy as a result. I wouldn't want to think of you as being unhappy.'

She smiled. 'You've no worries on that score. I'm loving my new life, especially now that I've mastered the art of driving.'

'When I return I hope you get posted near me, so that we can see more of each other.'

'It certainly would be nice,' agreed Cadi. 'We'll just have to keep our fingers crossed.'

'So what about me?' asked Jez. 'Have you missed my handsome face?'

She laughed. 'As well as your modesty!' She hesitated before continuing, 'Of course I've missed you. But if I make corporal they'll be sending me all over the country, and with Lincolnshire having the most air-fields, it only stands to reason that I should come close to you at some stage or other, when you're back in Blighty, of course.'

'So *that*'s why you want to be corporal,' teased Jez, 'so that you can be near yours truly.'

Cadi agreed wholeheartedly, albeit tongue-in-cheek. 'I can see you've got me down pat.'

Leaning down, Jez kissed her tenderly. 'God, I've missed you.'

They may have been joking, but in a lot of respects Jez had hit the nail on the head. Losing Carrie had made Cadi aware how precious their time together was, and being promoted to corporal – should she be lucky enough to achieve that position – would give her more chance of being closer to the people she loved.

Leaning back from their embrace, Cadi managed to utter the words 'And I've missed you too,' before Jez pulled her in for another kiss.

Softly caressing the back of her neck as his mouth met hers, Jez kissed her gently, before pulling away. 'When I come back from Africa we need to spend a weekend away together – but not in Liverpool, because we're never truly alone when we come here.'

'Sounds good to me,' said Cadi.

Jez smiled. 'Then it's a date.'

As they continued walking, Cadi looked to the lake. 'I love coming here, it reminds me of the time we used to go to the lake in Sefton Park.'

Jez slipped his arm around her shoulders. 'I remember teaching you to skim stones.'

She smiled. 'I got to be jolly good at it. I wonder if I've still got the knack?'

Jez looked towards the inky lake. 'We'll have to come back tomorrow and see.'

Cadi slid her arm around his waist. 'It's so peaceful. Where do you think everyone is?'

Jez stamped his feet. It had been cold in church, but it was positively bitter outside. 'In front of a warm fire, if they've got any sense.'

She looked up at the stubble on the underside of his chin. 'Is that where you'd rather be?'

He squeezed her shoulders. 'Not just yet. I prefer to get nice and cold out here, so that we can snuggle up in front of the fire when we get in.'

'I think I heard Maria say she's got some cocoa ...' said Cadi absent-mindedly.

Jez smacked his tongue against his lips. 'Now you're talking. I bet it's better than that watered-down stuff they give you in the RAF. That's more like dishwater with a hint of chocolate.'

Cadi grimaced. 'Sounds lovely.'

Holding her against him, Jez kissed the top of her head as they continued their moonlit stroll. 'Where do you think we'll be when all this is over?'

'How d'you mean?'

'Well, I don't intend to stay on in the RAF, but I don't think I'd like to go back down the docks, either.'

'You're a qualified mechanic – you could work anywhere,' said Cadi. 'It's different for me. Once the war's over, no one's going to want female drivers, so even if I wanted to continue, I wouldn't be able to.'

'I know Maria would welcome you back to the Belmont,' suggested Jez.

'Only I don't think that's where my future lies,' Cadi confessed. 'I rather fancy the idea of a tea room, myself. Pubs are all well and good, but the hours are long and unless you're lucky, like Maria, you could end up with summat like the Bear's Paw.'

'Sounds like you've thought this through?' mused Jez.

Cadi rested her cheek against his chest. 'It helps to look forward to the future, don't you think?'

He nodded. 'Definitely.'

Cadi gasped as the moon's reflection appeared on the lake. 'It's so beautiful.'

Jez turned to face her. 'Just like you.'

She gazed up at him. 'Beautiful it may be, but clear skies bring trouble.'

Leaning down, Jez kissed her gently. 'We're safe tonight.'

Wrapping her arms around his waist, Cadi nuzzled her cheek against his chest. 'How can you be sure?'

'Because even the Luftwaffe can't spoil *this* Christmas.'

She glanced up at him. 'Why? What's so special about this Christmas?'

'It's our first Christmas as an engaged couple, and the last one before I go overseas.'

Cadi listened to his heart beating steadily in his chest. 'I wish you weren't going.'

Jez squeezed her gently. 'Me too, but someone's got to go. We'll not win the war if we can't get our boys off the ground.'

'And are you certain they'll be sending you straight back?'

'That's what they've said.'

Cadi snuggled against him. 'I'm missing you already, and you haven't even gone.'

Jez leaned back from their embrace. 'If I could, I'd marry you tomorrow ...'

Cadi shook her head. 'That's what people do when they think they're not coming home.' With tears forming in her eyes, she closed her lids as Jez kissed the tip of her nose.

'Wild horses couldn't keep me from coming home to my Cadi.'

She gave him a wobbly smile. 'Glad to hear it.'

Placing his arm back around her shoulders, Jez led her alongside the lake. 'You're my Welsh rarebit.'

Cadi giggled. 'You do know that's basically cheese on toast?'

'Only more special, just like you,' said Jez.

'Ever the charmer,' smiled Cadi. She sniffed the frosty air. 'It really is awfully cold. I think we'd best go back whilst I can still feel my toes.'

Wrapping their arms tightly around each other, they had walked back to the Belmont, where Maria greeted them with a cup of cocoa. They had spent the evening playing rummy, three-card brag and charades. Izzy had had a wonderful time, and Cadi had enjoyed seeing their friend so happy. They were enjoying themselves so much that no one wanted to go to bed, and Cadi had fallen asleep on Jez's knee as they sat in front of the fire, only to wake up in his arms as he carried her up the stairs. How she wished she could end every day that way.

Now, as she lay in her bed, Cadi hoped fervently that something would happen to keep Jez in England, because the thought of him so many miles away in Africa was more than she could bear.

It was Christmas morning and Cadi was wide awake. Looking across the room, she saw that Poppy too was stirring. Leaning up on one elbow, she gained Poppy's attention. 'Pssst!'

Poppy gave her friend a sleepy wave. 'Mornin',
Cadi.' Then, remembering what day it was, she added,
'Merry Christmas.'

Sliding from beneath her sheets, Cadi donned her
dressing gown as she headed over to Poppy. 'Did you
sleep well?'

Poppy stifled a yawn behind the back of her hand.
'Like a baby. What time is it?'

'Just after six.'

Poppy nodded. 'Reveille.'

'I still wake up at half-past five,' said Cadi. 'Kitty and
Ronnie used to ask me to wake them early, so that they
could get a head start on the other women in our hut.'

'When was the last time you spoke to them?' asked
Poppy.

'Shortly before I left for Liverpool. Kitty's loving
serving the officers in their mess – she says the food's a
lot better than the stuff they give us—'

Poppy interrupted. 'Sounds about right.'

'As for Ronnie, she's still enjoying the WAAF, but
it'll be six months before she's fully trained as a wireless operator.'

'Blimey!' breathed Poppy. 'It must be a lot harder
than driving.'

Cadi nodded. 'Ronnie's very clever, so I'm sure she'll
pass the course with ease.'

Izzy spoke, whilst yawning. 'Is it Christmas yet?'

Cadi laughed. 'It certainly is! Although it sounds like
you could do with getting your head down for a bit
longer ...'

Izzy, however, had no intention of going back to
sleep and was already up and walking towards them

with her hands outstretched. 'I got you both a little something. I've never done this before, so I don't know whether I'm doing it right or not?'

Cadi beamed as she lifted the bar of scented soap to her nose. 'You're doing wonderfully, Izzy. I love it, thank you.'

Poppy opened the small bag of sweets and smiled. 'Liquorice Allsorts, my favourite!'

Cadi hurried over to her bag and pulled out two small packages, which she handed to the girls. 'Merry Christmas!'

Izzy looked up sharply. 'Pan-cake! How did you manage to get your hands on this?'

Cadi smiled. 'Sheer luck.'

Poppy looked up from her present. 'A manicure set.'

Cadi grinned. 'I was told it was an essential bit of kit for any WAAF driver.'

Poppy laughed. 'It certainly is. I need a new nail file, after snapping my old one getting into one of the cars.'

Cadi chuckled. 'You've got to stop locking yourself out.'

Poppy gave her friend a smug smile. 'Only this time it wasn't me, but some poor girl who was fresh off the course.'

Leaning over the side of her bed, Poppy pulled out two items. She handed the first to Izzy, who took it eagerly.

'I must say, this Christmas thing is fun, isn't it?' said Izzy. She was carefully removing the envelopes that Poppy had used as wrapping paper, to reveal a tube of lipstick. Smiling, she looked from Cadi to Poppy. 'You got me this because my father never allowed me any, didn't you?'

Both girls nodded. 'You've missed out on a lot,' said Poppy, 'and we think it's high time you caught up.'

'And you're already seeing the benefits of make-up,' noted Cadi.

Izzy nodded. 'It helps hide the scar, which gives me more confidence in front of people I don't know.'

Cadi opened her gift from Poppy. Inside was a photograph of herself and Poppy the day Cadi had been crowned Rose Queen. 'Poppy!' she gasped. 'Where on earth did you get this from?'

Poppy beamed. 'Do you like it?'

Cadi held it to her chest. 'I *love* it.' She turned the photograph, which was beautifully presented in a wooden frame, for Izzy to see. 'This photograph was taken at the Rose Queen Fete. Every year they choose someone to be the Rose Queen, and that was the year it was my turn. My mam made the dress out of old sheets, and the roses out of lace doilies.'

Izzy admired the photo. 'You look beautiful.'

Cadi ran her finger down the length of the frame. 'I loved every minute of that day, but it wasn't enough. I knew I wanted more out of life, and I was determined to get it.'

'Hence the move to Liverpool,' said Poppy, popping a sweet into her mouth.

'And the rest, as they say, is history,' finished Cadi.

Someone knocked a brief tattoo on the door to their room. 'Can I come in?' It was Jez.

Cadi called back. 'Only if you're tall, dark and handsome.'

There was a brief pause. 'I'll take that as a yes.' He entered the room with a beaming smile on his cheeks. 'Merry Christmas, one and all.' He held up a jug of warm water. 'Where would you like this?'

Standing up on tiptoe, Cadi kissed his cheek. 'Merry Christmas, Jez.' She took the jug and poured the water into the basin. 'Is anyone else up?'

'Maria's in the kitchen, making toast and porridge, and Bill's fiddling with the volume on the wireless, to see if he can stop it from crackling.'

'Flippin' heck!' exclaimed Poppy. 'Looks like we'd best get a shuffle on.'

Jez shrugged. 'Maria said not to rush.'

Izzy took her towel, soap and flannel over to the basin. 'Who's rushing? I can't wait to get downstairs and see everyone.'

Cadi handed Jez the empty jug. 'Thanks for the water. Tell Maria we'll be down in a mo.'

When they had finished their breakfast of toast and porridge, Cadi and Jez headed into the small parlour to exchange presents. Jez handed Cadi a small piece of tissue, which she carefully unwrapped.

'Oh, Jez! It's beautiful.' She laid the blue glass-beaded bracelet on top of her wrist and Jez fastened the clasp.

With the bracelet in place, he said, 'I'm glad you like it,' before kissing her softly.

Breaking their embrace, Cadi looked down at the bracelet. 'I don't just like it – I love it.' She pushed her hand into her pocket, removing a small package, which she handed to Jez to unwrap. 'I know you said the bristles were falling out of yours …'

Beaming, Jez ran the new shaving brush over his chin. 'It's perfect, as mine's nigh on bald.'

Cadi breathed a sigh of relief. 'I did worry you might've already bought one.'

He shook his head. 'Never seemed to remember, or find the time.' He turned as Izzy entered the room.

'We're going to the carol concert in Newsham Park, are you coming?'

Jez looked to Cadi, who nodded. 'I'll get my coat. Are Bill and Maria joining us?'

Izzy grinned. 'They certainly are. The veg is prepped and ready to cook, and Maria's put Peter in the oven on low …'

Cadi grimaced. 'It's a good job there're no kiddies living in the pub.'

A voice called through from the kitchen. 'Are you lot coming?'

Cadi and Jez followed Izzy back into the kitchen, where Bill, Maria and Poppy were standing in their coats, ready for the off. 'Those Nazis might've ruined last Christmas, but they aren't going to ruin this one,' said Maria firmly. She was, of course, referring to the Christmas blitz of 1940.

'That's the spirit!' said Poppy.

Izzy beamed happily as she buttoned up her coat. 'Nothing could ruin this Christmas.'

With the last person out, Bill locked the door to the pub and they set off for the park. Within minutes of leaving, the small group found themselves entering the gates.

'It must be lovely living so close to the parks,' remarked Izzy.

Maria smiled. 'I'm afraid we don't get to enjoy them much – not with the hotel on top of everything else.'

They gravitated towards a large gathering of people. 'Good turnout,' said Jez as he surveyed the carollers.

A man at the front of the crowd cleared his throat, then called for silence so that they might start the first carol, 'Deck the Halls'.

Jez placed his arm around Cadi's shoulders as they started to sing. Feeling his warmth, Cadi once again wondered how she would cope with him being so far away. The very thought made her lean closer in to him.

With the final carol sung, the crowd slowly dispersed, and they were just about to leave the park when Izzy asked the question uppermost in her thoughts. 'Would it be all right if I went to see my old home?'

Poppy and Cadi exchanged surprised glances. 'Of course,' said Cadi swiftly, 'but why would you want to?'

Izzy grimaced. 'Morbid curiosity?'

'I'd have thought you'd want to leave that place as far behind you as you could,' said Poppy.

'I do, but I've been thinking about this all night. You see, the last time I was there I ran away.'

Bill frowned. 'Exactly, so why go back?'

'I *say* I've changed, and I *say* I'm not scared of Dad, but that's easy to say when you think you're never going to run into him again. I want to *prove* to myself that I don't fear him any more.'

Cadi puffed out her cheeks. 'Do you not think it's best to leave sleeping dogs lie?'

'Or, if you really feel you have to, go another day,' reasoned Maria.

'If I go now, while the pubs are still shut, I know Dad won't be leathered, and I want him to hear every word I have to say, while sober,' explained Izzy.

'You're thinking of confronting him?' asked Poppy, her eyes growing wide.

Izzy nodded. 'How can I prove I'm not scared of him if I don't even see him?'

'Well, you're certainly not going on your own,' said Cadi firmly.

Izzy arched a single eyebrow. 'It won't be the same if I have all my friends around me.'

'You don't have to prove anything to anyone,' said Cadi.

'If I'm really going to leave my past behind, then I need to do this,' said Izzy plainly.

Jez pushed his hands into his pockets. 'I can see why you don't want us going along en masse, as it were, but why not let me tag along?'

Maria put her thoughts across. 'Being away from your father's obviously done you the world of good, but you seem to have forgotten quite how nasty he can be.'

Izzy's brow shot towards her hairline. She pointed a finger at the scar that ran high on her cheekbone. 'Believe you me, I could *never* forget how violent my father can be, because he left me with a permanent reminder. But men like him are bullies who cower when someone stands up to them – and I want to

110

prove to myself, as well as him, that I *am* that someone.'

Cadi intervened. 'How about if Jez walks you down to the corner of your road and then stands back? You could go and see your father on your own ...'

'But Jez would still be there.'

'But Eric wouldn't know that, would he?' said Poppy reasonably.

'And we'd all feel a lot better knowing you had help nearby, should you need it,' confirmed Maria.

Izzy turned to Jez. 'Do you promise to let me go to the house on my own?'

He nodded solemnly. 'I'll do whatever you want.'

She turned to the others. 'Thanks for letting me do this. I know it must seem like I'm courting danger, but it's the opposite – or it is for me, at any rate. Once I've spoken to Dad, explained that he can't touch me any more, I know I'll feel better for it.'

Cadi embraced Izzy. 'Just make sure you take care of yourself, and if it looks like things are getting iffy, or if Eric's three sheets to the wind, walk away.'

'I promise.'

Jez gestured towards the park gates. 'Best to strike while the iron's hot.'

Izzy turned to the others. 'I promise to be sensible, and do try not to worry, I know my father better than you think.'

With that being said, the pair strolled out of the park, with Maria calling after them, 'Don't forget, dinner will be served at one o'clock sharp.'

Waving a hand of acknowledgement, Izzy turned to Jez. 'Do you understand why I have to do this?'

Pushing his bottom lip out, Jez hazarded a guess. 'It sounds like you're laying your ghosts to rest?'

She nodded. 'Precisely.'

'And you're doing it on your terms,' finished Jez.

'Yes. I'd hate to bump into him down Paddy's market, or taking a stroll around the shops. I don't like it when people cause a scene, and I know Dad would positively revel in doing so.'

'Draw a crowd, so that he can embarrass you in front of everyone,' said Jez.

'Exactly. Maria thinks I'm underestimating my father, but I'm really not. I know him well, and he only picks on people he thinks are weaker than him. It's up to me to show him that he can't pick on me any more and, by proving it to him, I can also prove it to myself.'

Jez looked at her quizzically. 'What if Eric doesn't wait to hear what you have to say, but ploughs in, fists first?'

Izzy gave him a reassuring smile. 'He won't – trust me. Dad's worse when he's had a drink, but it's only half-past ten. Even *he* doesn't start drinking before the yardarm's up.' She chuckled. 'He can't afford to.'

Jez mulled over her words. The first time he'd had an encounter with Izzy's father was when he had gone to approach Izzy at the bus stop. Eric had raced over and pulled her far away from Jez, before turning on him. With spittle forming around the older man's mouth, Eric had warned Jez that he was to stay away from Izzy or suffer the consequences. Being only eight at the time, Jez hadn't needed telling twice. But years later, when he saw Eric dragging Poppy, Jez had rushed to her aid. All it took was one punch, and Jez felt like he'd not only rescued Poppy, but had vindicated his younger self. He supposed this was a similar situation for Izzy. He eyed her curiously. 'Has Eric *ever* picked on anyone equal to himself?'

Izzy laughed scornfully. 'Only once. I remember it well. He came flying home one afternoon, scared to death because he'd punched some captain aboard a merchant ship. He was terrified they were coming after him. It was the first time I'd ever seen him scared, and I suppose I knew then that he was nothing but a bully who'd bitten off more than he could chew.'

Jez frowned. 'It takes guts to hit someone like a captain.'

Izzy gave a mirthless laugh. 'Not if you're bladdered.'

'Oh ...'

She tucked her hands into her pockets. 'He hates being a docker, but he's too thick to do anything else,' adding as an afterthought, 'and too scared.'

Jez furrowed his brow. 'Scared?'

'He's worried they'll call him up if he leaves the docks – that's the only reason he stays.' Suddenly remembering that Jez used to work down the docks, she added quickly, 'When I say he's too thick to be anything other than a docker, I mean he's not like you – cos you worked the cranes, didn't you, and then you became a supervisor.' She grinned apologetically as Jez waved a dismissive hand.

'You're right. You don't have to be Einstein to work down the docks, and that's why they pay the poor sods peanuts.'

Izzy remembered the large amount of cash they'd found hidden in her father's box the day she ran away.

113

'That's why I can't understand where he got all that money from.'

'Not the docks, that's for sure,' said Jez, adding, 'Cadi thought he might be part of a smuggling ring.'

'Maybe – he's got some pretty shifty characters as friends.'

Jez rubbed his chin. 'I suppose it's possible. I'd always assumed Eric didn't have any friends, but if you're right, then yes, he could be making serious money as part of a gang.'

As they continued on their way the pair mulled over the possibilities of Eric's smuggling ring, and the feasibility of him getting away with it for such a long time. They were so deep in conversation that Izzy hadn't realised how close they were to her former home. She placed a hand on Jez's arm, drawing him to a halt. 'We're nearly there.'

He gave her an encouraging smile. 'It's not too late to change your mind.'

'Thanks, Jez, but this is something I have to do, and I think you know it.'

He pushed his hands into his trouser pockets. 'I'll be right here, should you need me.'

Leaning forward, Izzy kissed him on the cheek. 'Thank you, Jez, you're a real gent.' As she turned she found herself standing face-to-face with her father, who had rounded the corner, nearly colliding with the pair of them.

Snorting his disgust, Eric was about to pass them by, when the penny dropped. He backed up, staring at Izzy as though she were a ghost.

114

Izzy stepped towards him. 'Dad?'

He pointed a trembling finger. '*You!*'

Izzy nodded mutely. This was *not* how she'd envisaged her first encounter with her father.

Eric's jaw tightened. 'If you're thinking of crawling back, then you can sling your 'ook – you burned your bridges the day you nicked all me money.'

Izzy rolled her eyes. 'I did no such thing; well, not on purpose at any rate. I only wanted what was rightfully mine, and once I realised my mistake I returned the money, although I sincerely doubt it was yours in the first place …' She fell silent, because rather than listening to her, Eric was staring at Jez in horror.

'It was *him* – he was the one who snuck into my house!' He looked from Jez to Izzy and back again. With his eyes still darting wildly between the two, he backed away from them, his hand partly covering his mouth. 'You mean to tell me that you've been together all this time?'

Izzy wagged a reproving finger. 'Don't you dare try and change the subject—'

But Eric cut her off. 'Plottin' behind me back. I see the apple didn't fall far from the tree for him, neither.'

Izzy had had enough. 'Stop trying to blame me mam for all of this, when it's your fault she left in the first place.' She walked forward, the tip of her forefinger inches away from her father's nose. 'I *pity* you, Eric Taylor, you're nothing but a great big bully who's going to die a sad and lonely old man, and all because you never learned to say "sorry".'

Once again Eric didn't appear to be listening, seeming to be more interested in darting his attention between the two friends. The colour slowly drained from his face. 'It weren't my fault ...'

Izzy stared at Eric, open-mouthed. 'What *are* you on about?'

Eric gaped at her. 'Everyone knew your mam was a slapper – what was I supposed to think?' Without another word, he pushed past the two of them, calling over his shoulder as he went, 'If you want to blame anyone, blame her.'

Izzy stared at Jez. 'What on earth was all that about?'

He raised his hands. 'I haven't the foggiest.'

'Me, neither.' She hesitated. 'Do you think living on his own has caused him to go doolally?'

'Maybe. It's hard to tell.' He gave her a sideways glance. 'Do you feel any better?'

'I suppose so. I got to tell Dad what I thought of him, whilst letting him know I wasn't afraid of him any more, and that's why I came.'

'*And* you let him know you thought your mum left because of him.' Jez watched as Eric rounded the corner at the top of the road. 'Do you think you'll ever see him again?'

Izzy shook her head. 'No. It might have been different if he'd apologised and tried to make amends, but he'll never change, I realise that now.'

As Eric strutted down the road, his mind was racing. Did they know? Was that why they'd come to see him? He paused mid-step, shook his head and said 'Nah'

116

beneath his breath, before continuing on his way. He was letting his imagination get the better of him. *It was the shock*, Eric told himself, *that's what it was. A good stiff drink – that's what I need.* A shiver ran down his spine as he envisaged Izzy kissing Jez on the cheek. The very thought made him feel sick to his stomach. Anger welled inside him. Everyone made mistakes, and if he was right, he'd made his biggest one so far, but it was nothing compared to the one his former wife had made.

When Jez and Izzy returned to the Belmont, they found themselves the centre of everyone's attention, all of them eager to hear the news.

'Sounds to me like Eric didn't know which way to turn,' said Bill. 'You obviously caught him un-awares, which is why he tried to wriggle out of it by making out like you and Jez were plotting behind his back.'

'I understand that,' said Izzy, 'but he was looking at me as though he'd seen a ghost.'

'Probably because he wasn't expecting to see you,' said Cadi reasonably.

Izzy wasn't so sure. 'It was more than that, although I don't know what.' She turned to Jez. 'You know what I mean, don't you?'

Jez nodded slowly. 'He was acting peculiar – even for Eric. He said summat that didn't sit right, but I can't remember what.'

Maria, who was busy doling out the vegetables onto the plates, tutted beneath her breath. 'I'm not even going to try and work out what goes on in that man's head. As far as I'm concerned, Izzy got to say her piece, and that's all that matters.'

Izzy reached for the gravy. 'And I feel a lot better for it.'

Bill watched as she poured the gravy over her potatoes. 'It's a shame Eric didn't try and fight for you, Izzy. I would've, if you were my daughter.'

Maria's brow rose. 'If she were your daughter, you wouldn't have behaved like that in the first place.'

Having finished with the gravy, Izzy passed it over to Bill.

'Too right, I wouldn't,' he said. He poured the gravy sparingly, before placing the jug on the cork mat in the centre of the table. He looked around the seated diners. 'Shall I say grace?'

Maria took her husband's hand with a small nod. When Bill had finished, they began to tuck into the hearty meal of rabbit, vegetables, roast potatoes and bread sauce.

Izzy leaned over to Cadi, who was staring at her portion of rabbit, and whispered in a voice loud enough for everyone to hear, 'Close your eyes and pretend it's chicken.'

Cadi blushed as a ripple of giggles swept through those around her. 'I *know* it's silly, but it doesn't help when Izzy keeps calling him Peter.'

Bill roared with laughter. 'Is that right, Izzy?'

She grinned sheepishly. 'She knows I'm only pulling her leg.'

Cadi pushed the meat around with her fork. 'I keep expecting to find a piece of waistcoat in my gravy.'

Maria shot her a wry smile. 'Don't be daft. I took his waistcoat off before he went in the oven.'

'Maria!' cried Cadi.

Reaching over, Jez coddled Cadi's hand in his. 'Think of it this way. Lots of folks aren't having any form of meat for their Christmas dinner. So when all's said and done, you're quite lucky really.'

Before she could talk herself out of it, Cadi took a bite of the meat and tried not to laugh as everyone stared to see her reaction. Swallowing, Cadi smiled graciously at Maria. 'It's lovely – you've done us proud.' She then turned to Jez. 'And you're right: we are lucky.'

Bill rested his fork against the plate. 'In my day, rabbit was considered good fare; it's funny how things change.'

'Sign of the times,' agreed Maria.

'Does anyone else keep expecting to hear moaning Minnie go off at any second, because I do,' said Poppy. 'They did it last year and I'm kind of expecting them to do it again, just to see if they can break our morale.'

Bill hesitated, a glass of beer poised before his lips. 'They'll *never* break our morale, and do you know why?'

Shaking her head, Poppy looked at him expectantly. 'No, why?'

He rested his glass on the table. 'Because we've got summat worth fighting for, and that's why we're going to win this war – it might take time, but we *will* win, especially now that America's joined us.'

Cadi, having eaten all of her rabbit first, so as to get it out of the way, reached for the pepper cellar. 'May God forgive me, but targeting Pearl Harbor was the best thing the Japanese did, because if they hadn't, I don't know what would've happened.'

'And once we've solved the engine troubles in Africa, our boys will be back in the air, doing us proud, and we'll get the job done in half the time,' conceded Jez.

Maria glanced at him from across the table. 'You make it sound easy.'

He grinned. 'When I know I've got this one waiting for me,' taking Cadi's hand in his, he kissed the back of her knuckles, 'it'll take more than some silly engine to stop me.'

Bill raised his glass. 'To our boys in Air Force blue.'

Raising their glasses, they all echoed his toast.

Placing her glass back on the table, Cadi eyed Jez as he continued to eat his dinner. She had no doubt that he would solve the problems they were having in Africa. Cadi's concern was the long sea voyage. That was when Jez would be in real danger.

It was 2 January 1942 and Cadi stood on the platform with Jez, Poppy and Izzy.

'It's gone too fast,' murmured Cadi.

Jez pulled her close, so that he was resting his chin against the top of her head. 'Time always flies when you're having fun.'

Cadi tightened her grip around his waist. 'Are you *sure* you have to go to Africa?'

Jez drew a deep breath before letting it out. 'I'm afraid so, queen – unless someone solves the problem in the meantime, of course.'

Cadi crossed her fingers. 'Let's hope they do.'

Poppy rubbed Cadi's back soothingly. 'He'll be back before you know it, Cadi.'

Lifting her head from Jez's chest, Cadi gazed at Poppy. 'I wish I was getting a few extra days, like you and Izzy.'

'We arrived after you,' Izzy reminded her, 'ergo we leave later too.'

Cadi's eyelids fluttered as she heard the train pull into the platform behind her. 'Trust it to be on time, for once,' she murmured softly.

Jez kissed the top of her head. 'Poppy's right: it's not going to be for ever, and the sooner I get there, the quicker I'll be back.'

Worried that looking at Jez might cause her to lose control of her emotions, Cadi continued to rest her cheek against his chest whilst looking at Poppy and Izzy, both of whom were eyeing her sympathetically.

'How about we meet up for a forty-eight in a couple of months?' suggested Poppy.

Cadi smiled. 'That'd be nice.'

Jez gave her another squeeze. 'There you go. It's good to have summat to look forward to.'

Watching the other people as they began to board the train, Cadi sighed. 'I suppose I'd best get myself a seat – it looks pretty busy.'

Leaning back from their embrace, Jez kissed her goodbye, whilst Izzy and Poppy turned their attention to the train, in a bid to appear discreet.

Melting into his arms, Cadi wished their kiss would never end, but the guard brought her back to the present when he blew his whistle. Taking Cadi by the hand, Jez led her over to the train, with Izzy and Poppy.

'I hate goodbyes.' mumbled Jez as they stood outside one of the carriages.

Cadi slipped her hand from his so that she might embrace her friends. Smiling brightly, she tried to hide the emotion in her voice. 'I'll telephone the Belmont as soon as I get back to base.' She turned to Jez – she had been determined she would stay strong and board the train, but her strength deserted her as soon as her gaze settled into his deep-brown eyes. Dropping her bag, she rushed into his arms and studied his face; she wanted to remember every inch, from his laughter lines to the dimples that formed whenever Jez smiled. Gulping back the tears, she smiled weakly.

'I love you *so* much, Jeremy Thomas.'

Kissing her gently, Jez squeezed her tightly before letting her go. 'And I love you too, Cadi Williams.' He cleared his throat as his emotions threatened to get the better of him. 'Now, get you gone before I run away with you.'

Nodding, she picked up her bag and boarded the train without so much as a backward glance. Heading for the nearest carriage with a window seat, she quickly stowed her bag, then searched for her friends on the platform. Seeing Jez with his arms around Poppy and Izzy as they stared up at her, teary-eyed, Cadi dabbed away her own tears with the handkerchief that Bill and

Maria had given her for Christmas. The guard blew his whistle and the train inched its way forward. As it began to build momentum, Cadi placed a hand against the window, mouthing the words 'I love you' to Jez, who shouted them back.

Chapter Three

January 1942

Since arriving at her new base Cadi had barely set-tled in before she found herself on the move once more. Acting as a courier meant that she was forever flitting from one place to another, rarely spending more than one night in the same location. It was hard work and tiring, but she loved every minute, mainly because it helped take her mind off Jez's imminent departure.

After completing her training at RAF Cardington, Cadi had assumed she knew everything there was to know about the MT, but she soon realised that she still had a lot to learn. Corporal Moses had been right when she said the MT needed Waafs who could think on their feet without supervision. Poppy had also hit the nail on the head when she said that map-reading was nigh on impossible when most of the road signs had been taken down. Cadi had reasoned that while the signs might be down, it didn't change the road layout itself, but she soon discovered that bombs altered everything, in-cluding roads and landmarks, which weren't where they used to be. Hoping to rely on strangers for directions, she had been disappointed to learn that most people preferred to remain tight-lipped.

'I know they say "Loose lips sink ships",' complained Cadi in a telephone conversation to Poppy, 'but I'm driving round in a staff car wearing a WAAF uniform – how much proof do they need that I'm legit?'

Poppy laughed down the phone. 'Show 'em your passion-killers – that should prove you're true blue.'

Cadi rolled her eyes. 'I am *not* showing anyone my knickers, Poppy Harding. And besides, I don't see how that would prove anything.'

'I can't see anyone else wearing them, bar us,' remarked Poppy. She leaned against the wall. 'Have you heard from Jez?'

Cadi smiled. 'He telephones every day for a chat, because we don't know whether he'll be able to, once he's left Blighty.'

Poppy sighed breathily. 'I'm keeping my fingers crossed that they're going to find a solution *before* he leaves for pastures new.'

'Me too,' said Cadi. 'Talking of pastures new, I've heard from Kitty and Ronnie.'

'That's nice. How are they?'

'Very happy – especially Kitty. She's been posted to somewhere called RAF Little Snoring—' She stopped speaking as Poppy cut across her.

'Well, blow me down!'

Cadi hesitated. 'What's up?'

'I'm going there tomorrow.'

Cadi's brow rose. 'I must admit, I thought Kitty was pulling my leg at first, but she was adamant that she'd got it right.' She hesitated. 'You simply must seek her out and say hello when you get there. She knows who you are because I've told her all about you, Izzy and Jez.'

'It'll be nice to meet her—' Poppy began, before being cut short by the telephone operator, who informed the girls their time was up.

'Let me know how you get on, won't you?' said Cadi.

'Will do – ta-ra, Cadi.'

'Ta-ra, Poppy.'

Cadi left the telephone for the next person in the queue. Calling loved ones kept everyone's spirits up and she would really miss her daily chats with Jez. Even though no one had said as much, she felt certain that telephoning from Africa wasn't going to be easy.

Poppy pulled up outside the gate to RAF Little Snoring and flashed her identification to the guardsman, who let her through. As usual, she was only delivering documents for signature before returning to Fiskerton, but she found this preferable to ferrying around grumpy officers who spent the entire journey complaining about the state of the roads, as though Poppy was personally responsible for every pothole.

When she had parked up, she handed over the documents and was told to go and grab herself some lunch in the NAAFI whilst they did the necessary. Poppy was about to turn on her heel when she remembered Kitty.

'Where's the officers' mess?'

The guardsman, who'd tucked the paperwork under his arm, appeared intrigued. 'Why would you want to know that?'

'I'm looking for ACW Kitty Brown, she works as a cook in the officers' mess,' explained Poppy.

He pointed out of the window to a large building further down. 'Same place as it is on most bases.'

Poppy wasted no time in seeking Kitty out. She knew, from experience, that the papers could be returned within minutes or hours, but either way they would expect to find her waiting in the NAAFI. She knocked tentatively on the door to the kitchen.

'Come in,' called a voice from inside.

Poppy opened the door and addressed the woman inside. 'Hello. I'm looking for Kitty.'

The woman nodded knowingly. 'She's on her break – you'll find her in the NAAFI.'

Thanking the woman, Poppy exited quickly. Standing with her back to the mess, she got her bearings. The RAF set most of its bases out in the same fashion on purpose, so that people could navigate their way around each new station with relative ease. Only buildings such as the officers' mess seemed to change. As her eyes fell on the familiar sign for the NAAFI she made her way to the door.

Once inside, she lined up with everyone else and, when it was her turn, ordered a cheese sandwich along with a cup of tea. As she handed over the money she asked the woman serving her whether she knew of Kitty's whereabouts.

The woman handed Poppy her change. 'That's her over there,' she said, jerking her head in the direction of a brunette sitting on her own, a few tables in from the door.

Thanking her for her assistance, Poppy approached Kitty. 'ACW Kitty Brown?'

Kitty looked up. 'Can I help you?'

'I'm Poppy Harding – Cadi's friend.'

Smiling, Kitty gestured to the chair opposite hers. 'Hello, Poppy. I must say, this is a nice surprise. Are you here for a while or is it a flying visit?'

Placing her lunch on the table, Poppy settled into the chair opposite Kitty's. 'Flying visit, I'm afraid.'

'Sounds about right. I think most of the drivers in the MT are the same. From what Cadi told me, she spends most of her day in the car.'

As they continued to chat, Poppy became aware of a fair-haired woman who had sat down at the table next to them. She did not look at all happy, and Poppy could see that her knuckles were smeared with oil – a sure sign of a driver in the MT.

Poppy began to eat her sandwich as Kitty talked.

'How's that fiancé of Cadi's?' she enquired. 'I know she was missing him terribly when she was in Innsworth.'

Poppy grimaced. 'They're sending him to Africa.'

'Oh dear, Cadi must be dreadfully upset.'

Poppy nodded. 'She is, but she's been putting on a brave face, for his sake.'

They both looked towards an airman who was approaching. It was the same one who'd taken the papers off Poppy. He smiled as he handed them over. 'All done.'

Poppy held her hands up to retrieve the documents. 'Thanks.'

As he walked away, Kitty indicated the papers with a nod of her head. 'Is that it, then?'

Poppy swigged the last of her tea. 'It is, but I don't have to rush off yet.'

The woman on the table next to theirs leaned across. 'Sorry, but am I right in thinking you're a driver in the MT?'

Nodding, Poppy stowed the mouthful of sandwich that she had taken into the corner of her cheek. 'Mmm.'

Standing up from her table, the woman came over to join them. 'I hope you don't mind my butting in, only I'm in a bit of a fix.'

Poppy quickly swallowed her mouthful. 'Oh?'

Beckoning Poppy and Kitty closer, she bent down in a conspiratorial fashion. Raising her voice just above a whisper, she eyed Poppy grimly. 'I've locked my keys in the car.'

Poppy wrinkled the side of her nose in sympathy. 'What car is it?'

'A Morris Eight – why?'

A smug smile graced Poppy's cheeks. 'Some cars are easy to break into, others not so much. Luckily for you, the Morris Eight is a piece of cake, and I'm a master at breaking into them.'

The woman let out a gusty sigh of relief. 'Really?'

Poppy went to slide her chair back, until her eyes fell on the remainder of her sandwich. 'Have you got time for me to finish my lunch or are you desperate to be off?'

The girl looked anxiously towards the door of the NAAFI. 'I really don't want to rush you, but this was only meant to be a fleeting visit.' She held up some papers. 'I got these half an hour ago.'

Poppy picked up the remainder of the sandwich in one hand, and her own papers in the other. 'Lead on.'

The Waaf smiled gratefully. 'Thanks awfully. I do feel rotten for disturbing your lunch, but I really didn't want to ask one of the fellers for help.'

Kitty and Poppy followed her out to the car, which was parked a little way off from Poppy's own. 'Don't worry about it, it's a common error – or at least it was for me.'

'Is that why you say you're a master at breaking in?' asked the Waaf.

'When I first started driving I used to lock myself out at least twice a week,' admitted Poppy, 'and the fellers got fed up of having to come to my rescue, so they showed me how to pick a car lock.'

The Waaf sighed wretchedly. 'It's the first time I've ever done it, but I wish someone would've taught me. I've been sweating cobs, worried sick that someone was going to realise what I'd done.'

'Why worry?' asked Poppy casually. 'It's not the end of the world.'

The Waaf blushed. 'It is when you're trying for a promotion.'

Poppy took the small manicure set that Cadi had bought her for Christmas from her handbag and removed the nail file. Squatting down, she placed the file into the lock and, after a couple of trial twists, they all heard the lock click open. Poppy stood up. 'Ta-dah!'

The Waaf shook Poppy firmly by the hand. 'Thanks ever so.'

Poppy waved a dismissive hand. 'It's easy when you know how. Would you like me to show you?'

'Would you?'

Without further ado, Poppy locked the car door and handed over the nail file. 'Slide it in and twist until you hear a click – you'll have to make a few attempts before you get the knack —' She stopped speaking as the door clicked open on the Waaf's first attempt. 'Blimey!' breathed Poppy approvingly. 'Ever thought of becoming a mechanic? I reckon you'd be a natural.'

Standing up, the Waaf handed Poppy the nail file. 'Maybe I should. At least I wouldn't be rushing round the country like a headless chicken.'

Remembering Jez's imminent departure to Africa, Poppy spoke her thoughts. 'True, but at least we get to remain in good old Blighty.'

The woman raised an inquisitive eyebrow. 'Why do you say that?'

'Our pal's fiancé's being sent to Africa because he's a brilliant mechanic.'

The woman pulled a face. 'Tough luck. I take it she doesn't want him to go?'

Poppy shook her head. 'What with him being ground crew, she always believed he was safe, but Africa? The journey alone is fraught with danger ...'

'I can see why she's so worried.' She opened the car door and pulled out the crank handle. 'I was the same with my boyfriend. He was desperate to become a pilot, but I was the exact opposite – better off on the ground than in the air.'

'I think we should see if there's summat we can do to put a spanner in the works,' suggested Kitty, 'you know, to stop him leaving.'

The woman's face clouded over as she shook her head in earnest. 'Don't. Take it from one who knows: these things are best left well alone, because you could end up making things a hundred times worse.'

Poppy and Kitty exchanged intrigued glances.

'What do you mean by that?' asked Poppy.

She sighed miserably. 'I knew my boyfriend would make pilot unless I stepped in, so that's exactly what I did.'

Kitty looked round to make sure they couldn't be overheard. 'What did you do?'

Colour flushed the woman's cheeks and, when she spoke, she was so quiet Poppy could barely hear her. 'I've got a cousin who works in the administrative offices,' she lowered her voice further still, 'and she fixed his papers.'

Poppy could scarcely believe her ears. 'She did *what*?'

She nodded wretchedly. 'I couldn't lose him – and we all know that air crew ...' She fell silent, before adding, 'I did it for him as much as myself.'

Kitty took pity on the Waaf, who was blowing her nose into a handkerchief that she had fished out of her handbag. 'I take it he found out?'

The woman looked at Kitty, aghast. 'God no, and I pray he never will.'

Poppy spoke slowly, considering each word before it left her lips. 'If he doesn't know, and he never made it to pilot, then I don't see the problem?'

The woman hung her head in shame. 'He didn't make it as a pilot, but he *did* get into air crew.'

'All that palaver and you're still no better off,' said Poppy. 'Talk about being caught between the devil and the deep blue sea.'

The woman was staring, stony-faced, at Poppy. 'He's tail-end Charlie.'

Kitty's jaw dropped. 'Rear-gunner?' she breathed.

The Waaf nodded brusquely. 'The most dangerous position in air crew, and I put him there.'

Poppy, realising her mouth was open, closed it again. 'Is he still your boyfriend?'

'He is, but only because he doesn't know what I've done, and I'd prefer to keep it that way. But it's why I urge you not to interfere.'

'We won't,' promised Kitty.

Poppy smiled kindly. 'And I'm sure your boyfriend will be all right.'

The woman put the handle into the slot and cranked the vehicle into life. 'I hope so.' She climbed into her car and closed the door. 'We seem to know an awful lot about each other, yet I don't even know your names.'

'I'm Poppy, and this is Kitty.'

The Waaf, who was already pulling away, called out to them from her open window, 'Nice to meet you. I'm Daphne by the way.'

Poppy stared, open-mouthed, at the retreating car. 'Did I just hear right? Did that woman say her name was Daphne?'

Kitty nodded. 'Yes, why?'

Poppy looked at Kitty, her eyes growing ever wider as Daphne's words sank in. 'I think I know her.'

Kitty watched the car as it pulled through the open gate. 'I don't understand?'

Poppy looked awkward. 'I don't *know* her exactly, but I think Cadi does.' She stared fixedly at Poppy from hollow eyes. 'And, if I'm right, I know who her boyfriend is.'

'Do you know him well?'

'Very.'

Aware that she was gawping, Kitty closed her mouth. 'How can you be sure it's the same feller?'

Poppy glanced in the direction of the NAAFI. 'I can't, and that's why I need to make a phone call.'

Kitty looked towards the officers' mess. 'I'd better get back to work – but will you let me know what happens?'

Poppy nodded. 'I'll have to make tracks before your next break, but I promise I'll telephone as soon as I can.'

'If you're right, and you *do* know her boyfriend, what then?'

Poppy ran her tongue over her bottom lip. 'I haven't the foggiest.'

With nothing more to be said, the girls parted ways: Kitty for the mess, and Poppy for the NAAFI. Seeing the queue of people waiting to use the telephone, Poppy tutted beneath her breath as she joined the back of the line. Whenever she was the one on the phone it seemed as though three minutes was over in a jiffy, but when you were waiting for others, it seemed to take for ever. By the time she got to the head of the queue, she had begun to fear that Cadi might be out on her travels, and indeed that was the case, but luckily for

Poppy, being last in the queue meant there was no one waiting and she was able to make another call, to the base where she hoped Cadi would still be. She waited with bated breath and almost cried out with delight when Cadi's voice came down the line.

'Poppy? Is everything all right?'

Poppy spoke hastily. 'Everything's fine. I've met Kitty and she's lovely.' She paused momentarily before continuing, 'I've also met a woman called Daphne, whose boyfriend wanted to be a pilot, but he's now a tail-gunner – does that make any sense to you?'

'Boyfriend?'

Poppy briefly described Daphne. 'She's taller than me, with fair hair and blue eyes; she's quite trim too.'

Cadi's voice came hesitantly down the line. 'Why didn't you just ask her if her boyfriend was Aled?'

Poppy swallowed. She would have to be very careful what she said. 'Because she told me something, but I've realised I can't tell you it over the phone.'

Cadi laughed. 'Poppy, you aren't making any sense – surely it can't be that bad?'

Poppy fell silent as she tried to find a solution to her predicament. 'I can't go into detail. Is there any chance we can meet up today, no matter how briefly?'

'I'm at RAF Syerston until tomorrow. Is there any way you can call on your way past?'

Poppy racked her brains as she tried to place RAF Syerston on her mind's map. 'It'll be a bit of a detour, but I think this is too important to ignore. I should be with you in a couple of hours.'

Hearing the click as Poppy hung up, Cadi handed the receiver to the aircraftman who was next in line.

135

What could be so important that Poppy would go out of her way to come and see her? She had mentioned Daphne and Aled, and something about Daphne being Aled's boyfriend. Cadi cast her mind back to Aled's last letter and the lack of information regarding his personal life. Perhaps this was why he'd been so guarded: he knew that Daphne and Cadi didn't see eye-to-eye. Maybe he hadn't mentioned Daphne in his letter because he knew the two of them didn't get on? With no obvious answer presenting itself concerning the urgency of Poppy's call, Cadi had no choice but to sit and wait.

Poppy cursed as she went back down the road she had just come up. Time was of the essence if she was to see Cadi *and* make it back to Fiskerton in good time. She stopped the car and examined the map for the ump- teenth time. She looked at her surroundings, then back at the map. With a squeal of triumph, her index finger landed on the road to her left. She was on the right track at long last.

Cadi paced the area in front of the gate to her tem- porary base. Poppy was running late, and Cadi had begun to wonder whether she would turn up at all when she heard someone tooting their horn. She ran to the end of the lane and waved at Poppy, who was waving madly back.

Pulling the car to a halt, Poppy apologised to Cadi, who had opened the passenger door. 'Sorry I'm late.'

Cadi jumped into the passenger seat. 'Never mind that. What happened in Little Snoring?'

Poppy told Cadi of the encounter with the Waaf called Daphne and of the revelations that had come from their meeting.

Cadi blew her cheeks out. 'Blimey! I can see why you daren't say anything over the phone.'

'Exactly,' said Poppy. She eyed Cadi anxiously. 'So what do you think? Is it the same Daphne?'

Cadi shrugged. 'It's too much of a coincidence for it not to be, but that doesn't give us the right to go in all guns blazing, *especially* if we're wrong.'

'And if we're right?'

Leaning her forehead into her hand, Cadi placed her elbow against the passenger door. 'If we're right, then Aled needs to know.'

Poppy swallowed. 'That's what I thought.'

Cadi grimaced. 'I don't see what other choice we've got. Fixing someone's papers just isn't on, no matter how good their intentions. Not only that, but if this *is* Aled we're talking about, then I think he needs to know exactly how devious Daphne can be.'

'What are you going to do?'

Cadi's eyes rounded. 'What am *I* going to do?'

'He's *your* friend,' said Poppy firmly.

'Hardly!' retorted Cadi.

'He writes to you,' said Poppy reasonably, '*and* you've met up a couple of times.'

'You spoke to Daphne, not me,' retaliated Cadi.

'Yes, but Jez was the one Daphne wrote to, and that's all part of her deception. I never read the letter, so I've no idea of its true content, but Jez did and he told you.' Poppy shrugged. 'Not only that, but she nearly destroyed your relationship. In all honesty, I'd feel a real

137

heel going behind her back, because she only told us to stop us making the same mistake in the first place – she was trying to do us a favour.'

Cadi fell quiet whilst she tried to think of an excuse as to why she shouldn't be the one to break the news to Aled, but Poppy was right. With a resigned sigh, she swivelled in her seat, so that she was facing Poppy. 'All right, so it's got to be me; but as you already know, it's not the sort of thing you say over the telephone or in a letter, so that leaves me with one alternative. I shall have to go and see Aled in person. I'll have a quiet chat, see if I can find out whether it's *his* Daphne and go on from there.'

'What if it isn't? Won't he be suspicious as to why you've gone out of your way to see him?'

Cadi mulled this over. 'I'll have to tell him the truth.' She shrugged. 'Aled's going to have to hear the full story, but it's *how* he hears it that concerns me, which is why I shall tread carefully.'

'Is he still at RAF Speke?'

'Yes.' A sudden thought entered Cadi's mind. 'What a good job I haven't written to him yet.'

'Indeed,' agreed Poppy, adding as an afterthought, 'are you going to tell Jez?'

'Not until I know what's what. There's no sense in telling him half a story, *especially* when he's going to be sailing halfway around the world in a few days' time.'

'I'm sorry to lumber all this at your door,' said Poppy.

'Hardly your fault,' said Cadi. She got out of the car and leaned in through the open door. 'It's time you made tracks.'

Poppy placed the car in gear. 'Ta-ra, Cadi. Let me know how you get on, won't you?'

'Of course I will. Ta-ra, Poppy, drive safely.' She closed the door and stood back to wave to Poppy, who tooted her horn as she drove off. Cadi turned back towards the gate. If Poppy was right – and Cadi rather thought she was – then Aled was in for a nasty surprise.

It was a couple of days after Kitty and Poppy's chance meeting with Daphne, and Kitty had telephoned Cadi to see if there was any news.

'I've had a marvellous stroke of luck,' Cadi informed her friend.

'Oh?'

'Mary – she's one of the WAAF drivers in Coningsby – was due to go to Liverpool on the fourteenth, which just happens to be her birthday. She'd really hoped to spend the day with her parents who are travelling up from Norwich, so I suggested we ask Sergeant Jenkins if we could do a swap and she agreed, as long as I didn't mind losing my day off.'

'Lucky all round,' agreed Kitty.

'It certainly is. I know I won't have an awful lot of time to myself, but it means I get to say goodbye to Jez *and* speak to Aled.'

'Two birds, one stone,' mused Kitty. 'Have you told them of your plans?'

Cadi hesitated before replying. 'I've told Jez I'm going to be able to say goodbye, but I've *not* told him I'm going to be seeing Aled. I rather think that might put a dampener on things, don't you?'

Kitty giggled. 'Just a bit.'

'I've written to Aled telling him I'll be in Liverpool and would like to meet up for a quick chat, if at all possible. He wrote back saying he couldn't guarantee anything, as he doesn't know what he's doing from one day to the next at the moment.'

'Are you staying at RAF Speke?'

Cadi nodded. 'Only for the night, so I should have a good chance of catching him at some time or other.'

'Where's Jez travelling from?' enquired Kitty. 'Surely not Speke?'

'No, they'll be travelling straight from RAF Finningley on the fifteenth, but as I'll be staying in Speke overnight I'll get time to see him before he goes.'

'Perfect timing.'

'It certainly is,' agreed Cadi.

'Well, I can't say I envy you,' admitted Kitty.

'Saying goodbye to Jez is going to be bad enough, but if we're right and the Daphne you spoke to *is* Aled's girlfriend,' Cadi blew her cheeks out, 'that's going to be opening up a whole new can of worms.'

Kitty tentatively nibbled her bottom lip. 'What are you going to tell Aled? Only Daphne's bound to know it was me and Poppy who blabbed, and whilst I don't agree with what she did, she really was remorseful – that's the whole reason she told us in the first place, so that we wouldn't make the same mistake.'

'I'll *have* to tell Aled the truth,' said Cadi, albeit a tad ruefully, 'but I'll ask him if there's any way he can leave our names out of it. I know how poisonous Daphne can be, and I wouldn't want her having a word with Jez – not after last time.'

'I hope he agrees,' said Kitty fervently. 'I feel sly, like I've been telling tales, which I suppose I have.'

Cadi felt desperately sorry for Kitty, who had unwittingly been dragged into her affairs. 'I know, and if it's any consolation, I feel the same way. I have no doubt that Daphne rues the day she interfered, and I very much hope I don't live to regret my own actions – after all, Daphne thought she was doing the right thing too.'

'That's what makes it so hard,' said Kitty. 'I feel sorry for her, but at the same time I also feel sorry for Aled.'

'Like being stuck between a rock and a hard place,' reasoned Cadi, 'I'd like nothing more than to find out this is one huge coincidence, but I really can't see that being the case.' She sighed. 'Poor Aled's going to have his whole world turned upside down.'

Cadi spent most of the journey to Liverpool worrying what the outcome of her meeting with Aled would be, whilst listening with half an ear to the officer she was chauffeuring.

'Are we here already?' asked the officer as he spied the gated entrance. 'These long journeys can be awfully tedious, but that wasn't half bad. You've done well, ACW Williams.'

Cadi smiled briefly at him in the rear-view mirror. 'Thank you, sir.'

They passed through the gate and Cadi pulled up alongside many other cars. As the officer left the car he turned to her. 'I'll see you back here tomorrow at twelve o'clock sharp.'

Cadi's tummy turned a somersault. She knew that Jez's ship was due to depart at eleven-thirty, which wouldn't give her much time, should anything go awry. 'I'll make sure the car's ready.'

He patted the back of her seat. 'Good girl.'

Cadi rolled her eyes. She knew he didn't mean it in a derogatory fashion, but she couldn't help feeling as though he was praising a well-behaved dog. With the officer gone, she got out of the car and made her way to the office. Once she had found out which one of the many Nissen huts she would be sleeping in, she asked where she might find Aled.

The Waaf left her desk and walked towards the open door. 'See that building over there? The one next to the tower?'

Cadi nodded.

'If he's not on operations, you'll either find him there or somewhere nearby.' She arched an eyebrow. 'You know what fellers are like – if they're not in their beds, they're usually gettin' summat to eat.'

Cadi thanked the Waaf for her assistance before hurrying towards the building. Having been on the road since early that morning, they'd only managed to stop once for a sandwich in a café. Her tummy rumbled its objection, but needs must, and she wanted to get the business with Aled over and done with, before anything else.

She knocked on the door and spoke to the airman who answered.

'I'm looking for Aled Davies, is he here?'

The airman called over his shoulder. 'Aled?'

Within moments he appeared. 'Cadi! How's tricks?'

She grimaced. 'Have you got time for a chat?'

The airman nudged Aled. 'Does Daphne know about this?'

Aled shot him a withering look. 'We're not all like you, Tom.'

Chuckling to himself, the airman known as Tom walked back into the building.

Closing the door behind him, Aled looked towards the NAAFI. 'Have you had summat to eat yet?'

Cadi shook her head. 'I've only just arrived.'

His brow shot towards his hairline. 'And you came to see me *before* getting summat to eat? Sounds serious.'

She gave him a weak smile. 'I'm afraid it is, or at least it might be.'

Aled began walking with Cadi towards the NAAFI. 'Come on, Cadi, *nothing* can be that bad.' He faltered mid-step. 'There's not been another accident at the mine, has there?' Before Cadi could reply, he answered his own question. 'Nah, that can't be it – my dad would've been straight on the blower.'

When they entered the building Cadi approached the counter. She ordered a plate of stew, before turning to Aled. 'Are you having anything?'

He shook his head. 'I've not long eaten – a cup of tea will suffice.' He looked at the woman who had handed Cadi her meal. 'Two cups of tea, please.' As he spoke he gathered some change from his wallet and, despite Cadi's objection, paid for the lot.

Taking the tray, Aled went to place it on a table near the counter, until Cadi shook her head. 'Not here, over there.'

Aled followed her gaze. 'Oh.' The area Cadi had chosen was far from prying ears and eyes. As they took their seats, he stared fixedly at her. 'It's not like you to be so guarded. What's happened?'

Cadi drew a deep breath. She had thought of nothing else since getting into the car that morning, and the journey had given her time to plan her conversation.

'Does Daphne have a cousin in the WAAF?'

Aled stared stoically at her. 'Maybe …' He thought for a moment before nodding. 'I'm sure she does, why?'

'Does she work in admin?'

Aled pushed his chair back so that he might stretch out his legs. 'Now you come to mention it, I believe she does.'

Cadi drew a deep breath. 'There's something I think you should know …'

Aled listened casually at first, but as Cadi's explanation progressed, his features grew stern. When she had finished telling him of Poppy and Kitty's encounter, she told him about the letter Daphne had sent to Jez.

With her explanation at an end, she gave him an apologetic smile. 'I understand it must be a lot to take in.'

He raised his brow. 'That's an understatement! Blimey, Cadi, I knew Daphne wanted me on terra firma, but I never thought for one minute she'd do summat so irresponsible, not to mention downright malicious.' Placing his elbows on the table, he held his head in his hands. 'I always said that I was surprised I'd not passed the maths part of the process, but this explains why.'

Cadi spoke hastily. 'By all accounts, Daphne thoroughly regrets her decision and, even though it was wrong, she only did it to keep you safe. Surely you can see her reasoning?'

Aled glowered at Cadi. 'No, she didn't; it would be a lot easier to stomach if she did, but I know Daphne and at the time I sat my exams, she was hell-bent on finding herself a farmer for a husband. She *knew* I wouldn't be so eager to stay on in the RAF if I didn't become a pilot, because I told her as much. The only reason she "fixed" the results was because she needed a man to help her run her father's farm, and she thought I was that man.'

'That's not what she told Poppy and Kitty,' said Cadi, 'far from it.'

Aled gave a hollow laugh. 'Of course she didn't. Admitting you were only thinking of yourself, when playing with someone else's life, doesn't sound as good as saying you were doing it for their benefit.'

Cadi got to the next point on which she knew Poppy and Kitty were keen to hear his answer. 'Poppy, Kitty and I would rather keep our names out of this, if at all possible?'

Aled nodded, absent-mindedly. 'Of course.' He looked up. 'I've got a lot of thinking to do – do you mind?'

Cadi nodded. 'Just for the record, I really don't think Daphne meant things to go the way they did. And she really does rue the day she ever interfered – don't forget she had no idea who she was talking to, when she met Poppy and Kitty, and, if she had, she'd have kept shtum.'

Standing up, Aled placed the chair back under the table. 'Maybe she didn't. But, while I don't want to appear overly dramatic, her actions could have caused my demise, and I'm only lucky that so far that hasn't been the case.'

Cadi lowered her head, before gazing up at Aled through her lashes. 'I know what you're saying is true, but no one knows what the past could have held, had we done things differently. Had you passed the pilot's test, as you were no doubt meant to, you could have been one of many who never made it back.'

'That's of little consolation,' muttered Aled.

'Maybe, but you can't hang her for what could've happened.'

He rested his hands against the back of the chair. 'Why do you care what happens to Daphne?'

'She was desperate, Aled, and people do silly things when they're in love. And there's no doubt in my mind that Daphne loves you with all her heart – she'd not have shown such remorse otherwise.'

Aled leaned forward. 'She nearly ruined yours and Jez's engagement.'

Cadi blushed. 'Only because I'd tried to make her jealous in the first place. Had I not been so silly, I dare say she'd never have written the stupid letter.' She hesitated before adding, 'And we both know the letter wasn't the only thing that caused Jez to be jealous.'

Aled chuckled softly. 'Maybe not. But Jez had better get used to it, because you're a beautiful, kind, caring woman, Cadi Williams, and I won't be the only man to say so.'

146

Cadi cursed the blush that threatened to invade her cheeks. 'Always the charmer, Aled – it must be the Welsh in you.'

He winked at her. 'Jez is lucky to have you. I wish I had half his luck.'

Cadi pulled the tray of food towards her. 'What do you think you'll do now?'

Aled shrugged. 'Have a long think. I certainly won't dive in head-first, not until I've had a chance to find out the answers to a few questions. That way, I can suss out the lie of the land. I want to make certain I have all the facts before I say anything to Daphne.'

She eyed him inquisitively. 'You mean proof?'

Aled nodded. 'Definitely. I don't want to snooker myself, so I'll be sure to have all holes covered.' Seeing the rueful look on Cadi's face, he continued, 'In all honesty, this was bound to come out sooner or later.'

Cadi swallowed a mouthful of stew. 'How?'

Aled sat back down in the chair. 'I was going to keep it a secret, because I didn't fancy making a fool of myself second time around, but seeing as you've been honest with me ...' He grinned. 'I've been thinking about reapplying for my wings.'

Cadi eyes widened. 'Oh. Aled, that's wonderful!'

He twinkled at her across from the table. 'I've always been miffed about that bloomin' exam and, if I'm honest, I put it down to either nerves or cockiness.' He grinned mischievously at her. 'You, of all people, should be able to relate to that.'

Cadi laughed. 'What, you? Cocky? Never!'

'Exactly!' He rolled his eyes. 'Golly, I was a little twerp, wasn't I?'

Cadi pretended to straighten her face. 'No comment.'

Aled drummed his fingers against the table surface. 'Very diplomatic.'

She smiled. 'I've learned a lot in the WAAF.'

Aled roared with laughter. 'Like how to hold your tongue, because you never had that skill before – not as I remember it.' He eyed her affectionately. 'There never were any hairs on your tongue, Cadi Williams.'

She raised her brow fleetingly. 'I can't be like that in the WAAF, though.' Remembering the ride down with the officer, she added, 'Calling an officer a boring snore might be frowned upon.'

'Possibly, although I dare say they've been called far worse behind their backs.'

She watched him with great fondness. Cadi had once described Aled as a mean, spoilt, spotty little oik. But not any more. He had grown into a handsome man with a heart of gold. She gave herself a mental shake. 'Any road, I'm sure you'll make a wonderful pilot.'

He grinned. 'So am I.' His smile faltered. 'Especially with no outside interference.'

'Good job you decided not to tell Daphne,' said Cadi, 'although I wonder what she'd do second time round?'

'I'd hope she'd stay true to her word and not inter-fere again – that's if she's genuine, of course,' said Aled, somewhat doubtfully.

Cadi scooped the last bit of stew onto her fork. 'Just how do you intend to prove her guilt?'

Aled viewed her over steepled fingers. 'I'll have to get my hands on my old papers – they'll be archived somewhere.'

'How long will that take?'

He shrugged. 'That's the trouble; and not only that, but how will I lay my hands on them in the first place?'

'It might leave you with more questions than answers.'

He sighed heavily. 'I'm going to need to have a long, hard think on how to handle this, but no matter how I decide to go ahead, the outcome will remain unchanged.'

Cadi looked at him expectantly. 'How do you mean?'

'Daphne and I are over.'

It was the following morning, and Cadi – unable to use the staff car for anything other than military business – was haring down the road that led to Huskisson Dock. As she neared, she could see a few men in RAF uniform getting out of the back of a military truck. Her stomach lurched. It *had* to be Jez and his companions, unless he was already on board, of course. She cursed inwardly at the wagon driver who had double-parked, delaying the bus journey by a good ten minutes. Holding on to her cap, she ran down onto the dock, where she began desperately looking round the men, trying to see if she could catch a glimpse of Jez, but he was nowhere to be seen. Looking back at the truck, her heart soared when she saw him talking to a Waaf who Cadi presumed had driven them to their destination, but on closer examination, her heart plummeted as she realised the driver was Daphne. After gleaning the knowledge that she had in the past few days, Cadi really didn't wish to go anywhere near the other woman, but if she wanted to see Jez, she'd have to bite the bullet and make herself known. As she approached them she realised they weren't chatting, but arguing. She cleared her throat.

As he turned to see who was interrupting, Jez's frown dissipated. 'Cadi!'

Her eyes flickered towards Daphne before returning to Jez. 'We haven't got long.'

Nodding, he began to walk away, but Daphne grasped him by the elbow, stopping him short. 'I'm sorry! I don't know what else you want me to say.'

Jez spoke through thin lips. 'I don't want you to say anything. I was just letting you know, that's all.'

Daphne turned to Cadi. 'I swear I didn't mean to cause any trouble.'

Cadi held up a hand to silence her. 'My fiancé is leaving for Africa and I don't intend to stand here arguing the toss with you.' Taking Jez's hand in hers, she led him over to the gangplank. 'Trust her to show up on your last day.'

He grimaced. 'I know. I didn't recognise her at first, but as soon as I realised who she was, I couldn't hold my tongue.'

'I don't blame you, but you shouldn't let the likes of Daphne get under your skin.'

'I wouldn't normally, but I guess the thought of leaving Blighty put me in a bad mood.' He placed his arm around her shoulders. 'Let's forget about *her*. How're Bill and Maria?'

Cadi felt her cheeks begin to colour. 'I didn't arrive until late last night, so I've not had time to see them. What's more, Officer Faulkner wants to be off at twelve o'clock sharp, so I won't be able to pop in for even the quickest of hellos,' she said, although she knew this to be a fib. The real reason she hadn't called in on Bill and Maria was because she didn't want to lie to them, by not telling them what she was up to.

Jez looked at his wristwatch. 'We've got five minutes.'

Cadi glanced at the enormous ship that would be taking Jez to Africa. 'So, this is going to be your home for the next few weeks.'

Jez followed her gaze. 'It certainly is. In some respects I'm rather looking forward to seeing how the other half live.'

A thin line creased Cadi's brow. 'Other half?'

'The Navy, of course. I've often wondered how the services differ and whether I made the right choice in joining the RAF.'

A sudden thought entered Cadi's mind, causing her stomach to lurch unpleasantly. 'Can you swim?'

Jez laughed. 'Of course I can swim. I don't think there can be many lads who haven't gone for a dip down the Scaldies at some time or other.' Seeing the blank expression on Cadi's face, he elaborated, 'That's what they call the pools at the Tate and Lyle factory.'

Cadi felt her tummy settle. 'At least that's something.'

He turned her to face the ship. 'Try not to worry – she's a sturdy-looking vessel.'

Seeing the other men begin to board the ship, Cadi buried her face against Jez's chest. 'I wish we had longer.'

He enveloped her in his arms. 'Once I get back we'll have all the time in the world.'

'I guess that's the price you pay when you're the pick of the crop,' she said miserably.

Jez's eyelids fluttered guiltily. He dreaded to think what Cadi would say if she knew that he'd volunteered for the post.

Hearing an officer calling for everyone to board, Jez kissed Cadi, softly at first, but growing in passion as the seconds slipped away. Aware that he was the last man on the dock, he reluctantly parted from his belle.

'I'll be back before you know it, and I'll write every day,' he promised.

Wiping her eyes free from tears, Cadi tried to put on a brave face. 'Missing you already,' she murmured through trembling lips.

She watched Jez, who had joined his fellow ship-mates on the starboard deck. Her stomach dropped as a man pulled away the gangplank. There was no going back now. She waved furiously to Jez, who blew her kisses. Hearing the ship sound its warning that it was about to weigh anchor, Cadi allowed the tears to flow. This might be the last time she saw Jez for what would be months – if not longer. With the ship under way, she turned to head for the bus stop, only to be waylaid by Daphne, who had sunk into step beside her.

'I know you know about the letter, because Jez told me,' said Daphne. She flapped her hands in an exasperated fashion. 'It was a stupid thing for me to do, and I don't have any excuse other than that I was jealous of you.' She started to jog in order to keep up with Cadi, who was walking determinedly towards the bus stop. 'I was frightened that Aled liked you better than he did me and I wanted to put him off, but I never meant to cause trouble between you and Jez, no matter how it might have looked as if I did.' She laid a hand on Cadi's arm in a bid to slow her down. 'The last thing I wanted was to split you up – far from it. Please believe me.'

Feeling the colour growing in her cheeks, Cadi stopped abruptly. 'I know you didn't mean to cause a divide between me and Jez, but whether you meant to or not doesn't matter, because that's what happened.'

'I know,' said Daphne miserably, 'and I can't begin to tell you how sorry I am and ...' She fell silent.

'And what?' asked Cadi, who was interested, despite herself.

'And I've no right to ask you to keep quiet, but I really don't want other people knowing what I've done – especially Aled.'

Cadi raised an eyebrow. She knew Daphne was referring to the letter, but she herself was thinking about the exam papers that Daphne was responsible for fixing. 'I'm not surprised,' muttered Cadi.

Seeing the bus that she was due to catch approaching the stop, she began to jog towards it. 'I haven't got time for this. That's my bus and if I miss it—' She stopped speaking as the driver of the bus slowed briefly, before speeding up again. Waving frantically, Cadi began running, but neither the driver nor the passengers were looking in her direction.

She stamped her foot angrily. 'Bloomin' brilliant. I've got to be back at Speke before twelve – some hope of that now!'

Daphne smiled meekly. 'I could always give you a lift?'

For two pins Cadi would have told the other girl what she could do with her offer, but needs must, when the devil drives. Sighing heavily, she turned to face Daphne. 'Thanks.'

Daphne hurried over to the cab of her lorry. 'Don't worry, I'll have you there in a jiffy.'

Cadi rolled her eyes. This was not how she imagined her day panning out, and she wondered what the others would say if they could see her now. Climbing into the passenger seat, she waited for Daphne to start the engine.

Taking her place behind the wheel, Daphne pushed the lorry into gear. 'I'm sorry if you missed the bus because of me. It seems I can't do right for doing wrong lately.'

Cadi remained silent. If Daphne knew of the conversation Cadi had had with Aled the previous evening, she very much doubted Daphne would be offering her a lift.

With no conversation forthcoming from Cadi, Daphne continued, 'I think Jez is very brave, volunteering to go to Africa.'

Cadi frowned. 'Jez didn't volunteer. He got called upon because he's the best mechanic in the RAF.'

Daphne appeared perplexed. 'Oh? I assumed he'd volunteered, like the others.'

'Well, you assumed wrong then,' snapped Cadi irritably.

Realising that she had ruffled Cadi's feathers, Daphne waited until they were nearly at the station before speaking again. 'I don't know whether you know, but Aled and I are an item.'

Cadi wished the ground would swallow her up. The last thing she wanted was to discuss Daphne and Aled's relationship. Not wanting to give anything away, she kept her eyes on the road ahead. 'Congratulations.'

'You probably don't think I deserve him,' said Daphne quietly, 'but I swear to you I'll never pull another stunt like that.'

Cadi stared stoically at the road ahead, willing the station to appear. The woman had some nerve, considering that she'd done far worse to Aled – and for two pins Cadi would have said so, but she knew it wasn't her place. Resting her chin against her fingers, she mumbled, 'Glad to hear it.'

'I think the world of him,' continued Daphne, 'and I've great hopes for our future.'

Cadi turned to stare out of the window, hoping Daphne wouldn't see the blush that was creeping up her neck. To her enormous relief, she saw the base loom into view. All she had to do was hold her tongue for a couple more minutes.

As they neared the gate, Daphne pulled the lorry to a halt. She spoke hurriedly to Cadi, who was opening the door. 'Please don't tell Aled about the letter. I know you haven't, as of yet, because Jez told me.'

This was the sort of thing Cadi had been dreading. To agree not to say anything to Aled would be an out-and-out lie, but to admit she'd already spilled the beans? It didn't bear thinking about. She opted for an evasive answer as she vacated the vehicle. 'I can't make any promises.'

Daphne leaned across the seat as Cadi turned to close the passenger door behind her. 'I *promise* you'll never see or hear from me again, if you keep shtum.'

Cadi kept her head lowered as she spoke. 'Like I've already said, I can't make any promises.' Closing the door behind her, she hurried to the gate and, after showing her pass, raced to the hut to collect her things. She had five minutes before they were due to leave and she couldn't afford to waste another second. Inside the hut she collected her bag, which was packed and ready to go. Rushing out of the hut, she collided with Aled, who was staring at her in disbelief.

'Do my eyes deceive me, or did I just see you sharing a lift with Daphne?'

Cadi rolled her eyes. 'I've not got time, Aled, but long story short: yes, not that I wanted to, mind you.' She glanced at the staff car. 'I've really got to go, I'm already running late – that's why Daphne gave me a lift. I promise I'll call and explain everything properly as soon as I get back, but for the record, I've not said a word about the exam papers, or anything else for that matter.'

Aled nodded sternly. 'Glad to hear it.'

Still hurrying, Cadi arrived at the car moments before the officer. It had certainly been an eventful twenty-four hours, and not one she wanted to repeat in a hurry. Looking on the bright side, she'd done everything she'd come to do and even though she hadn't relished having to spend time in Daphne's presence, it had been worth it, to say goodbye to Jez.

Watching Cadi drive through the open gate, Aled wondered quite how she had come to be in the same vehicle as his girlfriend – he corrected himself, his former girlfriend. He knew Cadi wouldn't blab to Daphne, but his mind boggled to think about what conversation had passed between the two women. With no choice other than to wait for Cadi's call, he continued on his way back to his billet. He didn't like to admit it, but his father had been right when it came to Cadi: Aled had missed out on a cracking lass, and he often rued the day he'd allowed her to slip through his fingers.

Whilst Cadi had told Aled she would ring him as soon as she returned to base, she telephoned Poppy first, so that she might hear her friend's opinion, prior to talking to Aled. Only after hearing everything Cadi had to say did Poppy speak her mind.

'You've had one heck of a stroke of bad luck when it comes to Daphne and, quite frankly, I don't know what I would've said *or* done, had I been in your position.'

'It was really awkward,' admitted Cadi, 'but what choice did I have?'

'On the other hand, if she'd have kept away, you'd have made the bus on time,' said Poppy evenly.

'I know.' Something else that Daphne had said came to the forefront of Cadi's thoughts. 'She seemed to think they'd all volunteered to go to Africa, *including* Jez.'

'Perhaps some of them had,' said Poppy amiably.

'Maybe, but it annoyed me that she automatically included Jez as one of the volunteers, rather than acknowledge that he'd been selected because he's bloody good at what he does.'

'Makes no difference, either way,' said Poppy.

'Only that he'd have lied, if Daphne were speaking the truth,' ventured Cadi.

'Why would Jez do that?' scoffed Poppy. 'He is a brilliant mechanic. Ignore Daphne – she's stirring up trouble, like she always does.'

'That's what I thought,' said Cadi, but deep down she hadn't been convinced that Daphne had been lying, purely because Daphne hadn't tried to argue her point, instead shrugging it off as inconsequential.

Poppy cut across her thoughts. 'How was Jez?'

'Good – pleased to see me, obviously,' she sighed. 'He was very upbeat, but I think he was putting on a brave face for my sake.'

'Typical Jez,' agreed Poppy, 'always putting others first.'

'Talking of boyfriends, how's the amazing Geoffrey?'

Poppy was practically purring. 'He's wonderful. I knew he was, the moment we met on the train, but spending time with him has only confirmed my thoughts.'

'I must say, given all that's going on, it's nice to hear some good news for a change. I'm so pleased it's working out for you.'

'Me too. I did worry he might've had a change of heart, but as soon as he saw me, he came straight over to say hello and even asked me if I'd like to go on a date to the cinema.'

'What about Izzy?' asked Cadi hopefully. 'Has she had any luck?'

'Nope, Izzy's sworn off men, in case she ends up with someone like her father.'

Cadi twiddled the phone wire between her fingers. 'That's a shame – we'll have to see if we can find her the perfect feller.' Glancing around the relatively empty NAAFI, she remembered she still had to phone Aled. 'I'd best be saying TTFN whilst it's still quiet,' she said. 'At least that way I can speak to Aled, set the record straight and find out what his thoughts are.'

'Right you are,' said Poppy. 'Be sure to let me know how you get on.'

'Will do. Ta-ra, Poppy.'

'Ta-ra, Cadi.'

Cadi replaced the receiver momentarily before asking the operator to put her through to RAF Speke. As Aled had been expecting her call, it wasn't long before he was on the other end of the line. She explained how she had bumped into Daphne down the docks, and everything that transpired as a result.

Aled was smiling, she could hear it in his voice. 'I can't pretend I wasn't concerned,' he admitted, 'but only because I couldn't imagine a scenario where the two of you would meet up.'

'I couldn't believe my eyes when I saw her, and I rather hoped she'd keep her distance, especially after Jez confronting her over the letter,' confessed Cadi.

'Did she mention me?'

'She certainly did,' said Cadi. 'She told me how the two of you were an item, before begging me not to tell

159

you about the letter, saying that she'd only sent it because she thought you liked me more than her.'

'That's no excuse.'

Noting that he had done nothing to deny Daphne's claims, Cadi continued, 'It is to Daphne.' A half-smile twitched her lips. 'What did you think we'd been talking about?'

Aled blew out his cheeks. 'I couldn't imagine, but I was pretty sure it wouldn't be anything good.'

'I'm surprised she didn't call in to say hello,' said Cadi. 'I would've, if it were Jez.'

'She probably daren't, in case you saw the two of us together and decided to let the cat out of the bag,' said Aled.

'Maybe. Have you any thoughts as to what you're going to do?'

He grimaced. 'Not really. It would be a lot easier if I could mention names, but as I can't, I'm going to have to box clever and come up with a plausible plan.'

'Let me know if you need any help,' said Cadi, adding as an afterthought, 'We're really grateful that you're leaving our names out of this, by the way.'

'It's hardly your fault you inadvertently found out the truth,' said Aled. 'But I'm jolly glad you did, because had you not, I could have ended up married to a wrong 'un.'

'Married?'

'I hadn't planned to ask her, but who knows?' said Aled matter-of-factly. 'What did Jez make of it all?'

'I was already late, and I didn't want to spend what time we did have talking about Daphne, so I've not told him yet.' She pulled a rueful face. It wasn't exactly the truth, but it sounded better than admitting she thought Jez would be upset, if he knew Cadi and Aled were still in contact.

Aled cut across her thoughts. 'Cadi?'

'Hmm?'

'I was saying that Jez probably wouldn't be surprised.'

Cadi spoke absent-mindedly. 'No, possibly not.'

He frowned. 'Are you all right?'

'Just tired,' said Cadi. 'It's a fair old way from Liverpool to Coningsby.'

'Much quicker in a plane,' remarked Aled, adding kindly, 'I've kept you chatting long enough, and you've had a rare old time of it. I'll give you a call when I know what I'm going to do, unless that causes problems for you and Jez, of course.'

Cadi was grateful that Aled was unable to see her cheeks, which were turning pink. 'It's important we know what's going on, in case we bump into Daphne again. I don't fancy being on the receiving end of her wrath, without fair warning.'

'Fair dos,' said Aled. 'G'night, Cadi.'

'Goodnight, Aled.'

Why does life have to be so awkward? pondered Cadi as she headed for her billet. *It would be far better if everyone could simply tell the truth.* A grim smile etched her cheeks. Quite often the truth could be hurtful, even if there was no malice behind it. She thanked her stars that Jez was as honest as the day was long. She turned her thoughts to what she should do when it came to telling Jez that she had been to see Aled. *If you value him at all, you'll tell him the truth. He might not like the idea that you've been to see Aled, but he's bound to find out sooner or later,* she told herself, *because no matter how hard you try, the truth will always out, and it's far better coming from you than it is from someone else – you should know that better than most, Cadi Williams.* But when? Surely not whilst Jez was in Africa? That wouldn't be doing anyone any favours, and he certainly wouldn't appreciate hearing such news when he was so far from home. No. She would wait until he was back in Blighty before telling Jez everything.

Back at her own base, Daphne parked the cumbersome lorry before making her way to the cookhouse. Worrying about what Cadi might say to Aled, she automatically found herself turning to food as a source of comfort. She had forgotten all about the stupid letter until Jez brought it up. If anything were to drive a wedge between her and Aled, that would be it. With Jez out of the country, she needn't worry about him spilling the beans, but could she say the same for Cadi? Up until now Cadi had obviously decided to keep it to herself, but would her encounter with Daphne give her pause for thought? She would have to hope not, and that her good deed in getting Cadi back to the base on time would encourage her to remain quiet.

Approaching the cook, Daphne watched as he placed a large slice of Spam on her plate. Pointing to the mashed potato, she turned her thoughts to

Jez. Had she not seen him, then the matter of the letter would never have come up and she would have continued with her life as before. A frown furrowed her brow. Cadi seemed to think that Jez had been selected to go to Africa, but as far as Daphne knew, that wasn't the case at all. She eyed the cook inquisitively. Having only arrived on base the previous evening meant that no one was aware that she and Jez had history.

'The fellers that've gone to Africa?' she queried.

He nodded. 'What about them?'

'Am I correct in thinking they were all volunteers or were some of them specially chosen.'

He shook his head. 'All volunteers – why?'

She frowned. 'I could've sworn one of them, I believe his name was Jess or …'

'Jez,' supplied the cook.

'Ah, that's right, Jez. Anyway, I got the impression he was one of those who'd been called upon.'

The cook shook his head. 'Last I heard, he was one of the first to volunteer, on account of his nan dying when the Luftwaffe bombed the pub cellar she was sheltering in.'

Without thinking, Daphne's head shot up. 'The Greyhound?'

He eyed her sharply, a deep furrow wrinkling his brow. 'You know him then?'

Daphne mumbled, 'Not really,' before taking a seat far away from the cook's prying eyes. So *that's* why Cadi had joined the WAAF. Daphne sliced the Spam into quarters, when a horrid thought rocketed to the forefront of her mind. The women who'd helped her break into the car, hadn't they been trying to find a way to stop their friend's fiancé from going to Africa? Abruptly losing her appetite, she pushed the tray away as she thought back fervently to their conversation. Had they named Cadi or Jez? She shook her head. No, or she'd have realised who they were straight off the bat. That was all right then.

Her heart skipped a beat as she remembered the conversation she had had with the girls. Had she mentioned Aled's name, or where he came from? She racked her brains, and was thankful when the answer came back no. Her cheeks coloured. Had she told them who she was? No. She sagged with relief. They had been so busy trying to get into the car that they'd not introduced themselves; she certainly didn't know who they were ... She hesitated as an image of herself calling out 'I'm Daphne by the way', as she drove off, entered her mind. Thinking back, she realised the girls *had* mentioned their names, but she hadn't heard them above the car engine, so it was highly likely the same could be said in return, especially as she had been accelerating away from them. And even if the girls had heard her, could they really have worked out who she was, just from her saying her name? Surely not. And besides, if they were friends of Cadi's, then they'd have mentioned their encounter with Daphne. Cadi might have been willing to let sleeping dogs lie over the letter, but there was no way she'd keep quiet about the exam papers – far from it, she'd have jumped at the chance to tear a strip or two off Daphne, *especially* after the letter business.

Daphne shook her head. Whoever those girls were, they didn't have a clue who she was – and a good job too!

Chapter Four

Several weeks had passed since Aled had learned the truth, and whilst he had far more important things on his mind, every time he closed the blast-chamber doors behind him, he couldn't help but think that he should be in the pilot's position and *not* in the rear end of a plane. He had considered going to the powers-that-be and telling them of his findings but he knew that if he did, Daphne and her cousin would find themselves in a lot of trouble; he corrected himself, an *awful* lot of trouble. He might be angry with Daphne, and there was no doubt she'd done the wrong thing, but did she really deserve whatever punishment awaited? Aled might be a lot of things, but he wasn't heartless, and even though he knew she'd fiddled the results of his exam papers for her own selfish reasons, he also knew that Daphne hadn't intended him to end up in the tail end of a plane.

Deciding there was no sense in crying over spilt milk, he had gone to ask if there was any chance of retraining as a pilot, only to be told that the RAF needed him where he was for the time being. He had wanted to protest, to object at the unfairness of their decision, but it was pointless. It took nerves of steel to be a successful rear-gunner and they needed people like Aled – who was damned good at his job – to keep their kites in the air. Keeping his eyes peeled on the skies around him, he found his thoughts turning to what he should say to Daphne, when the time came. She had telephoned his base a couple of times, and up till now he'd made excuses not to take her calls, but he knew he couldn't avoid her forever. He would have to tell her the truth one day, but he had no clue how could he so without mentioning Cadi, Poppy or Kitty.

In his earpiece he heard the bomb-aimer liaising with those around him. He supposed he could tell Daphne that he was going to ask to see his old papers because he couldn't fathom how he'd done so badly. Would she confess, rather than run the risk of him finding out and reporting her cousin? He nodded slowly. That might actually work, especially if Daphne was as remorseful as the girls thought her to be. Hearing the pilot report that they were cleared for take-off, Aled decided he would write to Daphne telling her that he intended to reapply for his wings, but wanted to see his old papers first, so that he could see where he had gone wrong. That way, Daphne would have time to think things through, and he very much hoped she would come to the right decision and confess all.

Not that it would make any difference to the out-come. Aled had no intention of lying with wolves. He had questioned whether he should simply end things with Daphne and move on with his life, without telling her what he knew, but he couldn't. She had been getting away with murder, and someone needed to call her out.

Eric gave the three-whistle signal indicating the all-clear. In the distance he heard a low whistle in response to his. Turning his back to the men who were ferrying the goods off the ship, he kept a keen eye out for scuffers, mariners – or anyone who'd try to put a stop to their dealings. As his stomach rumbled, his thoughts turned to his supper. He was fed up to the back teeth with chip suppers, soup or cheese on toast.

An image of Izzy serving up a bowl of scouse entered his mind's eye. She might have been fit for nothing else, but the girl could cook – just like her mam. He switched the image to Izzy and Jez on Christmas Day. It had been a while since his last encounter with his daughter, but the memory still haunted him. Izzy had been the last person he had expected to run into, and seeing her looking so like her mother had come as quite a shock; in fact at first he had thought he was looking at his wife, and it was only when Izzy spoke that he realised his mistake.

Eric knew that his wife's affair had been the talk of the district, but he also knew something they didn't; for had they known the truth, they'd not have been so quick to judge him. His wife had lied, of course she had – not only about the affair, but about everything else.

He remembered how she had stood before him, pleading with him to see sense. He had spat at her feet; called her out as a slut, and a liar to boot. His jaw stiffened as he replayed the image of her standing with her clothes around her feet while she begged him to listen, promising that he would see for himself soon enough, but Eric wasn't interested.

Once again the image of Izzy and Jez entered his mind. He remembered the time the boy had tried to befriend Izzy. Just like any decent father, Eric had been quick to put a stop to their friendship – or at least he thought he had. He hesitated. Had they become friends behind his back? He mulled this over for a moment or two, before dismissing it from his mind. If they had, then he'd have known about it, for Izzy had been too frightened of her father to lie to him. He turned his thoughts to the boy's grandmother. He was almost positive she knew the truth, but had wisely decided to keep quiet. And quite right too. No one in their right mind provoked the wrath of Eric, and he knew it.

He took his tobacco pouch from his pocket and began rolling a cigarette. From what he'd heard, the old bat had died in the bombings. Could it be that Carrie had said something to the boy before she died? Again he quickly dismissed this thought. He had no idea why Izzy had come to see him that day, but he was certain that, had she known the truth, she would have wasted no time in running to the scuffers. As far as he was concerned, his wife had deserved everything she'd got. And whilst there was no doubt in his mind that she'd been having an affair with Colin, he supposed some might say that he'd overreacted. Even so, it was still her fault, for had she not lied in the first place, he wouldn't have had to take such drastic action. His wife was the one with blood on her hands – not him.

Daphne warmed herself in front of the tortoise stove that stood in the middle of their hut. She had been trying to get hold of Aled for weeks, yet it seemed every time she phoned he was either on operations, sleeping or off base. She had written several letters, but until today she hadn't received a response. She reread the letter in her hands:

Dear Daphne,

Sorry if you've been trying to get hold of me, but I've been frightfully busy of late. I think I should let you know that I'm considering reapplying for my wings, but after much deliberation I decided it would be best if I asked to see my old papers first – that way I can see where I went wrong the last time, so that I don't repeat the same mistake. I know from a pal of mine that they retain previous papers, so it should be easy enough for them to dig them out. I've run the idea past my PO and he thinks it's a good idea …

Folding the letter, Daphne placed it into the fire. Was Aled telling the truth – that he wanted to learn from past mistakes – or had someone, such as Cadi or her friends, tipped him off? It did seem a tad suspicious that she hadn't been able to get hold of Aled

170

since Cadi's trip to Liverpool. But all of this was by the by. If Aled got his hands on the papers, he'd know something was up. She knew that her cousin, Lisa, had been against the idea of fixing them from the start, but Daphne had assured Lisa that the idea was watertight and she would take full responsibility, should anyone find out. She nibbled the inside of her bottom lip. Perhaps she should she warn Lisa, give her the heads-up, so that she could find Aled's papers and destroy them? After all, no paper, no proof. Lisa would be furious, and quite rightly so, but at least she'd be in the clear, unless someone caught her in the act, of course.

Daphne's stomach lurched unpleasantly. It didn't bear thinking about. She heaved a sigh. This was a mess of her own making and she should be the one to sort it out. Only how? She could hardly tell Aled not to go searching, because he'd want to know why. If she told him the truth, then they would be over as a couple – and not only that, but he might end up reporting her. She moved from the fireside to her bed. How long had Aled been thinking of retrying for his wings? He'd not mentioned it before. She cast her mind back to see if there had been any clues or hints. It seemed to her that everything had been fine until recently – one minute Aled had been his usual self, warm, caring and attentive, and the next he'd been cold, elusive and distant. Was it coincidental that it had all happened around the time she'd seen Cadi and Jez?

She heaved a miserable sigh. What was she to do? Sit tight and hope for the best, or approach it head-on? A single word came to the forefront of her thoughts: Africa. She had been pushing it to the back of her mind, by pretending it was all a big coincidence, but it was high time she faced the truth. Those girls must have been friends of Cadi's and they'd spilled the beans. Daphne hung her head in defeat. There was no point in pussyfooting around. She would have to come clean. Her mind made up, she made her way out of the hut and over to the NAAFI, where she found the telephone unattended. Picking up the receiver, she asked the operator to put her through to RAF Speke and waited for Aled to come on the other end of the phone.

When he spoke, his tone wasn't light and upbeat, as usual, but low and serious. 'Daphne?'

Daphne sighed breathily. 'I think we need to talk.'

'Oh? What about?'

'Please don't pretend – I know that you know about the papers.'

There was a moment's silence before Aled spoke, and this time there was no denying his true feelings. 'What the hell did you think you were playing at?'

Daphne sniffed back a tear. 'I was scared of losing you. I know it was wrong, and if she'd told you the whole story, then you'd know that already.' She blew her nose gently, before continuing, her voice edged with bitterness, 'Only I dare say she didn't, did she, because she's only out to stir trouble.'

'Don't try and cast the blame on anyone else – *you're* the one who decided to play God with *my* life. You're the one who put me in the most dangerous position of all, no one else.'

'I didn't mean to,' wailed Daphne, 'I'm so sorry. *Please* believe me when I say I was doing it for your own good.'

Aled spoke through thin lips. 'How can I believe a word you say? Let's face it, Daphne, you wanted a farmer for a husband, and you *knew* I'd not go back to farming if I gained my wings. You only did this for one person – and that's yourself!'

He was right, and Daphne couldn't pretend otherwise. Only things had changed since then. She wasn't with Aled just so that she could run the farm when the war was over; she was with him because she had genuinely fallen in love with him. If she could turn back the hands of time, she would do anything to change the past and have him as a pilot, because she knew how happy it would make him. If it meant she lost the farm, then so be it. She'd rather have Aled than not. But that one action had ruined everything.

With tears forming, Daphne spoke quietly. 'Are you going to report me?'

Aled huffed down the phone. 'I should, but I won't.'

Daphne nodded. 'Thanks.'

'I'm not doing it for you and, believe me, if there wasn't a war on, it would be a very different story.'

Daphne swallowed. 'For the record, I really am sorry.'

'That's the only thing I *do* believe,' said Aled, his tone a little kinder. 'But what's done is done and I can't ignore that. It's a shame, because I *thought* we made a good couple.'

'We do!' cried Daphne. 'Still could ...'

'After what you did?' said Aled, his tone incredulous. 'I'd be forever watching my back.'

Desperate to try and convince him otherwise, Daphne spoke through her tears. 'No, you wouldn't! I swear I'd never do anything to hurt you.'

'I'm tail-end Charlie on an Avro Lancaster. Do you know how lucky I am to be alive? Yet according to you, you wouldn't do a thing to hurt me.' He tutted down the phone. 'You already have.'

'I didn't mean to—' Daphne began, but the operator cut across.

'The other caller has hung up.'

'Put me back through!' she sobbed. 'I hadn't finished what I was trying to say.'

'Your three minutes were almost up. Please replace the receiver, so the next person in the queue can use the telephone.'

Daphne spun round. She had been so engaged in her conversation that she had completely forgotten other people might be listening. Seeing the next Waaf in line coming forward, she hastily replaced the receiver. With tears still streaming down her face, she made her way to the parade ground, where she knew she could be on her own.

Going over Aled's words, Daphne realised that whilst he had not acknowledged it was Cadi who'd told all, neither had he done anything to deny it. Daphne had only referred to Cadi as 'she', but they both knew who she was talking about – otherwise Aled would have questioned her further. It certainly explained why Cadi had been eager to avoid Daphne; after all, no one wants to admit they've been the one telling tales, although Daphne was bemused as to why Jez hadn't taken the opportunity to give her a piece of his mind. Whilst it was none of his business, it would have added fuel to the fire. Unless Cadi hadn't told Jez of course, but then why not? The answer hit Daphne like a ton of bricks: Cadi had lied to Jez. The more she thought about it, the more it made sense.

Cadi might think she had the perfect relationship; the truth was far from that. In fact, as far as Daphne was concerned, Cadi was as big a liar as Daphne herself – if not bigger. *I've a good mind to speak to Jez and tell him how his fiancée has been sneaking around behind his back, stirring up trouble with his old adversary*, Daphne thought to herself. *Cadi lied to Jez once, and she's doing it again. It'll serve the cow right for not telling Aled the full story, because if she were being truthful, she'd have told him how sorry I was and how I very much regretted my actions.* But how would she tell Jez without some phone operator hearing what she'd said, or some censor reading what she'd done?

Wiping the tears from her cheeks, she sought out the corporal in charge of her billet. Seeing Daphne waving to get her attention, the corporal paused before the door to the cinema. 'What's up?'

Catching her breath, Daphne forced her lips into a smile. 'Nothing. I just wanted to ask whether it would be possible for me to pick up the lads who went off to Africa today – when they return, I mean.'

The corporal shrugged. 'Don't see why not. Any reason in particular?'

'I know one of them – he's engaged to a friend of mine – and I thought it would be nice to see how he got on, catch him up with the news from back home, that kind of thing.'

175

The corporal nodded. 'Can't promise anything, but I'll bear you in mind.'

Daphne thanked the corporal. She'd give Cadi a taste of her own medicine by filling Jez in on his fiancée's shenanigans as soon as his feet touched British soil.

Two months had passed since Jez's departure and Cadi was on her way to Lincoln, where she was looking forward to spending the weekend with Poppy and Izzy. Everything, as far as the business with Daphne was concerned, had come to a head, and even though Aled said he'd not mentioned the girls by name, he was pretty sure she had put two and two together. Cadi awaited reprisals – be it an angry telephone call or a spiteful letter – but much to her relief, neither of the girls involved had heard so much as a whisper from her.

Pushing Daphne to the back of her mind, Cadi turned her thoughts to the telephone call she had had with Jez before leaving for Lincoln. It seemed he was rather enjoying his life in a different country, although he did miss British cooking.

'It's even worse than me nan's,' joked Jez, 'and that's sayin' summat. I'm tellin' you, Cadi, you wouldn't *believe* some of the stuff they eat out here.'

'I can't imagine that it's very different from ours,' mused Cadi.

Jez spoke in a guarded fashion. 'Put it this way: anything that moves is up for grabs, and I mean *anything*.'

Worried that Jez was about to go into more detail, Cadi quickly changed the subject. 'How are you getting on – with the "you-know-whats"?' They had decided to refer to the engine troubles in this way to save being challenged by the operator every time they spoke.

Jez heaved a sigh. 'Every time we think we've got it licked, summat else crops up, but I'm hoping we'll get it sorted sooner rather than later.'

Cadi decided to voice Daphne's accusations, to see whether he'd heard from the other woman. 'That rotten Daphne tried telling me that you'd volunteered for the job.'

'Ignore Daphne, you know what she's like,' said Jez sullenly, before adding, 'If I never see that woman again, it'll be a day too soon.' He cursed himself inwardly. He hated lying to Cadi, but admitting that he'd volunteered wouldn't change the outcome. He'd still be in Africa.

Relieved that Daphne's words had been idle gossip, Cadi continued, 'Same here.' She deftly changed the subject. 'Have you acclimatised or are you still struggling with the heat?'

Now, as she looked out of the train window, she put all thoughts of Daphne from her mind as the station came into view. Glancing down at the stripes on her shoulder, she wondered what her friends' reaction would be when they realised she had made corporal. Her smile broadened. They would be happy for her, not to mention proud.

As the train pulled into the platform she looked for a sign of her pals and was delighted when she caught sight of Poppy, who was waving madly to gain her attention.

Collecting her things, Cadi made her way to the carriage door, where she stood waiting for the train to stop. Descending onto the platform, she embraced Poppy, who was already gabbling excitedly about the stripes on Cadi's upper arm. Leaning back from their embrace, Cadi looked around them. 'No Izzy?'

Poppy shook her head. 'She's going to join us for a drink after she's finished her shift.' She turned her attention back to the corporal's stripes. 'So come on, when did this happen?'

Cadi blushed. 'A couple of weeks ago. I must say I was rather surprised, because I didn't think I'd pass muster, but I passed with flying colours.'

'Anyone could see that you were destined for the top,' said Poppy loyally. 'You do far more than me. I've barely left Lincolnshire, but you're up and down the country like a yo-yo, which is why we never get to see you.'

Cadi shrugged. 'I'm on my own half the time. Apart from the people I meet on my travels, I never get to see anyone.'

'Precisely,' cried Poppy, 'they can trust you to do your job without supervision – believe me, they can't do that with everyone.'

Cadi linked arms with her friend. 'So how's Izzy?'

'Wonderful! She's well on her way to becoming sergeant. She's in a different hut to me, so we don't get to see each other as much as we did.'

'I wish her rotten father could see how well she's doing.'

'You and me both, but I doubt he'd be impressed or even show any interest, come to that.' She came to a halt on the concourse. 'You're staying in the Horse and Groom, aren't you?'

'Do you know it?'

Poppy grinned. 'I don't think there're many pubs Izzy and I don't know around Lincoln. The Horse and Groom is one of our favourites: lovely grub and reasonably priced too.'

'Sounds right up my street,' said Cadi. 'I've stayed in some right hovels on my travels. You never know what you're getting until you set foot over the threshold. It's like Russian roulette.'

'Well, you won't have that fear in Lincoln, as the city has lots of pubs, cafés and restaurants and they're all lovely,' said Poppy loyally.

'It sounds like you go into Lincoln a lot.'

Poppy smiled shyly. 'Geoffrey likes to spoil me.'

Cadi grinned. 'So I gathered from your letters. I take it things are still going well?'

Poppy nodded fervently. 'They certainly are. He's wonderful, Cadi, I've really landed on my feet. Izzy thinks the world of him, and has even said that if she could meet a feller like Jez or Geoffrey, she might consider dating herself.'

'Oh, that's marvellous news,' said Cadi. 'I really did start to worry that her father might have put her off men for life.'

'I think he had, but being surrounded by so many smashing fellers, even Izzy can see they're not all bad – especially the pilots. She has a real soft spot for them, but as you know, it's not easy meeting one.'

'Do you go dancing much?'

Poppy shot her friend a wry smile. 'Whenever and wherever we can. Which is most weekends. They've got some smashing dance halls in Lincoln. Why do you ask?'

'I've not been dancing since Jez left for Africa; it's difficult making friends when you're constantly on the move.'

Poppy patted Cadi's hand. 'It can't be all work and no play, so we'll have to make sure you make the most of your weekend. Talking of Jez, do you know when he's coming back?'

Cadi shook her head. 'He hopes it won't be too much longer.'

Poppy gave Cadi a sidelong glance. 'Have you heard any more regarding the Daphne and Aled business?'

'Nope, but it's been a while now, so I think we can afford to rest easy.'

'Poor Kitty's been having kittens,' said Poppy, 'thinking that Daphne's about to turn up and start shouting the odds.'

Cadi frowned. 'Why is it that everyone's worried about what Daphne has to say, when she's the one in the wrong?'

Poppy grimaced. 'Because we know how badly she felt, and she only told us to stop us making the same mistake – she was being nice.'

Cadi sighed wretchedly. 'You're right, although I suppose I knew it all along. It's one of the many reasons why I didn't say anything to Jez.' She glanced at Poppy guiltily. 'Do you think we did the right thing by telling Aled?'

Poppy nodded determinedly. 'I do. Because whilst I know Daphne regrets what she did, the consequences could have been dire, and even though she says she's remorseful, who's to say she wouldn't do something similar, or even worse, in future?'

Cadi looked doubtful. 'Do you really think she would, though?'

Poppy screwed her lips to one side. 'Put it this way, if Jez had done summat similar, would you want to know?'

Cadi didn't need to think before replying. 'Yes, because it would show how devious he could be and, like you say, who's to say he wouldn't do it again, should the need arise?'

'Exactly.' Poppy pulled Cadi to a halt and pointed to a sign above their heads. 'Here we are.'

Cadi followed Poppy into the pub and over to the bar, where a cheery-looking man was serving a customer. Seeing the girls approach, he beamed at Poppy. 'Hello, love. Bit early in the day for you, isn't it?'

'Never too early,' joked Poppy. She placed her arm around Cadi's shoulders. 'Alfie, this is my oldest and bestest friend, Cadi Williams.'

Alfie pushed the till drawer shut before walking towards Cadi, his hand held out. 'Nice to meet you, Cadi. Am I right in thinking that you're booked in for the weekend?'

Cadi placed her kitbag on the floor and shook Alfie's hand. 'I certainly am.'

He took a key down from a row of hooks on the wall. 'Room two,' he pointed to a door at the far end of the bar, 'through there, second on the right.'

Taking the key, Cadi looked at the diners seated around them. 'Are you still serving food?'

In answer Alfie pointed to a chalkboard behind the bar. 'We've everything bar the faggots.'

Cadi tried her best not to grimace. She'd never liked faggots and was quite glad they were off the menu. She turned to Poppy. 'What time can we expect Izzy?'

'She said not to wait, and to eat without her – she'll grab a sandwich en route.'

Cadi smiled at Alfie. 'In that case I'll have the fish and chips, please.' She glanced at Poppy.

'Go on then, you've twisted me arm. Make that two fish and chips, please, Alfie,' said Poppy.

Cadi picked up her kitbag. 'I'll just pop this in my room – shan't be long.'

By the time she returned a few minutes later, Poppy was sitting at a window table with two glasses of ginger beer.

She smiled at Cadi, who sat down on the chair opposite. 'Have you told your mam and dad about your stripes yet?'

Cadi rolled her eyes. 'You'd swear I'd been awarded the Victoria Cross, the way my dad was carrying on.'

Poppy grinned. 'You always said you wanted him to be proud of you.'

'I know, and even though he was proud of me for running the B&B, it's nothing compared to the way he is now I've been promoted to corporal. Mam says he's been telling everyone in the village – twice over!'

Poppy pouted. 'So my mam and dad knew, but never told me?'

182

Cadi nodded. 'I told Mam that no one was to tell you until I'd had a chance to do so myself.' She took a sip of the soft drink before continuing. 'I wanted to see your reaction first-hand.'

'I'd probably be the same,' mused Poppy, 'not that I think I'm ever likely to make corporal.' She gazed out of the window to the drizzle that was starting to run down the windowpane. 'I remember the first time I met your Auntie Flo, I thought at the time that the two of you were like peas in a pod, and I was right, because she's always rushing round like a headless chicken, much the same as you.' She looked back to Cadi. 'Do you ever get lonely?'

'Not really – I suppose I don't have the time. I enjoy meeting new people and seeing new places, it's interesting.'

'I like being based somewhere,' admitted Poppy, 'especially now I'm with Geoffrey.'

'I must say, I can't wait to meet him,' confessed Cadi.

Poppy shuffled excitedly on her chair. 'He can't wait to meet you, either.'

The girls fell silent as their meal arrived. Cadi closed her eyes as the delicious waft of freshly fried fish and chips entered her nostrils. 'I wish all the places I stayed in did nice food like this.' Shaking salt and vinegar over the chips, she continued, 'I'm not surprised the Greyhound did so well, when you compare it to some of the places I've stayed in.'

'Pretty grim?' said Poppy, taking the salt from Cadi.

'I've walked out of one or two without even approaching the bar,' Cadi admitted.

Poppy swallowed her mouthful. 'Not as bad as the Bear's Paw, though, surely?'

Cadi nodded. 'Believe it or not, some of them are even worse.'

Poppy tutted disapprovingly. 'I'm surprised the WAAF sends you to places like that.'

'It's hard to tell what a place is like when you've only got the name to go by ...' She stopped talking as a man in pilot's uniform entered the bar. 'Of all the—'

Poppy followed Cadi's gaze. 'Do you know him?'

'He's one of the Greyhound's old customers. He only stayed with us once, mind you, but he's the feller that recommended me for promotion, back in Innsworth.'

'That's *him*?' Poppy sliced a piece off her fish. 'I don't remember you saying anything about him being drop-dead gorgeous.'

Cadi pulled a downward smile. 'I never really noticed.'

'I didn't realise you were having problems with your eyesight,' quipped Poppy, 'you should get that checked.'

Cadi shot her friend a wry look. 'There's nowt wrong with my eyes.'

Poppy raised her brow. 'There must be, if you can't see how handsome he is.'

Cadi tilted her head to one side as she viewed the pilot. 'He must be in his late twenties, early thirties at best – too old for girls of our age.'

'Not for Izzy, though,' mused Poppy.

Perhaps sensing that he was being talked about, the pilot turned to face the girls. As soon as his eyes fell on

Cadi, his cheeks split into an enormous grin. 'Corporal Williams!' Taking his drink from the bar, he walked over to the girls. 'May I join you?'

Cadi nodded. 'Please do.'

Getting a chair from a nearby table, he sat down between them. 'Please carry on with your meals – I wouldn't want them to go cold on my behalf.' He jerked his head towards the bar. 'I've got something on order, so I won't have to nick any of your chips.' He glanced at Poppy. 'I don't believe we've been introduced. I'm Flying Officer Grainger, but you can call me Mike.'

Poppy introduced herself, adding shyly, 'It doesn't seem right calling an officer by his first name.'

He waved a nonchalant hand. 'I don't see the need for formalities whilst having a friendly drink.' He turned his attention back to Cadi. 'I must say I'm glad to see you made corporal – I hate it when hard work goes unrecognised.'

A pink tinge flourished Cadi's cheeks. 'I don't know about that.'

'You're a grafter and always have been. I knew that from our little chat in the Greyhound all those years back,' said Mike knowingly. 'You mark my words: women like you are as rare as hens' teeth.'

Poppy sliced her knife through the crunchy batter. 'That's what I've been telling her.'

Alfie approached the trio with a plate of sausage and mash, which he placed before Mike.

'That looks good,' observed Poppy. 'I'll have to try that next time.'

'It sounds as though you're based nearby,' observed Mike as he gathered his cutlery.

185

'RAF Fiskerton, so not too far,' said Poppy. 'You?'

'Waddington.'

Having finished her food, Cadi automatically stood up and took the plate to the bar. 'Would anyone like another drink?'

Mike indicated the full glass of stout he had brought over. 'Not for me, thanks.'

Poppy nodded. 'I'll have a pale ale.'

Cadi returned with Poppy's ale and a lemonade for herself.

Mike looked at the glass of lemonade. 'You're not a drinker then?'

Cadi shook her head. 'I'm always driving, so I don't see the point. I know I've got a forty-eight, but I guess it's become a force of habit.'

Seeing Izzy walk into the pub, Poppy placed her fork down and waved to get their friend's attention. 'Over here!'

Acknowledging their presence, Izzy ordered a drink from the bar before coming over to join them.

Cadi saw a hint of colour enter the officer's cheeks as she approached. Getting to his feet, Mike gave up his seat to Izzy and fetched another over for himself.

'I'll finish my meal, then get out of your hair. I didn't realise this was a reunion.'

Izzy smiled timorously. 'Don't worry too much. I'm rather afraid I'm about to break the party mood.'

Cadi tutted. 'Don't say you've got to shoot off?'

Izzy grimaced. 'I have indeed.'

'Not for long, though?' asked Poppy hopefully.

Izzy eyed her friends in a meaningful manner. 'I've had a telephone call from Lethia.'

Cadi's and Poppy's jaws dropped.

'From the Chinese laundry?' Cadi asked in disbelieving tones.

Izzy nodded.

Poppy wrinkled her brow. 'What on earth did she want you for?'

Izzy was silent for a moment as she thought of the best way to break the news. 'It's Dad ...'

Poppy sighed breathily. 'Oh God, what's he done now?'

The corner of Izzy's bottom lip jerked downwards. 'Died.' Seeing the flying officer's face drop, she was quick to reassure him. 'Don't worry, I'm not about to burst into tears or owt like that.'

'Tears of joy maybe,' muttered Poppy under her breath.

Quick on the uptake, Mike arched an eyebrow. 'Not exactly Father of the Year, I assume?'

Izzy's features clouded over. 'You could say that.'

'Not a father at all,' snorted Poppy, 'but a thug who liked to throw his weight around.'

Mike drained his drink. 'I think it's best if I make myself scarce.' He smiled kindly at Izzy. 'Hopefully we'll meet again, only under happier circumstances.'

Izzy returned the smile. 'That would be nice. Are you local to Lincoln?'

'I'm based at RAF Waddington.' Gathering Poppy's plate with his own, he placed his empty glass on top, whilst continuing to gaze at Izzy. 'Perhaps we could meet up for a drink when you get back so that I can introduce myself properly – I'm Mike by the way.'

Izzy had always found pilots to be rather attractive because they were heroes who rushed off to save the day. However, this was the first time she had spoken to one outside a work environment.

Realising that she was staring, Izzy found her tongue. 'I'm Izzy,' she said, 'and I'd very much like to take you up on that offer of a drink.'

Mike smiled slowly. 'I'm free on Wednesday, if that suits?'

Izzy nodded fervently. 'It does indeed.'

His smile broadened. 'Wonderful. How about we meet here at nineteen hundred hours?'

Dimples formed in Izzy's cheeks as she tried to swallow the smile that was forming. 'I look forward to it.'

When Mike was out of earshot, Poppy turned to Izzy, an enormous grin etched on her cheeks. 'You've got a date, with a *pilot*.'

Looking slightly bemused, Izzy nodded. 'I have, haven't I?'

Cadi rolled her eyes. 'Never mind that – although it is good news. What happened to your dad?'

Poppy tutted irritably. Having previously been attacked by Izzy's brute of a father, she really couldn't care less what had happened to him. 'Hang Eric …' Hesitating, she turned to Izzy, her eyes growing wide. 'They didn't, did they?'

Izzy knitted her brows. 'Didn't what?'

'Hang him,' said Poppy plainly. 'We all know what he's like, and quite frankly it wouldn't surprise me if he'd found himself on the end of a noose.'

'Poppy!' hissed Cadi. 'I know we might not like him, but don't forget that he is, or rather was, Izzy's father.'

Poppy murmured a shamefaced apology to their friend. 'Sorry, Izzy.'

'Don't apologise,' said Izzy sharply. 'My dad was a brute, and I dare say you're not the only one who's glad he's gone ...' She shrugged helplessly. 'I can't even pretend I'm going to miss him because, as far as I was concerned, I was never going to see him again.'

Cadi laid a reassuring hand over Izzy's. 'I know, chuck, and I don't blame you for feeling the way you do, but it must still have come as quite a shock.'

'I've only just found out, so I suppose I don't really know how I feel.' Izzy glanced towards where Mike had taken a seat, not far from the bar. 'I hope I didn't sound heartless in front of Mike,' she began, but Cadi was quick to put an end to her worries.

'Not at all. He's a smashing feller, and he soon got the gist of what your dad was like.'

'Only we're getting off the topic,' said Poppy. 'I dare say you don't much fancy discussing what happened to your father, but ...'

Izzy drew a deep breath. 'From what Lethia said, they found him down the docks.' She grimaced. 'They reckon he'd been there for a few weeks ...'

Cadi clapped her hand over her mouth. Speaking thickly through her fingers, she repeated Izzy's words: 'A few weeks?'

Izzy nodded. 'I know – dreadful, isn't it? I can't pretend I liked my father, but the thought of anyone—'
She shook her head.

'Who discovered him?' asked Poppy. 'Surely not Lethia?'

'Gosh, no. Lethia found out through the grapevine.'

Morbid curiosity getting the better of her, Poppy asked the question uppermost in her mind. 'How do they know he'd been there for a few weeks?'

'Dad's landlord had been trying to get hold of him because he'd stopped paying his rent.'

'Bloody hell,' whispered Poppy.

'I know,' said Izzy, 'pretty grim, eh?'

'So why are you going to Liverpool, and in such a hurry?' asked Cadi curiously.

'Knowing the landlord was owed rent, Lethia told him that Dad had a box that supposedly contained money, and that the landlord should get it before the scuffers did.' She shrugged off Cadi's and Poppy's shocked expressions. 'Not all scuffers are straight and if the wrong person finds the box, it'd never see the light of day again. Not that it matters, because the landlord said he'd rather write it off as a loss than have anything to do with the money.'

Poppy leaned forward, intrigued. 'So he reckons it was dodgy?'

Izzy nodded. 'It seems that way. You see, whilst we don't know the ins and outs of Dad's demise, we do know that it was no accident. If the rumour mill is correct, then Dad was mixed up in a ring of smugglers; and when Lethia spoke to the police, they told her that they thought it was probably a bad deal gone wrong and that Eric bore the brunt of it.' She shrugged. 'Knowing him, he'd probably tried to double-cross them or ask for more than his fair share.'

'Do they know that he was mixed up with smugglers for definite?' asked Cadi.

'No,' admitted Izzy, 'but the tom-toms have been going hell for leather, and Lethia reckons the rumours are true.'

Poppy shuffled forward in her seat. 'So what happened to the money box?'

'Lethia's got it,' said Izzy. 'That's why I'm going to Liverpool, so that I can take it off her hands.'

'How did Lethia know about the money?' asked Poppy curiously.

Izzy shot her friend an incredulous look. 'Do you not remember Dad screaming blue murder the night I ran away?'

Cadi nodded. 'I certainly do – he was telling everyone that you'd stolen his money.'

'Of course!' said Poppy. 'I'd forgotten all about that.'

'Exactly. That's why Lethia took it. As she rightly said, better it go to me than the scuffers, or those responsible for Dad's murder.'

'Good for Lethia,' concluded Poppy. 'It's a shame you've got to go all the way to Liverpool, though. When are you thinking of leaving?'

'I'm afraid I'll have to go tonight. I don't know when I'll get another forty-eight, and Lethia wants it out of her house a.s.a.p., just in case anyone gets wind of what she's done.'

'Typical!' moaned Poppy. 'First time we've been together since Christmas and this happens – goodness only knows when we'll get another opportunity.'

Cadi was eyeing her friends thoughtfully. 'Why don't we all go?'

Poppy frowned. 'But you're booked in here.'

Cadi shrugged. 'I'm sure Alfie won't mind; not if we tell him the circumstances.'

Izzy looked dubious. 'It's a fair old trek, though, and you've not long arrived.'

'As long as I'm with my pals I don't care where I am.'

Izzy beamed. 'So is that decided?'

Poppy drained the last drop of ale from her glass. 'I don't see why not. We can stay at the Belmont, provided Maria and Bill haven't rented out our room, of course.'

Cadi stood up. 'Maria would never do that. She's said there'll always be a room for us in the Belmont, no matter what.'

Poppy stood to one side to let Cadi get through. 'You get your bag, and Izzy and I'll explain the situation to Alfie.'

It didn't take Cadi more than a moment to fetch her bag from the room, and as she entered the bar area she saw that Alfie was smiling at her. 'Don't worry about the room, love, some things are more important.'

Cadi handed over the key. 'Thanks for being so understanding. The meal was top-notch, and I dare say breakfast would've been just as good.'

He huffed on his fingernails before pretending to polish them against his shirt. 'High praise indeed, coming from you.' He glanced towards Poppy. 'Our Poppy's told us all about the Greyhound.'

Cadi beamed proudly. 'It was the best pub in Liverpool.'

Alfie hung the key back in its place. 'Who knows? Maybe I'll see you again.'

Bidding the landlord a friendly goodbye, the girls headed for the taxi rank outside the railway station. 'You might as well come with me and Izzy whilst we fetch our stuff,' Poppy told Cadi, as she and Izzy climbed into the back of the nearest taxi. 'Saves you waiting on your tod.'

It was a relatively short drive from the city to the RAF base, and the girls chattered continuously about the journey that lay ahead. As they exited the vehicle, Izzy instructed the driver to await their return.

'I reckon we'll be there no later than midnight,' said Izzy as they hastened across the yard to Poppy's hut, 'but we'll have to hurry, as the train leaves in half an hour – wait for me by the gate.'

Inside Poppy's hut, Cadi helped her friend pack the essentials. 'It's a shame I won't get to meet Geoffrey—' Cadi began, before being cut off by a sharp squeal from Poppy.

'Geoffrey! I nearly forgot,' she cried. Pushing the last of her bits into the bag, she raced out of the hut with Cadi in hot pursuit. 'If we hurry, we might catch him.'

Pelting along, Poppy skidded to a halt as a man exited one of the huts. 'Geoffrey!'

He furrowed his brow. 'I thought I was meeting you in the Horse and Groom?'

She shook her head fervently. 'I'm going to Liverpool with Cadi and Izzy. You see, Izzy's father's died and we've got to get his loot before the smugglers get their filthy mitts on it.'

193

Geoffrey's brow shot upwards. 'You've got to what?'

Cadi stepped forward. 'Hi, Geoffrey, I'm Cadi. What Poppy *means* is that we've got to retrieve Eric's money box from a friend of ours.'

Geoffrey nodded slowly. 'And the smugglers?'

Cadi continued. 'They don't know where the money is, which is why we have to get hold of it before they put two and two together. It's not fair on Lethia, especially as she took a risk by hiding the box in the first place.'

The frown on Geoffrey's face deepened. 'I don't like the sound of this. Are you sure you should be going on your own?'

Poppy nodded. 'We'll be fine – besides, there's three of us.' Stretching up onto her tiptoes, she kissed him on the cheek. 'Gotta dash. I'll tell you all about it when we get back.'

Geoffrey, who was much taller than Cadi had expected him to be, squeezed Poppy in his arms. 'Just you make sure you take care, Poppy Harding – you're a very precious commodity.'

'I will, don't you worry,' Poppy assured him.

Geoffrey turned his attention to Cadi. 'There's never a dull moment with our Poppy around. Look after her for me, won't you?'

Nodding, Cadi gabbled a quick 'Ta-ra' before grabbing Poppy by the hand and rushing her back to the taxi, where they found Izzy already seated in the back.

'Sorry,' puffed Poppy, 'I had to say goodbye to Geoffrey. He'd have wondered where we were.'

'Not to worry,' assured Izzy, 'we'll still make it in time.'

When they were eventually sitting on the train, Izzy was the first to realise they hadn't informed Maria or Bill of their plans.

'We'll have to tell them at the next station,' said Cadi. 'I'll nip off the train, if you two keep my place.'

'Make sure you hurry,' warned Poppy. 'You know these trains don't like to hang about.'

Izzy had been correct in guessing they would arrive in Liverpool before twelve, and because Cadi had been successful in informing Maria of their anticipated arrival, it meant the girls had a hot cup of tea, as well as a round of sandwiches, waiting for them when they entered the kitchen of the Belmont. Maria placed a finger to her lips as they greeted one another. 'I've got a full house, so we'll have to be quiet.'

Bill turned to Izzy. 'Cadi didn't have a chance to tell us much, but from what we gathered, summat's happened to your dad?'

Izzy took a long sip of her tea before answering. 'Lethia said some fellers had found his body down the docks and that he'd been dead for some weeks. I don't know the ins and outs myself, save for the conspiracy theories, of course.' She finished off her cheese-and-onion sandwich before continuing. 'We all know Dad had too much money for a docker, so smuggling makes perfect sense. He always did want more than his fair share, so it's obvious to me that he's said or done the wrong thing to the wrong person.'

'Does anybody else know about Eric's secret stash?' asked Bill slowly.

'*Everybody*,' said Izzy, 'because Eric went round shouting the odds, accusing me of stealing it from him. Even if they thought him a liar, there's no smoke without fire, and with Dad out of the way, it won't be long before people decide to see for themselves whether there was any truth in the rumours.'

'That's why Lethia fetched the box home,' stated Cadi.

'If Eric was mixed up with a rum bunch, they must know about the money,' said Maria fearfully, 'so what if they come looking for it?' But Bill was shaking his head.

'That's what I thought at first, but if Eric died a while before he was discovered, they'd have made their move pretty quickly, *before* anyone else had a chance to look.'

'So why didn't they?' mused Poppy.

'If the scuffers are right and it was a bad deal gone wrong, then the smugglers probably decided to bump Eric off so that they could take his share of the money,' suggested Cadi.

'And I bet no one seriously thought Dad saved his money, because they knew how fond he was of the drink,' said Izzy reasonably. 'It probably didn't occur to them that he really did have a private stash.'

Bill nodded wisely. 'Now that makes sense.'

Maria hid a yawn behind her hand. 'It's far too late for all this excitement. Shall we resume this conversation in the morning?'

With everyone in agreement, they retired to bed. Snuggled beneath her sheets, Poppy closed her eyes. It might have been a couple of years since Eric's attack, but she still lived with the memory of that night and what could have happened, had Jez not come to her rescue. She rarely spoke of her anxieties, not wanting Cadi to continue taking the blame, but Eric's actions had scarred her for life and even though he was gone, the memories remained. She didn't wish to appear heartless in front of the others, but she only saw Eric's death as a good thing, and she was pretty sure Izzy felt the same way. The knowledge of how easily a man can overpower a woman had left Poppy cautious when it came to the opposite sex. It was why she loved Geoffrey so much. He was a gentle giant, who wouldn't dream of raising his voice in anger, let alone his fists. She knew it was why Izzy steered clear of men, but she very much hoped that Izzy, too, would soon learn that not all men were like Eric – especially if she took Mike up on his offer of a drink. She turned her thoughts to the handsome flying officer. *He's just the sort of man our Izzy needs*, Poppy thought to herself, *someone who'll show her how wonderful love can be.* And with that thought, Poppy drifted off to sleep.

The next morning the girls left the Belmont as soon as they had finished helping Maria with the guests' breakfasts.

'I don't think I got a wink all night,' confessed Poppy as they made their way to Lethia's.

'Me neither,' admitted Cadi. 'I dreamed that the smugglers turned up whilst we were at Lethia's.'

'I can't pretend I'm not anxious,' Izzy admitted. 'I know it's highly unlikely they know about the money, but I can't stop myself from thinking: what if they do and they're waiting for the right moment to snatch it?'

Poppy gave a mirthless laugh. 'Bill's right. If they knew about it, there wouldn't *be* any money. Don't forget, the smugglers hid your father after murdering him in cold blood. People like that are ruthless.'

Cadi nodded. 'That money would be long gone.'

'I wonder how much money there is now?' pondered Poppy. 'You could be rich, Izzy.'

Izzy wrinkled her nose in distaste. 'Maybe so, but what am I meant to do with it?'

'Spend it!' cried Cadi and Poppy in unison.

'If that money has been made illegally – and let's face it, we all know it has – then I don't think it's mine to spend,' reasoned Izzy.

'You can hardly give it back,' said Poppy, 'especially when you don't know where it came from in the first place.'

'I could always give it to the police?' suggested Izzy.

Poppy's brow shot towards her hairline. 'Oh aye. You've already said they might pocket it for themselves. I'm not being funny, Izzy, but once that money's out of your hands, anything could happen to it …' She hesitated. 'They might even nick you.'

Izzy laughed this off. 'Don't be daft. Why would they do that?'

Poppy pouted defensively. 'They might think you had summat to do with it. It was a lot of money, after all.'

'Not if I'm handing it over, they wouldn't,' Izzy began. But, seeing the doubtful look on Cadi's face, she hesitated before continuing, 'They couldn't, could they?'

Cadi pulled a sceptical smile. 'They'd want to know where the money came from. If you told them the truth, they'd start asking questions.'

'Like what?' said Izzy.

'Like where's it been until now, and why you didn't go to the police sooner?' Cadi shrugged. 'I'm not saying you could go to jail, but I do think the WAAF would want to know why one of their soon-to-be sergeants has been involved in summat iffy.'

'So what am I supposed to do with the money?' cried Izzy. 'I can hardly leave it with Lethia. She can't wait to see the back of it.'

'Spend it,' said Poppy levelly. 'No money, no proof.'

'I shall give it to the war effort,' said Izzy promptly, 'make an anonymous donation.'

Poppy sighed. 'All that lovely dosh.'

'We don't even know if there *is* any money,' reasoned Cadi.

'Let's hope not,' said Izzy.

Cadi jerked her head towards a terraced house with an old black door, its peeling paint splintered by the sun. 'Looks like we're about to find out.'

Cadi and Poppy both stood back as Izzy rapped a brief tattoo on the weathered door.

Within moments they heard footsteps approaching from the other side, and Lethia called through. 'Who is it?'

'Izzy, Poppy and Cadi,' replied Izzy.

Lethia opened the door. 'Flippin' Nora, I didn't expect to see all three of you.' She stood to one side so that they could enter. 'Come on in.'

The girls trooped in and Lethia pointed towards the kitchen table. 'Take a pew and I'll fetch the box. Anyone fancy a cuppa?'

'Yes, please,' said Poppy. 'My mouth's drier than the Sahara.'

Lethia popped the kettle on to boil, before fetching Eric's box from under the sink. She handed it to Izzy. 'There's no key, so I don't know how you'll get it open.'

Poppy swiftly removed the nail file from her bag and pushed it into the lock, which sprang open after a few twists. 'Ta-dah!'

Lethia looked impressed. 'That's a handy trick.'

Pulling the box towards her, Izzy raised the lid. Staring at the contents, she murmured, 'Dear God!' beneath her breath, before turning the box to face the girls, who uttered various cries of surprise.

'I reckon there's a lot more in there this time,' said Poppy. She gave Izzy an encouraging nod. 'Count it.'

Emptying the contents onto the table, Izzy placed the box to one side as she separated the money from a few envelopes, which she held up for examination. 'I don't remember seeing these the last time.'

'Neither do I,' admitted Cadi. 'Maybe it was the shock of seeing all that money. After all, we were only really searching for your papers and they were on top of the money.

'Could they be bonds?' suggested Lethia.

Izzy pulled a doubtful face. 'Dad would hardly invest stolen money. Even he wasn't that stupid.'

'You never know,' conceded Lethia. 'I'd always assumed all his money went on liquor.'

Gathering the various notes, Izzy shuffled them to-gether. 'Even Dad couldn't have drunk this much.' She hesitated. 'And if he'd flaunted his wealth down the pub, folk would've got suspicious.'

Cadi glanced at the envelopes. 'Do you want me to take a look at these whilst you count?'

Izzy shrugged. 'You can, if you like.'

Cadi examined the writing on each envelope. 'Did Eric have a penpal?'

Izzy emitted a shriek of laughter. 'What on earth makes you say that?'

'Because these don't look like they're from an official body – they look more like letters,' said Cadi, 'and if Eric kept them, I can only assume they must have been important to him.'

Izzy stared at the envelopes in Cadi's hands. 'If they're letters, they'll be demanding money, cos there's no way my dad had a penpal.' Chuckling to herself at the very thought, she began to count the money.

Cadi pulled the letters out of their envelopes, all of which appeared to have been written by the same hand. Lining them up in a row, she glanced at the sig-nature at the bottom of each letter.

'Wasn't Raquel your mam's name?'

'Yes – why d'you ask?'

Cadi turned the letters for Izzy to see. As her eyes fell on the signature at the bottom of each one, Izzy stopped counting the money.

'She wrote to him?' she asked, her voice barely above a whisper.

Cadi pushed the letters towards her.

Seeing the date at the head of each one, Izzy placed the four letters in order so that she might start at the beginning. Clearing her throat, she began reading the first one out loud:

'Eric,

'I can see how it must've looked, but please believe me when I tell you you've made a terrible mistake. Colin Robins and I were never having an affair, and you should have known better than to listen to idle gossip. As I've already told you, I was only seeing him so that he could teach me how to read and write. I knew you wouldn't approve, which is why I lied about where I was going and who I was with, but I swear to you, Eric, that's where it ends. By refusing to answer the door, you're not even giving me the chance to put things right – explain my side of the story. You're cutting off your nose to spite your face because of one stupid misunderstanding.'

Izzy looked at Lethia, who was pouring the boiling water into the teapot. 'Is this true? Is this Colin the one they reckoned was having an affair with my mam?'

Lethia nodded. 'Colin Robins was a cobbler on the Scottie.'

Cadi pointed at the remaining letters. 'What do the others say?'

Izzy began reading the next in line:

'Eric,

'It's been months, and still no reply. I just want to know if Izzy's all right. I realise you're still angry, and

202

*in some respects I suppose I don't blame you. But
looking after a toddler whilst keeping down a job must
be difficult. I know you're only keeping Izzy to punish
me for what you believe I've done, but please don't
punish her for my actions. None of this is Izzy's fault.
You should've let me take her with me when I asked. It's
still not too late for you to reconsider, even if only for
Izzy's sake.'*

Cadi blew her cheeks out. 'So your mam didn't
desert you for another man.'

Izzy wiped a tear from her cheek. 'I said we shouldn't
believe a word that left Dad's lips, and I was right.' She
looked to Lethia. 'You knew my mam, what did you
make of the rumours?'

Lethia drew a deep breath before letting it out. 'No
one argues with Eric, you know that. He reckoned he'd
heard it straight from the horse's mouth. Did I find it
hard to believe? I suppose I did. But the proof was in
the pudding. Your mam had gone, and so had Colin.
With no one to say anything to the contrary, what were
we meant to think?'

Izzy wrinkled her brow. 'Colin left too?'

Lethia nodded. 'That's why we believed Eric when
he said they'd run off together.' She eyed Izzy cautiously. 'I know your mam's pleading innocence in
these letters, but she's hardly likely to admit to having
an affair – not when she was asking him to hand you
over.'

Cadi indicated the next letter. 'What does that one
say?'

Once again Izzy started reading:

'Eric,

'I don't know what you've done, but from what I hear, Colin's missing, and I can only think of one explanation for his absence. I pray to God that I am wrong, because that man is innocent – all he did was try and educate someone in need. I know first-hand that you've a filthy temper, and I also know how vicious you can be, which is why I ask you yet again to hand Izzy over to me. You've never had any patience, and children can be very trying. If you do decide to give her up, then I shall welcome her with open arms; not only that, but I promise you shall never hear from me again.'

Lethia stared at the reverse side of the letter, before turning hollow eyes to Izzy. 'Oh my God!'

'She was telling the truth, otherwise she'd not be questioning Colin's whereabouts,' said Izzy. She eyed Lethia accusingly. 'If it weren't for folk gossiping, my mam might never have left.'

'Be fair!' cried Lethia. 'Your mam either had an awful lot of shoes what needed repairing or summat else was going on. We all knew what a bastard Eric could be, and none of us blamed her for seeking a friendly face elsewhere. It never occurred to anyone ...'

Izzy's lips tightened. 'That my mam wasn't a tart?'

Lethia rallied. 'I never said that, nor did anyone else.'

'Might as well have,' said Izzy. 'My dad certainly thought so; he even tarred me with the same brush—'

Cadi cleared her throat before interrupting. 'You can't blame folk for getting hold of the wrong end of the stick, Izzy.'

'No, but I can blame them for gossiping. If they'd kept their mouths shut, my mam might never have left,' replied Izzy bluntly.

'Only we weren't the only ones who talked,' said Lethia defensively. 'Eric said he'd seen them together, so you can't blame us. If it was all so innocent, why didn't your mam tell Eric the truth from the start?'

'Because my dad wouldn't approve,' retorted Izzy. 'You said so yourself: no one argues with Eric.'

Poppy spoke quietly in a bid to calm the rising tension. 'So if you want to blame anyone, you should blame your dad, because this was all his fault. If he hadn't been so controlling, your mam wouldn't have had to lie in the first place.'

Izzy sighed heavily before apologising to Lethia, albeit a tad grudgingly. 'I don't blame you, not really; it's just hard when you've been told the same thing all your life, only to find out it wasn't true.'

Cadi looked at Lethia through hollow eyes. 'If Colin didn't run off with Raquel, then where is he?'

Lethia had turned pale. 'I dread to think. No one questioned it at the time because we all assumed Colin was with her.'

'You mentioned something about him being a cobbler,' said Poppy. 'What happened to his shop, his supplies, his tools?'

Lethia let out a staggered breath. 'Abandoned. Rumour was that he legged it before Eric got wind of their intentions.' She placed her head in her hands. 'All this was over twenty years ago. It made perfect sense at the time.'

Cadi's blood ran cold. 'Do we really think Eric *murdered* Colin? I …' She was about to say that she knew Eric had a temper, but murder? Then her eyes fell on Izzy's scar. 'Jez said summat about Eric only picking on people weaker than him. What was Colin like?'

Lethia turned her gaze from Cadi to the letters. 'I never knew him socially, but whenever I went into his shop to get owt mended, he allus come across as pleasant and mild-mannered. Certainly not the sort to get mixed up in a brawl.'

'What sort of build?' asked Izzy.

'Smaller than Eric,' considered Lethia, 'not only in height, but in weight too.'

Izzy held a hand to her stomach. She was beginning to feel sick. 'Just the sort of person my dad would challenge, *especially* if he thought he was in the right.'

Cadi indicated the last letter with a nod of her head. 'What does that one say?'

Izzy began reading:

'Eric,

'I've done what you asked, even though it pained me terribly. Denying me is one thing, but denying your own child? Surely even you can't believe that to be true? One of these days you'll see for yourself that you were wrong, and God help you when that day comes. I myself have to live with the consequences of my actions, which is why I've left Liverpool. I can't look after myself, let alone a child. I think it's best if I cut all ties. The pain of my actions is too strong for me to bear. No matter what you think, please let Izzy know that I love her with all my heart.'

206

Izzy wrinkled her brow. 'What does she mean by "denying your own child"? Dad never said I wasn't his – or not that I ever knew of.' She looked directly at Lethia. 'Does it make sense to you?'

Lethia, who had gone quite pale, shook her head vehemently. 'It would be wrong to start speculating, especially when we've just seen the trouble that can be caused by assumptions and rumours.'

'Too little, too late,' said Izzy primly, adding in kinder tones, 'Besides, all this was twenty years ago. I don't think it really matters now, especially with Dad gone.'

'He might be gone, but others aren't,' said Lethia levelly. 'To speculate could open a whole can of worms, and for what? These letters have proved two things. Your mother never had an affair, and an innocent man might be lying at the bottom of the Mersey because of something that never happened. And all because people cast suspicions on what they thought to be obvious.' She shook her head. 'Once bitten, twice shy. This is best left well alone, if you ask me.'

'And what about Colin Robins?' cried Cadi. 'You can't really be suggesting that we don't report our suspicions to the police?'

Lethia leaned back in her chair. 'And what do you suppose will happen, if you do? It's not as if Eric can be held accountable for his actions – and besides, where's the body?'

'She's right,' said Poppy, 'we've no proof, bar these letters.'

'But we know from the letters that Dad was lying. And with Colin missing, surely that only goes to prove ...' said Izzy, flourishing the last letter.

Cadi spoke grudgingly. 'Not really, Izzy. I know it looks like your mam's telling the truth, but we need more proof than these letters.'

Izzy stared, open-mouthed, at her friends. 'Is that what you all think?'

'I believe your mam,' Poppy assured her, 'but only because I know what your dad was like. If I were an outsider – like the police, for example – I'd probably say that actions speak louder than words.'

Seeing that Izzy was struggling to deal with their reasoning, Cadi made a suggestion. 'Your mam wrote her address on the top of the last letter, so why don't you write to her? At least that way you could meet up, get her side of the story first-hand.'

Izzy gave a triumphant cry. 'Of course! Why didn't I think of that?'

'Because you're still in shock,' said Lethia kindly. 'I think we all are.'

'So you do believe her?' asked Izzy, in tones that were almost begging Lethia to confirm this to be true.

Lethia nodded. 'And if it's any consolation, I'm sorry I ever doubted her. But Eric was pretty convincing, and everything he accused them of seemed to match up – or at least it did at the time.'

Poppy gestured towards the money. 'Now that we've sorted that out, how about you count the money and see how much you've got?'

They waited whilst Izzy counted the money into piles. 'There's forty-three pounds in total.'

'Flippin' 'eck!' breathed Lethia. 'What are you goin' to do with it?'

Folding the money, Izzy placed it back in the money box along with the letters. 'That's easy. I'm going to give it to me mam just as soon as I find her.'

Chapter Five

September 1942

Several months had passed since Izzy had written to her mother, and despite her hopes for a timely response, she had received nothing but disappointment. In fact Izzy had nearly given up hope when her own letter was returned to her, one balmy autumnal morning. Worried as to what might unfold, she had telephoned Cadi's base and the girls had arranged to meet outside All Saints church in the village of Ruskington, which lay midway between Coningsby and Fiskerton.

As soon as Poppy and Izzy alighted from the bus, Cadi, who'd already arrived, walked over to greet them. 'I'm surprised you haven't opened the letter already. I don't think I'd have your patience – not under the circumstances.'

Izzy held a hand to her tummy. 'I'm scared to, because I'm certain it's bad news, which is why I want my friends with me. Besides, we started this journey together and it only seems right that we end it the same way.'

Cadi raised a brow in query. 'What do you mean by "end it"?'

Izzy held up the envelope. 'It's the same letter I sent her, only with her address crossed out and mine written in.'

Cadi's face dropped. 'Oh, not looking too hopeful then?'

Izzy pulled back the Sellotape that had been used to reseal the envelope. Taking out the contents, she glanced at the short note before turning it to face the girls.

'"Not known at this address",' said Poppy. 'Oh, Izzy, I am sorry, but I suppose it was a bit of a long shot.'

Folding the note, Izzy was about to tuck it into the pocket of jacket when Cadi held out her hand.

'Do you mind if I take a quick peek?'

'Not at all,' said Izzy, handing it over.

Cadi stared at it. She had only seen the other letters fleetingly, but if she was right ... She looked up at Izzy. 'Do you still have the letters that your mam sent your dad?'

Izzy shook her head. 'I left them at Maria's, along with the money.'

'Of course.' Cadi held up the note. 'Would you mind if I kept hold of this?'

Izzy shrugged her indifference. 'Do what you like – I was only going to bin it.'

Cadi listened as Izzy and Poppy discussed the possibilities of finding out where Izzy's mother had moved to.

Her friends seemed satisfied with the returned envelope. But several things didn't sit right with Cadi, and she knew that the answer to her queries lay in the bottom of Eric's box.

Several weeks had passed since meeting up with her pals, and Cadi was currently making her way to the Belmont in Liverpool – or, rather, she was making her way to RAF Speke, but she was doing so via the Belmont.

Despite solving the issue with the engines, Jez remained in Africa, and Cadi's worst fears had come true. It seemed that Jez was so good at his job they had refused to send him home. He had broken the news in a telephone conversation a few days earlier.

'Darling Cadi. You've no idea how much I miss you.'

'And I you,' said Cadi. 'I wish you were on your way back already.'

Jez grimaced. 'It could be next year at this rate, although of course I can't say why.'

'I know, I know,' drawled Cadi. 'You still haven't—'

Jez cut her short. 'Only we have, that's not the issue.'

'That's not fair!' wailed Cadi. 'They promised ...'

'I know they did, queen, and I'm not happy about it, either, but my hands are tied. I wish I could say more.'

'I know,' mumbled Cadi. '"Loose lips" and all that.' She thought back to how tongue-wagging had caused major issues for Raquel and said as much, adding, 'Did your nan ever mention Izzy's mam?'

'God, no! Not because she wasn't one to gossip, mind you,' he chuckled softly. 'Nan loved a good natter as much as the next woman, but she was different when it came to Eric.'

'Why do you suppose that was?' asked Cadi.

'Probably because he was a nasty piece of work and she didn't want to get on the wrong side of his temper.'

'Granted, but that didn't stop the others,' said Cadi, adding peevishly, 'more's the pity.'

'Yeah, but Nan was on her own, so it would've been different for her.'

'Surely she would've said something to you, though?' ventured Cadi. 'Everybody has their own opinions and theories, so I'm surprised she didn't voice them to you, if to no one else.'

'I was still in nappies when Izzy's mam left.' He hesitated. 'Why all the questions?'

'I can't help thinking there's more to Raquel and Eric's situation than meets the eye. She wrote candidly in her last letter, and I got the distinct impression that she didn't want Izzy contacting her. Strange, when she'd appeared so eager before. It makes me wonder what happened to change her mind.'

'From what you told me, Raquel said it would be better if she cut all ties. Maybe she wanted to start afresh and move on with her life, instead of living in the past. Raking over old ground never does anyone any good, and wishful thinking can lead to nothing but heartache, if it never comes to fruition. So I should imagine Raquel decided to do just that. If she doesn't expect Izzy to come calling, then she won't be disappointed if she never does.'

'Very intuitive,' mused Cadi. 'What inspired you to come up with that?'

'When I arrived I was desperate to get the job done so that I could get back to Blighty, but each time I failed, I

213

got disheartened. When we finally had the breakthrough we needed, I was cock-a-hoop, only to have my hopes dashed when they said we'd not be going home for some time yet. That's when I decided it would be easier for me to accept that I could be here until the end of the war – that way I'm not living in constant hope, and anything to the contrary will be a bonus.'

Now, as Cadi pulled up outside the Belmont, she waved to Bill, who had appeared on the pavement.

'Come in, queen, our Maria's prepared you some scouse, and the tea's in the pot.'

Cadi followed Bill through to the kitchen. 'Golly, it's good to be back, even if it is only a flying visit.' She glanced at her wristwatch. 'I've got to pick up Officer Wendall at two, but even I'm entitled to a lunch break.'

'Good to have you back,' said Maria. 'How's Izzy? Poor thing must be awfully disappointed.'

'She always knew it was a long shot,' conceded Cadi, 'but it still came as a huge blow.'

Maria dished the scouse into a bowl and handed it to Cadi. 'You mentioned something about Raquel's letters in your last telephone call?'

Cadi dipped her spoon into the stew. 'Have you got them to hand?'

Maria looked at Bill, who disappeared up the stairs. 'We keep Eric's box under our bed – not the safest place, I know, but I don't want to put it in the bank in case they ask where I got the money from.' She hesitated. 'Why are you so interested in the letters?'

Cadi rolled her tongue around the inside of her cheek. 'I just want to check something.'

Bill reappeared with the box. 'There you go.' He glanced over at the pot of scouse. 'Is it only our Cadi gettin' summat to eat?'

Tutting, Maria proceeded to dole out a portion into another bowl. 'Honestly, Bill Shankley, you're a bottomless pit.'

Pulling the note from her pocket, Cadi held it next to each of the letters, before giving a small exclamation. 'I knew it!' She beckoned Bill and Maria over. 'What do you think?' Before either of them could answer, she continued, 'Pay careful attention to the letter "k": see the way she does a flick on the end? Also the letter "a" – they're both done in the same fashion ...'

'Not only that,' said Bill, 'but they all look like they've been written by a child.'

'And Raquel had only just learned to read and write,' concluded Cadi.

Maria pointed to the short response that Izzy had recently received. 'You think this note is from Raquel?'

Cadi nodded fervently. 'We know, from Raquel's last letter to Eric, that she'd made up her mind to cut all ties and move on with her life. Maybe hearing from Izzy now proved too painful.'

Bill speared a piece of carrot with his fork. 'Have you mentioned any of this to Izzy?'

'No, I needed to be sure before I started bandying my opinions around. There's been too much of that, when it comes to Raquel.'

'What do you intend to do, now you've seen the evidence with your own eyes?' asked Maria.

'I'm still not going to say anything. Not until I've found out why Raquel doesn't want to talk to her daughter. Izzy's had enough disappointment in her life, and I'll be damned if I'm going to add to it.'

'Well, writing to her has proved fruitless,' said Maria, 'which only leaves one other option.'

Cadi nodded. 'I shall either have to make a special trip or see if someone needs summat delivering down Portsmouth way.'

Maria joined Cadi and Bill at the table. 'What I don't get is why Raquel felt she had to go so far away?'

'Eric,' said Cadi simply. 'Raquel would've known he'd not rest whilst she was in the same city.'

'I reckon Cadi's right,' said Bill. 'Eric would've kept Izzy a prisoner, for fear she might bump into her mother.'

Cadi looked at her hosts. 'I know you never really knew Raquel or Eric socially, but what did you make of the gossip surrounding her sudden departure?'

Maria grimaced. 'We both knew better than to talk about someone like Eric behind his back.'

'That's what Jez said about his nan,' considered Cadi.

'She had Jez to protect,' said Maria. 'Carrie would've walked across hot coals for that boy.'

Cadi scraped the last morsels from her plate. 'I wish I knew more, because none of this makes sense.'

Bill leaned forward in a conspiratorial fashion. 'I didn't like to mention it in front of Izzy – not after all the speculation – but you know that Colin Robins?'

'What about him?'

'From what I remember, word had it that he went down the docks in search of Eric not long before he went missing.'

Cadi frowned. 'Why on earth did he do that?'

'At the time I thought there was no truth in it,' admitted Bill, 'but after seeing those letters, I'm guessing he went down to tell Eric that it was a load of rubbish and not to listen to the gossips.'

Cadi stared at Bill, open-mouthed. 'Colin must have realised Eric wasn't the sort of man who'd listen to reason?'

Bill shrugged. 'I'm only telling you what I heard. That doesn't mean to say it's true, but it might explain why Colin disappeared.'

'Did anyone see them talking?'

Bill shook his head. 'Nobody actually saw Colin go down the docks; it was a passing comment that he'd made to someone, which was overheard by someone else, and it went on from there.'

'Chinese whispers,' said Cadi, 'so we've no idea whether there's any truth in it?'

'Apart from Colin disappearing, of course,' Bill reminded her. 'Although that didn't look at all fishy at the time.'

Cadi breathed out slowly. 'Eric has literally got away with murder.'

Maria collected the empty dishes. 'It certainly looks that way.'

Realising the time, Cadi got up from her seat. 'I've got to dash.'

Maria fussed over her as they made their way to the car. 'Make sure you drive safely, and give us a holler if you need owt.'

Bill admired the car that Cadi was driving. 'Very nice!'

Giving her friends a hug goodbye, Cadi started the engine before taking her place behind the wheel. 'I'll give you a call if I hear any more.'

Bidding them a fond farewell, she pulled the car away from the kerb. As she drove through the streets of Liverpool she replayed her findings in her mind. If she could only see Raquel, speak to her face-to-face, Cadi felt certain she would be able to talk the older woman round.

As she approached the gate she showed her pass to the guard, who waved her through. Parking in one of the spots reserved for visitors, Cadi reported in, only to be told that the officer in question was running late and wouldn't be available for another half an hour, if not longer.

All that rushing, thought Cadi, *and for what?* With nothing else to do, she informed the office that she would wait for the officer in the NAAFI. Having already eaten, she only intended to get herself a cup of tea, but after seeing the cakes on offer she decided to treat herself to a scone. Selecting a table by the door so that she could be spotted easily, she had only just sat down when a familiar voice called out.

'Cadi!' cried Aled. 'What on *earth* are you doing here? You never rang to say you were popping by?'

She turned to greet him. Having taken a bite of the scone, she spoke thickly through her fingers. 'Sorry, you know how it is.'

He pulled a face. 'I do indeed – rushing round like a blue-bummed whatsit, only to have some old goat hold you up. Am I right?'

218

Swallowing, Cadi smiled. 'You are indeed.' She indicated the scone. 'I thought I might as well grab a bite to eat to pass the time.'

'Tea and cake?' mused Aled. 'Not the healthiest of lunches.'

Cadi chuckled. 'I had scouse at Maria and Bill's before I arrived. I've not seen them for a few months ...'

Aled gave her a shrewd smile. 'So that's two visits, and no "hello" to your old pal Aled. Should I be offended?'

'Not at all,' said Cadi, continuing by way of explanation, 'The last time we came was a spur-of-the-moment thing.'

He appeared intrigued. 'We?'

'Myself, Poppy and Izzy – you don't know Izzy. Her father died, and we came back to Liverpool so that we could get his things.'

'All three of you? How much stuff did he have?'

'A box,' said Cadi, before quickly explaining the situation.

'Blimey! Sounds like she's well rid of him – a bit like me with Daphne.'

At the mere mention of the other girl, Cadi's face dropped. 'I take it you've not heard from her?'

Aled shook his head. 'All's quiet on the Western Front. You?'

'Not a dicky bird; same goes for Poppy and Kitty. I must say I'm rather relieved. I had feared Daphne might try and get her own back somehow.'

'What could she possibly do? It's not as if you did anything wrong.'

Cadi pulled a guilty face. 'Not as far as you and Daphne are concerned, but I failed to tell Jez that I was meeting you the day before he left for Africa.'

Aled pushed his shoulders back. 'I already know this, you told me—'

Cadi cut him short. 'I know what I said, but I wasn't being entirely truthful. I didn't tell Jez because I was worried he'd think I was interfering in something that had nothing to do with me and, quite frankly, he'd be right. That aside, I still don't think Jez would relish the idea of me meeting up with you.'

Aled eyed her curiously. 'So why did you?'

Cadi looked at him through her lashes. 'Because I consider you to be a friend, and if the boot were on the other foot, I'd hope you'd have done the same for me.'

'Like a flash,' said Aled, adding after a moment's thought, 'Do you not think Jez would see it that way?'

'I think he'd agree that you should be told,' mused Cadi, 'but that Poppy or Kitty should have been the ones to do the telling, not me.'

'I suppose he might have a point,' considered Aled. 'So what happened? Did you draw the short straw?'

'The letter,' said Cadi. 'You knew nothing about it, and it was kind of proof as to how low Daphne would go.'

He roared with laughter. 'You didn't think fixing my papers was bad enough?'

Cadi blushed. 'When you put it like that ...'

'I reckon you wanted an excuse to see my handsome face one more time,' joked Aled, but Cadi wasn't laughing.

'That's what Jez would probably think, which is why I wanted to keep it quiet.'

Aled waved a carefree hand. 'I guess I can see where he's coming from, especially after all that business last time. Getting that poison-pen letter can't have done much for his confidence.'

'I know, which is why I'm keen to keep him in the dark until I can tell him myself. The *last* thing I want is for to him hear things second-hand.'

'Well, your secret's safe with me,' Aled assured her, then hesitated. 'Does this mean I won't be seeing you again?'

'It shouldn't,' said Cadi, 'not if Jez trusts me.'

'I know we haven't always seen eye-to-eye, but I consider you one of my closest friends—' Aled began.

Cadi interrupted without apology. 'When you started writing to me, was it to find out how things had gone after I left? Or were you genuinely interested in maintaining our friendship?'

Aled leaned back in his chair. 'Six of one and half a dozen of the other. Why?'

'It seemed that you went off the boil, after I confirmed that Jez and I were together. Like you weren't really interested in discussing your own life. In fact you only really talked about life back in Rhos, and not what was going on with you. I understand there's a need for secrecy, but surely you could have been a little chattier – told me what films you'd seen, what you'd thought of them, that sort of thing.'

He nodded slowly. 'I knew you didn't think much of Daphne and, like most couples, we did everything together. But looking back, I'm not sure I was being entirely truthful with myself.'

'How do you mean?'

Aled leaned forward and, cupping her hands in his, he gazed into Cadi's eyes. 'I'd far rather have been doing those things with you, even though I know there's no chance of that happening.'

Cadi gently removed her hands from his. 'And that's *exactly* why Jez doesn't like the idea of us meeting up.'

Aled rested his arm along the back of the chair next to his. 'Do you think we should draw a line in the sand?'

Cadi lowered her gaze. 'I think it's best, don't you?'

Standing up, Aled smiled ruefully. 'I'm afraid I do, but I want you to know that should you ever need me, I'll always be there for you.'

Cadi smiled up at him. 'Thanks, Aled. I hope you get your wings.'

He winked at her. 'All good things come to those who wait.'

And with that, he walked away. He didn't want to break ties with Cadi, far from it, but he knew it was the healthiest thing to do.

Breaking up with Daphne should have been hard for him, but in all honesty his heart had never been in the relationship. In fact the only woman he'd ever had feelings for was Cadi, and even though he knew she was with Jez, he had always lived in the hope that something would happen and Cadi would be free to be with him. It was something, he acknowledged now, that had been preventing him from moving on with his life. Kicking a stone with the toe of his boot, Aled resigned himself to the fact that, in order to move on, he would never be able to see Cadi again.

Poppy picked up the telephone receiver. 'Cadi?'

'Hello, Poppy, I thought I'd give you a call so that I could bring you up to speed, as it were.'

As Cadi explained, Poppy listened to her friend's trip to Liverpool, the discovery of the writing and her subsequent chat with Aled.

'Blimey, you have been busy.'

'I certainly got a lot sorted,' agreed Cadi, 'or at least I did as far as Aled and I are concerned.'

'I said he still had the hots for you. I *knew* he wasn't writing just to say hello; his feelings run far deeper than that, and a woman can always tell – well, this one can, at any rate.'

'You certainly saw more than I did. I thought he'd put all that behind him,' admitted Cadi. 'And even though it wouldn't make any difference, I'm glad my dad doesn't know.'

Poppy chuckled down the phone. 'You reckon he'd give you a good old dose of "I told you so", eh?'

Cadi grimaced. 'I think he'd want to, because even though he's accepted Jez, he always insisted that Aled was keen on me.'

'Well, your father will never get wind of it now – not with Aled out of the picture. That goes for Jez too, be-cause with Daphne off licking her wounds, and Aled steering clear, Jez need never know of your rendezvous and the subsequent outcome.'

Cadi tutted softly. 'You're right, I could've kept Jez in the dark. But as it stands, I've already made up my mind to tell him the truth ...' Hearing her friend cry 'Why?', Cadi continued, 'It was lying that got me into trouble the last time, and only a fool makes the same mistake twice.'

'Very noble of you. I just hope it doesn't backfire,' said Poppy. She hesitated. 'Perhaps hearing that you don't plan to pursue your friendship with Aled might soften the blow.' Her tone sharpened as a thought entered her mind. 'When you say you're going to tell Jez the truth, surely you don't mean the bit about Aled saying he'd rather be with you?'

Cadi breathed in sharply. 'No, I do not! Flippin' heck, Poppy, talk about adding fuel to the fire!'

Poppy sighed with relief. 'Thank goodness for that.'

'I shall tell him of Daphne's shenanigans and how I informed Aled of her dealings, although I won't tell Jez *when* I told him, because hearing that I'd spent the evening before he left with Aled might be the straw that breaks the camel's back.'

'Very wise,' agreed Poppy. 'Now we've sorted that out, what are your intentions regarding Raquel?'

'Softly, softly,' said Cadi. 'I don't want to scare her off before I've had a chance to meet her properly.' She hesitated. 'You won't mention any of this to Izzy, will you?'

'My lips are sealed,' Poppy assured her.

'Thanks, Poppy, only I don't want to get Izzy's hopes up, only to dash them further down the line.'

Poppy was grinning – Cadi could tell by the tone of her voice. 'I don't think she's even thinking about her mam, or not at the moment at any rate.'

'Oh?' said Cadi, her voice full of intrigue. 'Why's that then?'

'Flying Officer Grainger seems to be the only name on Izzy's lips at the moment.'

'Oh dear,' sighed Cadi. 'I do hope he doesn't let her down—'

Poppy interrupted without apology. 'Didn't you know?'

'Know what?'

'They've started dating,' said Poppy; with her tone rising to a squeak, she continued, 'It's so exciting, Cadi. I don't think I've ever seen Izzy smile so much.'

'Oh, Poppy, that's wonderful news. I'm so pleased. Izzy deserves some happiness in her life.'

'She's practically walking on air, Cadi – it's so lovely to watch, *especially* when you remember what she was like when we first met her.'

Cadi imagined Izzy on the arm of the handsome pilot as Cadi introduced Izzy to her mother. 'If I can find her mam, then it'll be the icing on the cake.'

'So when are you goin' to make a start?'

'Right away. I'll put myself forward for any trips down Portsmouth way. I'm not due any leave for another month or so yet, and to be honest I'd rather save it for Christmas if I can.' A sudden thought entered her mind. 'If I time this right, I could have Izzy reunited with her mother for Christmas. How good would that be?'

'The best Christmas ever!' sighed Poppy.

When Cadi heard the news of Jez's return to Blighty she had been cock-a-hoop. She had arranged a four-day leave, and their plan had been to meet at the Belmont, where they could spend their weekend celebrating his return.

Now, as Cadi sat in the cookhouse, she recalled the moment she had been told that Jez's ship was going to be delayed by more than a week. She had tried desperately to rearrange her leave, but the officer in charge denied her request, saying it was too late.

She glanced at the clock on the wall. Jez's ship would be docking at the same time as Cadi headed for Bristol.

To take her mind off Jez, she turned her thoughts to Raquel. Try as she might, Cadi had not been able to secure a trip to Portsmouth, and with one lot of leave wasted, she was desperate to save her last allocation so that she could spend Christmas with Jez. As a result, she would have to leave the business with Raquel on the back burner, at least for time being.

As she sat staring gloomily ahead of her she was approached by a Waaf who wordlessly handed her an envelope.

Thanking the girl, she glanced at the writing before slitting it open with her knife. It was from Ronnie. Cadi smiled. She knew, from her letters, that Ronnie was living life in the thick of things. The airfields and satellite stations that she worked on were often targeted by the Luftwaffe, and Ronnie would regale Cadi with tales of near-misses and hair-raising moments that left her lucky to be alive.

Cadi smoothed the paper down:

Dearest Cadi
We really are going to have to meet up one of these days. I've so much to tell you that I can't say in a letter or over the phone.

226

Life in Gosport, as ever, is entertaining, to say the least. Although I'm getting fed up to the back teeth with Jerry leaving his calling card. (This, Cadi knew, meant bombs.)

I have got some good news, though. I'm going to be moving closer to you and Kitty sometime in the New Year. Can't say where because it's pretty hush-hush, but it does mean we should be able to arrange a reunion sooner rather than later.

I won't miss being the bullseye of Jerry's main target, but I will miss the sea. I do love being close to the wide blue yonder, even if I can't go for a paddle. I guess it comes from growing up in Blackpool. I know I'm definitely going to miss the ability to nip into the city whenever the fancy takes me, because I'm pretty sure they haven't got much in the way of shops, cinemas and restaurants where I'm headed ...

Cadi stared open-mouthed at the page in front of her. Gosport was close to Portsmouth, which is where Raquel lived. She might not be able to check things out for herself, but she was almost positive Ronnie would do so for her, especially as she was only a stone's throw away – or at least she was at the moment.

Hurriedly spooning down the rest of her lunch, Cadi took her tray back to the counter, then dipped her irons into the hot water, almost scalding herself in the process. She had to get to the telephone and call Ronnie, post-haste.

Rushing out of the cookhouse, she made a beeline for the NAAFI. Crossing her fingers, she pushed the door open and trotted towards the phone, which was, as yet, unoccupied. Picking up the receiver, she wasted no time in asking the operator to put her through to Gosport. As soon as she heard Ronnie's voice, she relaxed.

'Cadi! Did you get my letter? Is everything all right?'

'Hunky-dory,' said Cadi, 'but I do need to ask you a favour, and as I'll shortly be travelling halfway across the country, I thought it best to speak now.'

'Fire away.'

Cadi explained, as briefly as she could, her predicament, ending with, 'So I could really do with your help.'

'It'll be my pleasure. I love all this cloak-and-dagger stuff,' said Ronnie excitedly. 'Will I need a disguise, do you think?' she said, thrilled at the prospect of her new adventure.

Cadi giggled before answering, 'Why would you need a disguise? It's not as if she knows who you are.'

'I suppose not.' She hesitated. 'What is it you want me to do exactly?'

'Verify that it's her,' replied Cadi simply.

'Only what's my excuse? It'll look a bit odd if I knock on her door and say "Are you Raquel Taylor" and then – if she says yes – walk off without saying another word.'

Having been in a rush to set the wheels in motion, Cadi hadn't thought this far ahead. 'True ...' She fell momentarily silent as she sought a solution, but Ronnie got there first.

'Got it! I can pretend I'm looking for women to join the Women's Voluntary Service and I want to see whether she's interested in joining.'

'What if she says no or that she's already joined?' asked Cadi uncertainly.

'I'll take a clipboard with me and write a load of names on it. When I see her, I'll ask her what her name is, so that I can tick her off on my list,' Ronnie said triumphantly.

A slow smile crossed Cadi's cheeks. 'Do you know, Ronnie, I think that might just work.'

'And is that all you want to know or is there summat else?'

'That'll be all for now,' said Cadi. 'Once I know for definite, I can plan my next move.'

'So you're not one hundred per cent certain about the writing then?'

'Raquel wrote to Eric twenty-odd years ago,' considered Cadi, 'when writing was still new to her. She'll have had a lot of practice since then, which is why I'm thinking the writing – although still childlike – looks improved.'

'I see. Well, I hope it is her,' said Ronnie, 'if only for Izzy's sake.'

'Me too,' agreed Cadi. 'And now that we've got that sorted, how're things with you?'

'Same old, still single – and that's how I prefer it. I see far too many war widows nowadays.'

Cadi grimaced. 'I can't argue with that, although not every marriage ends in tragedy.'

'A friend of mine wed a feller within a week of meeting him – stupid, I know, but she wanted to get everything done before he went overseas.' Ronnie paused briefly. 'Less than a week after him departing, she receives a telegram informing her that her new husband's ship was sunk whilst crossing the Atlantic.'

Cadi felt a sense of unease. 'I've always said I won't marry Jez until the war's over for that very reason. It's almost like an omen, don't you think?'

'It's bad luck, that's what it is – on top of which, the silly girl's lumbered herself with his surname, so she has a constant reminder of her impulsive behaviour.' Ronnie tutted irritably. 'You should only marry someone if you love them, and how can you possibly love someone if you've only known them for a week? It's different for you and Jez, as you've been together for years. Now *that's* love.'

The operator cut across their call, informing them that their time was up.

Cadi spoke with urgency, fearful the operator would cut them off before they'd finished talking. 'When do you think you'll have time to call on Raquel?'

'When I go into the city next, which should be this Friday.'

'Let me know how things go, won't you? I don't know whereabouts in the country I'll be, but if you write to me at Coningsby, I'll get it on my return.'

'Will do! Ta-ra, Cadi, safe journeys.'

Cadi managed to get her goodbye in before the operator cut them off.

Breathing a sigh of relief, she relaxed in the knowledge that she had set the wheels in motion, and she would soon know whether or not Raquel was indeed the person responsible for the note on the envelope.

*

Daphne sat in the lorry, waiting for the passengers to disembark. She had envisaged this day many times in her mind and there had been moments when she was uncertain as to whether she was doing the right thing. It was only when she reminded herself that Cadi had had no reason to tattle-tale that she confirmed her decision.

She did it out of pure spite, Daphne told herself now. *I reckon I was right when I said she wanted to get her claws into Aled, and this just goes to prove it. The only reason why she didn't tell him about the letter I wrote to Jez was because she knew there was some truth in it. She did kiss Aled – albeit on the cheek – and she also suggested that he take her for a personal tour around Lincoln. With wanton behaviour like that, I had every right to tell Jez what was going on.*

She continued to gaze at the vessel, which had been docked for the past ten minutes. It had occurred to her that Jez might not care if Cadi had met up with Aled behind his back, but then she remembered Jez's words, saying that Daphne's letter had caused a divide between himself and Cadi. A glimmer of guilt crossed Daphne's face, only to be replaced with a stony look of vengeance as she reminded herself, yet again, that she had only been speaking the truth.

When she saw Jez walking down the gangplank, her heart skipped a beat. He was looking older than he had when he left Blighty, which suggested that his time in Africa had not been easy. Leaning forward she wondered when would be the best time to accost him. It was going to be a long drive back to RAF Finningley and … She stopped short. Why was Jez waving goodbye to his shipmates? To her horror, she saw him peel away from the pack. It was now that the penny dropped: Jez must have applied for leave. With no time to spare, Daphne slipped out of her seat. Holding on to her hat with one hand, she ran towards Jez, calling out for him to wait.

Hearing someone calling his name, Jez half turned, hoping to see Cadi. When he saw it was Daphne, his jaw dropped. Surely she wasn't going to start harassing him again, not after all this time? Didn't she realise they'd been delayed for more than a week, with barely enough provisions? Or did she simply not care? Probably the latter, Jez thought bitterly. He heaved a sigh. He very much wanted to ignore her calls and continue on his way, but Daphne had drawn the attention of his shipmates, who had stopped to see what was going on. Not wishing to cause a scene, Jez waited for her to catch up with him.

'If you've come to have a go at me or beg for my forgiveness, then you've got it. I forgive you,' said Jez huffily. 'Now can you please leave me alone so that I can get on with the rest of my life in peace?'

Angered by his air of apparent self-importance, Daphne glared at him. 'I'm not here to do anything of the sort – far from it.'

'Oh?' said Jez, a trifle surprised. 'Then what do you want?'

'I'm here to set the record straight,' said Daphne. 'Your girlfriend's been at it again, spreading rumours behind people's backs. Rumours that don't tell the whole truth, I might add, and as a result Aled wants nothing more to do with me.'

Jez blinked in silent confusion. 'I don't know what you're on about. Cadi's not mentioned any of this to me.'

'Of course she hasn't,' cried Daphne, 'you're the last person she'd tell, because she knows what she's done is wrong. You don't go running off to someone else's boyfriend with half a story, and that's exactly what she did. She didn't even hear it with her own ears, but got the so-called facts from her pals. If anybody should've gone to Aled, it should've been them. But, oh no, Cadi couldn't wait to spill the beans.'

Jez placed his bag on the ground. He had no idea what Daphne was on about, but whatever it was it had clearly angered her. 'I don't even know what you're supposed to have said or done. You need to slow down and start again. I'm sure this is some sort of misunderstanding.'

But Daphne wasn't one for listening, or explaining what she'd done. 'I've not got time to go into all that now, but when someone says they rue the day they did summat and are truly sorry for their actions, you should hear them out, not rush off to tattle-tale! It was nothing to do with Cadi.'

Jez wrinkled his brow. 'You do know I've been in Africa, don't you?'

'Of course I know!' snapped Daphne. 'I'm not stupid.'

'Good! Then you should realise that Cadi's hardly going to start gossiping to me about the ins and outs of your and Aled's relationship when I'm halfway around the world.'

'She could've told you before you left,' said Daphne evenly.

Jez stared at her. 'This happened before I left?'

Daphne nodded. She had placed the knife in his breast, all she had to do now was twist it. 'That was the whole point in her coming to Speke, so that she could whisper in Aled's ear one minute and kiss you goodbye the next. Two birds, one stone,' said Daphne nastily. 'Surely you knew she'd stayed in RAF Speke the night before you left for Africa?'

Jez opened his mouth to speak, but a few of his shipmates had wandered over to tell Daphne they were ready to leave.

She flashed him a smile full of triumphant malice. 'Gotta dash!'

Ignoring Jez's cries for her to wait, she ran back to the lorry. She had well and truly set the cat amongst the pigeons and she was only sorry she wouldn't be there to witness the fallout.

As Jez watched Daphne drive away, her words rang inside his head and, try as he might, he couldn't mute them. He knew that Daphne was deliberately stirring up trouble, because that's what she did, but was she doing it because she was a woman scorned or was there a genuine reason for her anger? And exactly what had Daphne done that would cause Cadi to come all the way to Liverpool to see Aled? What's more, why hadn't Cadi filled him in? And why hadn't her friends – whoever they were – spoken to Aled themselves?

There was only one way to find out the answers to his questions. He would have to talk to Cadi. He picked up his bag and began walking. Daphne might be a troublemaker, but Cadi had given her the ammunition by keeping Jez in the dark.

He very much wanted to believe that it was all a big misunderstanding, but there was something in the way Daphne spoke that told him she was telling the truth, at least in part. He had no doubt that Cadi would insist she had only kept quiet because of his trip to Africa, but was that really the case? After all, it made no odds to him what Daphne got up to, so as far as he could see there was no plausible excuse for her silence. He felt his cheeks begin to warm. He didn't like the idea of Cadi and Aled having secrets that he knew nothing of. That wasn't how relationships were supposed to work – not in Jez's book. Swinging his kitbag over his shoulder, he pulled his cap further onto his head. It was not the welcome that he had envisaged, and the sooner he got to the bottom of things the better, although he wasn't sure it was going to have a happy ending.

Driving away from the docks, Daphne looked into the side mirror. Jez had only just picked up his bag, which meant he'd spent some time contemplating her words. Not that she was sorry about upsetting him – far from it. Jez deserved to know the truth, no matter how unpleasant it might be. And if that meant his relationship suffered as a result, well, so be it. As far as Daphne was concerned, Cadi was cold and calculating, and she had gone out of her way to split up Aled and Daphne, most probably to get revenge for that stupid letter.

Daphne shook her head. The letter had been stupid, but it wasn't as though it had been a total lie – not at all. Cadi might have thought she'd had the last laugh, but it was Daphne who would be laughing the longest.

As soon as she was parked up, Cadi rushed to the NAAFI, so that she could ring Jez.

'Belmont Hotel, Maria speaking.'

'Maria. It's me, Cadi – is Jez back?'

'Hello, Cadi love. There was an audible pause before Maria continued, 'I'll see if he's about.' Cadi could tell by the muffled sounds that Maria had placed her hand over the receiver as she talked to someone close by.

She knitted her eyebrows. What did Maria mean by 'I'll see if he's about'? Surely she knew whether or not Jez was there? Waiting patiently, she could hear a muffled conversation taking place and, from what she could gather, the participants seemed to be arguing.

She was about to call down the phone to remind Maria that she was waiting when Jez's voice came down the line, only when he spoke, it wasn't the happy-go-lucky, loving Jez she had expected to talk to, but a sulky, morose version of her fiancé and, in truth, it was more of a grunt than a greeting.

Thinking that Jez was annoyed she hadn't been able to meet him, Cadi was quick to reassure him that she had tried her best. 'Honestly, Jez, I tried my hardest, but they refused to move my leave.'

Jez gave a disbelieving 'Mmm' in acknowledgement.

Cadi blinked. It was most unlike him to behave in such a petulant manner. Something was obviously amiss, but with nothing coming forth, she decided to cut to the chase. 'For goodness' sake, Jez, what's up?'

'You tell me,' said Jez in clipped tones.

Cadi was perplexed; she couldn't think of anything that could have riled him so. 'I would, if I knew, but if you're going to behave like a child, how can I?'

'What's the matter?' said Jez sullenly. 'Don't you like being kept in the dark?' He gave a sarcastic laugh. 'Funny, that.'

Cadi had last spoken to him a matter of hours before he left for Britain, and when she had done so, everything seemed fine. In fact he couldn't wait to come home and see her.

'Look, Jez, my hands were tied. Left to me, you'd have got a hero's welcome ...'

Jez tutted angrily. 'A hero's welcome would have been more favourable than learning that your fiancée's been sneaking around behind your back with another man.'

Cadi was stunned. How on earth did Jez know? What's more, who'd told him and what exactly had they said? She swallowed before attempting to speak. 'Who've you seen and what have they said?'

'So you're not denying it then?' said Jez, and he was so angry he was practically spitting the words out. 'And who do you think told me?'

Cadi hung her head. 'Daphne.'

'Ten out of ten,' he replied sarcastically. 'Although you would know the answer to that one, wouldn't you, because unlike yours truly, you're fully in the loop.'

'If you'd give me a chance, I can explain,' Cadi began. 'What Daphne did was—'

Jez cut her short. 'I don't give a monkey's what Daphne did. You're the one who decided to keep me in the dark – unless you're telling me that she held a gun to your head?'

'No, but—'

'There are no buts,' insisted Jez. 'From what she told me, it was your friends who were privy to the information, *not* you. Yet you took it upon yourself to break the news to Aled. Why didn't you tell me what was going on? At least that way I wouldn't have been standing on the dock feeling like a complete and utter fool. Have you any idea how humiliating it was to hear Daphne tell me how my fiancée was keeping secrets from me with another man? And not just any man, but the one you kissed in order to spite her.' He drew a deep breath before letting it out in a staggered fashion. 'Sometimes I wonder if I know you at all. But if you are the sort of person who sneaks around behind her fiancé's back, then quite frankly I'm not sure I like what I see.'

Cadi felt her heart sink. The last thing she had wanted to do was offend Jez or shake his trust in her. 'You do know me, Jez, and I *was* going to tell you, but not when you were about to leave for Africa.'

'Why?' asked Jez. 'Just how would Daphne's shenanigans affect my trip to Africa?'

Cadi fell silent before mumbling, 'Well, it wouldn't, but I didn't want to upset you.'

'Only you have.'

She sighed ruefully. 'I should've been straight with you from the start.'

He tutted irritably. 'Yes, you should.'

A tear trickled down Cadi's cheek. 'I don't know what to say, other than I'm sorry.'

'Sorry that you've been caught out, or sorry that you did it in the first place?'

'That I did it in the first place. I should've insisted Poppy tell him.'

'Then why didn't you?'

'Because I knew about the letter, and that added to the severity of Daphne's deception.' Cadi heaved an exhausted sigh. 'Daphne fiddled with Aled's exam results, Jez – that's why he failed his pilot's exam and ended up as tail-end Charlie.'

'And why couldn't you tell him that over the phone?'

'Because we weren't a hundred per cent certain that the girl Poppy had met was the same Daphne. She didn't actually mention Aled by name, so if we'd got it wrong,' she shook her head, 'it didn't bear thinking about – and *that's* why I went to see him.'

'And you used the letter as an excuse. Why? Because you thought he'd need convincing?'

Cadi's cheeks coloured. 'You're making it sound as though I took delight in breaking the news.'

'Are you telling me that it didn't feel good, getting your revenge on someone who'd unearthed your own skeletons?'

Cadi's emotions turned from guilt to anger. 'Why are you turning this round on me? I've apologised repeatedly for what I did, and I've explained why I did it. I thought you were fine with that?'

'So did I,' admitted Jez, 'but that's before I realised this seems to be a habit of yours.'

Cadi could hear someone – she suspected it was Maria – objecting in the background.

'I think it's best if we talk after you've had a chance to calm down,' said Cadi stiffly.

Jez muttered, 'Don't hold your breath,' before handing the phone to Maria.

'Cadi?'

She burst into tears. 'Oh, Maria! I've made such a dreadful mess of things.'

Maria's soothing tone calmed Cadi's wails. 'If it had been at any other time, Jez might not have taken the news so badly, but to be told as soon as your foot touches British soil ...'

Cadi sniffed audibly. 'Daphne was *waiting* for him?'

'It seems that way – she was the one driving them back to Finningley.'

'Only if Jez didn't board the lorry, how did she manage to speak to him?'

'According to Jez, Daphne ran over to him.'

'Sounds about right,' muttered Cadi. 'I bet she couldn't wait.'

'From what Jez said, Daphne took delight in telling him all she knew.'

'I'm sure she did,' said Cadi sullenly. 'As far as she's concerned it was tit-for-tat, but I didn't put anyone's life in danger for my own gain; the only thing I did wrong was not keep Jez in the loop and, no matter my intentions, that was the wrong thing to do.'

'Even so,' soothed Maria, 'it was hardly the crime of the century, and Jez'll see that, given time.'

'Will he?' asked Cadi, uncertainty clear in her voice. 'I thought we'd drawn a line under the last lot, but it didn't take him long to rake it up again.'

'He wants to hurt you the way you hurt him,' said Maria. 'I'm not saying that's the right thing to do, but love can be a funny creature at times. Makes us act out of character and do things we'd never normally dream of. You've hurt him, Cadi, and not for the first time, either.'

Cadi stared in disbelief at the receiver. 'Not you too!'

'I'm not having a go, love, simply stating the facts. There's an old saying, "Once bitten, twice shy." Well, Jez has been bitten twice now.'

Cadi spoke softly. 'I can't feel any worse than I already do, Maria. I thought being in love was meant to be the easiest thing in the world.'

Maria smiled. 'Then you thought wrong. Being in love isn't all chocolates and flowers – far from it. You have to work at it, learn to compromise, think of someone other than yourself and put them first. Your aim was to protect both Aled and Jez, but it was Jez who got caught in the crossfire.'

Cadi mulled over her friend's words. Maria was right: she should have concentrated on protecting Jez, before Aled.

The operator cut across her thoughts. 'Caller, you've had well over your three minutes. I'm afraid your time is up.'

Realising that the operator had used her discretion regarding the call, Cadi thanked her before saying goodbye to Maria.

'Give him time to lick his wounds. He'll soon come round.'

'Thanks, Maria.'

Cadi heard the operator terminate the call.

Putting the receiver down at her end, Cadi lifted it once more. As soon as she heard the operator's voice, she knew it was the same woman who had just been on the line, so she spoke quickly. 'It's me again. I know I had more than my fair share, but I really need to speak to my friend, and as there's no one else in the queue ...'

The operator paused, before asking Cadi for the connection.

Relieved that the operator had seen fit to give her a break, Cadi waited for Poppy's voice to come down the line.

'Hello, Cadi?'

Cadi burst into tears. 'Oh, Poppy, it's all gone horribly wrong. Daphne's told Jez everything and now he hates me.'

Poppy was quick to soothe her friend. 'I'm sure he doesn't hate you, Cadi. He's probably just angry.'

Cadi quickly told Poppy of their conversation.

Poppy tutted irritably. 'He's cutting his nose off to spite his face. If I see him, I'll give him a thick ear!'

'He's every right to be angry, though,' said Cadi. 'I knew I shouldn't have gone behind his back, but I did anyway.'

'You did what you thought was best,' said Poppy, 'and Jez will realise that, given time.'

'I hope so, because I can't bear the thought that I might have really gone too far this time.'

'Give him time to think things through,' advised Poppy. 'This is still very raw for him.'

'I know, I just wish—'

Poppy cut her off. 'There's no point dwelling over what's done – you have to concentrate on the future. I dare say it seems like you'll never come back from this, but you will, because Jez loves you, Cadi, and you love him. Believe me, this is merely another hiccup – albeit a big one.'

Feeling slightly better, Cadi raised a small smile. 'Thanks, Poppy.'

'That's what friends are for.'

The operator cut into their conversation.

'Time I was off,' said Cadi. 'I'll let you know what happens.'

'Ta-ra, Cadi, and look after yourself.'

'I will. Ta-ra, Poppy.'

Replacing the receiver, Cadi made her way over to the counter. She pointed to the apple crumble. 'I'll have that with custard, please.'

'None of my beeswax,' said the cook, 'but you look like you've lost a pound and found a penny.'

Cadi nodded.

The cook doled out a large portion and smothered it in custard. 'Get yourself on the outside of that – pudding always makes everything better.'

Cadi gave her a wobbly smile. 'If only it was that simple.'

The cook winked. 'There's nothing that a good portion of apple crumble and custard can't fix.'

'Maybe I should give some to my fiancé.'

'They do say that the way to a man's heart is through his stomach, so I suppose it couldn't hurt to try.'

Cadi chuckled without mirth. 'Somehow I think it's going to take a lot more than apple crumble and custard.'

The cook leaned against the counter. 'If he loves you – and I mean truly loves you – then he'll come soon come round; you've just got to be patient.'

Hearing the cook affirm Poppy's words, Cadi half smiled to herself. If there was one thing she was sure of, it was that Jez loved her. She would have to hope that, in this case, love would be enough.

As the taxi pulled up outside Hillcrest House, Ronnie began to feel a sense of unease. She had never ventured to this part of Portsmouth before, and she could see why. The area was rundown and neglected, with many of the properties having missing or boarded-up windows, whilst others stood derelict.

Leaning his arm over the back of his seat, the driver turned to Ronnie. 'Are you *sure* you've got the right address, love?'

Ronnie cast a doubtful eye over the building opposite. It was certainly better than the rest, but it didn't look as welcoming as the houses closer to town. 'If that's Hillcrest, then yes, I'm at the right address,' she replied. A slight frown creased her brow. The driver had already asked her this question when she first entered the back of his cab. Did he know something? She decided to pose the question. 'Why do you ask?'

Tilting his cap to the back of his head, he gave her a grim smile. 'It just didn't seem the sort of a place a nice girl like you would go, that's all.'

Again Ronnie's eyes flickered towards the house. Compared to the other buildings, it seemed reasonably well kept. The windows had curtains and the general façade seemed in good order. She glanced back at the driver; if he knew something about the house, perhaps he also knew who lived there. Taking the fare from her purse, she passed it forward.

'Do you know if there's a woman by the name of Raquel living here?'

Pushing the money into his pocket, his cheeks reddened. 'No idea,' he spluttered. 'I've never been in the place, and nor would I.' Speaking gruffly, he turned his back to her. 'I don't know what kind of feller you take me for …'

Realising that she had unintentionally offended him, Ronnie gabbled a hasty apology as she exited from the back of the cab. Holding the door slightly ajar so that she could ask him to wait for her, she gave an exclamation as he pulled the taxi sharply away, causing the door to slam shut.

Bewildered by his behaviour, Ronnie stared after him, before turning her attention to the building on the opposite side of the road. If she had asked to visit one of the other houses, she could have understood the driver's concern, but Hillcrest was quite an impressive building, size-wise, and it was certainly more appealing than the neighbouring properties. She knitted her eyebrows. In her opinion, the house was far too big for one person; maybe a family, but … It was at this point that realisation dawned. Raquel had left Liverpool more than twenty years ago. Why hadn't any of them considered the possibility that she might have remarried? For all they knew, she could be living in that house with a dozen kids. It would certainly explain why she wasn't keen to let Izzy know her whereabouts, especially if her new family knew nothing of Raquel's past.

Deciding that she needed to handle this one with kid gloves, Ronnie placed the clipboard that she had brought with her on a stone wall. Leaning against the lamp post, she was wondering what she would say to Cadi, should she find her suspicions to be true, when a man on the opposite side of the road approached the house. At first she supposed he might be Raquel's new husband, but on a second glance she dismissed the idea. He didn't look like the sort of man who could afford to rent somewhere as big as Hillcrest; not only that, but he was only a little older than Ronnie herself. *Perhaps one of her sons?* she mused. As he passed through the front door she hoped for a glimpse of the inside of the building, but the blackout curtain was already in place, obscuring her view. Supposing that now might be a good time to approach the house, Ronnie found another thought entering her mind. Finding out if Raquel lived there wasn't going to be the issue, but discovering *who* she lived there with might prove problematic. After all, she could hardly ask questions about the family – not without someone smelling a rat.

As she pondered her predicament, a man, different from the one who'd just entered the building, exited. He was a lot older than the first and, judging by his attire, he was also considerably wealthier. She watched as he walked briskly down the road.

That must be the husband, thought Ronnie. *Probably off to some posh club to meet his swanky pals.* No sooner had he gone from sight than another man appeared. Ronnie frowned. Like the man who had left the building, this one was well dressed and he, too, seemed in a rush to get to his destination. She watched as he climbed the few steps to the front of the building. As he hastened through the door, Ronnie felt her interest piqued. Was Raquel having an affair? It did seem rather odd that as one man left, another appeared, almost as if he'd been waiting for the coast to clear.

As she perused the probability of this, she was surprised to see yet another man approaching. He was not as well dressed as the other two, but better dressed than the first, and she saw him glance briefly around him before entering the house. Smiling to herself, Ronnie blew out a relieved sigh. Hillcrest was obviously some kind of office. Feeling as though a weight had been lifted from her shoulders, she leaned away from the lamp post. Picking up her clipboard, she was about to walk forward when a woman exited the building. Much to Ronnie's surprise, it seemed that the woman was walking towards her in a determined fashion. As she drew near, Ronnie saw that she was a quite a few years older than herself, with dark wavy hair, which hung loose around her shoulders.

'Hello, lovely,' said the woman. 'Are you here on a bit of business?'

The woman's assumption had given Ronnie the perfect way in. 'I am indeed.'

247

The woman, who had obviously been expecting Ronnie to say no, looked rather startled. 'Are you sure?'

Ronnie smiled in what she hoped was a confident fashion. 'Positive.'

Appearing to reach a conclusion, the woman leaned forward in a conspiratorial fashion. 'In a bit of trouble, are you?'

Ronnie shook her head fervently. 'Oh no, nothing like that.'

The woman wrinkled her brow. 'Then why are you here?'

Realising that they were talking at cross-purposes, Ronnie elaborated. 'I'm looking for Raquel Taylor. I'm thinking she must work in Hillcrest?'

The woman peered at Ronnie through thickly mascaraed lashes. 'Oh aye? And who are you exactly?'

Ronnie flourished the clipboard by way of explanation. 'I'm here to see if I can drum up some volunteers for the Women's Voluntary Service – someone said I should try Hillcrest House.'

The woman cackled sarcastically. 'The Women's Voluntary Service, eh? Well, I guess you could say we're all volunteers here.'

Ronnie smiled fleetingly. 'Would it be all right if I ran through my list with you?'

Linking her arm through Ronnie's, the woman began leading her towards the house.

'I can do better than that. You come along with Dolly and we'll see what we can do for you.'

Ronnie glanced towards the house. From what she knew, there were at least three men inside. Feeling the hairs prickling on the back of her neck, she stopped short. 'I don't mind doing it out here ...'

Dolly, however, wasn't listening to excuses. 'Don't be daft – you don't want to be stood on the street when you could be in the warm. Besides, I should imagine you'll need as many women to join as you can get.'

Ronnie looked startled. 'How many women are there?'

'Come in and see.'

Feeling as though she had no choice but to go through with her ruse, Ronnie allowed Dolly to escort her into the building. As they entered through the curtained doorway, Ronnie blinked as the curtain passed over her face. Expecting to be illumined by the light of the entrance hall, she was surprised to find the area bathed in a soft red glow. Casting an eye around her, she saw that there were lots of doors leading off from the hallway. She was about to ask which room Raquel worked in when a man, different from the ones she had previously seen, came out of one of them, still tucking his shirt in. Seeing Ronnie, he immediately pulled his cap down to obscure his face before hastening out of the front door. It was then that the penny dropped.

Ronnie stared open-mouthed at Dolly, who had picked up a black cigarette case. 'Is this place what I think it is?'

Dolly gave her a wry smile. 'Depends. What do you think it is?'

Ronnie wasn't about to say the word 'brothel', for fear she might be wrong. So she tried a more subtle approach. 'Would I be right in guessing there are a lot of women living here?'

Dolly was grinning wickedly. 'Try "only women" and I rather think you've hit the nail on the head.'

'Then I've made a mistake,' gushed Ronnie. 'The woman I'm looking for isn't ... isn't ...' She fell silent.

'Isn't what?' asked Dolly in clipped tones, before adding, 'I find it a bit odd that you're only askin' for this Raquel. And since when did a Waaf volunteer for the WVS?'

As she spoke, another man emerged from one of the many doors that lined the hall. Holding his hand up to hide his face, he muttered 'Excuse me' as he headed for the exit. Seizing her opportunity, Ronnie made a dash for the door. Pushing past the man, she fled from the house of ill repute.

Only when she was several streets away did she stop to catch her breath. Looking back over her shoulder, she chastised herself for getting herself into such a predicament. Worst of all, she was still clueless as to whether Raquel was one of the women living at the address. Still trembling after her narrow escape, Ronnie wondered what on earth she was going to tell Cadi.

Apologising for the disturbance, Dolly closed the door behind the man. Alone in the hallway, she called out to someone unseen, 'She's gone.'

A scrawny-looking woman with hollow cheeks peered cautiously from behind one of the doors.

Taking a cigarette from the black case, Dolly tapped the end to loosen the tobacco, before placing it between her lips. 'So? Was that her?'

The woman shook her head. 'I haven't a clue who she was. My Izzy's not a redhead.'

Lighting the cigarette, Dolly took a long pull before blowing the smoke downwards. She eyed the other woman in an accusing fashion. 'She seemed to know who you were.'

The woman shrugged. 'She knew my name, that's all.'

Dolly flicked the ash from her cigarette into an ash-tray that stood next to an oil lamp on top of a half-moon table. 'There's no need to be gettin' defensive with me, Raquel. I'm not the enemy here, as well you know.'

Raquel relented. 'I know you're not, but I'm stuck between a rock and hard place, and *you* know that better than most. If the Finnegans get wind that my daughter's been asking questions, they'll soon put a stop to her enquiries, and I don't want Izzy getting in-volved with them. On the other hand, if I'm right and the letter is from Eric, then I'm goin' to get it in the neck anyway. Quite frankly, I don't know who I'm more afraid of: the Finnegans or Eric.'

'I know you think it's Eric,' said Dolly, 'but what could he possibly gain from gettin' back in touch after all this time?'

Raquel stared woodenly at Dolly. 'Money – that's the only thing Eric's ever been interested in. He's probably been sacked for saying the wrong thing to the wrong person, or getting into a fight down the docks.' She gave a short, mirthless laugh before continuing. 'It's not as if it would be the first time. He's probably gam-bled away the last of his pennies, in the hope of making up for lost wages. After that, he'll be looking to make money any way he can.' She tutted irritably. 'He's as thick as two short planks, but when it comes to being underhand, he's as sharp as a knife. He's probably guessed what I do for a living, but to make sure he's sent that girl over for a gander.'

'He must realise you'd have no reason to hand over your money. It's not as if he can give you a hidin', like in the old days,' reasoned Dolly.

'Blackmail,' said Raquel. 'Either I pay up or he'll tell Izzy what's become of her mam.'

Dolly hissed between her teeth 'That's evil – there's no other word for it. But it sounds like an awful lot of effort to go through, on the off-chance. Surely there has to be an easier way to earn a few bob.'

'Easier than blackmail?' scoffed Raquel, her brow rising. 'Eric never did like workin'. If he can get summat for nothin', then that's what he'll do.'

'Bad enough that he drove you out of your own home when you'd done nothin' wrong,' seethed Dolly, 'but to hound you years later, just so that he can blackmail you, is—'

'Eric all over,' said Raquel. 'That's why I never believed that rubbish in the letter about him dyin'. Nothin' bad ever happens to men like Eric. You watch: he'll outlive the lot of us.'

'So what now?' asked Dolly.

Raquel fell quiet as she thought this over. 'Sit tight and see what happens. The girl he sent looked terrified, so I doubt she'll be back, no matter how much he threatens her. If I know Eric, it'll be him what comes next.' She shook her head sadly. 'Leaving Liverpool was the hardest thing I ever did. Looking back, I should've fought harder. I'd have got a damned good hiding, but I'd have got rid of Eric once and for all.'

Dolly arched a beautifully shaped eyebrow. 'Everything's easy with hindsight, but it's different at the time. I remember what you were like when I found you on the streets all them years ago.' She shook her head as an image of Raquel, cold, wet and bedraggled, formed in her mind. Dolly had been down the market when Raquel had been caught stealing a loaf of bread from one of the traders. Dolly had paid for the loaf, whilst reminding the stallholder that she could have a quick word with his wife if he carried out his threat to turn Raquel over to the police.

'You were at the end of your tether,' Dolly reminded her, 'even threatenin' to jump into the docks. You couldn't have looked after yourself, never mind a child. What do you suppose would've happened to Izzy, had you brought her with you? The Finnegans might be a rum lot, but even they'd draw the line at kiddies. So there'd only be one place you could've gone, and nobody in their right mind wants to end up in the workhouse, let alone put their kid in one. You'd have been subjectin' her to a life of misery.'

'I know you're right,' conceded Raquel. 'I just wish things could've been different.'

Dolly smiled kindly. 'I know you're sure that the letter was from Eric, but what if you're wrong and it really was Izzy that wrote it? I know you wrote back denyin' your existence, but it doesn't seem to have put her off.'

Raquel stared down at herself in disgust. 'Look at me, Dolly. I'm a mess. What sort of child wants a prostitute for a mother?' Tears brimmed beneath her lids. 'I'm an embarrassment. If that letter really was from Izzy, then she's better off without me – which, I might add, is the whole reason I broke contact in the first place.'

Dolly eyed her darkly. 'It's not only about Izzy though, is it?'

Raquel turned as the door to the house opened. The man who entered nodded expectantly at her. Wiping her tears away, Raquel smiled brightly at him. 'I'll be with you in a minute.'

She waited until he walked into her room before turning to Dolly.

'I know you think I'm doing the wrong thing, but trust me, it's better this way. I've already ruined one life, and I'm not about to make the same mistake twice. If *anyone* comes looking for me, they're to be told that Raquel died twenty years ago.' She shrugged, before adding, 'In some respects that's true.'

Disappearing into the room, Raquel closed the door behind her.

Dolly walked over to the front door and pushed the curtain back into place. She could understand why Raquel was eager to cut ties with the past, but if Izzy really was trying to find her mother, then Raquel should count herself lucky. Dolly walked into her own room and gazed out of the window onto the street where Ronnie had been standing. All the women who ended up at Hillcrest did so out of desperation. She tutted beneath her breath. The Finnegan brothers only

254

preyed on girls who were in dire straits. They would pretend to befriend them, luring them with the promise of a warm bed, food aplenty and the chance to earn good money. All this sounded a lot better than the workhouse, but in truth it was just as bad. Not that the girls realised this at first. The brothers were keen to keep up the pretence by spoiling them with new clothes, hot baths and plenty of food. For the first couple of weeks the girls would spend their days enjoying the brothers' company, but all that would change on the third week, when they would be coaxed into sleeping with a man – just this once – in payment for all the brothers had done for them. If they refused, the brothers would demand back all the money they had spent on the girls – something they knew the girls couldn't possibly manage. With no one to turn to, the women had no choice but to do as they were told. The brothers had the girls right where they wanted them, with no way out. Which is why if any of them had been lucky enough to have a loved one looking for them, Dolly knew they'd leave Hillcrest without a backward glance.

Aled gazed out of the café window, hoping for a sign of his latest conquest, a fair-haired radio operator by the name of Marnie. The two had met over the wireless, when she had been guiding their craft back to base after they had lost the use of one of the engines.

Seeing Marnie enter the café, he stood up to greet her as she shook the rain from her umbrella. 'Sorry I'm late, but you know what it's like,' she said. 'Have you been waiting long?'

He waved a nonchalant hand. 'I've always said: all good things come to those who wait.'

'Charmer,' said Marnie as she placed her umbrella in the stand. Taking the seat opposite his, she perused the small menu.

'I try my best, though I often fail,' joked Aled. He pulled down the top of the menu with his finger, so that he might see her properly. 'Shall I order a pot of tea for two?'

'Yes, please.'

Aled waved at the waitress, who walked over towards them. 'Pot of tea for two, please, love.'

Acknowledging his order with a nod of her head, the girl disappeared behind the counter.

'So where've you been that's more important than spending time with your handsome tail-gunner?'

Marnie batted her eyes flirtatiously. 'You know I have to go when duty calls.'

Aled winked. 'I love a woman who's not afraid to take charge.'

She wagged a reproving finger. 'You certainly know all the right things to say.'

Holding her hand in his, Aled kissed the back of her fingers. 'Give me the right woman and I'll say the right things.'

Appearing by their side, the waitress emptied the tray of its contents. 'Are you ordering anything to eat?'

Aled looked expectantly at his date. 'Do you know what you want – apart from me, that is?'

The waitress giggled. 'Someone sees themselves as a bit of a bobby dazzler.'

He flashed her a cheesy grin. 'What can I say?'

Marnie looked up at the waitress. 'Sausage and chips for me, please.'

'I'll have the pie and mash, please,' said Aled, adding, 'and a round of bread and butter to go with it.'

Having written their order down, the waitress took the empty tray.

'Have you thought any more about Christmas?' asked Aled hopefully. 'My folks are keen to meet you, and I know you'll love the farm.'

'I have,' began Marnie slowly, 'and even though my parents are disappointed ...'

Aled was grinning. 'You're coming?'

She nodded. 'I am indeed.'

'Splendid!'

She wrinkled the side of her nose. 'My dad wasn't frightfully impressed.'

He wrinkled his brow. 'Oh?'

'He wanted to know where I'd be sleeping, so I assured him that I'd be in the spare room.'

Aled poured a dash of milk into his tea. 'Spoilsport.'

Marnie gasped before giggling, 'Aled Davies! What are you like?'

He raised an eyebrow. 'Hopeful?'

Wagging a reproving finger in jest, Marnie left behind the subject of Christmas, explaining instead the problems they had had in the control tower that morning, which had led to her being late.

Aled eyed her fondly as she chatted merrily away. There wasn't a bad bone in Marnie's body and, unlike Daphne, she played everything straight. As far as Aled was concerned, he was quite possibly looking at the future Mrs Davies. The fact that Marnie looked similar to Cadi was purely coincidental.

It was very late in the evening when Cadi was called to the NAAFI. Thanking the Waaf who had passed on the message, she spoke into the receiver. 'Hello?'

'Hello, Cadi, it's me – Ronnie.'

Cadi's eyes widened. With all the upset surrounding Jez and Daphne, she had completely forgotten about Ronnie's quest to track down Izzy's mother.

'Ronnie! How'd it go?'

'I know I said I'd write to let you know of my find-ings, but' – she sighed irritably – 'I think this is too important to relay by mail, especially if it falls into the wrong hands.'

Cadi held her breath. 'Oh my God, you found her.'

'Not exactly.'

Cadi was confused. 'What do you mean by "not exactly"?'

'I didn't see Raquel, and Dolly neither confirmed nor denied that there was a woman called Raquel living there.'

'Who's Dolly?'

'She's the woman who first approached me whilst I was standing outside, gathering my nerves,' explained Ronnie.

Cadi frowned. 'Does she live there too?'

'Kind of.'

'What do you mean, "kind of"—' Cadi began, before being cut off by Ronnie, who blurted out the truth.

'Hillcrest House is a brothel.'

Temporarily struck dumb by her friend's revelation, Cadi sieved through the multitude of questions that

258

entered her mind, asking only the one uppermost in her thoughts. 'Are you *sure*?'

'I'm afraid so,' said Ronnie, 'I wish I was wrong ...' She went on to explain how she came to enter the building, and the conclusion that the house was one of ill repute. 'The penny didn't drop until I was inside; that's when all became clear, and Dolly more or less confirmed my suspicions by saying that it was *only* women who lived and worked there.'

'Oh God,' mumbled Cadi, 'what on earth am I meant to tell Izzy?'

'Nothing, or at least not yet,' said Ronnie hurriedly. 'Not until someone's gone back to investigate properly. I don't mind goin', but I don't want to go on my own.'

'Too right you won't be going on your own,' said Cadi fervently. 'I'm only sorry I asked you to go it alone in the first place.'

'You weren't to know,' Ronnie assured her. 'I was standing outside the place for a good ten minutes, yet even I didn't realise until I got inside.'

Having thought she would be spending Christmas with Jez, Cadi had already booked leave, but as things stood, it didn't look as though that was likely to happen – not with Jez in his current frame of mind at any rate. Her mind made up, she voiced her thoughts. 'What are you doing for Christmas?'

'Working, why?'

'I've got a week's leave around Christmas time,' explained Cadi.

'What about Jez?' asked Ronnie. 'Don't you want to spend it with him?'

Cadi felt her bottom lip tremble. 'I can't see that happening – not this year, at any rate.'

Sensing that something was awry, Ronnie trod softly. 'Problems in paradise?'

'To cut a long story short, yes,' said Cadi. 'I'll explain everything properly when I see you.'

'Oh dear. I do hope it turns out to be a storm in a teacup.'

'Me too, but you know how it is: things get said that can't be unsaid – we'll just have to see.'

'Won't Poppy and Izzy expect to see you over the Christmas period?'

'Possibly, but with five days off, I should be able to squeeze them in at some point, preferably *after* we've sorted things out with Raquel,' said Cadi.

Ronnie rolled her eyes. 'Or not, depending on what we uncover.'

Cadi grimaced. 'I suppose Christmas wouldn't be a good time to find out that your mam's a prostitute.'

'I don't think *any* time's a good time to find out that kind of news,' conceded Ronnie. She glanced at the queue that was building up behind her. 'It's getting pretty busy in here. Shall we call it a day, and you can telephone when you've sorted some dates?'

'Sounds good to me,' said Cadi. 'I'll get back to you as soon as I know what's what.'

'Ta-ra, Cadi.'

'Ta-ra, Ronnie, and thanks – for everything. You're a real pal.'

'That's what friends are for!'

Cadi replaced the receiver before asking the operator to put her through to Poppy's base. Waiting for

Poppy's voice to come down the line, Cadi prayed that Izzy wouldn't be nearby.

'Cadi?'

'Is Izzy with you?'

'No, why – should I get her?'

Cadi shook her head fervently. 'No, I'd rather she knew nothing of our conversation.'

Poppy listened quietly as Cadi told her how she'd arranged for Ronnie to visit Hillcrest House and everything that had transpired as a result.

'No wonder you don't want Izzy knowing,' said Poppy quietly.

'It's awful, Poppy. Never in my wildest dreams did I think Raquel would be' – she hesitated – 'one of *those*.'

'What are you going to do?'

'Take my Christmas holidays in Portsmouth so that I can see for myself,' said Cadi, adding, 'I would ask you to come too, but I don't want Izzy coming along, for obvious reasons.'

'Not to worry,' said Poppy. 'I'll keep Izzy entertained here whilst you play detective down there.'

'Thanks, Poppy, I knew I could rely on you.'

'I don't suppose you've heard from Jez?'

'Not a dicky bird.'

Poppy sighed heavily. 'Men and their pride, eh?'

'I think he has reason, this time,' said Cadi.

'He'll come to his senses sooner or later,' replied Poppy.

'Let's hope so.'

'I know so,' said Poppy. 'But I think you've got quite a lot on your plate at the moment, without worrying about Jez, don't you?'

Cadi rolled her eyes. 'You're right there.'

Hearing her yawn, Poppy ended their conversation. 'You sound like you're dead on your feet. Go and get yourself some kip, and give me a ring when you can.'

'I will. G'night, Poppy.'

As Poppy said her goodnight, Cadi heard the line go dead and she returned to her hut so that she might mull things over undisturbed. Hearing that Izzy's mother could be a prostitute had been a lot to take in, although it did explain why she had cut all ties after moving to Portsmouth. If Cadi were Raquel, she wouldn't want her children to know the levels to which she'd had to stoop in order to keep a roof over her head.

Entering the hut, she sat down on her bed. This was going to take a great deal of consideration, not only about what they'd tell Izzy, should their suspicions be confirmed, but also concerning what would happen afterwards? They could hardly walk away, leaving Raquel to continue her life as a . . . Cadi shook her head; she couldn't even process the word. Taking her washbag, she headed for the ablutions and within ten minutes she was curled up in her bed. Visions of Raquel – an older version of Izzy, beaten and bruised by men who were no better than Eric – kept entering her mind. Cadi wondered how on earth the woman had got herself into such an awful situation. Surely there must have been something else she could do?

She hesitated. As far as she knew, Raquel hadn't worked before leaving Liverpool, which meant she'd been thrown out of her house with no money, or clothes or personal possessions. She brought her knees to her chest. Where on earth would that poor woman have spent the nights? More to the point, how had she earned the money to pay for her passage down south? She couldn't have got it from Colin Robins, because he hadn't gone with her. She furrowed her brow. If Eric really had murdered Colin, then he knew that Raquel hadn't run off with him, which meant all the tales about his wife running off with another man were completely fabricated. Or maybe he'd just said that to throw everyone off the scent? She nodded. No one had questioned Colin's disappearance because they believed he was with Raquel. She wondered what conversation, if any, had taken place between Eric and Colin. There wasn't a doubt in her mind that Colin would have maintained his innocence – not that Eric would have listened, of course. She envisaged Eric walking towards Colin, who was standing with his back to him. Raising his hand, Eric swung.

Cadi's eyes flew open. Breathing heavily, she tried to banish the vision that had presented itself to her. Eric was a coward; they all knew it. He wouldn't have given Colin the chance to fight back. A tear trickled down her cheek. She didn't know him, but the thought of someone being murdered purely for trying to help a woman like Raquel chilled her to the bone.

There had been a lot of toing and froing, but after many false starts, everything had been arranged for 23 December. Cadi had got in touch with Kitty, who

263

said she would very much like to join her friends, and so the two women had booked a twin room in the Castaway B&B, but that's as far as their plans had got.

Now Cadi had the dreaded task of telephoning her mother and explaining why she wouldn't be with them for the fourth Christmas in a row.

'But why Portsmouth?' said Jill. 'Surely we're closer?'

Cadi had been dreading this question. 'You are, but I've not seen the girls for ages, and I need to sort out this business with Izzy's mam.'

'You've not seen your family for far longer,' Jill reminded her. 'Is Jez going with you?'

Cadi grimaced. 'Not this time.'

'Oh? Why not?'

'We've had a bit of a falling-out,' admitted Cadi, 'so he's spending Christmas with Maria and Bill.'

'Honestly!' breathed Jill. 'You two need your heads banging together.'

'Mam!' protested Cadi.

'You're behaving like a couple of kids, and I bet it was over something and nothing,' Jill muttered irritably.

'Can we not talk about it?' pleaded Cadi.

Jill nodded wisely to herself. If her daughter didn't want to moan about how awful and unreasonable Jez was being, then it could only mean one thing: the argument, whatever it was, had been Cadi's fault.

'Well, I hope you see fit to come home next year,' said Jill, 'because Christmas isn't the same without you.'

Cadi pulled a guilty grimace. 'Sorry, Mam, I promise I'll be home next year.'

'Make sure you are.'

Having said her goodbyes, Cadi replaced the hand-set. She felt terrible about not spending Christmas with her family, but she would move heaven and earth to ensure that she was with them the following year and, if she was lucky, Jez would be by her side.

Chapter Six

December 1942

It was 23 December, and Maria was busy doling out porridge into three bowls.

'Cheer up!' she told Jez.

He smiled fleetingly. 'Sorry, Maria. I am trying, honestly I am, but it's not been the easiest of years.' He looked at the sparsely laid table. 'Christmas was always Nan's favourite time of year – she'd get all the neighbours round for a drink and have them singing carols until the small hours.'

'I think Cadi rather enjoys Christmas too,' said Bill. 'Do you know where she's spending it this year?'

Jez shook his head sullenly. 'It appears I'm not privy to that kind of information.'

'You've no one to blame but yourself,' counselled Maria.

'Thanks for reminding me,' said Jez, before adding in sulky tones, 'Given that all this seems to be my fault, Cadi's probably chosen to spend Christmas with *him*.'

Maria tutted impatiently. 'I don't reckon you believe that for one minute! Besides, Cadi's not like that – you know she isn't.'

Jez prodded the porridge with the back of his spoon. 'I'm not sure I know anything when it comes to Cadi, save for the fact that she'll always go running to *him* over me.'

Bill voiced his opinion. 'She warned Aled that his girlfriend was a snake in the grass, which is a pretty valid reason, if you ask me.'

'She should've run it by me first,' said Jez. But, on seeing the stern look on Maria's face, he instantly rued his words.

'And just why should Cadi have to ask your opinion every time she does something?' asked Maria tartly.

'She doesn't,' said Jez, adding petulantly, 'unless *he's* involved.'

Bill took a large swig of his tea. 'Why? What's Aled got to do with the price of fish?'

Jez scowled at Bill from across the table. 'He's wanted Cadi for himself ever since he walked into the Greyhound – probably before. He even admitted it.'

Taking a bite of his toast, Bill chewed thoughtfully before replying. 'Did Cadi tell you this?'

Jez nodded.

'So she was up front and honest with you?'

Jez put the spoonful of porridge back down into his bowl. 'About that mebbe, but not about her kissing him, or accepting his offer of a personal tour around Lincoln.'

Bill's brow shot towards his hairline – this was certainly news to him. 'Cadi snogged Aled?'

'Not snog, exactly,' Jez admitted, 'but she did kiss him on the cheek.'

'Oh,' said Bill, deflating a little. 'And how did her tour of Lincoln go?'

'She never went,' said Jez, 'or not that I know of. According to Cadi, she only said it to annoy Daphne ...'

Maria fixed Jez with a steady gaze. 'I believe her. More to the point, I reckon you do too.'

'Of course I believe her!' snapped Jez. 'But that's not the point. Cadi shouldn't have lied to me in the first place.'

Maria's patience had run out. She had put up with Jez's bellyaching ever since his return, and even though she'd tried to be understanding, he refused to listen to reason. It was time to take off the kid gloves.

'You joined the RAF to impress her, despite saying that you didn't. You then tried to persuade Cadi to join up, because you knew Aled was being posted to Liverpool.' She held up a finger as Jez tried to interject. 'Let me finish. After that, you proposed to her, purely to keep Aled at bay. And last but not least, you lied about volunteering to go to Africa. From where I'm standing, you've told far more porkies than Cadi.'

Jez stared at Maria. 'There's nothing wrong with wanting to impress the girl you love ...'

'Of course not,' snapped Maria, 'but you only joined the RAF because you hoped to become a pilot, which would be one up on Aled.'

Jez continued without addressing her reply. 'And as for marriage? I wanted to marry that girl from the day I set eyes on her. When it comes to volunteering, that was a spur-of-the-moment decision, which I don't regret, but I do regret that I didn't come clean when Cadi assumed that I'd been selected.'

'So it's one rule for you and another for Cadi?' said Maria. She eyed him coolly. 'And you never denied the fact that you tried to persuade Cadi to join the WAAF to get her away from Aled.'

'Because I can't,' said Jez miserably. 'And that's why I retracted my words, because I knew I was only asking her to ease my own stupid insecurities. Something that I bitterly regret.'

Maria cupped his hand in hers. 'You've always thought she was too good for you, and your biggest fear is that she'll realise it for herself one day. But Cadi loves you for who you are, not because of some fancy uniform, or because you've got pots of money.'

'But I'm not even a nice person,' said Jez. 'If I were, I'd not have done any of the things I have.'

Coming round to his side of the table, Maria enveloped him in her arms. 'You are a wonderful young man, Jeremy Thomas: kind, caring, considerate and loving. You were the apple of your nan's eye *and* mine.'

'Why, though?' said Jez. 'When my own parents didn't want me?'

'They didn't *know* you, Jez; you were a newborn when Carrie found you. You can't possibly have done anything wrong. It's your parents who were at fault, not you.'

Jez rubbed his nose. 'That's what I thought, but Nan was always very defensive when it came to my parents.'

'In what way?' asked Bill.

269

'She said that we shouldn't blame them because we don't know their circumstances.'

Maria pulled a face. 'Very gracious of her, but that was your nan to a tee. And I suppose to some degree I agree with her, as there's plenty of young girls who find themselves with child when they're nowt but kiddies themselves.'

'Only I'll never know the truth, will I?' said Jez sullenly.

'True, but you mustn't let that rule your life,' said Maria, 'because it's holding you back, Jez, surely you see that now? Quite frankly, you're pushing Cadi into Aled's arms, and I reckon you're doing that because you believe you're unworthy of her love.'

Jez hung his head. 'I've been a complete and utter twit.'

Bill gave him a wry smile. 'You're a man – it kind of goes with the territory.'

Jez gave a soft chuckle. 'My poor nan, she put up with an awful lot.'

'Nonsense,' said Maria. 'Having never been blessed with any of her own children, Carrie saw you as a gift-child. A bit like me and Bill. I know I'd welcome a foundling with open arms, if it were to happen to me.'

'You'd make a brilliant mam,' said Jez. 'It seems wrong that you and Bill don't get to be parents, when there's people out there giving their babies away.'

Maria smiled. 'You're a dear, Jez, and you deserve Cadi's love.'

Jez stood up from the table. 'Can I make a telephone call?'

Maria gestured towards the telephone. 'You've no need to ask.'

Bill gave him a cheery wink. 'Good luck, mate.'

Jez picked up the receiver and dialled the number for Cadi's base. When the person on the other end picked up, he asked for Cadi and was disappointed to learn that she had gone away for Christmas. Assuming that she had gone to see Poppy and Izzy, he tried there.

'Sorry, Jez,' said Poppy, 'but she's not here.'

He frowned. 'Then where is she?'

'When I spoke to her last, she said she would be working over the Christmas period,' said Poppy, crossing her fingers behind her back.

'When I telephoned Coningsby, they said she'd already left on a week's leave?' Jez ventured.

Poppy fell silent. 'I don't know what to say to you, but she's definitely not here. If it's any consolation, I think she'd have loved to hear from you.'

'Can you think of anybody else she could be with?'

'Only Kitty, but I know she's spending Christmas with her friend Ronnie in Portsmouth.'

'Do you think Cadi might have gone there?'

Poppy sighed wretchedly. 'I really couldn't say.'

Jez fell silent. There was no way Cadi would do anything without running it by Poppy first, yet Poppy claimed ignorance as to her oldest friend's whereabouts. In his opinion, Poppy was lying – not that he could say that, of course. 'Can you do me a favour and telephone me, should she show up?'

Poppy nodded. 'Straight away.'

'Thanks, Poppy.'

'Ta-ra, Jez.'

'Ta-ra, Poppy.'

Jez replaced the receiver and headed back to Bill and Maria, both of whom were eager to know how he'd got on.

'She's got a week's leave and nobody knows where she is.'

Maria did a double-take. 'What do you mean, nobody knows where she is?'

'She's not on her base, and she's not with Poppy, Izzy or any of her other friends.'

Bill shot Maria a sidelong glance. 'Maybe war business?'

Maria nodded. 'That must be it. They wouldn't tell you where she was, because it's a secret. We all know Cadi's been flitting round the country taking all sorts of people to all kinds of places.'

Jez smiled briefly before fetching his greatcoat, which was hanging on the back of the kitchen door.

'Where are you going?' said Bill.

'Out,' said Jez. 'I need to clear my head.'

He swung out of the kitchen, into the cold and grey. *There was one place Cadi could be*, Jez thought bitterly, *and that's with that flamin' Aled.* He shook his head angrily. Had Maria been right? Had he pushed Cadi into Aled's arms? Buttoning up his coat, he lifted the collar against the wind. There was only one way to find out.

Poppy went to sit back down by Izzy, who was reading a letter from Mike.

'What did Jez want?' asked Izzy, barely lifting her head.

'Cadi.'

She looked up expectantly. 'Ooh, do you think he wants to make amends?'

Poppy shrugged. 'Dunno, I never asked.'

'Why doesn't he ring her at Coningsby?'

Poppy crossed her fingers below the table. 'He did, but she's not there.'

Izzy rolled her eyes. 'Surely he could wait until she came back? She can't have gone far.'

'Maybe,' said Poppy. She lowered her gaze to hide the blush that was creeping up her neck. She didn't like keeping secrets from her friend, but she knew from Cadi's telephone conversation that she didn't want Izzy to know what she was up to.

She turned her thoughts to Cadi's last phone call. 'I'm goin' to Portsmouth for the twenty-third,' Cadi had said. 'We'll investigate and see what's what, before I come and see you and Izzy.'

Poppy had pulled a rueful face. 'I wish I could be with you.'

'Me too, but like I said before, I need you to stay with Izzy. There's only you, me, Kitty, Ronnie and me mam that know the truth, and if anyone should ask, tell them you know nothing.'

Now Poppy looked at Izzy, who was writing her reply to Mike. She had a sinking feeling that bad news was coming Izzy's way.

Jez flashed his pass at the man on the gate. 'I'm looking for Aled Davies?'

The man shook his head. 'He's gone home for Christmas – can I help?'

Jez felt as though someone had ripped the rug out from underneath him. Why on earth hadn't he thought of that sooner? Cadi must have gone home to see her parents, *and Aled's gone rushing after her*, added his inner thoughts. Aware that the young man had asked him a question, Jez shrugged. 'It doesn't matter.'

Turning on his heel, he strode determinedly away as he wondered how long would it take him to get to Rhos from Liverpool.

It was the morning before Christmas Eve and Ronnie was having lunch at the B&B with Cadi and Kitty.

Cadi leaned back as Mrs Wiggs, who ran the B&B, placed a delicious-looking plate of pork, mash, vegetables and gravy in front of her.

'It's good to have the three of us back together again,' said Ronnie, shaking salt liberally over her meal.

Cadi picked up her cutlery. 'We've come a long way in a short space of time. Have either of you got any regrets?'

Kitty shook her head. 'I love my job – it's far better than the jewellery counter in Blacklers. I'm doing what I enjoy most and getting paid for it. What more could a girl ask for?'

'Same here,' said Ronnie. 'I love working on the airwaves, as you get to hear everything first.' She turned to Cadi. 'How about you?'

Cadi mulled this over before replying. 'I'm that busy I barely have time to think, and with everything that's been going on lately, that's probably a good thing.'

Kitty grimaced. 'Who'd have thought a chance encounter could open up such a huge can of worms? I sometimes wish Daphne had chosen a different table – that way, we'd have been none the wiser, and you'd still be with Jez.'

'It's nobody's fault,' Cadi assured her. 'I could have handled things differently, but I chose not to, and that's down to me – and me alone.'

'What do you think'll happen between you and Jez?' asked Ronnie. 'You don't really think he'll throw your relationship away over this, do you?'

'I would hope not,' said Cadi. She was looking at the engagement ring that encircled her finger. 'But I guess if he does, I'd have to wonder if he ever really loved me. Jez's nan said that relationships are full of arguments, misunderstandings and compromises, and that you couldn't chuck it all away at the first sign of trouble. I'll grant you this isn't the first hiccup we've had, not even the second, and we've got through worse.' She recalled Daphne's letter and the hurt it had caused. 'Far worse.'

'He's angry,' said Kitty, a forkful of mashed potato poised before her lips. 'Men are proud creatures. I dare say Daphne broadcasting his business in front of his mates was a real blow to his pride.'

Cadi grimaced. 'He'd only just got off the ship when she started running her mouth, and I'm willing to bet she made sure half of Liverpool heard her.'

'Oh dear,' sympathised Ronnie, 'it can't have been easy hearing that kind of news, but in front of your friends?'

Cadi was prodding her mashed potato with her fork. 'I need to speak to him.'

Kitty nodded. 'Do you know where he's spending Christmas?'

'Maria and Bill's,' said Cadi. 'Maria rang the base to see if I'd consider joining them, but I said at the time I didn't think it a good idea. I mean, who wants to spend Christmas with someone who's barely talking to you?'

'Perhaps she thought it would give the two of you a chance to make amends,' hazarded Ronnie.

'Probably,' conceded Cadi, 'but it's too late now. And besides, I've got all this business with Raquel to sort out.'

'*We* could do that, if you want to go to Liverpool,' Kitty volunteered.

'I know you could, and whilst I'm grateful for the offer, I really think it's my duty to see this through,' said Cadi flatly.

'In a strange way, I'm rather looking forward to it,' admitted Ronnie.

Cadi stared at her incredulously. 'I thought you hated the place.'

'I did, but this time we'll be able to ask Dolly – or whoever answers the door – outright. And we won't leave until we've got answers, unlike the last time, when I ran off like a frightened rabbit.'

Kitty giggled. 'Do you think they thought you were after a job?'

Blushing, Ronnie remembered how Dolly has asked whether she was there to do a bit of business – something that she now relayed to her friends. 'Do you think that's what she meant? Only she did look startled when I said yes ...'

Kitty smothered a shriek of laughter behind her hand. 'Oh, Ronnie, you didn't?'

Ronnie nodded miserably. 'I thought she was referring to the WVS; it didn't occur to me for a minute that she meant anything else.'

A look of horror crossed Cadi's face. 'Imagine if we turn up and there really is no Raquel living there?'

'New careers maybe?' quipped Kitty.

Ronnie was slicing a carrot into pieces when something dawned on her. 'You know the note – the one you think Raquel wrote?'

'The one she sent back saying "not known at this address"?' Cadi nodded. 'What about it?'

Ronnie placed her knife and fork down. 'Somebody must've read Izzy's letter, in order to reply.'

'And?' said Kitty, scooping peas onto her fork.

'Why didn't they mention it when I went to the house? You'd have thought she'd have said something like "Was it you who wrote the letter" or "Why have you come all this way when I'd already explained that Raquel doesn't live here?"'

Cadi was staring into space as a thought entered her mind. She glanced at her friends. 'If you'd received a letter for someone else, what would you do?'

Kitty was the first to reply. 'Write "not known at this address" and push it back into the letter box, which is exactly what she did, so why—'

Cadi was shaking her head. 'Only she didn't! She opened the letter and read the contents, before writing a separate note, saying that she didn't live at that address. But that's not what any normal person would do. They'd write it on the envelope itself, without opening the letter first!'

'Flippin' Nora,' hissed Ronnie. 'It really is her, isn't it?'

'I reckon so,' said Cadi, 'but why ask you in? You'd have thought that was the last thing she'd want, especially after trying to get rid of you with a note.'

Kitty coughed on a piece of pork that she had tried to swallow too hastily. 'Do you think Dolly *was* Raquel?'

Ronnie conjured up an image of Dolly in her mind. Strong, independent and fearless – not the sort of woman to hide behind a note. 'Nope. Whoever wrote that note, it wasn't Dolly.'

'I reckon she must've known about the note, though,' said Cadi thoughtfully, 'otherwise, why invite you in?'

'If she knows about the note, then she knew why you were there. So why ask you in, when she already knew the answer?' said Kitty. 'She could easily have said "no" and sent you on your way. And, let's face it, that probably would've been the end of that.'

'Curiosity?' suggested Cadi.

'Why? They knew who'd written the initial letter,' said Ronnie reasonably. 'Because Izzy signed it …' She glanced expectantly at Cadi, who nodded.

'Not only signed it, but gave her address, which is how they knew who to send it back to, and who the sender was,' confirmed Cadi.

'I wonder why they didn't simply ignore the letter,' mused Kitty.

'Izzy might have gone calling, and Raquel wouldn't have wanted that,' said Cadi.

'What if we go there and they say Raquel doesn't live there?' asked Kitty. 'We can hardly insist she does, when we've got no proof.'

Cadi began ticking off the evidence on her fingers. 'It's Raquel's last address; the handwriting's a match;

she read the letter rather than returning it unread. And if that's not good enough?'

Both girls were leaning forward, eager to hear what she had to say. 'What?' hissed Kitty excitedly.

'We'll say we're not leaving until we've spoken to Raquel. And if that doesn't work, I'll tell her that I'm going to ring Izzy and tell her that her mam's a prostitute.'

'You wouldn't?' cried Ronnie.

Cadi rolled her eyes. 'Of course I wouldn't, but she doesn't know that, does she? And if I were Raquel, I'd want to get my side of the story across first, wouldn't you?'

'It seems a bit cruel,' ventured Kitty cautiously.

'Cruel to be kind,' said Cadi evenly. 'I reckon Raquel's lying low because she's ashamed, and I don't blame her for that, but Izzy won't be bothered what her mam does, as long as she can have her back. It's tragic that they're both suffering for something Eric did. Not only that, but Raquel holds the answer to a lot of questions, and our Izzy deserves to know the truth.'

'And that's why we need you,' admitted Ronnie. 'You know poor Izzy and everything she's been through. If anyone can persuade Raquel to see sense, it's you.'

'And you knew Eric too,' Kitty reminded her, 'and if Raquel sees that you aren't judging her, but sympathise with her, she's more likely to come out of her shell.'

'Poor woman's in for one hell of a shock,' said Kitty, 'especially if she thinks it's all water under the bridge.'

'We've tried writing, and Ronnie tried calling,' said Cadi. 'I think Raquel must realise we're pretty determined to get to the bottom of things, don't you?'

'That's a thought,' agreed Ronnie. 'She must have been wondering who I was, because I never actually said. Assuming she's not a stupid woman, she'll have put two and two together by now, regarding the letter and my visit. She'll also know ...' She fell silent as a thought entered her mind; she mulled it over for a few seconds before nodding. 'I think Raquel was there the day I called by, and that's why Dolly wanted me to go inside, so that Raquel could take a good look and see if she recognised me.'

'So she knows you're not Izzy,' said Cadi.

'She must be really confused,' remarked Kitty, ''cos Ronnie here hasn't got a Scouse accent.'

'I wonder if curiosity has started to get the better of her?' said Ronnie. 'I know it would if it were me. But there again, I'm not a you-know-what, and maybe if I was I'd rather I was left well alone.'

'Which is all the more reason for getting Raquel out of there,' said Cadi. 'She only became one of them in the first place because she'll have had no choice, and the sooner we can confirm it's her, the sooner we can get her out of a bad situation.'

'I know you say that,' said Ronnie, 'but how?'

'Maria would have her like a shot,' affirmed Cadi. 'I know she would. And then there's the money.'

Kitty perked up. 'What money?'

Cadi lowered her voice. 'The money in Eric's box – it's a small fortune. But even if there was no money, I know Maria would happily pay Raquel to

280

help out at the hotel. She's been managing on her own ever since I left because she can't get the staff.'

Ronnie tutted. 'You'd think *someone* would be grateful for the work.'

'Conscription,' answered Cadi plainly.

Kitty spoke absent-mindedly. 'I'm surprised the women at Raquel's place haven't been called up.'

Ronnie grimaced. 'Probably too old or not on the census, as I very much doubt they pay taxes. Thinking back, that's probably why Dolly came over to me in the first place, because she saw the clipboard and feared I might be something to do with the authorities.'

'Do you think she still might think that?' said Cadi.

'Not the way I legged it,' said Ronnie. 'Hardly the actions of someone working for the government.'

'True.' Cadi automatically gathered and stacked their plates. 'Poor old Izzy hasn't got a clue where I am or what I'm up to.'

'You said you'd spoken to Maria. Where does she think you're spending Christmas?'

'She didn't ask, so I suppose she assumed I would be staying at Coningsby,' said Cadi.

'What if she calls to wish you a merry Christmas?' asked Kitty.

Cadi's cheeks coloured a little. 'I hadn't thought of that.'

'She might even persuade Jez to give you a call – you know, to make amends,' said Kitty.

Cadi's colour deepened. 'If he does, then he'll realise I'm not at Coningsby, so he'll telephone Poppy to find out where I am – only she's been sworn to secrecy.'

Ronnie spoke the thought that was on everyone's mind. 'That might look suspicious, don't you think?'

Kitty pulled a downward smile. 'I know what I'd think, if I was Jez …'

Cadi swallowed. 'You'd think I was with Aled.'

'Sorry, Cadi, but yes, that's exactly what I'd think,' confirmed Kitty. 'Wouldn't you?'

Cadi blew her cheeks out. She wanted to protest and say that any reasonable person would assume she was staying with her parents, but if that was the case, then Kitty would have said so. 'Not again!'

'Sorry?'

'I've made a complete pig's ear of things all over again,' said Cadi.

'It's hardly your fault,' soothed Ronnie. 'You're doing the right thing by protecting Izzy.'

'I know, but I should've seen this coming—'

Kitty cut her short. 'You've still got time. Ask Mrs Wiggs if you can use her telephone – I'm sure she'll say yes. That way you can phone Maria, let her know where you are and what's going on.' She smiled brightly. 'No harm done.'

Cadi stood up from the table. 'Shan't be a mo.' Within moments she was on the phone to the Belmont.

'Cadi! Is everything all right? Have you seen Jez?'

She frowned. Why did Maria think she might have seen Jez, when he was in Liverpool and, as far as Maria knew, she was at Coningsby. Her stomach dropped. Jez must have decided to pay her base a visit.

'I'm not at Coningsby.'

'I know,' said Maria, much to Cadi's surprise. There was an appreciable silence before she spoke next. 'Aren't you in Rhos with your mam and dad?'

Cadi shook her head. 'No, I'm in Portsmouth with my pals.'

Maria sounded exasperated. 'Then why on earth didn't Poppy tell Jez that?'

'Jez has spoken to Poppy?' Cadi asked Maria, her voice hollow.

'Yes. But she refused to say where you were – God only knows why. So Jez figured out you must have gone home to Rhos for Christmas.'

The penny dropped. 'Are you telling me that Jez is in Rhos?'

'We tried to stop him,' said Maria. 'We told him it was silly to go off on some wild goose chase when he didn't know for sure where you were, but after chatting to Poppy, it seemed obvious.'

Nodding miserably, Cadi went on to explain how she'd come up with the idea to confront Raquel, finishing with, 'I couldn't ask Ronnie to go again, and seeing as Jez wasn't even speaking to me and I still had my week's leave, I thought I'd kill two birds with one stone.'

'Leaving the rest of us to put two and two together, only to come up with five,' said Maria. 'Oh, Cadi love, what are we going to do with you?'

'Well, I've learned my lesson once and for all!' she replied firmly. 'No more lies, because no matter your intent, all you do is hurt the people you love most.'

'Poor old Jez has gone all that way for nothing,' said Maria. 'I really don't wish to rub salt into your wounds, but he too has realised the error of his ways – that's why he was looking for you in the first place. So that he could say sorry.'

'That's what he said the last time, yet here we are again—' said Cadi, only to have Maria cut across her words.

'That boy thinks he's unlovable because his parents abandoned him as a baby, so can you really blame him for looking at Aled – a handsome man in air-crew uniform – and thinking you deserve someone like him, over a foundling like himself?'

'I'd never think that!' cried Cadi, tears brimming in her eyes. 'I love Jez; he's all the man I want.'

'*I* know that, but Jez doesn't, or rather he didn't, until we had a real chat and I made him see that he was good enough for you.' She sighed. 'I loved Carrie to bits, but she told Jez not to blame his parents, saying that they might have abandoned him through no fault of their own, but unfortunately Jez took that to mean he was the one at fault. It's something he's been carrying around for a long time.'

'Poor Jez,' whispered Cadi. 'I had no idea.'

'Me neither,' admitted Maria.

'So what made him go to Rhos?'

'The natural answer, I suppose: every girl needs her mother during hard times. I must admit I was surprised when I heard you hadn't gone there, until you told me about Raquel, of course. It made sense then.'

'The question now,' said Cadi, 'is how we get word to Jez?'

'I don't suppose you told your parents where you were spending Christmas?'

Cadi went to shake her head, before giving a small cry of triumph. 'Yes! I told Mam. I didn't go into the ins and outs, just said that I would be spending Christmas in Portsmouth with my pals.'

'Did she ask why?'

'She did, so of course I told her that Jez and I had had a bit of a barney, although I must admit I didn't elaborate.'

'Oh? Why not?'

Cadi's cheeks flushed anew. 'Because I knew she'd say that I was in the wrong for keeping secrets.' She rolled her eyes. 'And boy, oh boy, would she be right.'

'So if Jez turns up at your parents', what do you think your mam'll say?'

Cadi pulled a face. 'Dunno really. Mam knows we've had an argument, so I dare say Dad does too. And because I didn't go into detail, she's probably guessed it was my fault. So if Jez turns up looking for me, they'll telephone me here at the B&B.'

'Thank goodness you had the foresight to let them know where you'd be staying,' said Maria, the relief heavy in her voice.

'I always let them know where I'm at, in case something happens.'

'Very sensible too,' remarked Maria. 'So what's the plan? Are you going to send a telegram to your mam's?'

'I can do one better,' said Cadi. 'I'll telephone the bakery where I used to work and ask one of the girls if they'll pass on a message for Mam to ring me at the B&B a.s.a.p.'

'Good idea. Please stay in touch – I'll only worry otherwise.'

'Will do. And Maria?'

'Yes, love?'

'Thanks. You really are one in a million.'

Maria chuckled softly. 'You're welcome, love. Ta-ra.'

Cadi said her goodbyes, clicked the receiver down and hastily dialled the operator. Asking to be put through to the bakery, she was glad when she heard the voice of her old supervisor come down the line.

'Jeff!'

'Hello, Cadi. You after your old job back? You'd be more than welcome ...'

Cadi laughed. 'I don't think the WAAF would see it that way.'

'Of course!' he cried. 'How could I forget? Your old man's told us all about *Corporal* Williams.'

Cadi rolled her eyes. 'I'd forgotten that Dad had been singing my praises.'

'Quite right too,' said Jeff. 'I know I'd be crowing it from the rooftops if you were my daughter.'

Cadi blushed. 'It's nice of you to say that. How's tricks at the bakery?'

'Same old,' said Jeff, 'but I'm fairly sure you didn't telephone for a chat about buns?'

Cadi explained that she needed to speak to her parents and would be grateful if Jeff could pass on a message for them to telephone her.

'I'll do it on my way home,' he confirmed.

Thanking him for his help, Cadi replaced the receiver so that she could get back to her friends, who were awaiting her with eagerness.

'We ordered you a pudding,' said Kitty, 'apple crumble and custard. I hope that's all right?'

Cadi smiled. 'Of course it is; apple crumble and custard makes everything better.'

'We gather you must have got through,' said Ronnie, 'you've been ages.'

As Cadi started her pudding she told the girls of her conversations with Maria and Jeff.

'Sounds like you've thought of everything,' applauded Kitty.

Cadi crossed her fingers. 'I hope so.'

Ronnie smiled confidently. 'What could possibly go wrong?'

Jez stared out of the window to his carriage. He had telephoned Maria and Bill from the station, saying that he wanted to find out if Cadi had gone home for Christmas. Maria had warned him not to go, but Jez had already made up his mind.

'I need to put things right, and I can't do that from the comfort of an armchair' had been his excuse, but the reality had been far from that. Jez's inner caveman was convinced that Cadi was with Aled, and whilst he believed it was all his own fault, he couldn't bear the thought of the two of them together. Looking out over the bleak landscape put Jez in mind of his own mood. Having spent the longest time chasing Cadi, he'd been the happiest man in the district when she finally agreed to be his belle. So why had he let his jealousy get the better of him? And why did he keep comparing himself to a man Cadi had once detested? Was it really because he'd been abandoned when he was a baby? Or was it because he thought Cadi deserved better? A man with land, money and the intelligence to get into air crew seemed to fit the bill far better than pot-less Jez, without a home to call his own.

He shook his head. There was an age-old saying that if you truly loved somebody, you would let them go. Jez knew he loved Cadi enough to do what was best for her, and if he really thought that someone was Aled, he would have stepped aside. But in his heart of hearts, Jez knew he was the right man for her. Nobody could love her the way he did, nobody would take care of her the way he would. Cadi meant everything to him, and he wasn't prepared to let her go without a fight. He tutted, causing several of the passengers to look in his direction. Cadi was still engaged to him. She wouldn't rush into another relationship, and it was unfair of Jez to think she might.

So how would he explain his presence? *Truthfully,* thought Jez. *I shall tell her that I've been a complete and utter pleb and will apologise, kowtow, beg and plead for her forgiveness. As for Aled? He'd probably heard that Cadi was going home for Christmas and, just as he had with the mining disaster, had hightailed it over to Rhos so that he could be a shoulder for her to cry on. What's more, I've no one to blame but myself, for giving him the opportunity. Aled's the one at fault here and, like a fool, I've played straight into his hands. But no longer!*

With the train drawing to a halt, he looked around the empty station. Seeing another passenger get to their feet, Jez asked where they were.

'Wrexham,' said the man. 'Where are you going?'

'Rhos?' said Jez.

288

'You'll need to catch a bus. One of the guards will point you in the right direction.'

Having left on the spur of the moment, Jez had nothing but the clothes he stood up in. Descending from the train onto the platform, he spoke briefly to a rail guard, who informed him of the bus he needed to catch.

'And if you're lookin' for somewhere to stay over-night,' continued the guard, 'then you'll not go far wrong with the Coach and Horses; they do a nice pie and mash, and it's clean too.'

Thanking him for his help, Jez headed for the bus stop. As he waited, he wondered how he would find out where Cadi lived. Maria was right about one thing: rushing off at half cock meant he hadn't a clue where he was running to. Cadi had said she used to live in a ter-raced house with her family, but that's as much as he knew. Jez heaved a sigh. Not only was he rushing into things, but he was making a complete fool of himself in the process. For two pins he'd get on the first train back to Liverpool, but he'd come too far to turn back now. Besides, should he find her, Cadi might be pleased to see him, especially when she got to hear how sorry he was.

Mrs Wiggs knocked on the door to Cadi and Kitty's room. 'Cadi, dear? Your mam's on the phone.'

Cadi opened the door. 'Thanks for letting me know. I'll come down now.' She turned to Kitty before leaving the room. 'I'll be back in a mo.' Trotting down the stairs, she headed to the hall table where the telephone was located. Picking up the receiver, she spoke to her mother.

'Hi, Mam.'

'Is everything all right? Jeff said you wanted me to call, but didn't explain why,' said Jill. She hissed something to her husband, who was trying to talk at the same time as her.

'Sorry, Mam, I didn't mean to alarm you – everything's fine, I just wanted to talk to you about Jez.'

There was an audible silence before Jill spoke next. 'Why? What's happened to Jez?'

'Nothing, but he's coming to Rhos looking for me ...'

'Why on earth does he think you're in Rhos?' asked Jill, her tone incredulous.

Cadi heaved a sigh. 'Because I never told him I was going to Portsmouth.'

'I see. So what makes you think he's in Rhos?'

'Maria,' said Cadi simply. 'I telephoned the Belmont and she said he'd gone to Rhos, believing I'd probably come home for Christmas.'

'And what would you like me to say to him, should he turn up?'

'I'd be grateful if you could let him know where I am, to save him worrying.'

'That boy must be head over heels to have come rushing all the way to Rhos on a whim,' noted her mother.

A slow smile crossed Cadi's face. 'He must, mustn't he?'

'So why on earth aren't the two of you together at such an important time of the year?'

'Because I've been putting other people before him, and I shouldn't have,' replied Cadi truthfully.

Jill tutted softly. 'Cadi, that boy's worth his weight in gold.'

'I know, Mam, and I'll never do it again,' said Cadi fervently. 'From now on, Jez comes first.'

'I shall be sure to let you know, should I see him,' her mother assured her.

'Thanks, Mam.'

'Take care, Cadi love.'

'Will do. Ta-ra, Mam, love you.'

'Love you too, sweetheart.'

Cadi replaced the receiver and headed back to their room, where she found Kitty sitting on her bed. 'Well?'

Cadi briefly outlined the conversation, finishing with, 'Life is hard enough as it is, so why do I keep making things worse?'

Kitty smiled. 'Because you're trying to do the right thing by keeping everybody happy. I expect Jez realises that.'

'I feel such a heel. He's gone all the way to Rhos and I'm not even there.'

'Hardly your fault—' said Kitty reasonably, but Cadi cut her off.

'It is, though, isn't it? If I'd told Maria where I was going, he'd be here, not in Rhos.'

Kitty sighed impatiently. 'Stop beating yourself up. You've done the right thing, by trying to protect Izzy from what could be a horrible truth. Imagine if you'd told Izzy your suspicions, or if she'd found out via the grapevine? What do you think she would have done?'

'She'd have gone straight to the house and demanded to speak to Raquel; that's what I'd have done.'

'And how do you think she'd feel, finding out first-hand that her mother had been reduced to prostitution?'

Cadi shook her head; the mere thought chilled her to the bone. 'Devastated, heartbroken – who wouldn't be?'

'By doing the groundwork you're softening the blow. If your suspicions are right, you can get Raquel out from that hellhole and into somewhere decent. Izzy will still learn the truth, but she won't have to witness it with her own eyes, which is something she'd never be able to unsee ...' Kitty paused momentarily before continuing, 'I've a cousin what used to live in Liverpool. She wasn't there for the May blitz, thank God, but she came for a visit not long after. She cried, Cadi, because whilst she'd heard about it on the news, she'd not realised quite how bad it was. It's the same for Izzy; she'll hear the stories, but she won't have to see it for herself – it'll mean the difference between a peaceful night's sleep and nights of torment.'

Cadi stared up at the ceiling as she blinked the tears away. 'I helped rescue a woman after the blitz, whose baby had died in her arms.' She looked at Kitty, who gazed back sympathetically. 'I'll *never* forget what that looked like, and even though Poppy and Jez were with me and they knew that the baby had gone, it wasn't the same for them because they didn't *see*.'

'There you are,' said Kitty. 'No harm can come from Jez going to Rhos, so stop punishing yourself, because you've done the right thing. You really couldn't have risked Izzy getting wind of this, as the consequences are too great.'

*

292

With the snow falling steadily, Jez gazed out of the window as the bus he was travelling on made its way up the steep hill. For what felt like the umpteenth time he rehearsed his apology to Cadi. He would start off by telling her what a fool he'd been for letting his insecurities get in the way of their relationship. After that he would promise never to be so churlish again, before begging her forgiveness.

With the plan clear in his mind, he was just beginning to wonder if the roads were going to get any worse, when the bus trundled to a halt and the driver hopped out of his seat. The clippie, who had been at the back of the bus, spoke to Jez as she passed by. 'Won't be a mo.'

Jez stood up to see what was going on. The driver and the clippie were standing outside the bus, staring at the road ahead. When they returned the driver spoke directly to Jez.

'This is as far as I can take her. If it's bad here, it'll be far worse at the top of the village, and this old girl won't make it halfway up,' he said, patting the steering wheel of the bus.

Jez donned his gloves. 'Where do I go from here?'

The driver pointed to a lane that pared off from the main road they had been travelling on. 'Up there ...' He hesitated. 'Whereabouts in Rhos are you headed?'

Jez shrugged. 'All I know is she lives in a small terraced house.'

The driver raised his brow. 'She?'

Jez nodded. 'I'm here to surprise my fiancée.'

The clippie clapped her hands together as if in prayer. 'How romantic!'

The driver's brow furrowed. 'And you don't know where she lives?'

Realising how odd this sounded, Jez gave a short laugh. 'She was living in Liverpool when we met, and since then she's joined the WAAF.' He hesitated. 'My fiancée's Cadi Williams. I don't suppose either of you know her?'

'Sorry, but I don't live in Rhos,' said the clippie.

Jez looked at the driver, but he was shaking his head. 'I'm the same as Shirley here – Wrexham born and bred.' Taking a cigarette paper, he began to fill it with tobacco from his pouch. 'Try the post office. I'm sure they'll know who she is.'

Jez brightened. 'That's a good idea. Where is it?'

The driver placed the cigarette between his lips and lit the end. 'Now *that* I can help you with.' He pointed to the road. 'Straight up as far as you can go – you can't miss it.'

Thanking them for their help, Jez hurried off. As he walked up the narrow lane lined with terraced houses, it occurred to him that he was the only soul around, something that was unheard of in Liverpool. No matter what time of day or night, or how bad the weather, there were always a few people going about their business. Cadi had said Rhos was too quiet for her, and Jez was beginning to see why.

Glancing into the windows that he passed, he wondered if Cadi was living in any of those houses, and thought how wonderful it would be if she came rushing out to greet him.

As he neared the top of the hill, he saw for himself why the driver had decided not to attempt the rest of the journey. The virginal snow was far deeper up here and, with no other traffic using the road, the bus would have been no match for it.

Since starting his walk, the only noise Jez had heard was the sound of his feet crumping against the snow – until now, that was. Standing still, he closed his eyes, then smiled. In the distance he could clearly hear people singing carols, just as he and Cadi had done in Newsham Park last Christmas. *And where there's folk, there's hope*, thought Jez. *One of them is bound to know Cadi – heck, she might even be with them.* He strode forward, and it wasn't long before he spied the group of carollers clustered around the entrance to a church. As he neared them, his hopes began to rise as his gaze settled on a blonde woman in WAAF uniform. In his heart Jez knew it had to be Cadi. He was about to call out her name when the man standing next to her placed his arm around her shoulders. Jez's heart plummeted into his boots. He had only met Aled once, but he was certain it was him. Hurrying forward, he saw the WAAF tilt her head, as Aled leaned in for a kiss.

Fearing that the worst was about to happen, Jez yelled out, 'Cadi!'

The woman concerned didn't even turn to face him, but Aled did. As their eyes met, Jez opened his mouth to give Aled a piece of his mind, when the woman also turned and Jez saw, to his shocked delight, that it wasn't Cadi after all. Eager to skedaddle before Aled realised who he was, Jez quickly mumbled an apology, but it seemed he was too late.

Aled was eyeing him quizzically. 'Jez?'

With his jaw flinching, Jez glanced up at Aled, who was staring at him with confused curiosity. 'That's right,' he replied. 'Now if you'll excuse me.'

Stepping to one side, Jez made to leave, but Aled was already speaking the thought uppermost in his mind. 'What on earth are you doing all the way out here? I'd have thought you'd have been spending Christmas with Cadi.'

Feeling utterly foolish, Jez spoke without making eye contact. 'It's a surprise,' he mumbled.

Aled's brow shot towards his hairline. 'I should think it is, considering that she's not here.'

Wishing that the ground would open up and swallow him whole, Jez was grateful when a fair-haired middle-aged woman approached. 'Excuse me, but are you Jez?'

Grateful for her intervention, he nodded.

Smiling warmly, she introduced herself. 'I'm Jill, Cadi's mam. She said we might be seeing you.'

Thanking his stars that he didn't appear quite so foolish as he had a few moments ago, Jez tried to look nonchalant. 'She did?'

Placing her arm through Jez's, Jill turned him in the direction of a man who was watching them with a vague curiosity. 'She telephoned earlier,' Jill explained. 'Come with me and I'll introduce you to Cadi's father.'

She walked him over to the burly man, who was now eyeing them both expectantly.

'Jez, this is Dewi, Cadi's father,' said Jill.

Jez shook the other man's hand whilst wondering what Cadi had told her parents.

Aware that they were drawing attention from inquisitive onlookers, Jill jerked her head in the direction

296

of a row of houses. 'Unless we want everyone knowin' our business, I suggest we head indoors. You've come a long way, so I dare say you're hungry.'

Jez was indeed hungry, but right now all he wanted was answers.

'What did Cadi say when you spoke to her?' he asked cautiously.

'That the pair of you have been acting like children,' said Jill plainly. 'Not surprising, seeing as you're both still young.'

Jez's cheeks reddened. 'I dunno about Cadi.'

Jill pulled her scarf up around her ears. 'It takes two to tango. If Cadi hadn't been so secretive, you'd have known where she was and none of this would've happened.'

Dewi, who had been quiet until now, spoke thoughtfully. 'You must love my daughter an awful lot to come tearin' across the country in the middle of winter.'

'I do,' said Jez fervently.

Jill pushed open the door to the small terraced house that the Williamses called home. Walking through to the kitchen, she removed her scarf and gloves and placed them on the fireguard to dry. Turning to face Jez, she held her hand out for his coat.

Undoing the buttons, he handed it to Jill, who hooked it onto the mantel above the fire. Glancing down at the hems of his trousers, she pulled a seat forward. 'Sit there and get yourself warm – those trousers look wet through.'

Taking the chair, Jez watched the steam rising from his trouser legs. 'It's not snowing in Liverpool,' he said by way of explanation for his unsuitable attire.

Dewi chortled quietly. 'You haven't even got a bag, boy. Don't try tellin' me you considered the weather before taking off.'

Jez grinned sheepishly. 'It was what you might call a spur-of-the-moment decision.'

'Young love, eh?' grinned Dewi. 'Hot and impulsive. I remember them days, but only just, mind you,' he said, winking at his wife.

'Then you've a better memory than me,' she said teasingly. Taking a dish from the warming oven, she removed the lid. 'Does anyone fancy a bowl of veggie broth?'

Jez's nostrils flared as the smell of warm soup wafted over him. 'If you've got enough, then I certainly wouldn't say no.'

Fetching three bowls out of a cupboard, Jill doled out the broth. Passing one of the bowls along with a spoon to Jez, she encouraged him to stay by the fire in order to dry out.

Taking a mouthful of the delicious soup, Jez swore he could feel it warming him to his toes. 'Perfect!' he said happily.

'So what happens now?' asked Dewi.

'Cadi asked Jez to telephone her at the Castaway,' said Jill, adding for Jez's benefit, 'That's the name of the B&B she's staying at in Portsmouth, with her pal Kitty.'

Jez furrowed his brow. 'But I asked Poppy whether Cadi might be staying with her pals in Portsmouth. Why on earth didn't she just say yes?'

Jill sat down on the seat next to his. 'Because she's trying to find Izzy's mam, and she doesn't want Izzy to get wind of it before she's sussed out what's what.' She gave a weary sigh. 'Our Cadi always means well, Jez, but for one reason or another it inevitably seems to backfire on her.'

'She's got a heart of gold,' Jez agreed. 'And she'd do anything for anyone. It's one of the many things I love about her.'

Dewi scraped the last of the soup from his bowl. 'If you ask me, the sooner you speak to our Cadi, the better.' He glanced at the clock above the small Welsh dresser. 'Time's ticking on. If you're ready, I think we should head down to the pub so that you can phone Cadi.'

'And what's wrong with the post office?' said Jill, arching an eyebrow.

'They don't serve beer,' replied Dewi, with a mischievous grin.

Jez quickly finished his soup, before placing his bowl in the sink. 'Thanks for the broth, Mrs Williams, it's exactly what I needed.'

Having fetched his coat from the hook, Jill held it up whilst Jez slipped his arms into the sleeves, now wonderfully warm. He grinned as she began doing the buttons up as though he were a toddler.

'Don't fuss, woman,' said Dewi. 'He's old enough to do his own coat.'

'I want to make sure he's warm,' muttered Jill. 'It's freezing out there, and Jez isn't used to winter in the hills.' Standing back, she watched as her husband gathered his own coat and scarf.

'I'll admit it's a fair old trek,' said Jez, 'but I'm glad I came.' He glanced around the cosy parlour. 'You've a lovely home.'

She smiled appreciatively. 'That's kind of you to say.'

Dewi opened the door. 'C'mon, lad.'

Passing through it, Jez turned to face Jill before the door closed.

'Goodbye, Mrs Williams, and thanks again.'

'Enough with the formalities, you must call me Jill – why, we're practically family!' Venturing onto the doorstep, Jill leaned up to kiss Jez's cheek. 'Take care of her for me, won't you?'

'I will. Goodbye Jill,' said Jez, before turning to follow Dewi, who was patiently waiting for him a little way off.

To Jez's relief, the pub wasn't far from the Williamses' home, and within minutes they entered through a low-slung doorway. Stamping his feet free of snow, Jez looked around him. He had assumed that the foul weather had prevented the villagers from leaving the warmth of their homes, but he could see now that he was wrong and that most of them had decided to take refuge in the pub. As they approached the bar, Dewi said something in Welsh to the barman, who gestured for Jez to follow him through to a room at the back. Indicating the phone, he left Jez to make his call.

Waiting anxiously for the woman who'd answered the B&B's phone to fetch Cadi, Jez's heart gave a joyous jolt as he heard her voice coming down the line.

'Jez?'

'Cadi darling, I'm so sorry.'

'Me too,' said Cadi. 'I don't know what my mam's told you …'

Jez quickly filled Cadi in on his arrival in Rhos, and everything that had transpired as a result.

'Oh, how I wish I was there with you,' cried Cadi. 'I've been so silly, Jez, but I've learned from my

300

mistakes and I promise I'll never interfere in someone else's life ever again.'

'You mustn't say that,' said Jez bluntly. 'After all, where would Izzy be if you hadn't stepped in? Still at home with that beast of a father of hers, that's where. You're a wonderful woman, Cadi, with a heart of gold, and I wouldn't want you to be any other way.'

There was a long pause before Cadi spoke. 'But what about Daphne and Aled?'

'You had to tell Aled,' said Jez, 'even I know that. As for Daphne? She was acting out of spite and I should've known better than to take any notice, but I was too wound up in my own insecurities to listen to my heart.'

Sniffing quietly, Cadi spoke softly. 'I can't believe you're in Rhos with my family, whilst I'm down here in Portsmouth.'

'It doesn't have to be that way,' said Jez.

'I haven't seen Izzy's mam yet,' said Cadi, 'and I can't just leave the girls on their own, not after the last time. This is my doing, and I've got to see it through.'

'Who says you have to come to me?'

'You mean, you could come here?'

He nodded. 'Why not? I don't have to be back until the twenty-seventh, and I can always collect my stuff from the Belmont en route to Portsmouth.'

'That would be wonderful, Jez,' said Cadi. 'I know the B&B where Kitty and I are staying has spare rooms. Would you like me to book one for you?'

Jez was beaming. 'Like it? I'd love it!'

'When do you think you can get here?'

'In the small hours of tomorrow morning,' said Jez confidently. 'I can catch the late train from Liverpool.'

'But if you do that, you'll be travelling all night. Why not catch the morning train?'

'On Christmas Eve?' He shook his head. 'Besides, I've already wasted too much time and I don't intend to waste another second.'

'I'm not sure what time the trains stop running from Wrexham,' said Cadi uncertainly.

'Then I'll catch a train from Chester,' announced Jez. 'I'll walk there if I have to.'

'You'll do no such thing,' scolded Cadi, 'especially in the snow.'

Jez wrinkled his forehead. 'How did you know it's snowing?'

'Because it's December and it always snows in Rhos during the winter months,' laughed Cadi. 'Now promise me you're going to be careful, because whilst I want you by my side, I'd prefer it if you were in one piece.'

'I promise.'

'Good!' Her tone softened. 'I can't wait to see you.'

'Nor I you.' He hesitated. 'And Cadi?'

'Yes?'

'I love you.'

He could hear the smile in her voice. 'I love you too.'

The operator announced that their time was up, before terminating the call.

Replacing the receiver, Jez entered the bar. He soon made out Dewi, who was sitting by a table with his three sons, the nearest of whom turned to greet him.

'Hello, Jez. I'm Alun, and these are my brothers, Arwel and Dylan.'

Jez shook each of the men by the hand. 'Nice to meet you all.'

302

Dewi indicated an empty stool. 'Take the weight off whilst I fetch you a drink from the bar ...'

Jez was grinning. 'Thanks for the offer, but I'm off to Portsmouth, so I shan't be stopping.'

Arwel lowered his drink from his lips. 'I dunno how you're goin' to get there. From what I heard, the buses aren't running, due to the snow.'

Jez cursed beneath his breath. 'But if the snow gets any worse, they might stop the trains too and I'll never get there.'

A man who was sitting close by leaned over. 'Is it an emergency?'

'To me it is,' confided Jez. 'You see, I wanted to spend Christmas with my fiancée, but it doesn't look like that's going to happen, unless I can find a way of getting to Wrexham – if the trains are still running, that is.'

The man appeared thoughtful. 'Not from Wrexham they won't, but I reckon my lad would run you over to Chester, if that's any good to you?'

Dewi pulled a doubtful face. 'I'm not so sure that's a good idea, John.'

Eager to stop Dewi putting the other man off, Jez butted in, 'I don't mind paying for his time, and the petrol, of course – unless you think the roads are too treacherous?'

Adjusting his cap, John got to his feet. 'He's used to drivin' in the snow. I shan't be a mo.'

Thanking the man for his assistance, Jez looked at Dewi and his sons, all of whom were staring at him as though something were amiss.

'What's up?'

Dewi glanced after the man who had left the pub. 'I'm not sure you're going to want a lift off his son.'

'Why not?' asked Jez, adding as a joke, 'I take it his son can drive?'

'He can drive all right,' said Alun, 'in fact he's been driving tractors most of his life.'

'That's all right then,' said Jez, although his face dropped. 'He's not going to try and take me to Chester in a tractor, is he?'

Dewi shook his head. 'It's not that. You see, John is—' He was interrupted by the door which had swung open at the back of Jez.

Turning to see who had entered, Jez found himself face-to-face with Aled and his father, John.

Aled raised an eyebrow coolly. 'We meet again.'

For the second time that day Jez wished the ground would swallow him up. Of all people, why did it have to be Aled? Realising that he was expected to respond, he nodded. 'We do indeed.'

John looked at them in surprise. 'I didn't realise you knew each other.'

'Not as such,' said Aled. 'This is Jez – Cadi's fiancé.'

'I didn't know Cadi was home—' John began, only to be interrupted by Dewi.

'The longer these two linger, the worse the snow will become.' He addressed Aled directly. 'Are you sure this is a good idea? Only the snow's pretty deep, and it doesn't look as though it's goin' to let up any time soon.'

Jez stood in temporary torment as he waited to hear the verdict. Would Aled still give him a lift to Chester or had he changed his mind, now that he knew who the passenger was?

Aled shrugged. 'I've driven in worse.' He turned to Jez. 'I'll start the engine.'

Jez turned to Dewi. 'It was good meeting you, albeit briefly.'

Dewi cupped his hand on Jez's shoulder. 'I hope you make the train.' Glancing outside, he grinned sympathetically. 'You must *really* love our Cadi.'

Jez laughed softly. 'Believe you me, I'd not be doin' this otherwise.' Looking over his shoulder, he bade Cadi's brothers goodbye before leaving the pub. Outside he saw that Aled was waiting for him in a flat-nosed Morris.

Jez settled into the passenger seat beside Aled. Not knowing what to say, he took some time before he actually spoke. 'I appreciate your help, especially as I know we haven't always seen eye-to-eye.'

Aled checked that the coast was clear before pulling slowly onto the main road. He turned to Jez. 'Haven't we? I wasn't aware we'd had words.'

Jez thought hard before speaking again. He was going to have to choose his words carefully if he didn't want to find himself walking the rest of the way.

'Cadi's a very honest woman,' he said. 'She tells me everything.'

Aled gazed steadily at the road ahead. 'I don't wish to appear flippant, but if that's true, why did you think she was in Rhos?'

Jez cursed himself inwardly. He hadn't been referring to Cadi's whereabouts, or even the business with Daphne. He'd been talking about Aled's feelings for

Cadi. He now said as much to Aled, adding, 'I don't know of many men who wouldn't get their dander up at the thought of another man pursuing their fiancée.' When he had finished his piece, he was pleased to see that Aled's cheeks had coloured ever so slightly.

'It's not as if I ever acted on my feelings,' said Aled defensively.

'Believe me,' said Jez, 'I'd not be sitting in the same car as you, if you had.'

Aled turned the windscreen wipers off as the snow eased. 'I know it's none of my business, but it's pretty obvious the two of you have had a falling-out. Would I be right in guessing it has something to do with Daphne?'

'She paid me a visit, just as soon as I got back to Liverpool,' said Jez. 'She couldn't wait to tell me how you and Cadi had been whispering in corners.'

Aled's jaw stiffened. 'Spiteful, vicious ...' He glanced at Jez. 'We wondered whether she'd try to get her own back, but I had no idea she'd turned on you.'

Jez hesitated. 'Didn't Cadi mention it?'

'I haven't spoken to Cadi for ages,' confessed Aled. 'In fact the last time we spoke, we decided to go our separate ways – friendship-wise.'

This was music to Jez's ears, but he wanted to delve a little further. 'Why's that?'

'Because she loves you and she didn't want there to be any misunderstandings.'

Jez's heart sank. He really had acted like an idiot.

Aled continued, 'I'm glad you've managed to patch things up with her, because Daphne isn't worth falling out over.'

'Did you ever blow the whistle on Daphne?' asked Jez, curious despite himself.

Aled scratched the back of his head. 'Nah, she's not worth it. I tried applying for my wings again recently, but they need me where I am.'

'I don't think I'd have taken it quite as well, had someone done that to me,' confessed Jez. 'After all, a pilot's position is nowhere near as dangerous as that of a rear-gunner.'

'Granted, but no one knows what might have been,' said Aled. He rested his elbow against the sill of the car window. 'Supposing I'd got my wings, who's to say my plane wouldn't be rusting at the bottom of the Channel? Or even shot down over France? No one knows what might have been; we only know what is, and so far I've been lucky. I'm bloody good at my job, and I'm not sure I'd trust someone else to keep me safe whilst I did the flying.' He hesitated before adding, 'Cadi taught me that.'

Jez smiled softly. 'Typical Cadi, always trying to look on the bright side.'

'She's right, though, and that's one of the reasons why I decided to let sleeping dogs lie.'

'So Daphne's going to get away with it?' said Jez bitterly. 'Hardly seems fair, after all the angst she's caused.'

'That's where our opinions differ,' said Aled. 'I don't think she's got away with it – not really. Daphne told me that she bitterly regrets fixing my papers, and I believe her.'

Jez was surprised to find himself warming to Aled. 'I think it's a good thing you found out.'

'Me too,' said Aled. 'No one wants to be married to a liar.'

'Lucky escape indeed …' Jez hesitated as the meaning behind Aled's words caught up with him. 'I didn't realise the two of you were that serious?'

Aled stared doggedly at the road ahead. 'There wasn't anyone else.'

Jez pulled his coat further around him. 'I see you've got yourself a new belle. I take it she's nothing like Daphne.'

'Marnie's as honest as the day is long,' said Aled. 'That's why I brought her home to meet the folks.'

'So it's serious then?'

'I'd not have brought her back otherwise,' said Aled. He shrugged. 'And I wanted her to see what it's like to be a farmer's wife.'

'Does that mean you're thinking of moving back, once all this is over?'

Aled nodded. 'It might have been different if I'd got my wings, but as it stands?' He looked at Jez. 'What about you? Do you think you'll stay on?'

'There's always a call for mechanics, so I shouldn't struggle to find work. As for Cadi, I know she wants to open a tea room or something similar.'

Aled jerked his head at the road ahead. 'Not much further.'

Jez settled into his seat. 'Thanks for this.'

Aled turned to face him. 'I know you weren't in Rhos for long, but what did you think?'

'Very quiet and olde-worlde,' said Jez. He glanced at the snow-covered trees that lined the side of the road they were currently on. 'Beautiful, though.' As he spoke, a large lump of snow fell from the branches, landing with a whump on the window. Blinded by the snow that covered the windscreen, Aled cursed loudly as he slammed his foot on the brake, but it was no use. The car didn't stop skidding until it hit something with a sickening crunch.

Cadi apologised to Mrs Wiggs for accepting yet another telephone call.

'No need for apologies,' said the older woman, 'that's what the phone's for.'

Taking the handset, Cadi addressed the unknown caller. 'Hello?'

'Cadi?'

She smiled. 'Hello, Dad. Is everything all right?'

There was an audible pause before Dewi spoke. 'It's Jez and Aled—'

Sighing irritably, Cadi cut her father short. 'What now? Please don't tell me they've had words' – an image of Jez clocking Aled formed in her mind – 'or worse.'

'We don't know,' replied Dewi truthfully.

'What do you mean, you don't know?'

'Aled was giving Jez a lift to Chester train station ...'

'So they've been getting on well then,' said Cadi tartly, annoyed at her father for worrying her unnecessarily.

'Not exactly,' confessed Dewi, 'the atmosphere was quite frosty when they met earlier in the day, and neither of them looked thrilled at the thought of getting into the same car.'

'Then why on earth did you let them?' cried Cadi. 'You must've realised things wouldn't go well! Where are they now?'

'That's what we're trying to find out,' said Dewi. 'Aled should've been back hours ago, but there's no sign of him. What with petrol rationing the way it is, nobody else has got enough fuel to get there and back. The villagers have got together and they're siphoning vehicles for any drop of petrol they can find, so that we can go and look for them.'

'Do you think Jez and Aled might've run out of petrol?' she asked hopefully.

'Maybe,' said Dewi doubtfully, 'but it's been snowing pretty heavily, and you know what the roads are like between here and Chester.'

'I do indeed, and quite frankly, Dad, I'm surprised you allowed Aled to leave.'

'He's a grown man,' objected Dewi. 'I can hardly take his keys off him.'

Sighing heavily, she held a hand to her forehead. 'Sorry, Dad, but I'm that worried.'

'I know you are, cariad, and believe me, we're doing everything we can to find out what's happened and bring them home safely.'

'Who's going?'

'Myself, Alun, John and Trefor.'

'The butcher?' cried Cadi incredulously. 'What on earth are you taking him for? Wouldn't you be better taking Dr Floyd, in case summat really has happened?'

'His car's not big enough,' answered Dewi simply, 'and if they've gone off the road' – hearing Cadi whimper, he continued hastily – 'and that's a big "if", then we need summat big that'll pull them back out, and Trefor's van's got more chance of doin' that than the doctor's Imp.'

310

Hearing someone calling for Dewi to join them, Cadi spoke hastily. 'Please telephone as soon as you know what's happened to them.'

Dewi nodded. 'Will do, love.'

'And take care,' said Cadi.

Hearing the click of the receiver, she placed her handset down. She was so deep in thought that she didn't hear Mrs Wiggs approach.

'Is everything all right, dear? Only you've gone quite pale.'

Nodding, Cadi elaborated. 'I'm expecting another phone call this evening. I'm afraid it might be quite late on, is that all right?'

Mrs Wiggs guided Cadi through to the room at the back of the B&B. 'More than all right. Now sit you down and I'll make you a nice cup of tea with plenty of sugar.' She glanced through to the dining room. 'I'll nip and get your pal first, though.'

She returned a few moments later with an anxious-looking Kitty, who took the seat next to Cadi. 'What's happened? Are you all right?'

Cadi quickly explained her father's side of the story. 'I'm really worried, Kitty.' She took the cup of tea that Mrs Wiggs had made her. 'Thank you. I'm sorry to be a nuisance.'

Mrs Wiggs tutted dismissively. 'You're not a nuisance, lovey.' She turned to Kitty. 'I'll serve your supper in here, so that you have a bit of privacy.'

'Thank you, this really is awfully kind of you,' said Kitty.

She waved a nonchalant hand. 'My pleasure, lovey. No one wants folk gawpin' at them when they're going through a tough time.'

Cadi smiled weakly. 'I really hope it's a case of something and nothing, but I know in my heart that things must have gone seriously wrong for Aled to be so late.'

'There's no point in speculating,' said Mrs Wiggs wisely. 'The best thing you can do is sit tight until you hear from your father.'

Jez slowly opened his eyes. His head was throbbing and his whole body ached. Wincing every time he tried to move, he became aware of something slowly trickling down the side of his face. Lifting his hand, he dabbed his fingertips against the liquid. He squinted at his hand to see if it was blood, but it was no use – he could barely see his hand, never mind anything else. Desperately trying to remember what had happened, he started as something moved in front of him. As it moved again, he realised it was the windscreen wipers. As they cleared more of the snow off the windscreen, moonlight flooded the vehicle and, to Jez's horror, his eyes fell on the recumbent form of Aled, who lay slumped over the steering wheel. In an instant Jez's memory returned. They had crashed.

He placed his hand on Aled's shoulder and shook him, gently but firmly. 'Wake up, Aled!'

But it was no use. Aled wasn't responding to any of his efforts. Jez's nostrils flared as the faint scent of petrol wafted towards him. Having attended many a crash site, he'd seen first-hand how quickly the flames could spread, and how explosive they could be if they ignited the petrol tank.

With the scent growing stronger, his fingers scrambled desperately along the car door until he found the catch. Grasping it firmly, he pulled hard at the same time as hefting his weight against it. To his relief, the door flew open and Jez tumbled into a bank of snow. Struggling to get to his feet, he took in his surroundings. There were no signs of life, and from what he could see, the car itself had come to a halt after colliding with a stone wall. He quickly stumbled his way round to Aled's side of the car and began heaving on the door handle. But it was pointless; the door was stuck fast. He thumped his fists on the window to see if he could wake him, but Aled didn't stir.

Jez made his way back round to the passenger side of the car and leaned in through the open door. He would have to try and pull Aled over to the passenger side in order to get him out. As he took hold of Aled's arms, he saw a large crack in the windscreen above Aled's head. For one horrible moment Jez wondered whether he was rescuing a body. He shook his head. Now was not the time for negative thoughts. Ignoring the pain that was searing through him, he managed to drag Aled's lifeless form over the seats and out of the car. Gasping from his efforts, Jez saw what he believed to be steam or smoke rising from the bonnet. Kneeling down, he ducked his head under Aled's arm and pulled him over his shoulder in the style of a fireman's lift. He didn't know where the strength had come from, but he was glad it had. Carrying Aled far from the car, Jez laid him down just as he began to stir. Disorientated and confused, Aled struck out at him.

Leaping back to avoid Aled's feeble attempt to protect himself, Jez spoke hastily. 'Aled, it's me, Jez. We've had a crash.' He pointed towards the car. 'I think the car's goin' to go up and, if she does, she'll attract every bomber from here to Berlin.' Without further explanation, he hurried back to the car and began piling snow onto the bonnet in a bid to stop the vehicle igniting. Seeing Aled stumbling towards him, Jez motioned for him to stop. 'Stay back. It's too dangerous,' he panted.

With the bonnet buried beneath the snow, Jez felt confident that he had averted disaster. Exhausted from his efforts, he sank onto the snow bank next to Aled. Looking around him, he raised a querying brow at Aled, who still appeared groggy. 'Do you have any idea where we are?'

Aled peered at their moonlit surroundings. 'I think we're near the Marford Hill.' He pointed weakly to the road they had been travelling on. 'The Trevor Arms is down there.'

Getting to his feet, Jez took off his coat and laid it over Aled. 'I'll go and get help.'

'You can't go on your own,' said Aled flatly. 'You haven't a clue where you are, and if you wander off the road we'll both be dead from hypothermia before they find us.'

Jez was going to object, but he knew Aled was right. Helping him to his feet, Jez placed his shoulder underneath Aled's arm, but Aled was determined that he could stand on his own two feet.

'I can manage,' he said obstinately, but as he tried to walk forward he sank to one knee, before Jez caught him.

Realising that Aled's pride was getting the better of him, Jez tried to make light of the situation. 'If you're going to insist on coming, we're going to do this together: agreed?'

Aled agreed, albeit reluctantly, and with Jez's support they began to descend the rest of the hill.

'I'm sorry about the car—' Jez began, only to have Aled cut him short.

'Nobody's fault, these things happen,' he said plainly.

'That's very generous of you.'

'It was my decision to take you,' said Aled. 'I could easily have walked away.'

Jez frowned. 'So why didn't you?'

Aled glanced sidelong at Jez. 'Because taking you to Chester would make Cadi happy.'

'So you did it for Cadi?'

Aled nodded, then winced. 'She's been a good friend. If it weren't for her, I'd still be with Daphne.'

'One good turn?' suggested Jez.

'Summat like that,' said Aled. But in his heart he knew he'd do anything to make Cadi happy.

Dewi's face fell as the van they were travelling in approached a large group of people gathered partway down the Marford Hill. With the crowd turning to see who was coming, one of the men waved them down. 'You can't go down there, mate.'

Dewi's heart dropped, as he feared he knew the answer to the question he was about to ask. 'Why, what's happened?'

'There's been a crash ...' the man began, before jumping back as Dewi leapt out of the vehicle and

315

began running down the hill as fast as his legs could carry him, with John hot on his heels.

Reaching the Morris, Dewi leaned in through the passenger door, which was still open. Looking back, he called out to the crowd, 'Where are they?'

One of the onlookers approached cautiously. 'Who wants to know?'

Dewi marched over and the man shrank back into the protection of the crowd. 'Just answer the bloody question,' Dewi snapped impatiently.

One of the women folded her arms across her chest. 'Not until we know who you are,' she said through pursed lips. 'You could be anybody.' She jerked her head in the direction of the car. 'Whoever drove that car didn't exactly hang about, so it's obvious they're up to no good.'

'Probably on the run,' called out another voice from the back of the crowd.

The woman arched an eyebrow. 'For all we know, they could be spies.' She looked Dewi up and down in a disapproving manner. 'You too, come to that.'

'Don't be so damned stupid!' blustered Dewi. 'They're no such thing.'

'You would say that, wouldn't you?' said the woman with a triumphant air.

He opened his mouth to give the woman a piece of his mind, when John hailed him from beside the Morris. Hurrying over, Dewi followed John's gaze towards two sets of footprints leading away from the car.

Dewi breathed a sigh of relief. 'Thank God for that.'

The woman had now bustled over, obviously intent on detaining them. 'Where d'you think you're going?' she barked, as the men climbed back into the van.

'To see if we can find our boys,' yelled Dewi, as Trefor drove off in the direction of the footprints.

As soon as they arrived at the pub the four men piled out of the van. Bursting through the doors, they startled Aled and Jez, who were sitting by the fire, each with a mug of warm cocoa. Aled viewed his father through the one eye that hadn't closed over. 'Dad!'

Seeing his son's condition, John hurried over. 'What happened? We saw the car ...'

'A bloody great lump of snow fell onto the windscreen, completely blinding us,' said Aled. 'I lost control and the rest – as they say – is history.'

Folding his arms across his chest, Dewi spoke in a chastising manner. 'You could at least have phoned to let us know you were all right.'

'We tried, but the phone lines are down because of the snow,' said Jez apologetically.

Stepping forward, Trefor beckoned to Jez. 'As we're here, I may as well give you a lift to the station.' He glanced at the others. 'I'm sure you fellows won't object to having a pint whilst you wait?'

Dewi shook his head. 'I'll come with Jez to see him off.'

John looked at his son. 'I think you should go to hospital – you've obviously taken a fair old crack to the head.'

'That's what I told him, but he won't have any of it,' said Jez.

Aled waved a hand dismissively. 'I've got a black eye that'll be a conversation starter for weeks to come, but apart from that I'm fine, honestly, Dad.'

'If you're sure ...' began John grudgingly.

'I am,' Aled assured him. He turned to Jez. 'Go on, and send my best to Cadi, won't you?'

Standing up, Jez turned to Aled, his hand out-stretched. He smiled as Aled shook it. 'Thanks for everything,' said Jez, 'you're a real gent.'

Aled chuckled softly. 'I bet you never thought you'd say those words.'

Jez grinned. 'Perhaps not, but then again, we all make mistakes.'

Dewi laid a hand on Jez's shoulder. 'C'mon, lad, you've not gone through all of this just to miss your train.'

Jez briefly shook hands with Alun and John. 'Thanks for coming to our rescue – greatly appreciated.' He turned to John. 'Sorry about your car. I know it was an accident, but even so.'

John shrugged. 'It's only a car. As long as you're both safe, that's all that matters.'

Leaving the warmth of the pub for the van, they were soon on their way to the train station.

'Our Cadi will be relieved,' said Dewi.

Jez raised his brow. 'Cadi knows?'

Dewi nodded fervently. 'Too right she does. She'd have my guts for garters if she thought I was keeping her in the dark. Besides, she was expecting you first thing tomorrow.' He hesitated. 'Aled told us how the accident happened, but he looked in a pretty bad way to me, and I saw that crack on his side of the windscreen.' He winced. 'It's a wonder it didn't knock him out cold.'

318

Jez explained the aftermath of the crash.

Dewi cocked an eyebrow. 'If you hadn't pulled Aled free, he might not be here.' He nudged Jez. 'You're a bloody hero.'

Jez rolled his eyes. 'Hardly.'

Dewi wagged a finger reprovingly. 'You might not think so, but I'm telling you, you are. Ain't that right, Trefor?'

Trefor nodded. 'But for your quick thinking, that car would've gone up – with Aled inside.'

Chapter Seven

Having received a phone call from her father the previous evening, Cadi knew all about Jez's accident and subsequent act of heroism. Delighted yet surprised to hear that he would still be travelling to Portsmouth, she was up betimes the next morning, so that she could meet his train when it arrived.

Now, as she stood on the platform, she peered along the track to see if there was any sign of the train. Seeing a cloud of white smoke puffing towards her, Cadi beamed. Jez was here at last. As the train pulled alongside the platform she desperately glanced into each carriage for a sign of her beau, but the passengers were crammed in like sardines, which she supposed was hardly surprising, considering that today was Christmas Eve.

After everything they'd been through, spending Christmas with Jez was going to be the icing on the cake. She gave a small gasp as she caught a glimpse of his smiling face. Waving excitedly, she walked alongside his carriage until the train came to a halt.

Clasping her handbag in both hands, she squeezed her way to the front of the crowded platform, where she waited with bated breath for the carriage door to be opened. To her delight, Jez was the first one off. Striding towards her, he dropped his kitbag to the floor before enveloping her in his arms and kissing her deeply. As Cadi melted into his embrace, she found herself wishing that the moment would last for ever. Lost in their love for one another, it was only when someone tripped over his kitbag that Jez reluctantly broke away. Apologising to the young man, Jez picked his bag up, swung it over his shoulder and placed his arm round Cadi. 'I've been waiting to do that since' – he puffed out his cheeks – 'since I got back from Africa.'

As they walked away towards the concourse, Cadi leaned her head against his chest. 'What a dreadful waste of time it's been.'

He nodded. 'But never again. What seemed important once is insignificant now, and if I can't learn from my own mistakes, then I should be paying more attention.'

Cadi nuzzled her cheek against him. 'I think that's a rule we could all abide by.' She glanced up at the underneath of his chin, flecked with the merest hint of stubble. 'Good journey? Apart from the first bit, of course.'

He kissed the top of her head. 'Dreadful. Every time the train pulled into a new station, it was all I could do to stop myself from being carried onto the platform.' He rolled his eyes. 'I lost count of the times someone had to apologise for stepping on my toes or elbowing me in the ribs. As for getting a seat, there was no chance – not with the number of women on board.'

Giggling softly, Cadi squeezed his waist. 'Ever the gentleman, that's my Jez.'

He glanced down at her. 'Don't you want to know what happened between myself and Aled?'

She shook her head. 'As long as you're safe, that's all that matters.' She stopped outside the entrance to the Castaway.

Looking up at the sign, Jez pulled her into his arms. 'I'd have done anything to spend Christmas with you.'

Cadi gazed into the depths of his eyes. 'I've missed you more than you'll ever know.'

'Oh, I know all right,' said Jez, 'because I feel the same way.' He brushed her hair back from her face before kissing her.

With his lips gentle against hers, Cadi dreamed of them running away together, leaving the war far behind them. She always felt safe in his arms and, with the familiar scent of his soap filling her senses, she was reminded of the first kiss they had shared on the dance floor of the Grafton. Oh, what she'd give to be back there right now.

Leaning away from the embrace, Jez kissed the tip of her nose. 'Shall we go in?'

Her arms still wrapped around his waist, she rested her cheek against his chest. 'Can't we stay just a moment longer?'

The answer to this came in the form of Kitty, who called to them from the door of the B&B, 'Coo-ee!'

Chuckling softly, Jez's eyes glittered as he gazed into Cadi's. 'I think we're wanted.'

Smiling, Cadi turned to face her friend. 'Kitty, meet Jez.'

Beaming from ear to ear, Kitty hastened down the steps that led to the front door. 'Hello Jez.' She jerked her head in a backwards motion. 'C'mon inside. I've left me cardie upstairs and it's brass monkeys out here.'

Following Kitty into the B&B, they joined her in the dayroom whilst they waited for Mrs Wiggs to come and show Jez to his room.

'What's gone on with Izzy's mam?' asked Jez. He was warming himself in front of the coal fire that burned merrily in the grate. 'Have you been to see her yet?'

Cadi shook her head. 'We thought it might be best if we waited for you.'

Jez's brow shot toward his hairline. 'Me? Why me?'

Cadi screwed her lips to one side before answering, 'To be on the safe side.'

Frowning, Jez looked from Cadi to Kitty and back again. 'What on earth do you think she's going to do?'

Kitty was staring at Cadi. 'Have you not told him?'

Jez was intrigued. 'Told me what?'

Both girls stepped towards him in a conspiratorial fashion. 'The house where Izzy's mam lives is a house of ill repute,' said Cadi. She had purposely lowered her voice when speaking the last two words, so much so that Jez had difficulty hearing her.

'It's a what?'

The girls immediately hushed him into silence. 'You know,' said Kitty, nodding frantically, 'it's a ...' she blushed crimson, more mouthing the word than speaking it aloud, 'brothel.'

The smile vanished from Jez's lips. 'Flippin' Nora, Cadi! Your mam never told me about this. Are you sure?'

'Pretty much,' confirmed Cadi, 'and Mam wouldn't have told you because I never told her.'

Jez asked the next question on his lips. 'How do you know?'

Cadi explained everything that had transpired from Ronnie's visit to Hillcrest House.

Jez eyed them from over the top of steepled fingers. 'You knew all this before I arrived, yet you were still intending to go?'

'We were pretty sure we'd be all right, with the three of us going,' said Cadi. 'But as soon as we knew you were coming, we figured you might as well come too.'

Kitty nodded fervently. 'We've got no experience when it comes to these types of places.'

'Neither have I!' cried Jez indignantly.

Hushing him into silence, the girls checked that they hadn't drawn any attention, before continuing.

'We know that,' said Cadi. 'What Kitty's *trying* to say is: we'd feel more comfortable with you there, in case things get heated.'

'I see.' He leaned back in his chair. 'So when are you planning on calling by?'

'Not tomorrow,' said Cadi. 'I don't think anyone would appreciate being knocked up on Christmas Day ...' She rolled her eyes as Kitty broke into a fit of the giggles. 'I don't mean in that way!' She glanced at Jez, who was looking stern. 'What's up?'

Shifting in his seat, he eyed her candidly. 'I could understand if you didn't want to get Izzy's hopes up unnecessarily, but that was before I knew her mam's profession, as it were. In my opinion, that changes everything, especially if it turns out to be true – it's not the sort of thing you want to hear second-hand. For a start, I think Izzy would want to play her part in rescuing her mam.'

Cadi looked at Kitty. 'We thought it would be kinder if we got her mam out of the situation first ...' She was about to continue, but she could see by the look on her friend's face that Kitty appeared to be having second thoughts. 'Kitty?'

Kitty sighed irritably. 'I can see things from both sides of the coin. Originally I thought it best if we saved Izzy from seeing her mam in those surroundings, but now I'm not so sure. If Jez is right, Izzy might feel as though everyone's in on it bar her – and that's not on, not when it's her mam.'

Cadi stared fixedly at Kitty, before sagging dejectedly. 'Once again I've put my oar in where it's not wanted.'

Jez clasped her hand in his. 'You've done no such thing. You're the most wonderful woman I know, Cadi Williams. You always put others first and try and do what's best for them. But no matter how much you try, you can't protect Izzy from the truth, not this time.'

'I knew I was right the moment I laid eyes on that note,' admitted Cadi. 'I was so excited that I might have found her mam, I didn't stop to think *why* she'd lied about her whereabouts. And when Ronnie telephoned, my heart sank into my boots because I *knew* it was Raquel, and I understood why she was being so evasive – but, without proof, I could kid myself that I'd got hold of the wrong end of the stick.' She sighed miserably. 'How on earth am I going to tell Izzy?'

'Is she working over Christmas?' asked Kitty thoughtfully.

'She's working Christmas Day, but she's got a couple of days off after that – Poppy too.' She hesitated before adding, 'Are you suggesting what I think you're suggesting?'

Kitty nodded. 'I think it's for the best, don't you?'

'Only what do I say to her?' A false smile etching her lips, Cadi pretended that she was talking to Izzy on the phone. '"Hi Izzy, it's me, Cadi. Guess what?"' Her face crumpled. 'I can't tell her over the phone – I just can't.'

'Tell her you've had your suspicions for some time, and you think she should come down to Portsmouth to see for herself,' suggested Kitty.

'And if she asks why I didn't say summat sooner?'

Kitty shrugged. 'Explain that you wanted to know for sure, before dragging her all the way to Portsmouth. And whilst you can't say for definite, you're fairly certain your hunch is correct.'

'That doesn't sound too bad, I suppose.'

'I agree,' said Jez. 'Don't mention the whole "house of ill repute" thing until Izzy's here, as it'll be a lot easier to explain when you're face-to-face.'

'But she's going to be so excited, and for what? Discovering what her mam does for a living will destroy her.'

'And you can't stop that from happening,' soothed Kitty, 'but you can be there to ease the pain.'

Cadi turned pleading eyes on Jez, then Kitty. 'Are you *sure* it wouldn't be better for us to soften the blow by finding out what's what first?'

Jez levelled with Cadi. 'Close your eyes and pretend you're Izzy.' Cadi did as he asked, so he continued, 'Imagine I'm telling you that I've rescued your mam from a brothel.'

As a surge of emotions swept through her, Cadi opened her eyes. 'If anyone's goin' to rescue my mam, it's goin' to be me.'

'Precisely,' said Jez.

Cadi smoothed her hair with the palm of her hand. 'Poor Mrs Wiggs, I bet she rues the day she had the telephone installed.'

As if on cue, Mrs Wiggs entered the room. 'Oh, hello! I didn't realise you'd arrived. It's Jez, isn't it?'

Picking up his kitbag, Jez shook the older woman's hand. 'That's right. And you must be Mrs Wiggs?'

Her cheery face broke into a smile. 'I am indeed. If you'd like to come with me, I'll show you to your room—' She broke off as Cadi gained her attention. 'Of course you can use the telephone, lovey, just leave the money in the box.'

'Thank you.' Cadi turned back to Jez and Kitty. 'Wish me luck.'

Jez hugged his kitbag close to his chest. 'Good luck.'

Echoing his words, Kitty followed Jez and Mrs Wiggs out of the lounge.

Cadi headed down the hallway and picked up the handset of the telephone. Crossing her fingers, she asked the operator to put her through to Izzy's base. As she waited, Cadi could feel her nerves rising, and when Izzy's voice came down the line she found herself at a loss for words. After a moment or two Izzy repeated herself, only louder and clearer, as though she thought Cadi was having difficulty hearing her.

'I said, "Is that you, Cadi?"'

'Yes,' said Cadi, her voice full of trepidation, 'it's me.'

Hearing the uncertainty in her friend's voice, Izzy spoke slowly. 'Is everything all right, only you sound a bit odd?'

Cadi held a hand to her forehead. 'I think we've found your mam. I've not seen her yet, but I'm pretty sure it's her.'

Cadi's heart dropped as Izzy gabbled excitedly into the phone, 'Where? In Portsmouth? Is that where you are?' She paused so briefly that Cadi didn't have a chance to answer. 'Why didn't you tell me? If I'd known, I could've come with you.'

This was the sort of response Cadi had been dreading. She sighed guiltily. 'I didn't want to raise your hopes in case I was wrong.'

'So you really think it's her then?' asked Izzy, her voice full of hope.

Cadi nodded miserably, only glad that Izzy couldn't see her face. 'Enough to say that I think you should come down, if you can.'

Izzy replied without hesitation. 'I can be there Boxing Day.'

'Will you be bringing Poppy?'

Cadi could hear the smile in Izzy's voice. 'Hang on a mo, I'll ask her – she's here with me now.'

Cadi turned pale as Izzy covered the mouthpiece with her hand. She would have to pray that her best friend wouldn't let the cat out of the bag until Cadi had had an opportunity to speak to her first. Within moments Poppy's voice came down the line.

'It seems we're coming to see you on Boxing Day. Is there anything I should know?'

'Yes,' hissed Cadi, 'I've not told Izzy about the house. We decided it was best to wait until we were face-to-face.'

'Right you are,' said Poppy.

Izzy's voice came back down the line. 'Talk about Christmas comin' early, this has to be the best news ever!'

Cadi grimaced. She hated knowing something that her friend didn't, but there was no way she was going to say anything over the phone. 'I'll see you on Boxing Day. Poppy knows where we're staying.'

There was an appreciable pause. 'Did Poppy know you'd gone in search of me mam?'

Realising that she had unintentionally dropped Poppy in it, Cadi spoke quickly. 'Yes, but I swore her to secrecy until we'd had a chance to investigate.'

'I can't wait to hear how you discovered me mam,' said Izzy. 'I'm that excited I don't think I'll get a wink of sleep.'

Cadi cursed herself inwardly. Hearing Izzy sounding so happy was more than she could stand. 'Can I have a quick word with Poppy before you put the phone down?'

'Course you can. Ta-ra, Cadi, and merry Christmas for tomorrer.'

Cadi just had a chance to say merry Christmas back before Poppy's voice came down the line.

'What's happened?' whispered Poppy.

Cadi filled her in on the conversation she had had in the lounge with Jez and Kitty. 'So what do you think?' asked Cadi anxiously. 'Am I doing the right thing?'

'Without doubt,' replied Poppy. 'Jez is right. It's never a good time to find out these things, but there is a right way, and I think you're doing it the right way.'

Cadi gave a weary sigh. 'I hope so, because now I've opened the bottle, there's no putting the genie back.'

'Well put.' Poppy's voice became muffled as she called out to someone over her shoulder. 'I'd best be off – Izzy wants to chat.'

'I expect she does,' said Cadi heavily.

'Ta-ra, Cadi, and merry Christmas.'

'Ta-ra, Poppy. Merry Christmas to you too.'

Hanging up the receiver, Cadi was about to go to her room when she saw Jez and Kitty descending the stairs.

'Jez has very sweetly asked if I'd like to join the two of you for an early lunch, but I think someone needs to tell Ronnie that our plans have changed, so I've volunteered to do that.'

'We could all tell Ronnie,' Cadi began, but Kitty was shaking her head.

'You and Jez have hardly seen each other since last Christmas.'

Cadi opened her mouth to insist that Kitty join them, but Jez pre-empted her thoughts. Placing his arm around her shoulders, he spoke teasingly. 'Are you not wanting to spend some alone time with your fiancé?'

Cadi slapped him playfully on the lapel of his jacket. 'You know full well that's not what I'm saying.'

'Then that's that sorted,' said Kitty brightly.

Realising that she was outnumbered, Cadi relented. 'All right, but can we meet back here later, so that I can introduce Jez to Ronnie?'

'We can indeed,' said Kitty. 'Now you two go off and enjoy your meal.'

As Cadi and Jez made their way down the steps of the B&B, Cadi looked down the street that led into the town. 'I'm afraid I can't recommend anywhere to eat because we've had all our meals in the B&B.'

Jez slipped his arm through hers. 'Portsmouth is a naval port, so we'll be spoilt for choice when it comes to pubs.'

'Did they have pubs in Africa?'

Jez laughed. 'Not that I ever saw.'

Cadi only knew two things about Africa: it was hot, and they had lots of wild animals roaming free. She imagined an elephant strolling past Jez as he worked on an engine. 'Did you see any elephants?'

'I don't think they live in Algeria,' mused Jez, 'but even so, we didn't see any wildlife – which isn't surprising, considering the conflict.'

Cadi gazed up at him. 'How bad was it?'

He squeezed her arm in his. 'It's how I imagine Armageddon would be.'

She swallowed. 'That bad?'

He nodded. 'There's nowt but sand for miles. The poor sods fighting on the ground are living in holes like rats.' He gave a brief hollow laugh. 'They even call them Desert Rats.'

Cadi's stomach gave an unpleasant lurch. 'Oh, Jez, how awful! I didn't realise ...'

He shrugged. 'You wouldn't, because you're too far away. All I can say is this: Bill's damned lucky he got out when he did.'

Cadi cuddled up to him as they continued to walk. 'I hope it ends soon.'

He gave a heartfelt sigh. 'You're not the only one.'

Hoping to steer the conversation in a different direction, she pointed to a sign above a pub. 'The Dolphin. That sounds nice; shall we take a look?'

Jez opened the door to let Cadi pass through.

As she entered, Cadi headed straight for the bar. If you wanted to know what an establishment was really like, that was a good place to start. Glancing along the bar's surface, she gave an approving nod, before turning to Jez. 'Clean bar, clean pub. I hope we're not too early for food.'

Jez pointed to a chalkboard that stood on the corner of the bar's top. 'Got to be fish and chips when you're staying so close to the sea, don't you think?'

Cadi smiled. 'I do indeed, especially if the batter's extra-crispy.'

Jez waited until the man in front had finished being served before making himself known to the barman.

'Can we order two fish 'n' chips, with a couple of rounds of bread and butter?'

The barman wrote the order down on a slip of paper. 'Anything to drink?'

Jez nodded. 'One' – he quickly surveyed the three pumps – 'Mild and ...' he looked at Cadi.

'Just a lemonade for me, please.'

With Jez's beer poured, the barman left it to settle whilst filling another glass with lemonade. 'There's a couple of empty tables on the far side of the bar. If you'd like to take a seat, I'll bring your food over when it's ready.'

Jez settled the bill before taking their drinks over to the table that Cadi had selected. 'The food smells delicious. I think we're in for a real treat.'

'Bet it won't be a patch on the grub we used to serve in the Greyhound, though,' said Cadi loyally.

Jez smiled. 'Nothing could ever compare to the meals you served in the Greyhound because it was you who made them, and that makes all the difference.'

She coughed on a sip of lemonade. 'Still the same charming Jez, I see!'

He gave her a cheesy grin. 'I guess it's in my nature, although in this case I was speaking the truth.' Cradling her hands in his, he gazed lovingly into her eyes. 'You make everything better.'

She smiled shyly. 'That's what I always say about you.'

'Do you know what that means?'

Cadi shook her head. 'Tell me.'

'That we're made for each other.'

Cadi glanced at his tanned complexion. 'I see you caught the sun; it looks good on you.'

Leaning forward, he wriggled his eyebrows suggestively. 'Wanna see my white bits?'

Cadi's brow shot towards her hairline as she whipped her hands out of his. 'No, I do not!' she cried, through smiling lips. She wagged a chastising finger. 'Honestly, Jez, what sort of woman do you take me for?'

He eyed her hopefully. 'One who wants to see my white bits?'

Giggling like a schoolgirl, Cadi shook her head. 'I think that sun must've gone to your head!'

Jez grinned without apology. 'Can't blame a feller for tryin'. I've not seen you properly for months and—'

'And we're not yet married, Jeremy Thomas,' Cadi reminded him.

His grin broadened as he held her hands in his. 'Would you like to see them, if we were?'

Chuckling softly, Cadi gave in to temptation. 'Let's just say things would be different if we were married.' Seeing the hope rise in his eyes, she added quickly, 'Although that's hardly a reason to march somebody down the aisle.'

His grin softened. 'I respect you too much to do that to you.' Rubbing his thumbs across the back of her hands, he added, 'I hope you know that.'

Gazing into his eyes, which sparkled lovingly at her, she murmured, 'I do.'

A kind-faced woman appeared by their table. Holding her tray up, she looked at them expectantly. 'Two fish and chips?'

Breaking hands, they leaned back so that she could place their meals down. 'That looks lovely!' observed Cadi.

The woman beamed proudly. 'Made with me own fair hands.'

Jez broke the batter on the fish. 'Extra-crispy, just how we like it.'

'There's spotted dick and custard for afters.'

'Go on then,' said Jez, 'you've twisted me arm.' He looked to Cadi. 'Are you havin' any?'

Cadi laughed softly. 'You've not finished your mains yet. How do you know if you'll still be hungry?'

He winked at her. 'There's always room for pudding.'

Cadi smiled up at the woman. 'Make that two. I'm sure he'll finish mine if I can't.'

Nodding, the woman left them to enjoy their meals.

Cadi blew gently onto a forkful of fish. 'Have you ever been full?'

Taking a slice of bread and butter, he folded it in half. 'Only when I was in Africa, but I'm not sure that counts.'

Cadi frowned. 'You told me you didn't like the food over there.'

He nodded fervently. 'I didn't – that's how you discover whether you're full or not.'

Laughing, she eyed him curiously. 'You never did say what it was that you didn't like; just that they'd eat anything.'

He shot her a dark look. 'Believe me, you don't want to know, especially when you're about to eat.'

A slow smile formed on her cheeks. 'It can't have been that bad ...'

Jez raised a singular eyebrow. 'Have you ever known me to refuse food?'

Shaking her head, she opened her mouth to speak, but Jez cut her off.

'Exactly! Now let's leave it at that or you'll not want to finish this lovely meal.' As a vision of the food that he'd seen in the Algerian markets entered his mind, he hastily turned the conversation to Izzy's imminent arrival.

'Have you thought about how you're going to break the news to Izzy?'

Cadi rolled her eyes. 'I've not thought of much else. I've decided to tell her as soon as she steps off the train. Any longer than that and I'd feel like I was lying to her. Does that make sense?'

'Perfect,' said Jez succinctly. He dislodged a piece of fish with his tongue. 'And if I were Izzy, I don't think I'd give a monkey's what me mam did for a living. I'd just be grateful to have one, and I'm damned sure she will feel the same.'

'You see?' said Cadi. 'There I was worrying about how Izzy will take the news, and you make everything better.' She gazed affectionately at him. 'I'm so glad you're back from Africa. I hope to God they don't call on you again, like they did the first time.'

Jez stopped chewing his mouthful. He had been lying to Cadi, and now was the perfect opportunity for him to come clean. He gained her attention by placing down his knife and fork. 'There's summat you need to know ...'

Cadi's face dropped. 'They're not sending you back?'

He shook his head. 'No – or at least, not as far as I know. It's not that. You see, I'm afraid I wasn't entirely truthful with you about being selected to go to Africa.'

Cadi nodded knowingly. 'Daphne wasn't lying, was she?'

Jez shook his head. 'When you assumed I'd been selected, I hadn't the heart to tell you I'd volunteered – mainly because I regretted doing so.'

'Oh, Jez!'

'I'm so sorry. I should've put you straight, especially when Daphne told you the truth, but I couldn't.'

She smiled kindly. 'I think we've done enough apologising for one day, don't you?'

'Aren't you cross with me?' he asked, incredulously.

Her smiled broadened. 'I'm proud of you for volunteering for summat when you didn't have to. I'm also grateful that you're back in one piece, because at the end of the day that's all that matters.'

Picking up his cutlery, Jez continued with his meal, but not before adding, 'I've made a lot of mistakes lately, the biggest one being Aled.'

She furrowed her brow. 'I don't understand?'

'I blamed Aled for all our troubles, but he wasn't really to blame. I *know* he's keen on you, Cadi, but that's hardly a reason to hang someone. And it's not as if he actually tried to steal you out from under me – even though I accused him of trying to do exactly that.'

She smiled. 'He's a charmer, much like yourself, but Aled would never try it on with a betrothed woman.'

'I know; that became clear on our journey to the station.'

'I must admit, I did wonder how the two of you got on, because my dad said that neither of you looked thrilled at the prospect of sharing a car.'

Jez laughed out loud. 'That's a good way of putting it, and indeed your father was right, but it did give us a chance to chat, speak our minds and clear the air.' He shrugged. 'Aled's a decent feller and, after our experience, I'd even go so far as to say he's a friend.'

Cadi was delighted. 'Now *that's* what I call progress!'

'He could've blamed me for wrecking his car – let's face it, he wouldn't have been out driving at all, if it wasn't for me – but it never even crossed his mind,' said Jez.

'And you saved his life, by all accounts,' Cadi reminded him.

'Sometimes it takes summat disastrous to make you see sense,' said Jez. 'I think that's what happened between me and Aled.'

'I'm proud of you, Jez, not only for volunteering to go to Africa, but for being brave enough to tell me the truth when you didn't have to. And not just that, but for getting into a car with Aled when you didn't want to, simply so that we could spend our Christmas together. It takes a real man to admit his mistakes, but a bigger one to sort them out.'

Jez beamed. It was going to be the perfect Christmas after all.

Izzy had been so excited with the news that Cadi had found her mother, she could hardly wait until Poppy was off the phone before announcing that she was going to phone Mike and tell him the good news.

'He'll be cock-a-hoop,' said Poppy. She glanced at the clock above the door to the NAAFI. 'Is that the time? I'll have to dash. I said I'd meet Geoffrey in the camp cinema.'

'Canoodling in the back row, eh?' teased Izzy.

'That's what back rows are for,' chuckled Poppy, before hurrying off.

Izzy picked up the receiver and asked the operator to put her through to Mike's base.

'Izzy?'

Just hearing his voice made her smile. 'It certainly is, and guess what?'

He hesitated. 'Not another promotion?'

'Better. I've found my mam.'

She could hear the exhilaration in his voice when he spoke. 'Darling, that's fantastic. But how?'

Izzy went on to explain how she had heard the news from Cadi, finishing with, 'So I shall be off to Portsmouth on Boxing Day. I don't suppose you could join me – only I'd love for Mam to meet you, and vice versa of course?'

Mike spoke ruefully. 'There's nothing I'd like more, but I think I've got more chance of flying to the moon.'

She was disappointed, but not surprised. 'I didn't think you'd be able to, but it's always worth asking, just in case.'

'I'll be with you in spirit,' said Mike, before voicing the thought uppermost in his mind. 'How did Cadi find her?'

'I'm not really sure,' Izzy confessed. 'She didn't say much, simply that she was more or less certain she'd found my mam.'

He hesitated. 'I don't mean to play devil's advocate, but if she's not seen your mam, how can she be sure she's got the right woman? I've always thought of Cadi as being extremely well organised as well as efficient, and this seems a bit ...'

Izzy finished the sentence for him. 'Wishy-washy.'

'Yes,' said Mike lamely. 'I don't understand why she waited all this time, if she was going to tell you anyway. It doesn't make sense.'

'You're right, it doesn't, which means that something must have happened to change her mind.'

'I wonder what?' mused Mike.

'I don't know, but I think I know a girl who might,' said Izzy softly.

'Oh?'

'Poppy,' said Izzy, 'because she knew Cadi had gone in search of me mam, but kept quiet.'

'But if something has happened to change Cadi's mind in the meantime, I doubt Poppy will be any the wiser,' said Mike pointedly

'Maybe, but Cadi asked to speak to Poppy after she'd spoken to me. What do you suppose that was about?'

Mike drew a deep breath before letting it out. He really didn't like getting mixed up in suppositions, but he thought Izzy had a point and he said as much.

'There's only one way to find out,' said Izzy.

'I understand that you have a lot of questions,' said Mike, 'and quite frankly I'd be the same, in your shoes. But remember, you might not always like the answers.'

'I know,' said Izzy, 'but I'll not settle until I've got to the bottom of this.'

Wishing him goodnight, she headed for the cinema, where she waited for Poppy and Geoffrey to come out of the movie.

*

340

Once Poppy had arrived at the cinema, she saw that Geoffrey was already waiting for her.

'Sorry I'm late,' she panted. 'We had an unexpected phone call.'

'We?' queried Geoffrey as the pair took their seats inside.

Poppy quickly told him of the phone call with Cadi. 'I had no idea that Cadi was going to call,' she confessed, 'and I'm rather surprised at how well Izzy took the news. If I were her, I'd have asked a lot more questions.'

'Perhaps she was just happy to hear that Cadi had found her mam,' said Geoff reasonably.

'Undoubtedly,' agreed Poppy, 'but that's because she didn't have time to think.'

'Are you worried she'll start asking questions when she has?'

Poppy nodded. 'Because I don't want to lie to her, but on the other hand, I don't want to be the one to break the awful news.'

'And Cadi's sure it's Izzy's mother?'

'I think she's always known,' mused Poppy. 'I reckon we both did, but hoped we were wrong.'

'Well, there's no going back now,' said Geoffrey. 'And you can only do your best. If she asks you summat outright, you'll have to answer truthfully. Better that than try and skirt around the issue or change the subject. Izzy's not soft – she'll soon realise summat's up.'

'I know she's not, which is why I'm not looking forward to the next couple of days,' confessed Poppy.

With the lights dimming, she leaned in to Geoffrey as he placed his arm round her. She was aware of the

341

film starting, but her mind was still on Izzy. If she purposefully avoided her friend, then maybe she could get away with it. On the other hand, that wasn't fair on Izzy. If the boot were on the other foot, Poppy knew she would definitely have a question or two, after having time to think. By the time the credits rolled, Poppy had decided that she would have to grin and bear it, should Izzy come asking questions. She said as much to Geoffrey as they vacated their seats.

Stepping outside, Poppy wasn't altogether surprised to see Izzy leaning against the fence.

Seeing her friends, Izzy stood up. 'I don't suppose you've time for a quick chat?'

Poppy nodded. 'Always.' As she kissed Geoffrey goodbye, she heard him whisper 'Good luck' into her ear.

'I thought it best if we chat on the parade ground,' said Izzy as she led the way. 'It'll be empty at this time of day and I don't particularly want to be overheard.'

A sudden thought entered Poppy's mind. What if Cadi had telephoned Izzy whilst they'd been in the cinema? Fearing that her friend might already know the truth, Poppy spoke with anticipation. 'Has summat happened?'

Izzy shook her head. 'Only I've had time to think, and it doesn't make sense that Cadi would try and bring me down to Portsmouth before she's seen my mam.'

Poppy ran her tongue over her lips. 'I thought Cadi was more or less certain it was your mam?'

'More or less isn't certain, though, is it?' said Izzy almost accusingly. 'And that's why it doesn't make sense.'

342

Poppy groaned inwardly. She might have agreed it would be better to not shirk the issue, but now that the time had come, she found herself doing just that. 'If Cadi says she's more or less certain, then I'd say the odds are stacked in your favour.'

Izzy looked at Poppy kindly. 'I'm sorry to ask, Poppy, but what did Cadi say to you after I got off the phone with her?'

Poppy was sunk. It was the outright question she had been dreading. She heaved a resigned sigh. 'You've heard the expression "Ask me no questions and I'll tell you no lies"?'

Izzy's face fell. She had suspected something was amiss, and Poppy's answer had confirmed her worst fears. 'Please, Poppy. I've been going out of my mind wondering what it is that's so bad Cadi can't tell me. Has my mam got another family? I wouldn't mind if she had; I suppose I'd kind of expect it, after all this time ...'

'Not as far as I know,' replied Poppy truthfully.

'Then what? Because something's not right.'

Poppy slipped her arm around Izzy's shoulders. 'As long as we find your mam, does it really matter?'

'It shouldn't, but I can't help the way I feel. And whilst I know I shouldn't keep asking, I can't help but think summat terrible has happened to her ...' As the last words left Izzy's lips, a truly awful thought entered her mind. She looked at Poppy, grey-faced. 'Is she dead? Is that what Cadi's found: a tombstone with my mam's name on it?'

'No!' cried Poppy. 'It's nothing like that – honest to God it's not.'

Izzy's mind began to race with possibilities. 'Is she seriously ill? On her deathbed in some hospital? Or ... or ...' She buried her face in her hands. But Poppy had had enough. Watching Izzy speculate, when she had the answer, was torturous for them both.

'Cadi thinks your mam might be living in a house of ...' Try as she might, Poppy couldn't bring herself to say the words.

Izzy's tear-stained face appeared from between her hands. 'Of what? Lunatics?'

Poppy was blushing madly. 'Women who work for their living.'

Izzy furrowed her brow. 'That doesn't sound so bad ...' But the intensity of the look on Poppy's face caused her to think again. 'You mean a workhouse?'

'No,' said Poppy, her eyes pleading with Izzy to get the answer right.

Izzy turned the words over in her mind, and looked up at Poppy sharply. 'Women? As in the plural?'

Hoping that her friend had formed the correct conclusion, Poppy nodded. 'Sorry, Izzy.'

'You say she's living there, but what you really mean is she's a working girl – the same as the others.'

Poppy held up her hands. 'I can't honestly say, because we don't know for certain that she's living there at all.'

'By "there" do we mean Hillcrest House?'

Poppy nodded. 'I'm afraid so.'

'But what made Cadi go looking for my mam there, especially when we'd already received a letter stating the contrary?'

'It was the letter that first caused Cadi to think ...' Poppy went on to explain how Cadi had examined the handwriting, drawing the conclusion that they had been penned by the same person. She then told Izzy of Ronnie's involvement and the subsequent outcome. 'Which is why Cadi went to Portsmouth,' concluded Poppy, 'as she needed to be sure before saying something.'

'So what made Cadi change her mind – about telling me, I mean?'

'Throughout this whole affair Cadi's been trying to protect you, hoping against hope that she was wrong. She's realised she's been kidding herself, and that no matter how hard she tries, you're still going to get hurt.'

Izzy's bottom lip trembled as she gave Poppy a rather watery smile. 'Typical Cadi, always putting others first.'

Poppy sagged with relief. 'I'm so sorry, Izzy. None of us wanted it to be true, but we don't always get what we want.' She eyed her friend through thick lashes. 'Are you mad at us for not including you from the start?'

Izzy shook her head fervently. 'All you and Cadi have ever done is look out for me. Had Cadi suggested the handwriting was similar, I would have dismissed the idea as being a fanciful waste of time.' A slight frown creased her brow. 'Was that the only thing that caught her interest – only it does seem a bit of a long shot?'

'That and the fact that whoever wrote on the envelope had opened it first, which is unusual in itself.'

345

'Unless they'd opened it by accident, only realising they'd made a mistake when they read the contents,' said Izzy simply.

Poppy's mouth fell open. 'We didn't think of that.'

Izzy smiled reassuringly. 'You see? I'd have put a spanner in the works straight off the bat. It's far better that Cadi went about this under her own volition.'

But Poppy couldn't stop herself mulling over Izzy's words. 'What if we've made a mistake?'

Izzy shrugged. 'Then we'll find out on Boxing Day.'

Poppy raised a surprised eyebrow. 'You still want to go then?'

Izzy's eyes glittered. 'Too right I do! I've not done anything this exciting since the day I done a runner from my dad's. And if my mam *is* in that house, then I'm going to be the one that gets her out!'

After the visit of the unknown woman to Hillcrest, Raquel couldn't shake the incident from her mind. Her first reaction had been to accuse Eric of trying to blackmail her, but something about that had been bothering her. Eric would have to know what went on at Hillcrest before he could even think of blackmailing her. If that was true, then how had he found out? She imagined him standing on the docks where he worked, chatting to a sailor. Her heart sank. Sailors were part and parcel of a working woman's life. It would only take someone to mention her by name ... She shook her head. Too big a coincidence.

Holding Eric's last letter between her fingers, she watched as a tear fell onto the page, smudging the ink.

She'd read it at least a hundred times and could probably recite it by heart. But for some reason, even though the words were cruel, she found herself reading it once more:

Raquel

How dare you make out like you're the innocent one, after everything you've done! Asking me to look after Izzy, as if you think I wouldn't! But don't you fret, I'll look after her all right, and I'll make sure she knows the truth about her mam whilst I'm at it. Because she needs to know that lies roll off your tongue with ease, and if it weren't for your sluttish behaviour, she'd still have a mother. You make out like leaving Liverpool is some big sacrifice, yet we both know you're only going to ease your own conscience. Hardly surprising, when you consider the truth. What sort of mother gives up her child for another man? You disgust me. I hope you rot in hell.

Raquel folded the letter and placed it with the others. Eric's words had reminded her just how nasty he could be. Blackmail wasn't beyond his capabilities – far from it. Yet there was still a niggling doubt in the back of her mind. The woman who'd come looking for her was wearing a WAAF uniform and, try as she might, Raquel couldn't envisage a scenario where Eric would have cause to talk to someone in the services; and even if he had, she felt certain they wouldn't do his bidding.

She turned her mind back to Izzy's letter. If it was genuine, then Izzy might really be looking for her; not

347

only that, but it also meant Eric was dead. The girl who called by wasn't a Scouser, that was obvious from her accent, but that didn't mean to say she didn't know Izzy. Especially if Izzy was in the WAAF. Briefly, she imagined her daughter, a grown woman in WAAF uniform. Could she really have escaped the clutches of her father? Hope rising, it quickly faded again as another question came to the forefront of her mind. How could Izzy possibly know her address? She couldn't – that was the simple answer. The only person who was privy to that information was Eric, and there's no way he would have told his daughter. He would've seen hell freeze over first. The thought of Eric keeping the letters entered Raquel's head briefly, before being dismissed. He would most likely have burned her letters as soon as he read them, if not before.

She held her head in her hands. Dolly had expressed the opinion that Raquel should at least look into the truth behind the letter, especially if it meant she could get away from the Finnegans. She gave a short, mirthless laugh. The thought of Eric trying to extort money from her was ludicrous. Every penny she earned went straight to the brothers. She slowly lifted her head. She might hate them, but if the Finnegans got wind that Eric was trying to blackmail her, they would pay him a visit and put an end to his shenanigans, perhaps permanently. If she were to write back, she could arrange to meet the letter-writer in one of the cafés. If it was Eric, she'd tell him to sling his hook whilst he still could. And if not? She'd be reunited with her daughter; and she might even escape from the Finnegans. After all, if Izzy never visited the house, she need never know the truth …

Her heart sank as she remembered the WAAF who'd already called by. There was no doubt the young woman knew where she was, and of course she would have told Izzy of her findings. In which case it was too late: the cat was already out of the bag. Raquel nodded decidedly. If she wrote to Izzy and got nothing back, then she'd know that her daughter had changed her mind about wanting to get in touch; if, on the other hand, Izzy did write back … A smile crept its way up Raquel's cheeks. It would mean that Izzy wanted to know her mother despite everything, and she could then be reunited with her.

It was Christmas Day and Cadi, Jez, Kitty and Ronnie were sitting in the guest lounge of the B&B, discussing their plans.

'I thought we could go for a walk through the city after lunch, take in some of the sights,' suggested Ronnie.

'Are you having your Christmas dinner with us?' asked Kitty.

Ronnie nodded. 'I didn't want to be a burden to Mrs Wiggs, but she insisted, saying that she'd already bought in extra.'

'She's a lovely old girl,' noted Cadi. 'We fell on our feet coming here.'

'She lost her son in the first lot – whilst he was fighting in France,' said Kitty. 'She said that knowing he was with his friends when he passed brought her great comfort. She likes seeing us all together, because it reminds her of him and his friends.'

'Poor woman,' said Cadi quietly. 'I had no idea.'

Kitty smiled fleetingly. 'You've been pretty busy, what with one thing and another, so me and Mrs W have had plenty of time to chat.'

Jez looked through to the area where their landlady disappeared whenever she wasn't busy with the B&B. 'Has anyone seen Mr Wiggs?'

Kitty grimaced. 'She's never mentioned him, so I've not asked. Sometimes it's better that way.'

'Why don't we ask if she'd like to join us at our table?' said Ronnie.

Kitty smiled happily. 'I think that's a marvellous idea.'

Standing up, Jez stretched. 'Anyone fancy a walk before lunch?'

Cadi nodded. 'I'll fetch my coat and hat.' She turned to the girls. 'What about you two?'

Ronnie shook her head. 'I've only just thawed my toes out. Take it from one who knows, it's brass-monkey weather out there.'

Kitty shivered. 'Sorry, but I'm also going to give it a miss. After all, I can't leave poor Ronnie on her own, sitting in front of a nice cosy fire, drinking cocoa.'

Jez finished knotting his scarf. 'Looks like it's just the two of us.'

'Shan't be a mo,' said Cadi. She disappeared to her room, where she hastily fished out the socks that she had bought Jez as a Christmas present. Being short of money, the girls had agreed that they would buy themselves a sweet treat instead of splashing out on a gift for each other.

'That way we get summat we want, without breaking the bank,' reasoned Ronnie.

Cadi had bought herself a bar of Fry's Chocolate Cream; Kitty had her favourite, Everton mints; and Ronnie had bought sherbet lemons.

Tucking the socks into her pocket, she headed down the stairs to where she saw Jez waiting for her by the front door.

As they descended the steps of the B&B, Jez breathed in the sea air. 'You can't beat that smell! Reminds me of home, so it does.'

Cadi smiled as she tucked her arm into the crook of his elbow. 'Lovely, isn't it?'

He twinkled down at her. 'Beautiful.'

Smiling coyly, Cadi gave him a playful dig with her elbow. 'Charmer!'

Jez produced a small package from the pocket of his greatcoat and passed it to Cadi. 'I know it's short notice, so I don't expect anything in return.' Stopping in her tracks, Cadi removed her gloves so that she could peel back the delicate tissue paper. Staring at the brooch in the palm of her hand, she looked up at him. 'It's beautiful, Jez, but it must've cost you an arm and a leg!'

Jez beamed. 'I'm glad you like it. I wasn't sure if it was your thing, as I've never seen you wearing a brooch before.'

Her brow shot toward her hairline as he pinned the delicate-looking brooch of roses to the lapel of her jacket. 'Only because I can't afford summat this beautiful.'

Jez's beam broadened. 'You're worth every penny – or should I say franc, because I bought it whilst I was in Africa.'

Blushing, Cadi handed him her present. 'I'm afraid I haven't got you anything anywhere near as grand ...'

Jez unfolded the socks. 'Nonsense! These are perfect, and much needed, I might add.'

Cadi lowered her gaze. 'Not the same as a brooch, though ...'

Jez nudged her playfully. 'I'd look silly sporting a brooch, don't you think?'

Cadi giggled. 'Possibly.'

He placed his arm around her shoulders. 'Besides, it's the thought that counts, and I'd far rather have summat practical. And if you could smell my old ones, you'd know I really needed socks.'

Cadi gazed down at the brooch, the petals of which caught the winter sunlight beautifully. 'Why roses?'

He smiled wistfully. 'I remember you saying how being the Rose Queen had made you feel special, and I rather hoped this might have the same effect.'

She smiled happily. 'It certainly does – especially coming from you.'

He kissed the top of her head. 'Are you looking forward to seeing the girls tomorrow?'

Cadi pulled a face. 'Yes, because I haven't seen them for ages, but I'm worried for Izzy.'

'I think she'll cope better than you think. Living with Eric for all those years has toughened her up.' He shrugged. 'She's probably realised summat's amiss.

After all, if we'd thought harder, we'd have asked more questions, and maybe the answer wouldn't have come as quite such a surprise.'

'You're right, as always. Why didn't we question how Izzy's mam was supporting herself? No one can afford to do a moonlight flit to the other end of the country and live there without money.'

'Do you think she might have been doing the same sort of thing in Liverpool?' asked Jez, his brow rising sharply.

'No,' said Cadi decidedly. 'She probably worked as a maid or cleaner, summat like that. The pay wouldn't be great, but it would be enough to get her to Portsmouth.'

Jez nodded slowly. 'That makes sense. I wonder what happened when she got to Portsmouth? I'd have thought the city was in need of maids and cleaners?'

'Of course, but maybe it's a case of who you know? Arriving in a different city with no friends might have been harder than Raquel thought.' She shrugged. 'Women don't have the same opportunities as men. That's why I wanted to go to Liverpool in the first place, so that I could make summat of my life, be my own boss and pay my own wage – one that's equivalent to a man's.'

'Do you still want to run your own business?' enquired Jez. 'It's summat me and Aled talked about before we had the accident.'

She eyed him curiously. 'You did?'

He pushed his free hand further into his pocket. 'Aled reckons he'll probably end up back on the farm, because it doesn't look as though he's going to pilot a plane any time soon, and I said I'd get a job as a mechanic.' His eyes glittered down into hers. 'I know you'll make a huge success out of whatever it is you choose to do.'

Cadi smiled. 'That's what my mam said before I left for Liverpool.'

'And she was right. You've hardly been in the WAAF more than five minutes and you've already made corporal.'

'If you're going to do a job, do it well,' said Cadi. 'I must admit I'm surprised to hear that Aled's decided to go back to the farm. Daphne's got a lot to answer for.'

'That woman's poison,' said Jez, 'and whilst I hate her for interfering in our relationship, it's nothing compared to what she did to Aled.' He gave a hollow laugh. 'And Daphne reckons she loved him.'

'I'm glad he's got himself a new girlfriend,' conceded Cadi. 'Aled deserves some happiness, after what Daphne put him through.'

'Just think,' said Jez, 'a year ago today we were in the park singing carols. Little did we know then how much our lives were going to change.'

'God, yes!' said Cadi. 'From Izzy putting Eric in his place, to learning the truth – at least in part – about her mother's disappearance.'

'An awful lot can happen in a year,' said Jez. 'That's why I reckon you should act now, as you may not have a tomorrow – or, to put it another way, strike whilst the iron's hot.'

'Too true,' said Cadi.

He smiled down at her. 'Does that mean you'll agree to be my wartime bride?'

She shook her head sadly. 'I know you think I'm being silly, but I feel like we'd be tempting fate, which is why I'd rather wait until we can do it properly. Besides, who wants to be walkin' up the aisle one minute and leggin' it down the nearest air-raid shelter the next, with moanin' Minnie instead of wedding bells?'

'As long as that's the only reason,' said Jez.

'You know it is, Jeremy Thomas,' chided Cadi. 'Besides, I want my whole family present when we marry, and I'm including Maria, Bill and the girls in that. The way the war's going, who knows when that will be.' She tutted beneath her breath. 'I rather hoped the whole thing would be over when America joined, didn't you?'

He shrugged. 'It's going to take a lot more than their presence to bring this thing to an end.'

'But surely there can't be any doubt?' said Cadi, her eyes full of hope as she stared eagerly up at him. 'The Americans have got a huge army, and loads of money. Quite frankly, I can't see how we could lose, with them on our side.'

'Only the Krauts have dug themselves deep into the heart of Europe, and they won't be easy to winkle out,' said Jez. Seeing Cadi's downturned mouth, he smiled reassuringly. 'But, yes, I do think we'll win. It's just going to take time.'

'Well, let's hope it's sooner rather than later,' said Cadi.

'Indeed,' agreed Jez, 'even if it's only to get you to walk down the aisle.'

Cadi laughed. 'Perhaps you should write a letter to that Roosevelt feller – tell him your dilemma and see if you can get him to pull his finger out.'

Jez shrugged as though this were the easiest thing in the world. 'If that's what it takes!'

Izzy and Poppy took their place on the train that would take them on the final leg of their journey. 'I'm glad I don't have to do this every day of the week,' muttered Izzy, turning her face away from a soldier's out-stretched armpit.

Poppy tried to swallow the smile that was threatening to grace her cheeks. Only when Izzy shot her a look of reproach did she allow the smile to form. 'I'm sorry, but it's better than the last train we were on.'

'Only because you were the one squished in the middle,' hissed Izzy, '*and* you weren't facing someone's' – she grimaced as she glanced towards the soldier who was holding on to the rack above her head – 'armpit.'

'Maybe not, but I did have that rotten little boy, covered in goodness knows what.' She pulled a disgusted face as the vision appeared in her mind's eye, and glanced down at her skirt. 'I swear he was using me as a hankie.'

Izzy relented slightly. 'All right, mebbe this isn't so bad ...' She fell silent as the soldier's distinctive body odour wafted towards her. Surreptitiously placing her hand over her nose and mouth, she spoke through her fingers. 'How long before we arrive in Portsmouth?'

'About half an hour or so, so not too long,' replied Poppy. 'Have you any idea what you're going to say to your mam? Assuming Cadi's suspicions are proved right, of course.'

'That I love her, and I don't believe a word that left me Dad's lips.' Izzy removed her hand from her face as the soldier shifted his position. 'I've made enquiries at our hotel to see if they've got a spare room, and they've said they'll pencil me in.'

'What did you tell them?'

A faint smile crossed Izzy's face. 'That my mam might be joining me.'

'That's all very well, but we're only stopping the one night,' said Poppy. 'Where's your mam goin' to stay after that?'

'According to Cadi, Maria's been having trouble getting help, and I reckon my mam would be perfect for the role.'

'How do you think your mam would feel about goin' back to Liverpool?'

'She's bound to feel apprehensive,' mused Izzy, 'but West Derby Road is miles away from where we used to live. So she's hardly likely to bump into anyone she used to know. Besides which, Maria can offer bed, board and a wage. I can't see her turning an offer like that down, can you?'

'I can't,' Poppy agreed, 'but going back's not going to be easy, no matter how far she is from Eric's old stomping ground.'

'Maybe she'll sign up, like we did?' suggested Izzy.

'I wonder why she didn't do that already?' supposed Poppy.

Izzy stared at her. 'Are you deliberately throwing obstacles in the way?'

'No,' Poppy assured her, 'but I think we need to think these things through before we go wading in.' She smiled sympathetically. 'If we have a decent plan in place, then your mam's far more likely to agree to leave.'

Izzy's eyes rounded. 'Surely you can't be suggesting she'd want to stay?'

Poppy raised her brow. 'A roof over her head? Somewhere to sleep? Food? Some things are preferable to a life on the streets – even I can see that.'

Izzy fell silent as Poppy's words sank in. 'Do you reckon we should telephone Maria first?' she ventured. 'To be on the safe side?'

'It's not Maria that's the problem,' said Poppy, 'as we both know she wouldn't dream of turning your mam away. It's getting your mam to go there in the first place.' She drew a breath. 'When your dad attacked me, I was scared of my own shadow for a long time afterwards. In fact I wouldn't go out of the pub unless someone was with me, and it took longer than I'd care to admit for me to feel safe. If I were your mam, the thought of going back would fill me with dread, which is why we need a plan B.' Staring at her feet, she drummed her fingers against the wall of the carriage as she tried to come up with an idea that would work. Her head jerked up suddenly. 'The bakery!'

Izzy stared blankly at Poppy. 'The what?'

'It's where me and Cadi used to work when we lived in Rhos,' gabbled Poppy. 'I know for a fact that they're crying out for workers there, because all the young girls have joined up.'

'Only where would Mam live? It's all very well having a job—' Izzy stopped speaking to allow Poppy, who was shaking her head, to interrupt.

'My mam and dad would put her up, no problem. It's not the biggest house in the world, but if your mam wouldn't mind sharing, she'd be more than welcome – I know she would.'

Izzy drew a deep breath before letting it out in a staggered fashion. 'How can you be so sure?'

Poppy smiled proudly. 'Because my mam's got a heart of gold. She knows how hard it was for me after the attack. There's no way she'd turn someone away who's been in a similar position.'

Izzy relaxed. 'So we've got a plan A and a plan B: do we need any more than that?'

Poppy shook her head. 'Like I say, I could see that your mam might object to Liverpool, but not to Rhos. It's a world away from all she once knew.'

'Then that's us sorted,' said Izzy in a satisfied manner. 'Now all we have to do is see whether my mam really is living in Portsmouth.'

Feeling her toes beginning to go numb, Ronnie tried to stamp the life into her feet. 'I thought they'd be here ages ago!' she complained to Kitty.

'It'll be the trains. They're dreadful at the best of times, but at Christmas?' She pulled a face. 'Hell on earth.'

'So what should we do?' asked Ronnie. 'Freeze to death?' She glanced in the direction of Hillcrest House. 'I'm sure I've seen someone peeking at us from behind the curtains. What are we meant to say if they come over before Izzy arrives?'

'Tell them the truth: that we're waiting for our friends.' She shrugged. 'I don't see what else we can do.'

'We could always head over to the station and see what's what,' suggested Ronnie. 'For all we know, their train might've been cancelled.'

Kitty shook her head. 'They'd have rung the B&B and told us, if that were the case.'

'Well, I wish they'd hurry up,' said Ronnie, adding as an afterthought, 'although I suppose one good thing's come out of this.'

Kitty looked curious. 'Oh? What's that then?'

'I'm that cold I'm not bothered about knocking on the door, not any more – in fact I can't wait to get inside.'

Kitty placed her arm round Ronnie's shoulders. 'You must be really cold to say that—' She stopped speaking as a man came out of the building, holding the door ajar for another man to join him.

Kitty tutted with disgust. 'On Boxing Day too – they should be ashamed ...'

Seeing the men heading towards them, Ronnie went rigid in Kitty's arms. 'Is it me or are they coming this way?'

Kitty instantly looped her arm through Ronnie's. 'If they ask, we're in the WAAF and we're waiting for our friends.'

Ronnie nodded before hissing, 'But we *are* in the WAAF.'

'I know,' replied Kitty, 'but I want to make sure they know that too – I certainly don't want them mistaking us for ... you-know-whats.'

As the men approached, Ronnie instantly made up her mind that she didn't like the look of them. They might be smartly dressed, but there was something in their features that she found unsettling. She glanced at the one who seemed to be taking the lead. His mouth might be smiling, but his eyes read differently.

'Can I help you ladies?' he asked in a thick Irish accent.

'We're in the WAAF,' said Kitty, her voice shrill, 'and we're waiting for our friends.'

'Oh, you are, are you?' said the second man, who had drawn level with the first. 'And why would you be wantin' to meet your friends here, I wonder?' He waved an expansive arm, whilst continuing to speak in a sarcastic fashion. 'Not a lot round here for girls like yourselves.'

'That's our business,' snapped Ronnie, who was too cold and tired to carry on being scared. 'What's it got to do with you anyway?'

The first man licked his lips. 'This is our patch, and anyone wantin' to work it had better be sure they know what they're lettin' themselves in for.'

Kitty puffed out her chest. 'You don't own ...' Seeing the man nodding, she followed his finger, which indicated the building behind him.

'I rather think we do, and we own everything in it too. And if you don't want to become part of that, I suggest you leave. And believe you me,' his voice lowered to a menacing growl, 'that's me askin' you nicely.'

'And who might you be exactly?' asked Ronnie primly.

The man stepped forward abruptly, but Ronnie held her ground. Smiling approvingly, he leaned forward until his nose was inches away from hers. 'We're the Finnegan brothers ...'

Chapter Eight

Raquel knocked on the door to Dolly's room before entering. 'What's going on? One of the girls said the Finnegans had a go at someone outside.'

Peering at Raquel around the corner of her curtains, Dolly beckoned her over. 'They did, but they've moved on.' She eyed Raquel sombrely. 'I could be barkin' up the wrong tree, but I reckon your daughter ain't takin' no for an answer.'

Startled, Raquel pulled the curtains back, only to have Dolly hastily close them again. 'Are you out of your mind?'

Raquel stared wide-eyed at Dolly. 'I'm not going to sit here whilst the Finnegans—'

'They aren't goin' to do nothin', because the girls have moved on.' She peered through the slit in her curtains. 'Not too far, but far enough. If it is your daughter, she's with the girl who first came here and they're both in WAAF uniform. The Finnegans might not think twice about settlin' a score with your average Joe, but

363

even they know better than to start a fight with the WAAF.'

Raquel didn't seem so sure. 'The Finnegans have no respect for women – whether they're in the WAAF or not, it makes no odds to them.'

'Them girls go missin', an' people'll start askin' questions,' said Dolly. 'And whilst the boys might be handy with their fists, they won't want to start explainin' themselves to the services.'

Raquel shrugged. 'Don't see why not – they'll just buy them off, like they do the scuffers.'

Dolly was shaking her head. 'You can't buy off the services, they aren't interested in backhanders – and the boys know that, even if you don't.' Hearing the front door close behind a customer, she indicated to Raquel that they should keep their voices lowered. 'I have a feelin' we're going to be seein' the girls again tonight.'

A half-smile graced Raquel's cheek. 'Really?'

'Really.' Lifting the curtain, she continued to watch them. 'They don't look like they're goin' anywhere, anytime soon.'

'But the Finnegans'll never let them in,' said Raquel dismissively.

'Then we must get you to them,' said Dolly.

Raquel started to shake her head in protest, then stopped. Why shouldn't she go out and speak to the girls? She could warn them about the Finnegans and ask them why they were there. If they said they were looking for Raquel, she'd come clean and go from there. She envisaged herself doing exactly that, but her cheeks bloomed as soon as she came to the part where she admitted who she was. She looked at Dolly, shamefaced. 'They're goin' to know that I'm a ... a ...'

'A whore?' said Dolly levelly. 'That ain't nothin' to be ashamed of – it's better than being a thief or a murderer.'

Blushing to the tips of her ears, Raquel nodded. 'I know that, but will she?'

Dolly smiled. 'She's here, ain't she? Besides, I rather think you'll find she already knows what you do for a livin'.' Having not taken her eyes off the girls, Dolly beckoned Raquel over. 'Is it me, or do they look like they're waiting for reinforcements?'

Raquel peered at the girls. 'I'd say so, judging by the way they keep looking around them.' She leaned back. 'I'll get my coat. If the boys ask where I'm going, I'll tell them I need a breath of fresh air ...'

Dolly was shaking her head slowly. 'I wouldn't go just yet, as we aren't the only ones who'll be keeping a keen eye on their movements.'

'When then?' asked Raquel, who was eager for the off.

Dolly stood up from her seated position. 'You stay here whilst I go and find out what's what.'

As she left the room, Raquel took up her position by the window. Dolly had only been gone for a few moments when she returned, a smile on her face. 'I was right about the reinforcements.'

Raquel stared at her. 'Why, what did they say?'

Dolly settled next to her. 'I asked Micky whether he was recruitin' from the WAAF and he just laughed and said the girls were there waitin' for their friends, so he told them to clear off.'

'And what about Micky and his brother: are they keeping an eye on them, same as us?'

'Micky's not, but I didn't see Paddy, so I can't say for sure what he's up to.' She smiled kindly at her friend. 'We've got to be patient. There's no point in goin' off half-cocked.' She indicated where the girls were standing. 'Even they know that, which is why they're bidin' their time. We have to do the same.'

'How will we know when the time is right?'

'I don't know, but in the meantime I think we should act like everything's normal. Which means you need to go back to your room. I'll keep an eye on things from here, and should anythin' else arise, you'll be the first to know.'

Cadi and Jez were waiting for Poppy and Izzy's train to arrive. Twiddling her thumbs, Cadi looked anxiously along the line as she repeated the same question she had been asking for the past twenty minutes. 'Where *are* they?'

Standing behind Cadi, Jez placed his arms around her shoulders. 'You heard the guard – it'll get here when it gets here.'

Cadi tutted her disapproval. 'Fat lot of good that does us. I need a proper time, not some wishy-washy excuse.'

'Only they can't give you a time …' Jez began, only to have Cadi finish the rest of his sentence.

'Because there's a war on,' she said huffily.

'There you are, then.'

Cadi was about to expand her thoughts on the rail system when she heard what she hoped was the sound of a train approaching in the distance. She glanced up at the underneath of Jez's chin. 'Did you hear that?'

'I certainly did.' He looked along the line that stretched into the distance. 'And I can see it too.'

Cadi gave a small squeal of delight, before placing a hand to her stomach. 'So this is what it feels like to be both excited and scared.'

'You mustn't worry,' said Jez soothingly. 'I'm right behind you, both figuratively and literally. And just remember: none of this is your fault. You weren't the one who put Izzy's mam in that place – Eric did that. If it weren't for you, Izzy wouldn't know whether her mam was dead or alive.'

Cadi grimaced. 'It sounds simple, when you put it that way.'

He shrugged. 'It's the truth. You tried getting to the bottom of things without involving Izzy, but that didn't work, so you've had no alternative but to call her in.'

'But what if she blames me?' wailed Cadi.

'Then I shall be the first one to tell her that she's bang out of order, whilst setting the record straight.'

'And how will you do that?' sniffed Cadi.

'I won't have to,' said Jez with certainty. 'Izzy's a decent sort, and she knows you'd never do anything to hurt her.'

As the carriages of the train passed them by, Cadi stared into each of them fleetingly. 'I can't see them.'

Jez, who was also looking out for the girls, spoke up. 'I'm not surprised – they're crammed in like tinned sardines.'

As the train drew to a halt, Cadi turned to face him. 'You do think she's come, don't you? I don't think I could stand to go through this again.'

With a smile etching his cheeks, Jez jerked his head towards the train. 'She's here.'

Cadi turned to see Izzy and Poppy walking towards them. She swallowed. 'Here goes nothing.'

Izzy strode towards Cadi and, with a tear trickling down her cheek, she took her friend in a warm embrace whilst whispering, 'I know everything, and I mean *everything*.' Leaning back, she smiled weakly. 'Poppy filled me in on Hillcrest,' she shrugged helplessly, 'and the type of women that live there.'

Cadi stared at Poppy, her eyes widening. 'But I thought ...'

Poppy was shaking her head. 'Izzy was beginning to think all sorts, and I couldn't stand by and watch her suffer. And, believe you me, sometimes the truth is better than fiction.'

'She's right there,' admitted Izzy. 'I'd begun to think we might be visiting a cemetery.'

Cadi clapped a hand to her mouth. 'Oh, Izzy, I am sorry.'

Izzy held up a hand, silencing Cadi's apologies. 'Don't worry your head none. You tried to do what was best by me, and I thank you for that.' She gazed into Cadi's eyes. 'Is there any way this could be a mistake?'

Cadi looked woeful. 'Sorry, but it doesn't look that way.'

'There's no need to apologise,' said Izzy. 'I'd rather my mam was a working girl than dead. I'm more concerned that they might have opened the letter by accident and we're merely clutching at straws.'

'We did think about that,' admitted Jez, 'but if that were the case, then why invite Ronnie in?'

368

'To see if Ronnie was you,' said Cadi, 'or at least that's what we reckon.'

Izzy picked up her overnight bag. 'Can we go there now?'

Jez indicated a taxi with a sweeping motion. 'Take your pick. We've arranged to meet Ronnie and Kitty there.'

Poppy huffed on her fingers before donning her gloves. 'Poor things will be like icicles, if they've been waiting all this time.'

Cadi grimaced. 'I'm glad they're wearing their greatcoats.'

The group walked to the first taxi and the girls climbed into the back, whilst Jez took the front seat next to the driver. 'Hillcrest House, please, mate.'

The man's brow shot upwards and he looked hastily at the girls in the rear-view mirror, before eyeing Jez dubiously. 'Are you sure you've got the right address, mate?'

Realising what he'd said, Jez coughed into his hand, a crimson blush sweeping across his cheeks. 'I ...' he began, until Izzy came to his rescue.

'It's not what you think, so if you wouldn't mind?'

Pulling the peak of his cap down to hide his embarrassment, the driver put the car into gear before pulling away from the kerb.

'I was about to say that I'm going to see my mam,' Izzy whispered into Cadi's ear, 'but I don't want to give him a heart attack.'

Snorting with laughter, Cadi did her best to quieten herself, whilst the driver stared doggedly at the road ahead.

The mercifully short journey was spent in silence, as each of the passengers – as well as the driver – wished themselves at the destination. When they arrived Jez paid the fare, before joining the girls on the pavement. Watching the taxi pull away, he blew out his cheeks. 'Never again.'

Poppy was pinching her nose in a bid to stop herself falling into fits of laughter. 'Do you think he thought you were our pimp?'

Jez's hairline turned beetroot. 'You might be laughing, but I reckon that's exactly what he thought.'

Cadi cupped the side of his face in the palm of her hand. 'I'm certain he didn't think that for one minute,' she soothed, before adding wickedly, 'He probably thought you were a customer.'

Poppy emitted a shriek of laughter so loud that the rest of them hastily hushed her into silence. Gasping to get her breath back, Poppy remembered Ronnie and Kitty. She began to look around her, but they were nowhere in sight. She knitted her eyebrows. 'Where are they? Do you think they got fed up with waiting?'

Cadi too was looking for the girls. 'No chance. I know we've been a while, but they're not the sort to abandon their post.'

Izzy, who had never met either of the girls, pointed to someone who was waving to get their attention. 'Is that them?'

Cadi peered at the rather squat figure who was now beckoning them across. 'I think so. It looks like Kitty, but what on earth is she doing all the way over there?' Frowning, she gestured for Kitty to come and join them, but Kitty was shaking her head adamantly whilst still beckoning them over. She turned to the others. 'Come on, we'd better go and see what's up.'

Once they reached Kitty and Ronnie, Cadi did a quick introduction before asking the question uppermost in all their thoughts. 'What on earth are you doing over here?'

Kitty glanced anxiously towards the house. 'Some fellers came out and told us to bugger off or else ...'

'They weren't here last time,' said Ronnie. 'They introduced themselves as the Finnegans. I've never heard of them, so I dare say none of you have, either?'

The others looked blankly at each other. 'No – why, who are they?' asked Cadi.

'They said they own Hillcrest and all the girls in it,' squeaked Kitty, 'and if we didn't want to end up inside, we'd best sling our hook.'

'Did they now?' said Jez. Puffing his chest out, he turned to walk in the direction of the house, but Ronnie laid a hand on his arm. 'No, Jez. They're not the sort who'll take notice of a feller in uniform.'

'They're a right nasty-looking pair,' agreed Kitty. 'The type to punch first and ask questions later.'

Cadi looked at Izzy. 'Maybe that's why your mam wrote back saying she didn't live there, because she was frightened of what they'd do to you if you turned up.'

'That sounds plausible,' said Izzy, 'but men like that don't frighten me – not after my dad.'

Ronnie shot her a dark look. 'I don't know much about your dad, but I'd wager these men would make him look like an angel.' Seeing the doubtful look on Izzy's face, she continued, 'They look like they're in their early thirties, whereas your dad was what – fifty, sixty?'

Izzy described her father. 'He was a fat old drunk who liked to pick on those weaker than himself.'

'Just as I thought,' said Ronnie, 'but these fellers aren't fat, they're lean, and I'd wager they get their exercise in the ring.'

Kitty gave a mirthless laugh. 'Boxing's meant to be a gentleman's sport, but there's nothing gentlemanly about those two. I'd say bare-knuckle fighting's more their kind of thing.'

Cadi looked towards Jez, a worried frown creasing her brow. 'Now's not the time to be playing the hero.'

'We can't just leave her in there,' he protested.

'And I'm not suggesting we should,' Cadi assured him, 'but we need to think this through and come up with a plan that gets her out safely – not march in, all guns blazing.'

'I've got an idea ...' said Ronnie slowly. She beckoned the girls to draw close as she discussed her plan.

Jez watched as they kept turning to look at him, before falling back into deep conversation.

After a minute or two Cadi called him over and the girls filled him in on Ronnie's idea.

Jez stared at them in horror. 'I can't! What if someone recognises me?' he spluttered, before adding hastily, 'Which leads me to another good point. If the Finnegans see that a man in RAF uniform is entering their premises, they'll soon put two and two together and it won't be long before they realise something's afoot.'

'I don't like the idea any more than you,' Cadi assured him, 'but you're the only one who can get in there with a legitimate excuse.'

'Besides, all sorts of people use them places,' said Poppy with an air of disgust, 'so I wouldn't worry about sticking out like a sore thumb. If anything, you should fit right in.'

'Oh, thanks! And just what am I meant to say?' asked Jez, desperate to find an excuse not to go in, posing as a customer.

There was a quick exchange of glances between the girls, before Izzy spoke. 'Dunno, really. I've never been in one of these places before ...'

'Neither have I!' objected Jez. 'And I'd prefer to keep it that way.'

Sliding her hand into his, Cadi gave his fingers a jiggle of encouragement. 'If you can think of any other way, then please tell us.'

Jez heaved a miserable sigh. The whole time they'd been talking he'd been racking his brains trying to think of a plan, but so far he'd drawn a blank. He shrugged in a hopeless fashion. 'Wait for Raquel to come out?'

'We could be waiting for ever!' cried Izzy. 'Besides which, we don't even know what she looks like.'

Taking his hand from Cadi's, Jez folded his arms across his chest in a resigned manner. 'All right, I'll do it, but I'm not promising anything.'

Izzy beamed. 'I can't ask for more than that.'

'What should he say, though?' said Kitty. 'There's no point in Jez going in and coming out with the wrong woman.'

Gently nibbling her bottom lip, Cadi let it slide out from between her teeth. 'I suppose men have their favourites? Perhaps Jez could ask for Raquel?'

'And what if they say there isn't a Raquel there?' enquired Jez. 'What then?'

Izzy grimaced. 'Say you've got the wrong address?'

'Hardly likely,' said Jez reasonably. 'And even if they do take me through to Raquel, what am I meant to do? I can't just walk out with her.'

'Explain why you're there,' said Izzy, 'and if it turns out we've made a mistake, apologise and leave.'

'What if she demands payment?' asked Jez. 'I don't even know how much these things cost.'

'You'll be in and out within a few minutes,' protested Cadi. 'How much could anyone expect for a couple of minutes?'

'It won't be down to her,' said Ronnie thoughtfully, 'it'll be them fellers what run the place. They're the ones calling the shots.'

'Perhaps you could say you've forgotten your wallet?' suggested Cadi.

Jez was looking doubtful. 'I suppose that could work, as long as this Raquel doesn't tell them fellers the truth as to why I'm really there.'

'I've been giving it some thought,' said Ronnie. 'If there's a Raquel living there, can you really see it being a mistake? Because I can't, and if I were Izzy's mam, then I'd want Jez to leave with as little fuss as possible.'

There was a general murmur of agreement.

'Go in and ask for Raquel – say she's been recommended to you,' advised Cadi. 'If they say you've got it wrong and there's no Raquel there, you should simply say you won't bother and walk out before they have a chance to argue. On the other hand, if they lead you through to her room, waste no time in telling her the real reason why you're there. If she's willing, see if you can arrange to meet her away from Hillcrest.' She shrugged. 'Even working women must go out occasionally. If Raquel says she's not interested, or denies being Izzy's mam, there's not a lot you can do, save walk away. If she truly isn't Izzy's mam, then I'm sure she'll take pity on you and maybe make an excuse on your behalf – say you got cold feet or summat similar.'

Jez clicked his fingers. 'I think you've hit the nail on the head. I bet plenty of fellers get cold feet.'

Izzy looked at those gathered around. 'Are we all agreed?'

There was a lot of head-nodding, with the occasional 'Yes' or 'Yep' thrown in.

Taking Jez to one side, Cadi wrapped her arms around him. 'If it looks as though things are getting heated, or if them fellers start throwing their weight around, leave. It's not worth getting into a fight for someone who might not even be there.'

Leaning down, he kissed her softly. 'I'm only doing this for you, Cadi.'

She gazed lovingly into his eyes, which twinkled with affection. 'I know you are, and please don't think I don't appreciate it, because I do.' She glanced towards the house. 'If you're not back in five minutes, we're coming after you.'

Jez held his hands up to disagree, but it seemed the girls had heard Cadi's words.

'She's right, Jez,' said Poppy. 'Them fellers might be a nasty bunch of so-'n'-sos, but there's six of us and they'd have to be fools to take us all on.'

'And if push comes to shove, I've got a mean right knee,' Izzy assured him.

Jez winced. 'I can see they'll be in for a shock if they try to tackle you lot.'

'Exactly,' confirmed Cadi. 'Now get you gone, and be careful.'

Nodding, Jez pushed his hands into his pockets before making his way up the street towards the house.

Unable to bear the waiting, Raquel slid into Dolly's room. 'Any developments?'

As Dolly turned to face her, Raquel could see from the grin on her friend's cheeks that something else had indeed occurred. 'When them girls said they was waiting for their mates, they weren't jokin' – there's six of 'em all told, and one of 'em's a feller.'

Raquel sank down next to Dolly. 'Good God, what on earth are they planning on doing, do you think?'

Dolly could barely contain her excitement. 'What do you think they're plannin' on doin'? If this isn't a rescue mission, then I'm Mother Teresa!'

Even though Raquel giggled, her face remained anxious. 'What's a feller doing, coming with them? They can't seriously think he's a match for the Finnegans?'

'I wouldn't have thought so. They've seen the Finnegans for themselves, so they've got a rough idea who they're dealin' with – which is why they left when they was told to.'

Raquel brightened. 'Maybe they already know who the Finnegans are and that's why they were waiting for reinforcements in the first place.'

Dolly shrugged. 'Probably, as there's not many in Portsmouth who haven't heard of them.' Dropping the curtain, she gripped Raquel's wrist. 'The man's walkin' this way.'

'Not on his own?' gasped Raquel.

Dolly looked back through the window. 'Maybe he's goin' to get more people?'

Raquel, who couldn't bear the tension, shifted Dolly over so that she could take a look for herself. 'I doubt it; it looks like he's making a beeline for the house.'

Seeing that Jez was, without doubt, making his way towards them, Dolly hastily dropped the curtain. 'What on earth is he thinkin' of?'

Raquel, her heart thumping in her chest, got to her feet.

'Where are you goin'?' hissed Dolly.

'To field him, before he gets himself into real strife.'

Jez's heart was thumping in his chest as he ascended the steps to the front door of the house. As he approached, he wondered whether he should knock or simply walk in. Cursing inwardly for not asking Ronnie what other people had done, the day she first called by, he decided to knock. Standing with his fist raised, he was about to strike when the door shot open and a scrawny-looking woman ushered him in. Taking him by the hand, she pulled him into a room before Jez had the chance to utter a single word.

Once inside, Jez broke free of the woman's grip as she closed the door behind them. 'Sorry, but I'm here ...'

Placing her ear against the wooden surface of the door, she held a finger to her lips, warning Jez to be quiet. She waited for a few seconds before making her way over to him. 'I know why you're here.'

Jez was shaking his head. 'You really don't—' he began, but the woman was adamant.

'You're here for me.'

Jez grimaced. This was proving more awkward than he first thought. He was about to explain himself when she spoke again.

'I'm Raquel.'

Jez's jaw nearly hit the floor. 'How ... how did you know?' he stammered.

Sitting on the bed, she patted the mattress, indicating for him to sit beside her. 'How do you think I know?'

Jez stared at the woman. 'So we were right,' he mumbled. 'It *was* you who wrote back.'

Nodding, she got to her feet and fetched one of the lit candles from her dresser. She held it up so that it illuminated his features. Letting out a soft gasp, she squeezed Jez's hand in hers. 'I'm so sorry. I knew Izzy was looking for me, but I didn't realise ...' Unable to continue, she buried her face in her hands. 'What must you think of me? I'm that ashamed.'

Jez laid a reassuring hand on her shoulder. 'You've got nothing to be ashamed of.'

Hugging herself, she gulped on her tears. 'I don't deserve your sympathy.'

Tutting, Jez clasped her hands in his. 'You mustn't punish yourself. This isn't your fault; if anyone's to blame, it's Eric.'

Raquel flinched on hearing his name. 'I should've stood up to him, refused to do his bidding.'

'Easier said than done,' replied Jez. 'Izzy only got away because she had help from her friends.' He smiled kindly. 'Not that it matters. With Eric gone, you've no need to fear him.'

Raquel placed a cold hand against the side of his cheek. 'I can see that you're a good lad ...'

Jez blushed. 'Let's not jump the gun. I haven't got you out of here yet.'

Raquel looked at him uncertainly. 'Getting out won't be the problem. It's what happens after – that's the hard part. Take it from one who knows. When you've got no money, no home to call your own and no friends—'

Jez cut her short. 'That's where you're wrong. You've a group of friends waiting for you outside, you've just not met them yet.'

Raquel eyed him doubtfully. 'I'm certain your intentions are good, but friends aren't everything, and there's not many people who'd want to employ a woman like me.'

'That's where you're wrong,' said Jez. 'Maria – she's another of our friends – would give you a job as well as bed and board in her pub.'

'But she's never even met me,' protested Raquel.

'She doesn't need to,' Jez assured her. 'You're Izzy's mam. That'll be good enough for Maria—' He stopped short as two men entered the room.

Realising that they had been caught red-handed, Jez leapt to his feet. Not knowing what he should say or do, he decided to play ignorant.

'Do you mind?' he said, eyeing them accusingly.

The taller of the two approached, a sneering grin on his lips. 'Yes, I ruddy well do. I'm Paddy, and this here is me brother Micky, and if you want to be with one of our girls, then you have to pay us first.'

Micky glared at Raquel through narrowing eyes. 'You know the rules: payment up front.' He glanced around him. 'Yet I see no money.'

Raquel licked her lips nervously. 'I can explain ...'

Paddy folded his arms across his chest. 'You're either givin' it away for free, which ain't allowed, or' – he hesitated – 'or this Romeo sees himself as more than a customer.' He laughed scornfully. 'Have I got it right? Have you come to rescue yer girlfriend from the 'orrible Finnegans?'

'Girlfriend?' squeaked Raquel. She stared at the shorter of the two men in horror. 'He's not my boyfriend.'

Paddy shot her a withering look. 'Boyfriend, fancy man – whatever you want to call him.' He turned to face Jez, his hand held out as if awaiting payment. 'So come on, chump, if you're not her boyfriend, I want to see the colour of yer money.'

Without waiting, Jez grabbed Raquel by the hand and together they ran towards the door. They had nearly made it into the hallway when Raquel suddenly jerked out of his clutch with a scream.

Jez turned back to see that Micky had hold of Raquel by her hair.

'Get your bloody hands off her,' Jez growled.

Hearing the commotion, Dolly ran to help her friend, but Paddy shot out a fist, knocking her clean across the hall. Hastening to the front door so that he could prevent Jez from leaving with Raquel, he roared, 'Enough!'

'She's a free woman,' snapped Jez. 'You've got no right to hold her against her will.'

Paddy had opened his mouth to speak when the door behind him shot open, causing him to stumble forward. Cursing loudly, he turned to see a group of determined-looking Waafs staring back at him.

Micky had tightened his grip on Raquel's hair. 'What's this, the soddin' cavalry?'

Without uttering a word, Izzy marched over to Micky and put her right knee to good use. He instantly released his grip on Raquel. Clutching the affected area, he crumpled to the floor, where he writhed in silent agony.

Paddy made to rush Izzy. 'Why, you little—'

But Cadi was quick to step in his path. 'She ain't the only one with a mean right knee.' Suspecting that he knew very little about the services, she added, 'They train us to do a lot more than that in the WAAF.'

Jez appeared at her side. Fixing Paddy with a steely glare, he spoke in leaden tones. 'Don't even think about it.'

Averting his attention to his brother, who was still bent double, Paddy shot Raquel a look of pure loathing. 'I dunno know what's goin' on here, but believe me, you're goin' to regret what you've done.'

Raquel looked at Micky, who was whimpering in pain. 'You're nothing but a pair of cowardly bullies. I don't know why I was ever scared of you.'

'Because we own the clothes you stand up in,' spat Paddy nastily. 'If it weren't for us, you'd still be in the gutter. We give you a roof over your head, and food in your belly. You're nothin' without us.'

Izzy was eyeing him in disgust. 'You make it sound like she should be grateful!'

'Because she should,' snapped Paddy. 'And if I'd known she was goin' to prove to be so ungrateful, I'd have left her fightin' for scraps with the rest of the dockyard rats.'

Izzy placed her arm around Raquel's shoulders. 'C'mon, Mam, you don't have to stand here and listen to his drivel, not any more.'

Paddy quickly stepped in front of the door to the house. 'You ain't goin' anywhere, until you give me back what's mine.'

'She hasn't got anything of yours,' said Kitty defensively.

A tear of embarrassment tracked its way down Raquel's cheek. 'He's talking about my clothes.'

Paddy folded his arms across his chest. 'She knows the truth, even if you don't.'

Raquel nodded. 'Only you don't tell me to take my clothes off – not any more.'

'They're mine!' roared Paddy.

Jez arched an eyebrow. 'Wouldn't you look a bit odd in them?'

Ignoring the murmur of nervous giggles, Paddy eyed him sourly. 'You know full well what I meant!' He pointed an accusing finger at Raquel. 'I bought them, to replace the rags she came to us in. She was beggin', practically on her hands and knees, pleadin' with me to look after her, so she was.'

Izzy slid her hand into Raquel's. 'If you call this looking after someone, then you're deluded. I'm leaving here *with* my mam, and you aren't going to stop me.'

She shot him a warning look. 'I've already got rid of one bastard in my life, I can easily make it three.'

Paddy spoke through gritted teeth. 'I wouldn't go makin' threats, little girl.' He shot a withering glance towards his brother, who was still in visible pain. 'You don't know who you're dealin' with.'

Raquel spoke quietly, her tone threatening. 'But I do; in fact I know an awful lot about you *and* your brother, and I reckon the authorities would be keen to hear what I have to say.'

Paddy threw his head back and laughed raucously, before snapping it forward. 'We *own* the authorities, you stupid bitch.'

'Then I'll go to the top,' said Raquel. 'And if that doesn't work, I'll go to the papers. I'm sure they'd love to hear exactly what goes on behind closed doors.'

Paddy's features turned thunderous, until his gaze fell on Dolly. 'Oh yeah? Well, you might think you're goin' to be wanderin' off into the sunset, but your pal's not.' He glared at Dolly maliciously. 'I shall enjoy makin' her pay for your words.'

Raquel quickly turned to Jez. 'This friend of yours, this Maria: do you think she'd have room for Dolly?'

He nodded. 'If it meant getting her away from here, then yes, I know she would.'

Paddy pushed his hand into his pocket. If word got out that he'd let two of his girls walk away scot-free, his reputation would be shot, and for men like the Finnegans, reputation was everything.

Believing that Paddy was donning the ferocious knuckledusters for which he was infamous, Dolly let out a cry of warning.

Fearing the worst, Kitty instinctively grabbed the nearest thing to hand and threw it at Paddy. The oil lamp missed its mark, but only by inches. Paddy ducked as the lamp sailed over his head. As it smashed against the front door, he leapt out of the way as it burst into flames.

They all stared in horror as the flames travelled up the blackout curtain and along the floor rugs.

Paddy tried to smother the flames with his coat, but instead of putting the fire out, he simply fanned them, making things ten times worse. Micky had got to his feet, although he was still bent double.

Someone, Cadi didn't know who, shouted, 'Get out!' And everyone – bar the brothers – ran through the flames that had engulfed the front door. Only when they were at the end of the street did they stop.

Barely able to breathe, Ronnie briefly introduced everyone whilst performing a quick head-count. 'Thank God for that, we're all here.'

Ronnie pointed back towards the house. 'Look!'

Kitty stared in horror as the flames spread to the downstairs rooms. 'What've I done?' she asked, in hollow tones.

Dolly placed her arm around Kitty's shoulders. 'Don't worry. Apart from the brothers, me and Raquel were the only ones in; the rest had gone to a ... party.' She uttered the last word with disgust.

'But you're not even meant to have a light shining through the window,' whimpered Kitty, 'and this is like a sodding beacon!'

Jez glanced meaningfully at the cloud-studded sky. 'No bomber's moon – not tonight.'

Kitty relaxed, but only a little. 'If he hadn't reached for a gun ...'

'Gun!' gasped Dolly. 'Is that what you thought?'

'When you shouted, I assumed he was reaching for a gun,' said Kitty defensively. 'Why shout otherwise?'

Dolly grimaced. 'He was reachin' for his knuckle-dusters. I've seen their handiwork first-hand and I was worried he was going to plough into one of us.'

Kitty's mouth slowly dropped open as she watched the flames coming out of one of the downstairs windows. 'All that, for knuckledusters?'

Dolly pulled a face. 'It wasn't your fault. You weren't to know.'

Izzy pointed to two men, both carrying suitcases as they ran into the night. 'They're running away!'

'Who in their right minds stops to pack their clothes when their house is on fire?' asked Kitty incredulously.

Raquel laughed. 'Clothes? Try money!'

Kitty's jaw dropped. 'I can't believe they're leaving their house to burn. Why don't they at least try and do summat to put out the flames?'

Raquel shrugged. 'It's too late, and once that fire's out, people will start asking questions that the Finnegans won't want to answer. I was right when I said they were nothing but cowardly bullies.'

'You certainly were,' agreed Dolly. She smiled at Raquel. 'And I was right when I said your daughter was comin' to your rescue.'

'And not only my daughter,' said Raquel, putting her arm around Jez's shoulders.

Dolly stared at Jez, then at Izzy, then at Raquel, before arching her brow. 'You mean ...?'

Raquel nodded. 'I certainly do.'

'But how?' said Dolly. 'I thought you said they didn't know each other existed?'

Raquel went to reply, before realising that she didn't know the answer herself. Taking Izzy and then Jez by the hand, she stood them side-by-side so that she could address them as one. 'Dolly's just raised a very interesting point. How *did* you find out? I'm damned sure Eric wouldn't have told you, and I swore Carrie to secrecy ...' She fell quiet, before speaking directly to Jez. 'It was Carrie, wasn't it?'

Dolly, seeing the blank, uncomprehending looks emanating from both Jez and Izzy, gained her friend's attention. 'Raquel?'

Still deep in thought, Raquel half turned to her friend. 'Yes?'

'I think you're singin' from a different hymn sheet to the rest of them.'

Raquel laughed. 'No, I'm not. Surely you can see the resemblance?'

Dolly nodded. 'I can, but I'm not sure about everyone else.'

Raquel turned to face her. 'Of course they can – that's why he's here.'

Izzy knitted her brow. 'Jez is here because he's our friend.'

Raquel looked at Dolly, open-mouthed. 'Oh dear ...'

Dolly smiled kindly. 'You've already set the cat amongst the pigeons, you may as well go the whole hog.'

Raquel turned apologetically to Jez and Izzy. 'I'm sorry, I thought you knew.'

'Knew what?' said Izzy, by now thoroughly confused.

Raquel smiled weakly. 'Jeremy is your brother.'

Chapter Nine

Jez stared at Raquel. 'I was abandoned on Nan's door-step as a baby – we don't know who my parents are ...' He looked at Cadi, who was staring at him as though she'd seen a ghost. 'Cadi?'

'I hadn't seen it before,' said Cadi softly, 'but it seems obvious now.'

'Like peas in a pod,' agreed Poppy.

With a line creasing his brow, Jez turned his attention to Raquel. 'What did you mean when you said you'd sworn my nan to secrecy?'

Raquel blinked as a tear left her lashes. 'That Carrie must never tell you the truth, in case Eric got wind of it.'

Izzy, who had been deep in thought, spoke slowly. 'In one of your letters you said summat about Eric denying his child.' She glanced at her mother. 'He wasn't referring to me, was he?' It was more of a statement than a question.

Raquel shook her head sadly. 'He was talking about your brother.' As Izzy's words caught up with her, she looked up sharply. 'You've read my letters?'

Izzy nodded. 'That's how we knew where you lived.'

Jez stared at Raquel, whilst speaking each word slowly and carefully to make sure there wasn't any possibility that he could be misunderstood. 'So ... you're my mam?'

Raquel's lips trembled as she tried to keep control of her emotions. 'I understand it's a lot for you to take in.'

Jez looked at Izzy. 'Which means you're my sister.'

Izzy grinned. 'Your *big* sister.'

Without uttering another word, Jez rushed forward, taking Izzy and Raquel in a firm embrace. 'I don't care what you did,' said Jez, in a whisper that was only audible to Raquel and Izzy. 'I've got my family back, and that's all that matters.'

With tears coursing down her face, Raquel planted a kiss on Jez's cheek. 'Thank you, son, you don't know what it means for me to hear you say that.'

'Jez is right,' agreed Izzy through quivering lips. 'Now that we're back together, nothing else matters.'

Raquel held Izzy and Jez by the hand. 'I hear what you're saying, but it's important to me that you hear the truth. That I loved you both with all my heart, and I only did what I did because I couldn't see another way round it.' Kissing the backs of their hands, she looked up to the heavens as she blinked more tears away. 'There's not been a single morning when I haven't woken up wondering where you both were, and how you were doing. I wanted to come back *so* many times, but not if it meant putting you in danger.' She turned specifically to Izzy. 'If I could've got you away from your dad, then I would've, but he kept a tight hold on you.' She looked to Jez. 'If it weren't for Carrie, I don't know what I would've done.'

'I still can't believe that Eric's my dad,' said Jez. Taking a handkerchief from his pocket, he offered it to Raquel, who took it gratefully.

She dabbed the tears from her eyes. 'He is – not that he believed it, of course.' She looked at Izzy. 'You say you've read my letters, but they only tell half the story. I think it's best if I start at the beginning.' She hesitated. 'Do you know who Colin is?'

Izzy nodded. 'He's the feller dad thought you were having an affair with.' She added hastily, 'We know you weren't, because we read the rest of your letters, including the one where Colin went missing.'

Raquel pulled a grim face. 'I was a few weeks off giving birth when your father heard rumours of our supposed affair. As you know, I tried to talk sense into him, but he wouldn't hear of it, instead accusing me of carrying Colin's baby and demanding that I give it up for adoption as soon as I'd given birth. Of course I refused. After all, why should I give my baby away when I'd done nothing wrong? That's when he threw me out. I had nowhere to go – no home, no job, no money, nothing.' Her face turned ashen as she re-called the memory. 'Colin got me a room on the far side of town, where no one knew who I was, but it was only a temporary solution. We agreed that it would be safest all round if we never saw each other again, and that Colin should leave town until things had calmed down. From that moment on, I was truly on my own. It was then that the gravity of my situation hit me. There was no way I could support myself as well as a baby. Women in my position usually only have two choices: the workhouse or the orphanage. Only I was lucky, because I had Carrie and I knew that I could rely on her to do the one thing I couldn't; to love my baby as her own. So I paid her a visit late one night and asked her if she would take care of Jez, for me. She agreed without hesitation – as I knew she would – but we had to come up with a story to protect you from Eric. That's when Carrie had the idea of finding a baby on her doorstep.' She shrugged. 'It was the perfect solution—'

Jez interrupted. 'How did you know Nan?'

'She was one of my neighbours,' said Raquel, 'the only one, I might add, who stuck by me when everyone else was calling me fit to burn.'

'Couldn't you have lived with Carrie?' asked Poppy innocently.

Raquel's eyes rounded. 'If Eric had thought his wife was living down the road for everyone to see, with another man's baby, he'd have swung for the lot of us – Carrie included. Which is why I knew it was safer for everyone if I left Liverpool for good.'

'That's why Nan always stuck up for my parents, despite the fact that they'd abandoned me,' said Jez, his voice barely above a whisper.

'Because she knew the truth,' said Raquel.

Izzy was shaking her head sadly. 'And all because you wanted to learn how to read and write.'

Raquel wiped the tears from her eyes, before nodding. 'If there was any other way, I *swear* ...'

'You don't have to convince me – I know exactly what my father was like,' said Izzy. She turned to Jez. 'That's why he was acting so strangely the last time we saw him. He must've realised the truth when he saw us together.'

Jez struck the side of his head with the palm of his hand. 'Of course! He even said that I hadn't fallen far from the tree. But how could Eric say that when he didn't know who my parents were? It didn't make sense at the time, but it does now.'

Raquel spoke thickly. 'For those of us in the know, it's obvious.'

'That must have been why Eric was so keen to get away,' said Izzy, 'because he knew he'd made a mistake when he saw the two of us together.'

'That wouldn't bother Eric—' said Poppy, but Cadi was quick to interject.

'It would, if he'd done away with Colin ...'

Kitty's eyes rounded. 'You think Eric murdered him?'

Cadi nodded sadly. 'It certainly looks that way.'

Raquel blew her nose quietly. 'Poor Colin. I assumed he'd left town until I'd had the baby, but when he failed to reappear ...' She fell silent, unable to utter the words.

'Blimey!' Kitty mumbled beneath her breath.

'Colin was a good man,' said Raquel, 'trying to do a good deed for a friend, just like Carrie.' She looked at Jez. 'Talking of Carrie, how is she?'

'I'm afraid she passed away over a year ago,' replied Jez quietly.

Overwhelmed with grief, Raquel wrang her hands. 'Why her? Why Carrie and not Eric? She was such a kind and wonderful woman, who'd do anything for anyone, and I can't even thank her for loving my child when I was unable to.'

Jez steadied his bottom lip. 'She would have known how grateful you were. She made sure I had the best life possible and that can't have been easy for her, knowing what she did, whilst living in the shadow of Eric. Especially when she saw what a terrible life Izzy had …' He fell silent as he realised what he was saying, and who he was saying it to.

Raquel viewed Izzy through eyes that glistened with tears. 'I'm so, *so* sorry.'

Izzy took her mother in her arms. 'It's not your fault. You did the best you could at the time and, believe me, if you'd turned up, Dad would have killed you where you stood rather than have the truth come out.'

'I should've tried harder—' Raquel began, only to have Dolly cut her off.

'We've been through this a thousand times. No matter which way you look at it, Izzy and Jez would have been seized by the authorities and placed in an orphanage, and we all know what that means.'

'The workhouse,' said Ronnie.

'It's like choosing the lesser of two evils,' said Raquel. 'Jez was definitely better off with Carrie, but I'm not sure the same could be said for poor Izzy.'

'I am,' said Izzy plainly. 'Some people never make it out of the workhouse, and I doubt I'd have had the will to leave.' She glanced at where Cadi and Poppy were standing. 'I didn't have the strength to leave Dad until I met these two.'

'Thank you for looking after her,' said Raquel. 'It must've taken real guts.'

Shivering with cold, Poppy smiled shyly. 'We'd have done anything to get her away from Eric. But perhaps we could carry on with this conversation somewhere a little warmer? I don't think I can feel my toes!'

'Come on,' said Cadi, 'let's get Raquel and Dolly booked in.'

Izzy gasped. 'I didn't realise we might have one extra when I made the booking.'

Cadi waved a dismissive hand. 'I'm almost certain they'll have room and, if not, Dolly can bunk with me and Kitty.'

'It's ever so good of you to offer,' Dolly began, 'but—'

'But me no buts!' said Cadi stiffly. 'That's what my mam used to say, and she was always right.' She glanced meaningfully towards Hillcrest House. The firemen had been in attendance for some time now and the flames were under control. 'You couldn't go back even if you wanted to, and I'm pretty sure you don't.'

'It's the last place I want to be,' Dolly agreed. 'But what will happen to the girls? We can't just leave them to fend for themselves.'

'They could always sign up,' suggested Ronnie.

Raquel raised her hands. 'How? They've got no identification, no clothes – nothing.'

Dolly explained the situation. 'The Finnegans take everythin' you have; it's their way of keeping control over you.'

'Not any more,' said Ronnie. 'The fire's put paid to that.'

'The girls are still no better off,' said Raquel.

'Yes, they are,' said Ronnie cheerfully. 'Because they've lost their home, on top of everything else.'

Raquel's frown deepened. 'You're making it sound as though that's a good thing.'

'It is, because they'll get rehomed,' said Cadi. 'And that means they'll have a respectable address to give out for correspondence; not only that, but they'll have a good excuse for why they haven't got any papers ...'

Raquel clapped her hands together. 'So all's well that ends well!'

Dolly turned to Kitty. 'And there you were, panickin' that you'd done the wrong thing.'

The smell of smoke was heavy in the air, and a slow smile crossed Raquel's cheeks. 'That, my dears, is what you call the sweet smell of success.'

Jez stood up from the wall that he'd been using as a bench. 'Now we know what we're about, how about we go to Izzy's hotel? I dunno about you lot, but I could do with a stiff drink.'

'I'm not coming,' said Dolly. She held up a hand to quell Raquel's protests. 'The girls will need someone here to tell them what to do, and I want to be that person.'

'But you've got the offer of a whole new life,' objected Raquel.

Dolly was smiling gratefully. 'And I appreciate it – I really do – but I want to make a difference, do summat good for a change.'

'But you did something good when you met me,' Raquel protested. 'If it weren't for you, I don't know where I'd be.'

Dolly took her friend in a warm embrace. 'I rescued you into the brothel, Raquel. I'd hardly call that doin' summat good.'

'It was, though,' insisted Raquel. 'I had nothing and no one, until I met you.' She gave a short, hollow laugh. 'The Finnegans were right about one thing: I was in the gutter; but it wasn't them that got me out, it was you. And whilst I hated being a working girl, it did keep me off the streets as well as give me an address, without which Izzy would never have found me.'

Dolly hugged her friend harder still. 'You've a heart of gold, Raquel, and you deserve better, just like the rest of the girls.' Leaning back, she smiled at her friend. 'They're only kids – barely nineteen, some of them – and they won't know what to do. If I don't help them, they'll end up back with the Finnegans and I'll be damned if I see that happen.'

'I'll never forgot you, Dolly Stephens.'

Dolly rubbed Raquel's back. 'Nor I you, and if you let me know where you're stayin', I'll be sure to write.'

At this point Cadi stepped forward. 'She'll be staying at the Belmont, West Derby Road, Liverpool.'

Dolly repeated her words two or three times, before nodding. 'Take care of each other. And, Kitty?'

Kitty lifted her head. 'Yes?'

She glanced at the house, then back to Kitty. 'Thanks for the misunderstandin'.'

It was the morning after the fire, and Izzy, Poppy and Raquel were having breakfast in the dining room of their hotel. Having spent the previous evening talking until the small hours, Raquel yawned behind her hand as she topped up their teacups. 'It's a shame you can't stay a little longer.'

'I wish I could,' agreed Izzy, 'but I'm afraid my hands are tied, although that won't stop me booking some leave as soon as I get back.'

'It would be lovely if I could spend some time with you and Jez.'

Izzy smiled. 'He thought the world of Carrie and he was devastated when he lost her in the bombings. Learning that he has a whole new family has come as a shock, but I'd say it's a welcome one.'

Poppy finished buttering a slice of toast. 'I saw his face as the truth hit home, and he was cock-a-hoop. I should imagine he's hardly had a wink of sleep, knowing that his mother and big sister are just down the road—' She broke off as the door to the dining swung open and Jez, Cadi and Kitty entered the room. Poppy grinned. 'Looks as if I was right.'

As they approached the table, Jez pulled up three more chairs. 'Hope you don't mind us joining you unannounced?' He caught the eye of the waitress who came over. 'Toast for three, as well as two more pots of tea, please.'

As the waitress went to fetch the order, Cadi grinned at the others. 'He's been up since five o'clock. I could hear him pacing the floorboards.'

Poppy's brow shot towards her hairline. 'Oh?'

Realising what her friend was insinuating, Cadi shook her head. 'Jez was in the room above mine, Poppy Harding, so you needn't go down that road.'

Raquel gazed lovingly at her children. 'I've still got so many questions. I don't know where to start.'

'We need time together,' said Jez. 'As soon as we get back to our bases, I suggest we make arrangements to meet at the Belmont for a few days, if not longer.'

'I said that!' cried Izzy. 'Is that great minds thinking alike or is it because we're siblings?'

'Siblings,' said Jez, and he savoured the word before adding, 'Or at least I'd like to think so.'

Raquel now spoke the thought that had been worrying her all night. 'I can't help feeling a tad apprehensive about meeting Maria—'

Jez intervened. 'I've already spoken to her, and she was delighted to learn the truth. She and her husband Bill will meet you at the station. I've been and bought you a ticket for the two o'clock train.'

Raquel stared, open-mouthed, at her son. 'You've already bought me a ticket?'

'He's been champing at the bit to come over,' said Cadi, 'so I suggested that we get things in order first, so that you could have a lie-in.'

Raquel smiled. 'He could have come over – I wouldn't have minded.'

'See?' said Jez.

'Your mam might not've minded an early-morning visitor, but I dare say the hotel staff would've had summat to say on the matter,' chided Cadi.

Jez gazed at Raquel. 'I've not had a proper mam before.'

Cadi rubbed his arm affectionately – seeing Jez so content was melting her heart. 'Carrie would be so happy, if she could see you now.'

The waitress came over with their order, and Cadi helped her lay the plates on the table. 'You're going to love it at the Belmont – it's not as big as this place, but it isn't far off.'

'I thought we could take Mam shopping before we leave,' said Izzy.

Raquel blushed as she held her hands over the plunging neckline of her dress. 'The Finnegans believed less is more. The staff have been very polite, but I know what they're thinking, because I'd be thinking the same if I were in their position.'

Cadi rummaged in her handbag, 'I've got some spare vouchers.' She gave Raquel a reassuring smile as she fished them out. 'I'm always in my uniform, so I really don't need them.'

Raquel accepted them gratefully. 'You've all been so kind.'

'You're worth it,' said Izzy, 'we all think so.'

There was a general murmur of agreement around the table.

Poppy peered around the table. 'Where's Ronnie?'

'Back at work,' said Kitty. She pulled a face. 'I can't believe we've got to go back so soon.'

'You and Ronnie must join us for a reunion,' said Raquel. 'Dolly too, if she can.'

'That would be lovely,' replied Kitty. 'It'll be good to meet Maria and Bill, as Cadi's told us so much about them.'

Discussing what they would do for their reunion, the group finished their breakfast before making their way into town. Cadi very much wanted Jez and Izzy to spend some time alone with their mother, but Jez wouldn't have any of it. 'I want you to share in every moment because, if it weren't for you, none of this would be happening.'

Raquel gazed gratefully at Cadi. 'Izzy told me all about your investigations and how you found me. My son is right: if it weren't for you, I'd not have my children, and I'd still be stuck in that hellhole.'

Cadi smiled shyly. 'I don't think I'd go that far.'

'I would,' agreed Izzy. 'You're always putting yourself down, and it's about time you stopped.'

Cadi laughed. 'You mean I should keep interfering?'

Izzy, Raquel and Jez spoke as one. 'Yes!'

Several months had passed since freeing Raquel from the Finnegans and a lot had happened in that time.

Raquel was now living at the Belmont with Maria and Bill but, wanting to make her own way in life, she too had applied to join the services. With both her children in the Air Force, there was only one choice, and Raquel was due to join the WAAF in a couple of weeks' time. They had all stuck to their word, and today they were meeting at the Belmont for the first time since leaving Portsmouth; and, to Raquel's delight, Ronnie had brought along a surprise guest.

'Dolly!' Raquel squealed as her old friend walked into the bar. 'How?' She looked at Jez and Izzy, who were grinning like a couple of Cheshire cats. 'Let me guess. These two had summat to do with it?'

Dolly nodded. 'You know what this lot are like when they get an idea in their head: the tom-toms start drummin' and, before you know it, I'm on a train to Liverpool!'

Ronnie was grinning fit to burst. 'Tell them about the Finnegans.'

Dolly took a seat beside the bar. 'After you left, the girls came back to find that the house had practically burned to the ground. Bein' young, they didn't know what to say when questioned, so they told the truth.'

Raquel's jaw dropped. 'There's the truth and then there's the *truth*. Which one are we talking about here?'

Dolly smiled happily. 'The whole nine yards. From how they'd met the Finnegans, to the company the brothers kept and the kind of things that went on behind closed doors.'

'Did the police believe them?' asked Raquel anxiously.

'It turns out a few of the girls' clients had birthmarks or tattoos in unusual places, and certainly not visible unless they were naked,' said Dolly triumphantly.

'Who exactly were these clients?' asked Cadi.

Dolly sighed happily. 'The Chief of Police and some of his sidekicks.'

Raquel gave whoop of joy. 'About blooming time too!'

Dolly was clapping her hands together in an excited fashion. 'Talk about the you-know-what hittin' the fan! Unsurprisingly, the authorities have bent over backwards in the hope that we won't go blabbin' to the local rags.' She rolled her eyes. 'As if we'd want anyone knowing our business!'

'Good, though,' said Raquel, 'because I'm guessing the girls are living somewhere nice?'

'Top hotel in Portsmouth, until their papers come through,' confirmed Dolly.

'So they are joining the services then?' said Raquel.

Dolly nodded. 'They were a bit dubious at first, but like I told them, they'll get a skill as well as a wage. What've they got to lose?'

Still beaming, Raquel introduced Dolly to Maria and Bill, who were listening with interest.

'Pleased to meet you, Dolly,' said Maria. 'Raquel said you were toying with the idea of joining up yourself?'

Dolly wrinkled her nose. 'I was, but I've been approached by other workin' women who are also lookin' for a way out. I've got a nice little flat on the outskirts of town – paid for by those who wish to remain nameless – and I let the girls use my address as a safe house whilst they get themselves out of bother.'

Cadi eyed Dolly with admiration. 'I think you're marvellous.'

Dolly smiled shyly. 'I'd want someone to do that for me if I were still in their position.'

'We've got so much to celebrate,' said Jez, 'I feel like I've won the pools!'

The reunion was staggered, with some of them leaving before others, and it seemed to Cadi that she was in a perpetual state of having to say goodbye to someone she loved.

As she waved Dolly and Ronnie off, she spoke to Raquel and Jez. 'When this is over, I hope we all come back to Liverpool, so that we can be close to each other. I hate having to say goodbye.'

With the train out of sight, Raquel turned towards the concourse. 'Do you not miss your family?'

'I do, but Jez and the girls have been my Liverpool family for a long time.' As they descended the steps, Cadi linked her arm through Jez's. 'Dad and the boys are always working, so there's only Mam at home, and even she's not there any more.'

'How so?' asked Raquel.

Cadi smiled. 'She's set up her own business making dresses and doing sewing repairs. She's always been a brilliant seamstress, but she didn't know how to run a business properly, so I gave her a few tips. Now she's got a little shop in Wrexham and she's earning a decent wage, on her own terms.' She glanced at Raquel from under her lashes. 'I've not asked until now, but how does it feel to be back in Liverpool? I must say, you seem to be taking it all in your stride.'

Raquel thought this over before answering. 'Appearances can be deceptive. I'll admit I'm a lot better now than I was, but when I first arrived, just hearing the Scouse accent was scary because it reminded me of times gone by. Maria was brilliant, escorting me everywhere – even though she didn't have to – and it wasn't long before I felt comfortable going into the city on my own. I know it's silly, because I'll never see Eric again – thank the Lord – but the thought of seeing someone I used to know was equally daunting. The last thing I wanted to do was explain my whereabouts for the past twenty years.'

'And did that happen?' asked Cadi curiously.

'Nope, but I suppose I've changed a lot since the old days, so people might not recognise me, nor I them.'

Jez gave his mother an approving glance. 'You've changed a lot in the past few months.'

'I smile more,' said Raquel. 'I hadn't realised until Dolly pointed it out.'

'You look healthier too,' noted Cadi. 'In fact you very much remind me of Izzy after she'd been in the WAAF for a few months.'

Raquel winced. 'Every time I think of Izzy having to live with *him*, I feel sick to my stomach. I know in my heart that I was powerless to reverse the situation, but I still can't forgive myself, even if she can.'

'You have to forget about the past and look to the future,' said Cadi, 'otherwise you'll never move on.'

'And I will,' reasoned Raquel, 'but it'll take time – just as it did for me to go out alone.'

'What gave you confidence to do that?' asked Cadi curiously. 'I only ask because I know Poppy had problems for ever such a long time after Eric's attack, not that she let on, of course.'

'You can't control the future,' said Raquel simply. 'I can't keep asking Maria to come with me "just in case", because that's simply not feasible. You can't live your life on "what ifs", else you'll never do anything.'

Jez gave Cadi a shrewd smile. 'Bit like you refusing to marry me before the war's over, in case it tempts fate.'

'That's different,' said Cadi a tad defensively. 'I've seen too many war widows—'

Raquel interrupted. 'Sorry, Cadi, but Jez is right. You marry for love, not for what might or might not happen. Those men or women would have met their maker whether they were married or not. When you think about it, marriage might have been the best thing that ever happened to them, and if that brought them

404

comfort in their final hours, then surely that can only be a good thing?'

Cadi closed her eyes. The very thought of Jez dying a single man broke her heart. 'I never thought of it like that.'

Jez stopped in his tracks. 'Does that mean we can set a date?'

Cadi nodded slowly. 'As long as it's a winter wedding. I've always dreamed of getting married in the snow, and it means everyone has time to—' She was about to say that everyone would be able to book time off work, or leave, but Jez, overcome with joy, had kissed her before she could say another word.

The year might not have started well, but he now had a mother, a sister and, before the year was out, he would make the woman he loved more than anything his wife.

Epilogue

December 1943

Cadi stood staring at her bouquet of hellebores, the deep-purple colour perfectly matching the beautiful shawl that her mother had knitted to keep her warm on her wedding day.

'Your mam's done you proud,' said Dewi as he admired his daughter in all her glory.

'She has that,' agreed Cadi. 'I remember the dress she made me when I was crowned Rose Queen all them years ago. No one would've guessed it was made from old bed sheets.' She lifted up the skirt of her wedding dress. 'She's a real whizz when it comes to making plain material look special.'

Smiling broadly, Dewi winked at her. 'I think the model has quite a lot to do with that. You could wear a coal sack and still look good in it.'

Cadi laughed. 'You're biased.'

Dewi shrugged. 'Maybe, but I don't think you'd find anyone who'd disagree with me.'

Cadi looked towards the vicar, who was trying subtly to gain their attention. Her stomach gave an anticipatory lurch as she nodded. Hearing the organist strike up Mendelssohn's Wedding March, Dewi gently pulled the veil over Cadi's head and lowered it down over her face. 'I can't believe I'm saying goodbye to my only daughter.'

Cadi slid her arm through the crook of his elbow. 'That happened a long time ago, Dad.'

Dewi patted her hand as they prepared to take their first step up the aisle. 'You're taking another man's name, cariad, and that makes all the difference.'

Cadi had been thinking about this for the past few days. She knew that taking Jez's surname meant she was no longer a single woman, and that tonight she would be sharing the same bed as her husband, the thought of which filled her with a mixture of emotions. Having never lain with a man, she had no idea what to expect, especially since none of her friends had gone further than a kiss. She swallowed as the questions came forth. *Would it hurt? Would she enjoy it? What if …?* Before the last thought could present itself, Jez turned to face her, a warm smile filled with love etched upon his face. Feeling the affection and reassurance coming from her fiancé, Cadi instantly knew that she had nothing to fear, not with Jez.

Because she had wanted a winter wedding they had agreed to get married in Rhos, where they would be sure of a white Christmas, with the reception being held in the Coach and Horses. It meant that her entire family could be present, and Cadi would be home for Christmas for the first time in years.

'I bet this brings back memories!' said John, as he came over to greet the newly-weds.

Jez nodded guiltily. 'Don't remind me! I still feel awful about what happened.'

John waved a nonchalant hand. 'You saved my son – believe me, you've nothing to feel badly about.'

Jez lowered his drink from his lips. 'How is Aled?'

John rolled his eyes. 'Still gung-ho, flyin' by the seat of his pants and treatin' the whole thing like it's a game.'

'Perhaps that's the best way,' mused Jez. 'There's a lot to be said for having confidence in what you do, and Aled has it in abundance when it comes to his role as rear-gunner.'

John smiled proudly. 'He's never been shot, but he's taken plenty down, and if that ain't summat to be proud of, I don't know what is.'

'He's doing his country a marvellous service,' conceded Cadi. 'Without men like him, I don't know where we'd be.'

Jez agreed with his wife. 'We owe men like Aled a debt of gratitude.'

John sniffed loudly, before clearing his throat. 'Aled doesn't see it like that. He says the RAF is like a well-oiled machine and if you take one part out, the whole thing breaks down.'

Cadi smiled wistfully. She knew that her father had invited Aled to the wedding, because the Davies were old family friends, but Aled had declined, using his schedule as an excuse. She recalled the telephone conversation she'd had a few days prior to the wedding.

'Cadi?'

'Aled!' She had felt her stomach jerk. Having not heard from him since before the accident, she had expected it to stay that way – unless something had gone wrong of course. 'Is everything all right?'

'Apart from hearing that you're getting hitched, I'd say everything's fine and dandy ...' Hearing the shocked silence, Aled chuckled softly. 'I'm only joshing. I couldn't be more pleased to hear the good news.'

Cadi gave a quiet sigh of relief. 'Thanks.'

'Although I must say I was rather surprised. I thought you said you wouldn't marry until the war was over?'

Cadi quickly ran through the conversation she'd had with Jez's mother and, in so doing, also explained her time in Portsmouth.

Aled blew his cheeks out. 'Flippin' Nora! What exciting lives you all lead.'

Cadi laughed. 'If that's what you call exciting, then I've had enough excitement to last me a lifetime.'

The operator had interrupted the flow of conversation to let them know their time was up and Cadi had replaced the receiver, content with the thought that Aled really had moved on this time.

But that was only because she didn't know his real thoughts. When Aled hung up, he had congratulated himself on a part well played. The truth was that he would always love her, and if Cadi was happier with Jez, then Aled loved her enough to let her go.

'Cadi?'

She jerked herself back to the present as Jez gave her a nudge.

'Sorry – I was miles away.'

Smiling, he gently smoothed a curl that had escaped its grip back behind her ear. 'I must be the luckiest man in the world.'

Cadi glanced around the guests, who were tucking into the sandwiches that Maria, Jill and Raquel had prepared. 'It's been such a wonderful day, I don't know why I ever worried it would tempt fate – it's not as though we rushed into things.'

Jez let a chuckle escape from his lips. 'Rush into things? We've been engaged for over a year!'

Cadi gave him a wry smile. 'Better to be safe than sorry?'

Sliding both arms around her waist, he gazed adoringly down at her. 'No matter the reason, you're worth the wait.'

He was about to kiss his wife when Poppy, Izzy, Ronnie and Kitty came rushing over. 'They want to know if you're ready for the first dance?' asked Poppy excitedly.

Jez arched an eyebrow, to which Cadi nodded. 'We're ready.'

With Kitty trotting off to inform the pianist, Poppy gazed lovingly at her friends. 'I said you were the perfect match, from the very first time I saw you together.'

Jez encircled Cadi in his arms. 'She might be my wife, but that doesn't mean to say she's lost her sense of independence.'

Cadi grinned. 'I wouldn't be me otherwise.'

'Exactly! And I wouldn't want you any other way.'

Hearing the pianist strike the first chord, the pair hastened to the area that they were using as a dance floor. Taking Cadi in his arms, Jez guided her to the music with ease. 'This is just the beginning of our new life together,' he said, 'and I can't wait to see what it holds.'

'Me neither,' agreed Cadi. 'I know we've had our share of ups and downs, but all that's behind us.'

He placed his cheek next to hers. 'With you being so fiercely against war marriages, I did worry you might get cold feet.'

Leaning back, she gazed into his eyes. 'Why would I worry, when I know you'll take care of me.'

Kissing her softly, he murmured, 'Until my last breath.'

KATIE FLYNN

If you want to continue to hear from the Flynn family, and to receive the latest news about new Katie Flynn books and competitions, sign up to the Katie Flynn newsletter.

Join today by visiting
www.penguin.co.uk/katieflynnnewsletter

Find Katie Flynn on Facebook
www.facebook.com/katieflynn458

HAVE YOU READ
KATIE
FLYNN'S
LATEST BESTSELLING NOVELS?

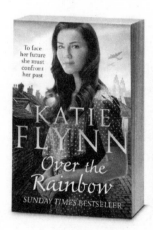

AVAILABLE IN PAPERBACK AND E-BOOK